Deadwater

A Gina Lindsey Mystery

by

Virginia Ann Work

Other Books Written by Virginia Ann Work

The Keys to the Kingdom Series:

Sirocco Wind from the East
Mistral Wind from the North
Zephyr Wind from the West
Lavento Wind from the South
Alexius, His Crown and His Curse, True Story from Mistral

Jodi Fischer Mystery Series:

The Mystery of the Missing Message
The Secret in the Silver Box
The Curse of the Broken Feather

Gina Lindsey Mystery Series:

Deadlocked
Deadwater

Digging Deeper Bible Studies:

The End of the Beginning, A Bible Study on the Book of
Revelation

I dedicate this book to my loyal fan and faithful readers who have waited patiently for the second Gina Lindsey novel. I am happy to present this second book for your enjoyment!

I want to thank my husband for his patient help, for the many trips we took to the areas in the book, and for his continued prayers for me. He is truly God's gift of grace to my life. I also want to thank my daughter, Vicki Lucas, for her painstaking editing work, and thanks to my other daughter, Sherry Sauskojus, for her input into EMTs and ambulances.

Chapter 1

A Beautiful Day to Die

A gunshot shatters the quiet sunshine. Something brushes my hair. I drop to the sand like I'd been hit and flatten myself behind a log. The roar of the discharge echoes across the river, and a crow explodes into flight with a cry of indignation. My heart thuds heavily in my ears. That bullet was meant for me.

Is Chance target practicing? Is he trying to scare me? No. He wouldn't do that. He's up there somewhere – I don't know where, but he'd never play around with guns that way.

The only other scenario is one I don't want to contemplate. Someone is trying to kill me.

I hunker down behind the log, keenly aware that this isn't the best shelter in the world if I'm trying to hide from an unseen assailant. Cautiously, I lift my head and peer around. Where did the shot come from? That thicket of laurel bushes across a stretch of sand?

At least I have my rifle, a Winchester Model 70 Sporter that Dad gave me for my fifteenth birthday eight years ago. It's a good weapon for deer hunting, but today it seems small against the firepower that blasted my quiet afternoon to bits.

A sudden silence falls over the forest. The Columbia River rushes past my feet six feet away. A bee buzzes my head, circles, and decides I'm not interesting.

I wish the person in the bushes would come to the same conclusion.

An army of ants march toward me in a line over the uneven, sandy ground. I inch closer to the log, bringing my legs closer to my chest and swipe at sweat trickling down my forehead.

Brushing away the ants, I grit my teeth. The silence wears on my nerves. Someone is hiding over there with their sights trained on any part of me that appears into view. Has my assailant moved? Is he like a cougar, creeping through the brush, ready to spring?

Was someone target practicing? But who would shoot toward the river? It's not hunting season, not even for ducks. Which means only one thing. Someone was aiming for my head and missed by a fraction of an inch.

Where is he? Why doesn't he do something?

Waiting in the scorching heat, my thoughts return to how this perfect day had gone so wrong.

All I'd wanted to do today was to find a good hunting area and be with Chance. I know, it's early to be thinking about hunting. This is only June and hunting season doesn't start until September. But Chance and I like to be outside, and what better reason than scouting out a good hunting area?

This morning, the skies were robin-blue, there was hardly any wind, and the weatherman promised warm sunshine after a spell of wet weather. I could almost *hear* things growing. I stepped out of the house and stretched, remembering to thank God for such a day.

By the time I got to Chance's house near Chewelah, the sun peered over Quartzite Mountain. I beeped the horn and climbed out of my dark blue Honda pickup. He jumped down the front steps of his farmhouse, looping his backpack over his shoulder and cradling his rifle under his right arm. He glanced at me and smiled that crooked grin of his that caught my heart the first time I saw him about a year ago.

He has to work tonight, but he said he'd come with me to a place north of Kettle Falls. Someone told him about the national forest in the area around Northport and said it was a good for both mule deer and white tail deer. And elk, too, if we could get a permit.

I walked over to his white Silverado truck where he strapped my rifle into the rack behind the seat. Tossing my backpack and jacket on the seat, I clambered into the high cab.

"You do this just to annoy me," I said in way of greeting, scowling at him.

His honest blue eyes twinkled as he brushed straight, brown hair from his forehead. "What? What'd I do now?" He frowned like he was offended, yet his eyes twinkled.

I slammed the door shut. "You park beside an incline so it feels like I'm scaling Mount Everest to get into this beast." I clicked on the seat belt and grinned at him, relenting. "Hi. How ya doin'?"

He laughed and shook his head, putting the truck into gear. "I'm doin' fine. I park here all the time. Hey, you get up on the wrong side of the bed this mornin'? Or haven't you had your coffee yet?" He chuckled and cast me a glance, pulling onto the highway, heading north.

I lifted my coffee mug and grimaced. "Wrong on both counts, cowboy. You got your lunch?"

"Shore do. What'd you bring? Some of those chocolate chip cookies you make?" He looked at my backpack like I was going to pull one out right then.

"Yeah. I might have. But you can't go wandering off if we're going to share lunch."

I've been with him before on hikes, like when we went picking huckleberries last summer, and he has a tendency to wander off without even knowing he's doing it.

"If you've got chocolate chip cookies, I'll stick to you like glue."

After driving through Chewelah, we continued north on 395, through Colville and Kettle Falls. After we left that little burg, we crossed the northern end of Lake Roosevelt and continued on the Northport/Flat Creek Road on the west side of the river.

About fifteen minutes later, Chance turned onto a dirt road that led through dense forest west up into the mountains. The road climbed over a ridge. I admired the view of the valley below and the river through the trees as I studied the country for possible places to hunt.

The road ended in a small meadow. Chance parked and hopped out. It was a little chilly, so I pulled on the new gloves I'd gotten at Cabela's – Montana Gloves by North Face, guaranteed to keep my hands warm in the coldest weather. I wondered if I should wear them. They could hinder my trigger finger if I had to go for my gun in a hurry.

You can't get away from being a police officer. I've been with the Special Intelligence Unit in Spokane for over a year now, and I love it, even though I have to deal with the under-belly of humanity in the city every day. I like helping those who can't fight for themselves, bringing some sort of justice in a world that is unjust.

"Which way are we heading?" I shrugged into my backpack and grabbed my rifle.

He nodded to the right. "Up over that ridge is my best bet for where game might hang out. You got any ideas?"

"I'd like to check out that lake we saw coming in. Animals need water and always come down for it."

"Okay. You do that. My gosh, this day has God stamped all over it."

"You're right about that." I inhaled a deep breath of fresh mountain air. "Let's go."

A crow called out his raspy croaking cry and took wing from his perch on the tall pine over our heads. A breeze stirred my hair. We started out.

Summer was here at last. The sunshine's rays warmed my back and kissed the grasses that would soon turn golden. The branches of the tall firs that towered above us sported tender new growth, and the air was scented with pine and moldy piles of dead leaves in places where the sun rarely comes.

After winding up the mountain, the trail leveled off, and we emerged in a meadow. It was bursting with new life, yet a growing sense of unease crept into my consciousness. *Is there someone out there, watching us?*

I didn't want to say anything to Chance because I figured he has good observation skills. But he wasn't thinking about danger lurking in the forest eaves – he was thinking about that trophy mule deer rack he would hang on his barn.

"You still want to go check out that lake?"

"Yeah. Where are you headed?"

"I'd like to take a look from that rocky point over there. How about if we meet down on the river in about ... an hour? You think you can find your way to the river?"

I nudged him with my elbow. "I can find my way anywhere. See you in an hour. But if you're not there, the cookies are mine."

"I'll be there, don't worry. Hey. Stay out of trouble, okay? I don't want to have to come and rescue you."

I snorted. "It'll be the other way around. See you."

I didn't wait to watch him walk off, but turned abruptly and started down the deer trail that led to the lake below. After crossing a creek on stones that were strung out like an irregular necklace, I followed a path that wound through a stand of tall pines.

Twenty minutes later, I came to the lake. It was a pretty little pond. When I scanned the ground, I saw no deer or elk tracks or any of their droppings. Hm. They must not have come down from their wintering places yet. I peeled off my gloves, shoved them in my pocket, and continued on.

It wasn't long before I found a new trail. Following it, I circled the small lake, looking for animal signs. I found some on the northern bank. Ok. They've been here. It looked like deer.

A while later, when I figured my hour was about up, I trotted downhill and crossed the highway. After I descended another hundred yards, I found a comfortable spot on the river. Some old deer droppings were scattered around at my feet.

Right here, the wide Columbia River flows south toward Coulee Dam and a series of other dams on its approach to Portland, Oregon. Further north, the Pend Oreille River joins it at the Canadian border.

I checked my watch. It had been exactly forty-nine minutes since I told Chance good-bye up there on the hill. My stomach grumbled about the fact that breakfast had been a long time ago, so I sat in the sunshine on a convenient log that faced the river, leaned my rifle next to my knee, and took off my backpack.

I tell myself that Chance won't mind if I eat my sandwich and apple. I'd save the cookies for when he joined me. I unwrapped my slightly squished ham and cheese sandwich and made short work of my lunch.

When I was finished, I stowed the papers in my pack, then wandered down by the water and studied the sandy ground. Picked up a rock and chucked it into the water.

The river made a bend right here – I couldn't see too far to the north, but across the river, I spotted a cliff side of shiny white rock, exposed to the sun. I'd seen another place on this side of the river that was white rock. Maybe there was a rock quarry there, or someone had a mining operation.

Returning to my spot by the log, I glanced at my watch again. *Where's Chance?* He should've been here by now. It was when I was standing there, perfectly outlined against the sky and the river, when that the shot came.

Now, getting tired of the cramped position I'm forced to hold, I glance right and left from my position behind the fallen tree, trying to work out a way to crawl to safety and shelter.

I had not chosen my perch very wisely – no cover, front or back. Yet I couldn't have known that someone would take a pot-shot at me, and worse, would wait for me to show myself so he could finish me off.

Dry brush crackles under the weight of the person in the bushes. He's working his way carefully to the right. After risking a quick look around, I understand. There's a big pine at the edge of the bushes. If he can get to it, he can shoot on my right. This time to kill.

While he's busy working his way through the thicket, I have to do something.

With a lunge and a roll, I dive over the log and scoot behind a rock. It isn't nearly enough cover for my whole body, but at least my head and shoulders are out of the line of fire. Another shot blasts through the quiet air. This one cracks off a big chunk of rock about six inches from my face. I flatten myself on the ground and peer around the boulder.

Thinking I can see a shape in the thicket, I aim and shoot. The sound echoes off the river behind me, and another crow cries noisily from the pines. Other than that, there is no sound. No movement. I didn't even wing him.

Darn. Now he knows my exact location.

Sweat burns my eyeballs. I plant my elbows into the soil and peer through the sights at the gap between the tangle of bushes and the tree. If he emerges even for a second, I'm ready to send another bullet his way.

Now I hear something else. A canoe approaches the river bank, coming from the north. There's the splash of paddles, the grating of the boat against the shale on the bank, the plunk of feet in the water, and the sound of someone pulling the boat up higher on the ground.

I risk a glance. It's a man carrying a rifle under his arm. Hope surges through me like adrenalin, thinking that he might be coming to help me, until I see him nod to my assailant in the bushes. Now I'm really sweating.

The man is dressed in camouflage and is wearing a wide-brimmed hat that shades his face. I think he has a beard. There's no time to notice all the details, because he's walking toward me, and he isn't smiling.

They must have been communicating with two-way radios since there isn't any cell service here. I scuttle back to the scant cover of a bush and a small tree, hoping they're more concerned with freaking me out than killing me.

Well, they'd accomplished their purpose concerning scaring me, and when I get frightened, it makes me mad. I'm prepared to shout at the man on the beach and tell him to stop in his tracks when the person in the bushes fires at me.

Tree bark sprays my face and something pings into my shoulder, spinning me backward. I regain my balance and see blood oozing from a rip in my jacket on my left shoulder.

The man on the beach yells, "All right! Come out! We have you covered. I don't want to kill you. Just throw down your gun, and we'll have a talk. We won't hurt you."

Yeah, right.

I scoot further into the brush, maybe three feet, and find a snug little place below a stump. The vantage point is good, and I think I'm concealed with the bushes. I can see the beach man's head and shoulders, but there are lots of branches between me and him. I aim and shoot.

He drops, and I think I got him. He's out of sight. Maybe I winged him. I don't know. How could I miss a shot that easy?

If I was a swearing person, I would blister the air with profanity, but I only dig my feet into the soil and reload. Twigs snap and brush crackles. Someone is coming for me. There's more of them. How many? Three?

The second man approaches on my left. From my peripheral vision, I guess his location and swing my rifle around, sending a bullet into the brush, shooting with more abandon and hope than precise aim.

He yelps and goes down with a crash of underbrush. Another shot explodes from a rock near the water, splintering the tree trunk near my face. I shake my head and glance around, searching for a way out. If I don't move, I'm dead. That's all there is to it.

Chapter 2

Ready to Kill

I have to do something.

Leaping from my position, I hightail it out of there as bullets whiz around my head. I head up the bank towards the road, scrambling through bushes and over dead trees on the ground, my desperation driving me forward despite the danger of being hit.

Panting, I get to the road and hope I can flag down a car, but the chance of one passing by is slim.

They'll follow me. That's a given.

I climb the hill on the other side of the road in the direction of where we left the pickup. After about a hundred yards, I stop and strip off my jacket, and my plaid shirt, going down to my t-shirt. The wound is high on my left shoulder and hurts like a stab wound. It's bleeding freely, and I need all my blood inside me right now.

After I assess the wound, I decide it's not too deep. I tie the plaid shirt around it, wincing with pain. That will have to do until I can get better care for it. That's about the time I hear brush crackling close by and look up to see Chance emerge from a dense cover of bushes.

"What's going on, Gina? It sounds like you've got a war in progress. You been shot?" He looks at my arm. "You need somethin' more on that?"

I'm so relieved at seeing him, I almost collapse. My speech comes in short gasps."No ... I'm ... fine. We gotta ... get out of here, though. They're coming. Arm's okay for now. Stopped the bleeding."

"Who's after you? What's happening?"

"Someone tried to kill me. Darn near succeeded. Can't explain now. Come on."

I put on my jacket and zip it closed. Taking a glance around, I note the landmarks. There's a giant Ponderosa pine down by the river. I should be able to find that again. And behind me on the mountain there's that sheer rock cliff that's white. We're about five miles south of Northport.

I lead the way toward the truck in a slow run and hear him sprinting behind me. I don't stop for about ten minutes. When we halt for breath, I remember my backpack by the log. *Shucks!* It was my favorite, too. But hell or high water wouldn't make me go back for it. I'm thankful I hadn't stuck any personal information in it.

Chance points through the trees. "The truck's over that way. Bear more to your right."

I nod. I'm usually pretty good at directions, but today my mind is messed up, and I'd gone astray a little bit. I'd have missed the meadow by a mile if I'd kept going the way I was headed.

I slow down and tell him in a low tone what happened. After my summary, I conclude, "That man who came in the boat, the one with the Aussie hat, was coming to meet his friends, I'm sure of that. I must have interrupted a meeting. But I can't understand why they started shooting. If they'd left me alone, I wouldn't have thought anything other than that there were some men who were coming ashore in a boat."

He nods, swishing back a tree branch for me. "They couldn't let you see who they were. Maybe they're smuggling drugs from Canada." He glances at me. "We've never had anyone try to do it on the river, but I suppose it's possible."

We climb the hill and pause at the top, studying our back trail. It doesn't seem like anyone's following. He brushes back his blond hair from his forehead and pierces me with his clear blue eyes.

"There's a lot of drugs coming into the US from Canada, but ... well, it seems there's more to this than that."

"I agree with that. Those men were ready to kill. Trained to kill. Terrorists, you think? But why here? What's drawing them?"

10

"You think?"

"Yeah. Who else would do that? But here? In this empty corner of the state?"

He nods. "Exactly. I've heard of people coming down further west of here around unpopulated ports to get across the border, smuggling. Got anything on your news feeds at work about extra crime activity?"

"No. Nothing. But I don't check the FBI reports or CIA. That's federal."

He shakes his head. "Seems like you stumbled into a bee's nest, Gina."

"And you came to rescue me."

"Well, let's get home before we start patting each other on the back."

Picking our way carefully, we get down off the hillside and approach the meadow where his truck is parked. Chance puts a cautionary hand in front of me.

I stop and hold my breath, listening. Are they here, waiting for us? His white truck is parked maybe a hundred yards away. It looks like a sanctuary. A haven. But we have to get there first.

Someone is here.

Cold chills race up and down my back and prickle my arms.

"What are we going to do? We have to get to the truck." My whisper sounds whiney, even to my ears.

Chance nods. He's gripping his rifle until his knuckles are white. "Don't know. Pray."

"I am." It's one of those short, urgent pleas to God. *Help!*

We wait in the shelter of the big pines. My mind returns to the puzzle. If it was a shipment of drugs, I wonder where they were headed with it. Maybe south, through the forest, someplace where they could load it into a car or a van.

Even with the legalization of marijuana, there are plenty of people who are producing, packaging and selling drugs for huge profits – heroin, black tar, which is a lethal concoction of heroin, cocaine, and meth.

Bringing my mind back to the business at hand, I hold my breath, listening. Besides a squirrel scolding us from the treetops, nothing is stirring. A twig snaps. All the forest creatures, even the birds, are silent.

Big black clouds are forming overhead, and a wind begins sighing through the treetops. A pine cone drops nearby. I jump, whirling, bringing my rifle around. Chance remains steady, staring at the forest across the meadow. How long will we have to wait? Are those men truly here, aiming to kill us when we step out of the trees?

"We're going to make a run for the truck, Gina. Get ready. On the count of three." He has his gun held firmly under his arm and a finger on the trigger. He's carrying the keys in his other hand. "This is going to be tricky."

I bring my rifle up. "Okay. I'm ready." But am I? Ready to die? I know where I'd go, but I desperately want to live. I have things to do. My mind flashes to the search I've been making for my mother. To the cases we have pending in the police force. To the girls I'd like to save from the sex trade. To the little house I'd like to paint, and the horse I'd like to train.

What are the chances for our survival?

Plenty slim. Chance's body stiffens. He draws a sharp breath. It's a sure bet our assailants don't want us telling anyone about what happened on the river bank. The fact that the man walked toward me without concealing his face showed they were planning to kill.

I take a gulp of fresh air.

"Okay." He says in a murmur. A second later, we're in motion.

We dash out of cover, guns held up, level. It's hard to hold the rifle steady when you're sprinting across uneven ground, but I'm scared, and almost anything is possible when you have adrenalin flooding your system. It doesn't take much imagination to feel the searing heat of a bullet between my shoulder blades.

Gunfire begins when we approach the vehicle. Slugs kick up the dirt around us. I jam it into high gear, but I can't catch Chance.

He moves out in front of me. He knows the line of fire, and he's taking the heat for me. But I'm not far behind him. We reach the truck and cower down beside it. Heavy rifle fire roars, and following that, another shot from a smaller gun blasts the air. The back window, where my head was a moment ago, explodes with shattered glass.

Chance mutters something under his breath as he fumbles for the key. I clench my teeth. The men stay hidden, but the firepower coming our way from an embankment across the meadow hasn't lessened. They are bent on eliminating us, and I'm bent on staying alive.

Chance drops the key. I scramble for it and retrieve it in one desperate swoop.

He fits it to the lock. It won't open. While he wrestles with the lock, I sense more than see them coming out of cover. Four of them. Sweat almost blinds me, but I don't bother to wipe it off.

"They're coming," I say quietly and turn, bringing my rifle around. When they're close enough, I'll shoot. I can hardly hear anything over the roar of gunfire and the pounding of my heart. My mouth is so dry, I couldn't spit if my life depended on it.

Finally, what my life *does* depend on happens. The key turns.

He opens the door and in one quick, fluid motion, shoves me up into the driver's seat. I scramble across. He leaps up beside me and swings shut the door. The motor is running before I can get my feet out of his way. He slams it into gear and pours on the gas, wrenching the steering wheel sharply. The truck skids in a circle, sliding in the soft dirt.

A sinking feeling in my gut tells me we're not going to make it — they will blast out the tires, kill us, and someone will find a burned vehicle in the meadow, and our bodies tossed under a pile of leaves. I hear myself sobbing. Please, God! Please! I want to live! Help us!

More shots reach the truck. The front windshield shatters.

"Get down!" He presses the gas pedal harder and wheels around a corner. We're out of their line of fire for a moment, on the rutted road. Chance eases up on the gas.

"You ... okay?" He says, gasping for air.

"Yeah. I can't believe we did it. It was ... a miracle. Thank You, God!"

He nods grimly. "Yeah. Now let's pray they don't have a vehicle nearby."

I don't breathe freely until we get to the highway. I pull out my cell phone when we get close to town and call 911. The dispatcher says they'll send an officer to the scene right away.

Half an hour later, we pull into a gas station in Kettle Falls. I climb out and almost fall flat on my face – my knees are like butter and my hands are shaking.

Chance gasses up the pickup, but we do it like we're at a pit stop on a race track. He keeps a sharp watch on the traffic on the highway. "We can't stay here. Let's get back home."

We climb into the vehicle. My shoulder starts to scream at me, pain radiating down my arm and up my neck. I put my hand on the wound. It's oozing more blood. "Maybe we could stop at the hospital in Chewelah. My shoulder might need a couple of stitches."

"Yeah." He nods. "My nerves could stand a cup of coffee. You okay? Can you make it that far?"

"Sure. Just drive and try to stay on the road."

He laughs and reaches over to pat my knee. "You're a trooper, Gina. I'm glad we got out safely."

"Me, too." I squeeze his hand.

My nose needs blowing, so I dig in my pocket for a tissue. Out comes my Montana Made Doeskin gloves! I have an urge to scream right there in Chance's Silverado pickup from sheer relief.

"Look. I still have my gloves," I say, lifting them up.

He smiles. "So, you do. Your favorite gloves. Congratulations."

"I almost lost my life," I say in a shaky voice, "and I lost my backpack. But I didn't lose my gloves."

Chapter 3

On the Prowl

June 4th

It was late before Chance pulled into his driveway. Gina's shoulder required a little more than a couple of stitches, but the ER in the hospital in Chewelah wasn't busy and he got his cup of coffee.

At the farmhouse, he stepped out of his damaged truck and walked her to her pickup. He lingered by the vehicle, reluctant to say good-bye, admiring the way the setting sun brought red highlights to her hair. She turned and looked up at him, her mouth tilting in that cocky grin of hers, her eyes snapping with her droll Irish humor.

"Well, that was quite a day. Sure appreciated your help. If it hadn't been for you ..." She sniffed and turned to fit the key into the lock of her pickup. "Well, I might not be here." She touched him lightly on the arm and hopped in the vehicle.

"I just wish you'd stay here tonight," he said, leaning down. "I'll be a gentleman. What if they find you? Come after you tonight?"

She laughed. "I'm fine, cowboy. No need to be babysit me. All I need is a hot shower, a couple of pills, and my bed. Then I'll be good as new."

He straightened, glancing around uneasily. "Keep your eyes open, okay? Those guys were determined to make an end to us. Call me tomorrow. Are you going to tell your boss about what happened?"

She started the motor. "Probably. Let me know what the sheriff says when you talk to him."

"Will do. Take care." He wanted to protect her, yet he knew it was useless to offer help. She wouldn't accept it.

He doubted that the sheriff would take this seriously, especially since no one was killed. Gina was hurt, but her injures would be deemed minor. Well, he might have to hike back in and take a look around. And while he was at it, he would visit the sheriff in Republic.

The next morning, he got a shower, and after packing a lunch, climbed in his truck, ready for work. After a twenty-minute drive to Colville, he parked in front of the US Border Patrol office building.

"Mornin', sir," he called when he entered the office.

The man behind the desk, Supervising Agent Stuart McCurry, held a sandwich in one hand and a radio in the other while studying the screen of the computer. The sandwich would be ham with mustard and lettuce, no mayonnaise, and that an empty bag of Salt and Vinegar chips would by the computer or on the floor. A paper cup from the Jamin' Java Drive-through Espresso stood near his elbow on the desk.

McClurry grunted and nodded. "Hey, Marshal. I got something here you might be interested in." He waved a brochure in the air, not taking his eyes from the screen.

Chance took it and glanced at it. "A survival camp?"

"Yeah. But there's more to it than that. Classes on how to shoot guns. On weapons of all kinds. Tracking. Martial arts. It's located right in your neck of the woods. Chewelah."

"You're kidding me." The brochure was a slick presentation with first-class pictures. The title read, "Forward Guard Weapons and Military Training Camp."

In smaller letters, there was more information. "A five-day retreat for individuals who are gun enthusiasts, who would like to learn martial arts and more about weapons, and who like challenges. The food is superb, the training is tough, and the setting is matchless. Guaranteed money back if you are not 100% satisfied."

He looked up. "Forward Guard? I didn't know something like this was in the area." He set the brochure on the counter top. "What do you know about them?"

"Not a thing. Just thought you'd like to go, that's all." McClurry lifted his eyes and grinned. "Someone left it on my desk."

Chance opened the brochure. "I'll take a look at it. Might be interesting, a week of shooting guns and learning some new techniques. Yeah, I'll check it out. But it's next week. Isn't it too late to sign up? And how about time off?"

"Oh, we can work something out. Give them a call."

"Okay." Chance pocketed the brochure. He nodded to the secretary and went back outside, around the back of the building, to the long barn and corrals where the horses were kept.

It was a large, airy indoor stable that smelled of horses, hay, and manure. This was the holding barn for Project Noble Mustang, begun in the spring of 2007, in which wild mustangs, brought from Wyoming, were trained to ride for the patrol in the rugged wilderness area in the Spokane Sector.

Dynamite was a sturdy black horse with white markings on his body and legs. Chance clomped down the long aisle with the bridle, halter, rope and saddle. A nicker of welcome greeted him when he approached the stall. He set to work grooming, saddling and bridling the horse.

Awhile later, his partner, Dusty, entered the barn and began preparing Laredo, his favorite mount, the same way. He was an older agent, gray-haired, seasoned with many years on the border.

They loaded the horses in a trailer, got in the Border Patrol SUV, and headed north. It was almost 1100 hours when they arrived at the staging area behind the Patterson border station on Highway 25, north of Northport.

There they unloaded the horses and mounted.

Chance settled his hat more firmly and glanced over at Dusty. The man met his eyes with a kind of glimmer in them like he enjoyed a joke at Chance's expense.

17

Chance loved the horse patrol, riding in the woods, protecting the country he loved. Yet realized he could be heading straight into the mouth of a firefight. There was danger out there. He couldn't afford a moment of laxity like he was taking a pleasure ride.

He wanted to make a success out of this, to prove himself. *But why? And to whom?* The answer came readily – to Dad, the man he barely knew growing up. The man who was always too busy. The man who could never give any kind of approval, even now.

He shrugged off the depressing thoughts and brought his mind back to the task.

A brisk wind, holding a hint of summer, stirred the treetops and carried the scent of pine and fir. The sun was hidden behind a cover of heavy clouds that threatened to bring a summer's storm on its front.

Calming his fidgety mount with a hand on his neck, he looked around, trying to determine which way to go. They'd been informed that one of the border guards had seen tracks crossing the border west of their position.

"Let's head over that way," he said, motioning with his head to the west. "I heard there's been some activity over there."

"Sounds good."

It was rough terrain, but the mustangs were strong, agile and able to navigate fallen logs, steep hillsides, and tangled brush. Chance liked to see the border swath from a high point, stretching east and west, a straight line through dense forest. They wouldn't be riding in the actual swath but would follow trails that ran alongside it.

The wind picked up, moaning eerily in the trees, and the sun peeked out from behind a bank of high clouds. Besides the wind, the forest was silent. There were coyotes and wolves in the area, but Chance had never seen them on a patrol.

They ate lunch as the storm grew closer, bringing the sound of thunder on the wind. Without much conversation, they mounted and continued on their patrol.

Chance was riding easy, Dynamite's hooves thudding on the pine-carpeted trail, when something landed on a rock beside the trail about twenty paces ahead, a tawny streak in the dim light. He made out its yellow eyes and lashing tail. A cougar!

Chance couldn't take much time to look at it because he was busy trying to stay in the saddle. His mustang was living up to his name, bucking and fighting the reins like a rodeo bronc.

He slid to the ground and held onto the reins. The horse reared. "That's okay, fella," he said, knowing it probably wasn't. Dynamite didn't believe him, either. Chance laid a calming hand on his neck when he came down.

When he had time to look around, the cougar had vanished. Evidently Dynamite smelled the cat again because he jumped back and snorted. The reins wrenched Chance's wrist and burned through his gloves. He gritted his teeth and hung on, reaching for his department issued pistol, a Berretta 96D Brigadier.

He tried to locate the cougar, but it remained hidden. It was close. Very close. A chill raced down his spine. Maybe he'd interrupted the feline's dinner. Maybe dinner was supposed to be a horse and man.

He waited, his heart pounding heavily, sweat prickling his neck. *Ah.* There he was, crouching beside a big stump, preparing for a spring. Chance lifted the pistol and everything faded from his consciousness. He only saw the animal, heard its deep, throaty growl. He pulled the trigger.

The cat leaped away an instant before the bullet left his gun. Dynamite jumped when the pistol discharged, pawing the ground and fighting Chance's hold on the reins with eyes rolled back and teeth bared.

"Easy, boy. We have to make sure that cat's gone." Another thought struck him. What would happen when Dusty, his partner, came around the bend?

Chance was ready to remount when the sound of horse's hooves beat a steady rhythm on the ground. It was Dusty on his buckskin.

19

"Got trouble?" Dusty called.

"A cougar," Chance replied. "Don't know where he's at, but he's close."

Dusty jumped off his horse as Laredo caught the cat's scent and pranced to the side. The agent landed on his feet and maintained his hold on the reins. Chance sensed more than saw Dusty hunch down beside the horse and draw his gun.

They waited, breathing hard. After five minutes, Chance straightened. Dynamite had calmed down and so had Laredo, a sure sign the cougar had moved on.

"Let's go." Chance looped the reins over Dynamite's neck and mounted, trying to appear composed, even though his heart was beating itself out of his chest, and his breathing was harsh in his throat.

Dusty nodded. "Sure." He mounted and waited for Chance to take the lead.

Chance tapped Dynamite on the flanks and started out, saying over his shoulder, "Let's keep our eyes open. I don't like the idea of that mountain lion stalking our trail. Maybe we should head back."

"No, we have to go on. We got somethin' worse than a cougar to worry about. I got a call from dispatch. That's why I was laggin' behind you. We got visitors from the north. They set off the seismic sensor about two miles west."

The border guard used three kinds of sensors to identify illegal activity. Seismic sensors could be set off with footfalls, infra-red sensors detected movement, and magnetic sensors alerted the guard to a vehicle passing over or nearby.

Chance groaned. "Okay. Let's angle south and intercept them on the logging road." The road was located in a narrow valley where two mountains met, a place where a person was forced to descend to the path, and so providing a perfect funnel to catch illegal activity. "How many?"

"Didn't say. She thought it was one, but it could be two."

Dread knotted Chance's stomach as he urged the horse to a trot. Along with that came a rush of adrenalin, flooding his veins like a shot of whiskey. He never knew what to expect when he started out on one of these patrols, and when they had to apprehend people, anything could happen.

He directed Dynamite onto a dim trail by a creek. After a while, he turned southwest. In about ten minutes, they emerged on the logging road. He pulled back on the reins and slid to the ground. Dusty did the same. They tied the mustangs to slender birch trees and made their way silently toward the road.

Chance eased his pistol from its holster as he spotted movement through the brush. He nodded. Dusty didn't move a muscle, but Chance knew he was ready for anything.

A dark figure appeared briefly, disappeared, then came into full view when the clouds moved apart and allowed the scant sunlight to shine briefly on the scene. One person of small build marched straight ahead. He wore dark clothing and a back pack. Dispatch said two. He waited to see the second, but no one appeared.

Chance reached up and pressed a button on his radio that would alert dispatch that they had a visual. He clutched the revolver in his right hand. It was hard to wait, but he knew they couldn't flush the quarry too soon and cause them to turn tail and run back over the border. Of course, from here it would be a long run, but some people thought they could do it.

No, it was better to wait until they were so close there was no possible way to escape. The person hiked purposefully forward with his head up and arms swinging. Still there was no sign of the second one.

Blood pounded hard in his ears. He gripped his gun and glanced over at Dusty. The older agent nodded. When the hiker came parallel to their position, Chance stepped out quickly from the brush and moved into position, blocking his progress. Dusty was behind him.

"Hello, there," he said conversationally. "Out for a stroll?" He stood in front of the person, blocking the path.

The walker chuckled. "Yes, sir. Any law against that?"

Chance drew in his breath, surprised. It was a woman. She was slender with dark hair tucked up under a wide-brimmed hat. She kept her head bent like she didn't want him seeing her face. Someone else emerged from the cover of forest about twenty yards back. It was a boy.

"No law against taking a walk, ma'am, but there's plenty of laws against crossin' the border illegally." Chance stepped closer to get a good view of her face, but she turned away from him, looking back over her shoulder at the boy who approached cautiously.

"Come on up here, youngster," Dusty called to him. "We have something we need to talk about." But still the boy hung back. It made Chance nervous because now he had to watch both of them.

"You came from Canada. We have proof of that, ma'am. We're going to ask you to show us what is in your backpack. After that, you'll come along with us to headquarters for a talk."

The woman laughed. She turned slightly to speak to the boy behind her. "Get down. They're bluffing. I don't think they can ..."

At that moment, several things happened at once. The woman bent over like she was going to tie her shoe lace. From the corner of his eye, Chance saw the boy drop to his haunches and pull something from his pocket.

Light gleamed on the black muzzle of a revolver.

These things registered in Chance's brain like a zap of lightning, but before he could react to the information, the boy fired. Dusty groaned and crumpled to the ground.

The woman screamed at the boy, "No! You fool!"

Chance shoved her aside, jumped ahead to the youngster, and kicked the weapon from his hand. The woman staggered but did not fall, and when he turned to her, she lashed out with her foot, connecting solidly with his *solar plexis*, a blow that would have taken out a heavy weight boxing champion.

He slumped to the ground, not unconscious, yet gasping for breath and unable to lift a finger, let alone the pistol that was still in his hand. There was no way he could defend himself or Dusty if they decided to shoot again.

The woman and the boy fled south, disappearing into the dark eaves of the forest. It was several moments before he could move, and when he struggled to his knees, he bent over Dusty's body, wiping his eyes with his sleeve.

There was a bloody hole in the back of the man's green jacket the size of a quarter. Chance turned him over. Another hole in his chest was where the bullet exited his body. It was laced with black powder. Blood flowed freely from it. It had been a big revolver with a lot of fire power to drive a bullet straight through his partner's body.

Chance folded his kerchief into a neat square and pressed it hard on the wound. He felt for a pulse in the neck and found one. Blood oozed from the kerchief. He'd have to find something more.

Dusty moaned, and his eyes fluttered open. "Can't see ... Chance. You there? You ... okay? It's ... dark. Did they get away?"

Chance stripped off his jacket, his shirt underneath, and tore off his undershirt. It didn't take more than twenty seconds to rip it into strips. These he folded into a square and pressed onto the wound.

"Yeah, they got away. I'm sorry, Dusty ... so sorry. It was my fault. Should've seen it coming. Couldn't stop it. So sorry."

Chapter 4

A Boyfriend Named Jim

A girl pulled out a worn blue notebook and lifted a pen from the desk. Turning the pages, she came to a blank one and began to write.

I decided to write about my life, boring as it is, because I don't have no one else to talk to, and they said in school that a person should write things down to make you feel better.

I started my story awhile ago, but I haven't written in my notebook for a long time. I was meaning to write every day, but I got too busy and forgot about it. Way to go, Sanora Brooks. I should have remembered to write. Paid better attention to things. I'm always so forgetful and stupid. My birthday and everything else important has gone by since I wrote last.

Now I'm almost fourteen and Mom says I'm nearly grown up.

When I look in the mirror, I see a little girl who's scared and stupid looking. She has mousy blond hair, an ugly nose and watery blue eyes. No one ever notices me, except for Angie Somners, my BFF.

You probably wouldn't notice me in a crowd, either, except that I have a bruise over one eye, and so I let my hair fall down to cover it. It's like I don't really have a face, you know what I mean? And if I did, I'd want to hide it.

My life up to this point has been extremely boring. I don't do anything exciting or fun, except like one time when my class went to a museum. Oh, there was the time we went skiing at Mt. Spokane and that was like cool. It wasn't fun when someone pushed me into a snow bank, and the other kids laughed.

When I think of it, I feel bad because I hear about other people having fun and going places and playing sports and being in the school play. I don't get to do things like that because I have to go home and take care of the little kids. We don't have any money for that stuff anyway. Like I said, it's just work at home and school.

I daydream about being someone else, like Kitty Belfounte who is like the most popular girl in the school. She has boyfriends, money, clothes and everything. Besides, she's cute and has a really good figure that the boys drool over.

Well, I got a boyfriend. Not like a real boyfriend. No guy in the real world would even look at me unless they was making fun of me. I connected with this guy, Jim, on the internet several months ago, and I really like him. We text all the time, and I can talk to him and he understands me. I tell him about my life, and he listens.

Like the other day when I told him how Buster, Mom's boyfriend, he came home mad drunk because he'd lost another job, so he went and wasted all his ending paycheck on booze. Mom was still at work. She'd told me to fix some macaroni for dinner, but I didn't get around to it, and before you know it, the door slams open and Buster comes staggering in.

The little kids, Jamie and Bonnie, ran and hid. I didn't have anywhere to go because they locked the bathroom door. I would have gone to the bedroom, but the door is off, and no one has fixed it yet. So I kind of like hunkered down, making myself small, and hoped he wouldn't see me. But he did, of course, and stomped over and yanked my hair.

I screamed, and he slapped me a couple of times. I didn't mind the slapping, even though it hurt, but I did mind the names he called me. I ran outside, but I didn't go far, because I knew if he didn't have me to torment, he'd yank the bathroom door from the hinges and get at the little kids. I couldn't allow that to happen. I had my phone in my pocket, so I called Mom.

She didn't answer at first, and when she did, she sounded tired. "Whad'ya want?"

I was sobbing, trying to breathe. When I could talk, I choked out, "It's Buster, Mom. He lost his job ... and he's drunk ... and he was hitting me like he did the last time. I can't take it. I'm going to call the cops."

"Don't you dare!" Her screech filled my ear. "They'd take you away from me." She started to cry. When she recovered, she said, "I'm ... busy, but, well, okay, I'll tell them I'm sick. I'm coming, sweetheart. Be there in about ten minutes. Don't call the cops. Just try to stay away from him."

I hid in the old shed in the back yard, but I was shaking and so terrified that my teeth were chattering because I knew he could find me in there. I hoped he wouldn't remember the shed and that he wouldn't get to the little kids and take out his anger on them.

Why does Mom stay with him? I can't figure her out. He beats her, abuses all of us, cheats and lies, yet she stays with him. I think it's because he says he has money. He told Mom he has a lot stashed away somewhere, and that if she's good to him, he'll share it with her. It's another lie, but she believes him.

Mom got home that night and things settled down. Sometimes she can calm him, kind of scolding him like she's his mom. We boiled macaroni but didn't have anything to put on it, not even any margarine. Oh, we did have a little bit of peanut butter, so Jamie and Bonnie put it on their macaroni and said it was good. Go figure! There wasn't a single solitary thing in the house to eat after that.

We live in an old house with mice and spiders and all sorts of things living with us. Mom pays for the rent, and Buster's supposed to pay for the food, which is why we go hungry a lot. He drinks it all up before he gets home.

At least I don't have to wonder what I'm going to wear to school. I only have a couple of shirts, two pairs of ripped jeans, and one skirt. I was still hungry that night when we went to bed. I cried into my pillow like I do most nights, and I knew when I got up in the morning, there would be nothing to eat.

That's when I thought about Jim. He leads a totally different kind of life. His folks don't fight, and they give him stuff. He has food to eat and nice clothes to wear. He sent me pictures of their house and his bedroom. It was so sweet. I was almost drooling, wondering what it would be like to live like that. I didn't know people lived that way, so peaceful and happy, and that they love each other and don't fight that much. And having that much money. I couldn't believe it!

He said he'd like me to go over to his house sometime. He goes to college to become an electrician, like his dad. His mom is a receptionist in a dental clinic. He drives his own car, and they have a boat, a four-wheeler and an RV. They have a large flat-screen TV. Each one of them has an I-pad, and they have three or four computers and smart phones.

Like my mouth waters when I think of a closet full of clothes, more shoes than I know what to do with, food to fill my stomach and lots left over, soda and chips and candy all the time, and nice jewelry to wear.

Jim says that if I come to live with him, he'll give me all this. He says his folks don't mind if I come. They have several bedrooms they don't use, and if I clean the house, they'll pay me enough so I can buy stuff.

I'd hate to leave Mom and the kids alone with Buster, to face his temper tantrums and drunken fits. But I figure if I can like earn enough money, I'll come back and get the kids, and we can rent an apartment. If I can get a good job, we'll be free of Buster once and for all.

This morning I made up my mind to meet Jim. I can't stand it any longer. Jim texted me, and we set up a date. I'm scared because it's the first time I've seen him face to face. I'm afraid he won't like me when he sees what a loser I am, but he says he already loves me and wants the best for me. Like, wow.

I washed out my best shirt and borrowed Mom's black skirt and shoes. I'm glad she's small, and we're the same size, more or less. I haven't told her about the date because I'm afraid she'll say I can't go out with someone I haven't met before.

But I have met Jim! On the internet... He's nice and funny, and he cares about me. He's the only one that does, as far as I can tell. Anything is better than this with Buster drunk most of the time and no food in the house and Mom crying all the time.

I made the date for tonight at six because Mom will still be working, and Buster said he was going to be gone, too. I'll fix something for the kids, probably cold cereal, then tuck them in bed. I'll meet Jim down by the drug store on Division Street. Oh, man! I am so scared and excited! I'll write in here tomorrow night and tell you all about it.

I'm sooooo excited!

Chapter 5

A Long, Lonesome Night

Near the Canadian border, June 4th

Chance knelt in the damp grass beside Dusty's prone body and sucked the cool air in through his teeth. This was going to be touch and go. The wound was high, so maybe it hadn't damaged his heart, but it most definitely pierced his partner's lung. He'd stopped the bleeding, but shock was setting in and that could kill a man fast.

He'd called dispatch and related the incident but hadn't had time to talk to his boss.

What made it more difficult was that the storm had arrived. Lightning split the sky and thunder followed. The rain came in a deluge, soaking both him and Dusty to the skin.

Dusty grasped his arm. "Don't be sorry, pal. Hey, who would've guessed a kid would be packing that kind of heat?" He paused, and Chance thought maybe he was unconscious again. But in a few seconds, he said, "You're religious ... ain't you? Can you say a prayer?" The man clung to his hand with more power than he thought possible, given his condition.

Chance closed his eyes and prayed for Dusty and that the storm would abate. He ended with, "And help him know Your love, Lord."

Dusty groaned. Chance leaned over him. His face was as white as snow, and his breathing was raspy. His pulse fluttered.

"Dusty? You there, buddy? Stay with me, okay? I'm gonna get help." He didn't let up on the pressure he was applying to the open wound below his hand.

The man's eyes fluttered open, and he shuddered. "That ... hurts a powerful lot, you know."

"I know. All I can do." He felt like weeping when he heard the rough voice, but he couldn't give into tears. He tied down the bandage and after donning his shirt and jacket, he leaned closer to the wounded man. "You stay with me. Can't do this job alone. I need you."

The storm moved on, rumbling across the mountains like a grumpy old man, and the rain let up. Weak sunshine filtered through frayed clouds as the sun sank behind the horizon.

Chance found a rock and propped Dusty's feet on it. Then he checked his breathing again. It seemed stronger, but he had to get help, or his life would ebb away in the night watches.

It took only about five seconds to get dispatch on his satphone. He reported the incident, hung up, and checked on Dusty again.

Two minutes later, Supervising Agent, Stuart McClurry, called back. "What happened?" The man's voice was taut, abrupt.

Chance knew this would cause him hours of paperwork and conversations on the phone. Maybe even an investigation from the national office. But more than that, McClurry cared for his men.

He told McClurry what happened. His boss said they'd send someone to pick up the smugglers at a lower point near the main road. "Don't worry about them. Just keep Dusty warm. Someone will be along shortly."

"Send a chopper. Tell them there's a meadow here. I'll have a fire going."

"Will do, Chance."

After Chance attached the phone to his belt, he got the horses. Both of them seemed pleased to see him. He led them to a stand of brush about twenty feet from their position. After taking off the saddles and bridles and attaching a rope to their halters, he rummaged in the saddle bags for water, food and emergency rations.

The fire he started was small, but he kept adding sticks and larger pieces of firewood to it until it was actually giving off some heat. He gave Dusty some water. After that, he gently rolled his partner to one side and edged the saddle blanket underneath him. When that was done, he spread the other saddle blanket over him, hoping it was enough protection from the cold.

When all was done that he could do, he found a rock and rolled it near the fire, shivering. How long would it take for the chopper to arrive? An hour? Someone had to get out of bed, drive to the pad, and get it going. That could take several hours.

Sitting with his back propped against the rock, he stared into the fire, a sense of despondency sweeping his soul. Why does everything have to go wrong? A conversation he'd had with Dad about a year ago returned to his mind. Chance called to tell him he'd been accepted for the job with the US Department of Homeland Security Department with the Customs and Border Patrol.

Josh Marshal just grunted. "It's a dead end job, Christian, you know that." He always used Chance's formal name when he was upset. "Why don't you come home and work for me in the office? There's lots of opportunities here for young men who want to rise in the party. It pays well. I'll see to that."

Since Dad had won the election last year, there was no stopping him. He was so focused on his position he could hardly talk about anything else. It seemed his life was spiraling downward, away from God, away from his family. Chance suspected he had even given up some of his morals to please his party friends.

Now he wanted Chance to come and work for him? Chance shook his head, remembering. *No way.*

"It's not about pay." Chance paused and searched for the right words, words that would convey to his father why money and prestige didn't matter to him anymore. "I like the work here. I like being out in the forest, and I like to think I'm doing something to protect our country. That's all there is to it, I guess."

"Yes. I guess so." He heard dismissal in his father's tone. "Well, I have a call coming in. I'll talk to you later."

He hadn't heard from Dad much after that and seen him even less.

He tossed a stick on the fire. *I'm such a colossal failure!* Now Dusty might die, and I should have done something to prevent it.

He sighed and settled back against the rock, the dampness of the ground seeping through his jeans. It would cause a firestorm back in headquarters. He imagined the media blitz, the interviews, the questions, the bigwigs who would descend on Spokane Sector.

Will I be put on administrative leave? But it's not my fault. It was no one's fault. Yet it happened, and no one would thank him when they had to mop up the mess. How could he have known that the kid would have a gun and be ready to kill?

He shivered. A branch snapped behind him in the woods. Was it one of the smugglers, coming back to finish him off? Or the cougar? If that cat smelled blood, it would come around, sniffing out the dinner it had missed. In fact, Chance felt it had never really left them.

After several tense moments, he leaned back against the rock and drew a deep breath. A cougar and armed smugglers all in one shift.

He hefted himself from the ground and paced the area. Checked on Dusty again. *This is going to be a long night.*

***

A man sat behind a large desk and tapped on the keyboard of a computer. His shirt was rumpled and sweaty and his hair a mess. Coffee cups, along with stacks of paper, littered the desk, and the mess extended to the carpet at his feet.

The door opened cautiously, and a young woman entered, carrying a sheaf of papers. "I think we have it, sir," she said, tiptoeing closer to the desk. "Do you want to take a look at these? I think you might find them interesting."

He shoved back from the desk and grabbed the papers from her hands with an impatient gesture. "What do you have here? I don't want ..." He glanced through the material in his hands. Most of it was data, but here and there he saw black and white photos. He stared at them.

They showed a young man in his late twenty's and a woman about the same age.

The girl said apologetically, "The pictures are a little fuzzy, but they're the best we can do."

"Yeah. This might be it. Send in Williams. I want to go over some of the details with him."

She turned and started for the door.

"Good work. I'll see you get a bonus, Cindy."

She flashed him a smile. "Thank you, sir."

He grinned and stood up, stretching. At the picture window, he admired the view he'd seen for five years – a little meadow with a creek rippling through it. The sun was rising over the mountain to the east, casting a golden glow on the dark scene. Just like what he wanted to happen in his life – a river of gold flowing into his bank account and people serving him. Well, it would come.

He opened the window and breathed deeply.

It had been a long night's work, but he'd bet his new Hummer on the fact that his people had nailed the target.

Williams entered without knocking. He was a lone wolf, a back-country type of guy who could get the job done if there was enough money in it. He wore a handle-bar mustache and a beat-up wide brimmed hat.

"Well, hello. Have a good drive?" The boss offered the man a cup of coffee.

Williams accepted the coffee and plunked into the chair opposite the desk. "Yes, sir. What's the job? I don't like to be kept in suspense."

The boss laughed. "Sit down. I'll line it out."

The young man elbowed up to the desk and studied the papers and the photos carefully. The top one was labeled Christian Jonathan Marshal. The boss tapped it with his finger.

"This is the owner of the vehicle. Nice looking fella. Looks stupid, like all those religious nuts do, but he's dangerous. Has worked for the FBI. Took out a drug cartel a year ago."

Williams picked up the paper and studied the face. "A border guard? One of those dudes who ride mustangs up into the woods and smoke weed while they're on patrol?" He laughed and tossed the picture down. "Piece of cake."

The boss wiped a hand across his forehead. It made him nervous to talk to this guy, despite the fact that he needed his services from time to time. "Yes, he'll not cause you any trouble. Here's his address, social security number, phone number."

"Okay. I can do it with no problem. Who's the woman?" Williams lifted the second sheet of paper. A good-looking brunette looked up at him.

"Name's Gina Moyia Lindsey. The fellow that came in the boat, Brown, said he recognized the photo, although he didn't get a real good look at her. We have her address and phone number. She's with the Spokane Police Department, a sergeant with the Special Intelligence Unit. Was from New York." He leaned back and rubbed his eyes. "Can you do it? A police officer?"

Williams gathered the papers into a bundle and stood. "You'll be getting my bill when the job's done. It shouldn't take long." He took a couple of steps toward the door.

The boss followed him, cracking his knuckles. "No trails. No evidence. A nice, clean job, huh?"

"You got it." Williams turned to glare at him. "What's the matter? Cold feet?"

"No, not that. I just want to be sure the job is done, and no one can trace it back to me."

Williams laughed, showing yellow teeth beneath his shaggy mustache. "Now, wouldn't that make me cry? You'll be hearing from me." With that, he marched out of the room.

The boss poured himself a cup of coffee and returned to the window where he watched the sun climb higher into the heaven. It was done. He had no doubts that Williams could take care of the two busy-bodies who threatened his operation.

When they were out of the way, he would proceed with his plans. He smiled and brushed his hand through his dark hair, wondering what they were making for breakfast.

Chapter 6

The Moment They Attack

I'm always grumpy when I have to work on the weekends, and today is no exception. I didn't do much on Saturday, mainly caught up on Facebook and rested. This morning, my shoulder aches, and my body registers other scratches and bruises I'd received from my excursion on the Columbia River on Friday.

The drive from home to the Spokane Police Department downtown takes about an hour. I settle down to work in my office.

After I've finished the daily reports and checked on my team, I pour myself another cup of coffee and look at the reports from the sheriff offices that come in on the internet feed.

Nothing from Pend Oreille county, but there is a report from Ferry County, from Sheriff Stevenson in Republic.

It's brief. "Reported shooting south of Northport on the Columbia River, off the Flat Creek/ Northport Road. Some property damage to a truck. Gina Lindsey, one of the people involved, suffered a slight injury to her shoulder. Two officers sent to investigate scene." The sheriff listed our names, addresses and locations, but that was all.

"Slight injury!" I mutter as I scroll down to find anything more. "A gunshot wound is *not* slight."

A few minutes later, I see Chief Smithers across the common room in the police headquarters and corner him, coffee still in my hand.

"Sir, did you hear any reports of a shooting up on the Columbia River yesterday?"

He shakes his head. "Can't say that I have, Lindsey. What's going on?" He's older, with graying hair that's cut short, a wide smile when he favors you with one, and deep blue eyes, sometimes almost black when he's mad.

"I was up there with my friend, Chance Marshal. We were checking out a good hunting spot. I went down to eat my lunch on the bank by the river when someone shot at me. Three men came after me. I got out of there, but they got me high on the shoulder" I touch the bandage.

I continue, "Then we headed for his pickup, but the assailants got there first and shot it all to pieces. We jumped in and took off. It doesn't look to me like the sheriff in Ferry County is taking this very seriously."

He shrugs. "I'm sorry, Gina, but you have to wait for the sheriff to investigate it. Sometimes it takes them awhile. The county sheriffs are always under-staffed. I can't do anything about it. It's out of my jurisdiction." He raises his eyebrows. "And out of yours, too. Let it go."

"That's a little hard to do when I'm carrying around a souvenir." I point to my bandaged shoulder. "If you'd been there, you would have a different opinion. They were aiming for us. They hunted us down, and they were going to eliminate us if they could."

"Okay, you got shot at." He's edging away from me. "I know. But you have a job to do here. Let the officers up there handle it." He gives me a sideways glance with a glimmer of a smile in it. "Probably someone was annoyed that you'd stumbled onto their property. You got out alive, that's the main thing."

That's the main thing for him, I suppose. But not for me. I'm trying to find something else to say when he turns abruptly and walks away.

I return to my office, plowing through a stack of paperwork. By the time I'm finished work and head north on Division, I've had it. My head aches, my body aches, and worst of all, my soul aches.

When I get down, I find myself thinking about Mom a lot. I'd wanted for so long to find her, and only just recently gathered my courage to begin the search for her. But my search produced nothing. Uncle Elton said he knew very little about her since she'd left my dad. The trail ended in Butte, Montana, and I hadn't had time to pursue it further.

Besides that, I'm anxious about the repercussions of what happened on the river. Will they trace Chance? And me? Surely, they'd seen Chance's license plate. I pull into the long driveway that leads to my house, trying to shake the eerie feeling that someone is watching.

My neck muscles start to relax when I see the house. It's nothing special – a small, white two-story farmhouse. But I think it looks quaint, like something out of a magazine, sitting in a framework of firs and pines, surrounded by a charming little meadow that has a stream chattering through it. A chain link fence borders my front yard and two mammoth cottonwoods stand beside the house like giant guards.

Long shadows lay across the pasture where my two horses graze. I scan the dark, hidden places where someone could hide in the forest and feel exposed like I did when I was on patrol on the streets in New York City.

They won't let me get away. They are here. How could they find me this fast? I answer my own question – there are ways, plenty of ways, to find things out.

Shivering from the goose bumps that rise on my arms, I pull into the garage and roll up the window. Inside the garage, I wait for a minute and listen, knowing from my training that the moment when you get out your car is when an attacker will strike because your mind is elsewhere, not on your immediate surroundings.

Are they lurking in the darkness behind the rack of coats near the door? Did I see one of them move?

The phone buzzes, and I jump. Taking it out, I see it's a text from Aunt Bobbi from Ekalaka. She chooses the worst time to text me. "Is this a bad time for you? I need to talk. Something really awful has happened." I shake my head. I'm leery of her dramatic pleas for help because usually they are trumped-up excuses to get my attention.

I text back, my eyes still roving the garage. "What's going on? Can't talk right now. Give me half an hour."

She replies, *OK.* Smiley face.

Getting my Glock from my shoulder holster, I leave my purse and jacket on the seat. I ease open the door and step out, my head up, holding my breath, straining to hear the slightest noise.

Something scratches the roof. I freeze. After a few seconds, I realize it's the tree limbs of the old maple tree, rubbing against the roof in the wind.

I let out my breath and creep forward, walking on the balls of my feet with the gun in both hands. Slanting sunbeams blind me as I step from the garage. Something shuffles in the grass. I shade my eyes. It's only the horses over by the corral. Gypsy Rose nickers. She wants her grain.

"I'll be out in a minute, girl," I call to her. She shakes her head like she understands me and turns to glare at Pecos Bill who approaches the rail fence.

I got Gypsy, my Arabian mare, when I first arrived here, and added Pecos Bill, the little paint, when a neighbor gave him to me.

I creep down the stone-paved walkway and enter the side gate that leads to the back door, studying the fields around the house, looking beyond them to the forest and trees ringing the pasture and meadow. I take a deep breath as I pass the lilac bush by the back door, pulling out my keys. I unlock the door.

My phone buzzes again. I glance at it. *Bobbi.* Shove it back in my pocket.

My two cats, Rikki and Susie, are not waiting for me inside the door as they usually are, begging for their dinner. I stop and listen, smelling the air, but all I detect is the slightly moldy smell of an old house. Nothing is moving, not as far as I can tell. Even the ancient timbers in the attic aren't creaking like they often do.

Working my way carefully through the rooms, I enter my bedroom and find the cats curled up on the bed. They awake, stretch, and deign to greet me, rubbing against my hand and purring.

"Why didn't you guys meet me at the door?"

They don't answer or show any guilt for letting me down that way. I smile as I rub their chins. They follow me to the kitchen, meowing for dinner. I get my stuff from the pickup and after making sure the doors and windows are locked, I hop in the shower, wincing at the pain from the wound on my shoulder.

It's not a deep cut and only took five stitches, yet it's still painful. A wave of weariness sweeps over me as I climb into my sweats, hoping I can sleep tonight.

Lately, I've been having awful dreams of people dying, of blood, and of the end of the world. In my dreams, everyone asks me questions, but I don't know what to do, and I'm just as confused and afraid as they are.

I call out for my mother. She's out there somewhere in the wreckage of the world, but I can't see her. I hear her sometimes, though, and that's when I start to weep like a broken-hearted little girl. I jerk awake and can't get back to sleep for a long time.

Mom left us when I was only three, and I have forgotten the way she laughed, the tone of her voice, the songs she sang to me.

By the time I was old enough to know anything, Dad removed all her pictures and things, and he refused to talk about her. I have one picture of her. It's a newspaper clipping that I found in a scrapbook at the bottom of a box in the attic I went through after Dad died.

Her dark, curly hair frames a round, smiling face with an upturned nose. She's wearing a hat that shades her eyes. The headline announces, "Moria Lindsey Installed as New Librarian," and the article says that she was tackling a mammoth job of cataloging all the books with a new system. The picture and the dreams only make my questions more acute.

Where did she go when she left? How can I find her?

There's a huge, empty room in my heart that has *Mom* written over the doorway, and no matter how hard I try, I can't ignore the pain and anguish that comes from that vacant hole. It's a haunted feeling that gnaws at my consciousness. I can't shake it – I just try to ignore it.

I pull on my rubber boots and head out to the corral, keeping a wary eye on the area around the barn where shadows are growing and someone might be lurking. As I get the grain from inside the sweet-scented barn, I jump when the wind brushes one of the tree limbs against the roof and the old timbers groan.

Holding the grain pans in my hands, I freeze and listen. That's when I remember that I hadn't brought my pistol with me. I feed, water and groom the horses, talking to them all the while, hoping someone isn't going to jump me with my back turned.

Returning to the house, I wash my hands and scramble two eggs in butter. Then I make some toast, load it with mayo and mustard, and place the eggs on the toast. Perfect! I grab a container of yogurt from the fridge and make a pot of mint tea.

After carrying my dinner to the living room, I snuggle down on the couch with my afghan and watch a rerun of CSI. While I'm eating and watching the show, I text Aunt Bobbi. "Have time now. What's going on?" I hope it doesn't sound too abrupt.

In two minutes, she replies, "Cows got out. Think someone cut the fence. Called the sheriff and he came out. Couldn't find anything. Scared."

I sigh. Bobbi has a good nature and always wants to help, but she demands more of me than I'm willing to give. Like now. What does she expect me to do? I text her back, "Sorry about that. I hope you found the cows. Where's Uncle Elton? Did you pray about it? God will help you." I grin as I punch in the words. She used to preach at me all the time. Now I'm returning the favor.

Her answer doesn't come back immediately. My attention returns to the show, yet I can't get into it tonight, mainly because I'm listening for the sound of a car or any other unusual noises that would mean an intruder has arrived. When the phone rings, I jump.

At first, I think it's Bobbi, but it's Chance. "Hi, ya," he says in his breezy, off-hand manner. Yet his voice is low and scratchy like he has a cold.

"Hi, yourself," I reply. "What's wrong?"

"Did I say somethin's wrong?"

I hear exhaustion and tension behind his casual words. He's in trouble. A sinking feeling creeps into my bones. "No, but you don't need to. What happened?"

"Well, my partner got shot while we were on patrol Friday, and I had to stay up there with him most of the night. The chopper came at two in the morning, so I slept when I got home."

He takes a deep breath. I visualize him rubbing his head. "Thank God, Dusty made it. He's in Deaconess Hospital in Spokane in critical condition. They tell me he'll pull out of it." He clears his throat. "I think he will. He's a tough."

"Oh, wow. I'll be praying for him. I can't believe that happened. Who shot at you? And why? Smuggling drugs?"

"We intercepted two people. It was a kid who shot Dusty. But they got away, unfortunately." His abrupt answer makes me think he's covering up, that he doesn't want me to know how serious this is. Which of course makes me more worried than ever.

"What are you going to do?" I tuck the afghan closer around my feet.

There's a pause, like he's thinking of what to say. "I ... uh, I don't know. I imagine I'll be put on administrative leave for a while. They do that anytime you've been involved in a shooting incident. The boss gave me a brochure about a weapons and martial arts retreat at a ranch outside of Chewelah. I called them, and they said I can register."

"When is it? Right away?"

"Next week. McClurry said the department will pay my way. It's an outfit called the Forward Guard. Don't know anything about them. You okay? No one came around? How's the shoulder?"

"I'm okay, Chance. Shoulder's fine. I had to work today. Wish I had a dog." I stand and pace to the window, lifting the curtain. "Did you call the sheriff?"

"Yeah, but they didn't take it very seriously. They said they'd send an officer up there. I called this afternoon, but he didn't find anything."

I sigh. "Do you think what happened last night to you is connected with what went on down by the river?"

"Don't know, but I hate leaving you with this. They may find us, you know, and they're ready to kill."

I laugh. "They might find me a little hard to kill. Hey, I'm going back up there and look around. You wanna come?"

"I can't. But don't go over to the river by yourself, you hear? They might still be there. I want to ride into the place where I was with Dusty and search. I couldn't see anything last night."

"Okay. Call me if you find out anything, okay?"

"Sure thing. Same thing for you, too." He sneezes. "Take care of yourself, Gina, and call if you need me. I just saw my partner get shot, and I don't want to lose you."

"I'm fine. Got my Glock handy and my 30.06 rifle by the bed." I chuckle. "I'll see you when you get time."

I'd tried to sound cheerful and upbeat, but I wonder about this training camp. I get out my iPad and Google Forward Guard, but all I find is about a million sites on basketball.

Bobbi sent two texts while I was talking to Chance. "Elton at a church board meeting. Got the cows home. How are you doing? Did you go up to that place on the river? How did that go? Are you home?" Then a few minutes later, "Oh, forgot to tell you we got a new four-wheeler today."

I text back, "Sounds good. Send a picture, okay? Went to the river and had a good time. Found some great hunting places. Tell Uncle Elton he'll have to come. Everything else is fine. I'll call sometime tomorrow. Take care. Love you."

"Love you, too. Bye!" She sends the reply with a heart emoji.

43

By the time I crawl into bed, I'm not only tired and sore, my shoulder is hurting. I want to go somewhere away from all this. Like Hawaii. I chuckle.

The wind is moaning in the big cottonwood near the bedroom window and branches are scraping against the side of the house.

I listen for the creak of a board that will signal an intruder. Or the squeak of the door. A soft footfall. A window being lifted.

Oh, God! Help me know if they come.

Chapter 7

Now I Know

The girl sorted through a box filled with old clothes and withdrew a tattered blue notebook. She grabbed a pen and plopped into a bean bag chair. She began to write.

Well, my date with Jim was fantastic. Jim is older than I thought he would be, but he's nice, and I think he likes me. We had fun. He took me to dinner. I couldn't believe the food they served at the restaurant. I ate until I was almost sick. Then we walked for awhile, and he held my hand and told me how pretty I am.

"You have beautiful eyes," he said.

I laughed, but I could tell he meant it.

I wanted to see his house, but he said he couldn't take me over there right then as his Mom was having a party with some of her friends.

He's tall and has dark hair and a nice smile. He wears glasses. He took me for a drive in his car. We went out toward Colville. I'd never been that far out of the city and couldn't believe how beautiful it was with all the stars twinkling and the smell of the firs and pines. We stopped at a lake.

There was a resort there, but they didn't mind if we walked along the beach. I twirled in a big circle with my arms out, and he laughed at me, but it was a nice sort of laugh, like he thought I was really cute and funny.

He listened when I told him about the time Buster beat me up and threw me out the door into the snow. That time he broke my arm and Mom had to take me to the ER. He said I should have called the police. But I told him I couldn't, or they'd take me away from Mom and the kids, and they need me.

"Well," he said with a slow grin. "After you've moved over to my house, I'll help you get your family away from Buster. He won't bother you ever again. I mean it, Sanora."

He put his arm around my shoulders. I about bawled right then. I just can't believe Jim would like me. I asked him why he was bothering with me. He said he likes helping people.

I found my Prince at last. I am totally in love with Jim. He makes me feel <u>so special</u>! I wanted him to kiss me when he told me good-night, but he seemed tired and said he had to get home.

I didn't want to go home to that dumpy, stinky house. But of course, I had to.

***

Well, another week has gone by, and I got to go out with Jim again. This time we went to the mall. He bought me some new shoes, and an outfit – jeans and a top – at Forever 21. I never shopped there before. Mom gets all of my clothes at the second hand store.

When I wore the new clothes to school, Angie was surprised and said they looked good on me. I'm starting to feel like a real person. Like I'm somebody.

We also went to Panda Express and he bought me dinner, then we went to Dairy Queen and got an ice cream cone. I love this!

Buster's been doing better since he got a new job. He says he likes it. He's also been going to some meetings for alcoholics. I think it's helping him.

Life is still bad here. Now that I know how other people live, I can't stand to be here anymore. Jim has been getting anxious for me to leave and go live with his folks. He says he's worried about me.

I've been doing a lot of thinking about how to get away. Mom said it's okay for me to stay overnight with my friend, Angie Winters. Angie knows about Jim and says she'll cover for me for a few days so they won't be looking for me right away.

I've got all my things packed in an old backpack of Mom's. She has to work late tomorrow night, so I'll tell her good-bye in the morning. It won't be so easy to tell the kids good-bye. They depend on me, and I'm going to miss them a lot. But I'll go back soon and get them out of there. I'll take them over to Jim's.

Jim says they have a whole basement that nobody uses and maybe we could rent it.

I still haven't gotten over to see his house or met his folks. He said his mom really wants me to come. His dad is working away from home right now, and when he gets home and sees I'm there, he won't make me leave.

I was scared before about seeing Jim for the first time, but this is worse! But I have to get out of here, and this is the only way I know how to do it.

***

I can't believe it's been so long since I wrote in this! I stuffed this beat-up old notebook at the bottom of my backpack the day I left home and found it today. I read what I'd written and cried my eyes out. I better explain what happened. I don't know how to put this, even in my own diary, but here goes.

It seems so long ago, that night I met Jim down on the street about three houses from mine at the corner of Jefferson. I had my backpack clutched tightly in my hands, and my knees were shaking.

Jim pulled up in his black and red sports car. It has black leather seats and a nice sound system. He grinned at me as he opened the door and beckoned me in. I looked back over my shoulder at my house. The lights were on. I could see, in my mind's eye, Jamie curled up with his book on the sofa and Bonnie playing with her doll on the floor. That's what they were doing when I told them good-bye.

"C'mon, sweetie," Jim called to me. "We got places to go tonight."

"Okay. But I feel bad, leaving them alone. Jamie and Bonnie, I mean." I got in the car, shut the door, and strapped on the seat belt. "Do you think they'll be okay without me?"

"Sure, darlin'," he drawled. "You can come back any time. It's not like you're leaving forever." There was something in his voice and in his eyes when he glanced my way that made me feel funny, like I was scared, but I knew I wasn't.

I looked at him to see if maybe I'd imagined it, and yes, I had. He was his old jovial self in a blink of an eye, turning up the music and laughing at a joke he told me. We started out, driving around like we usually do.

"I can't wait to meet your Mom," I said, my voice a little wobbly. I shoved down the jitters in my stomach. "And I can't wait to see my bedroom. You painted it mint green, my favorite color. Remember picking out the paint at WalMart?"

I thought he'd laugh with me, but he didn't.

He gave me a funny look and kind of shrugged. "Oh. About that. I forgot to tell you that the plans have changed. I can't take you home right now. Dad's there, and he's not in a good mood. He and Mom, well, they're fighting about something. So I thought we'd go out for dinner and a movie. After that, I'll take you to my friend's house. He has a big place. He said you could stay there until things settle down at my house. How about that? You don't mind, do you?"

My heart fell to my toes. Of course, I minded! I wanted to meet his folks and move into that wonderful home he'd told me about. Why was he putting me off like this?

Then I knew. This was a lie. I knew it because I'd been lied to so much. I stared at him like he'd turned into a monster. My heart shattered into a million tiny pieces. I tried to gather them into my hands, but they kept falling out and crashing to the floor with the awful sound of a broken heart.

This can't be happening!

I batted my eyelashes to keep the tears from my eyes. I had to believe. Maybe I was wrong. I clung to that hope.

Smiling, I said, "If you love me like you say you do, take me over to your house. I don't mind if it's not quite ready for me. Please?" My voice shook. I gulped, hoping he wasn't going to be mad at me.

He wasn't. He laughed like I'd told the best joke in the world. In a calm voice like he was taming a wild horse, he said, "Don't worry about it, babe. You'll meet them soon enough. I want everything perfect for when I introduce you to them. Okay?"

He patted my hand. "I'll make it up to you, I promise, Sanora. You'll really like Bud's house. There's some other girls there, and you'll make new friends. It won't be more than a couple of days, I promise, darlin'. Cross my heart." He grinned at me, that special grin of his that melted my heart, and kissed me on the forehead.

Tears stung my eyes. I'd been lied to so much that now it seemed the cruelest thing in the world that he would do it to me. I trusted and believed him.

Oh, well, I thought with clenched teeth. I'm going to do this anyway. I don't care what happens. Anything will be better than living another day with Mom's boyfriend.

"Okay, Jim." I kept my voice steady and pasted a smile on my face. "I'll try it for a couple days. Can I go back if I want to?"

"Of course, sweetie. Sure. Why not?"

"Okay." I sighed.

He stopped at a red light. "Now, where should we eat?"

We headed up Division Street. I perked up, and my heart did flip-flops inside my chest. This is going to be just like I thought it would be, I thought. He pulled into a Thai restaurant and parked.

"Let's celebrate," he said, laying his hand on my arm. "C'mon. We'll make a night of it. Dinner. A movie. Shopping at the mall. Then I'll take you over to Bud's place."

I grinned at him in acceptance of his plans. But my heart was still crying inside me. I hoped he wouldn't see the worried frown I tried to hide. I shouldn't have worried because he was talking on his phone.

49

While we ate, he spent most of the time on his phone. I asked if we could skip going to the movie and shopping, as I said I was tired and wasn't feeling very good. It was like around 8:30 when he turned left off Maple and pulled up to a drab two-story house on Gardner Street.

He grabbed my backpack and opened the door for me. I walked in front of him up the cracked walk and broken steps toward the house.

If I'd known then what I know now, I would have tore away from him right then like there was no tomorrow. But hope was a little spark of fire inside my head, telling me that maybe I was wrong and things would work out and that the future was going to be as bright as I thought it would be.

That hope kept me walking up those steps and into the house. But my little flame died after I'd been in the house for ten minutes. Someone grabbed me and shoved me into a room. I tried to get out, crying and screaming.

The door was locked and guarded. I am a prisoner.

Chapter 8

Unwelcome Visitors

June 5th

I can't get to sleep. I try every trick I know, but it does no good. After tossing about a dozen times and getting tangled in the sheets, I sit upright in bed and shove back my hair. Switching on the lamp, I reach for my Bible.

I turn to Psalms 32. My eyes see the words, but my mind doesn't take them in. *Memories.* They play like an unwanted movie before my eyes – a mixed bag of happy and painful, many of them I'd rather forget, but here they are, popping up when I want to sleep.

There were the happy times when I went hunting with Dad, and times when we had picnics and went to ball games, but I could never get close to him.

After a while, I stopped trying. It was like he shut part of himself down when Mom left. When I went to college and started my career as a cop, we worked together in the department, but he was always busy and pre-occupied. He never had time for me. I didn't mind because I'm like that, too. Not too big on relationships – I just want to get the job done.

Now it seems like I'm falling into the same pattern. I don't have hardly anyone to talk to, except for Chance. The few friends I've made are so new that I can't even call them friends yet. Sure, I could phone or text Aunt Bobbi and hear her talk for awhile, but I can't bring myself to share my life and problems with her.

There are people I've met at a Bible study I attend, and I have my neighbors. I'd hardly share my life with them, though. I need to talk to someone. *Mom.* The old empty space in my heart yawns open, and I decide right then that I'm going to keep trying to find her. I'd heard of other people who found their parents and families through the internet.

Yet it's frightening. What if I find her, and she doesn't want me? Can I handle being rejected again? What if she's dead?

But nothing can be as painful as not knowing.

The wind lashes the trees outside, things are bumping around, and branches are scratching the house. I listen, waiting, wondering if the men from the river will come. Nothing happens.

Turning off the light, I fluff up my pillow, roll over, and stare at the ceiling. What's wrong with me? I'm not usually like this. With a prayer, I pull up the covers and close my eyes.

Thud! My eyes fly open. Something hit the house. A tree limb? The wind seems worse. I look at the clock's glowing dials. It's two-fifteen in the morning. I get up, shove my feet in my sandals and pull on my robe.

Picking up the flashlight and my revolver, I creep to the window and peer out into the darkness. The big cottonwood in the yard sways in the winding, its limbs moving like an exotic dancer. *What was the big thump?*

Then I see my big garbage can rolling across the driveway near the garage. *Oh, great.* Now I have to go get it before it ends up in Mrs. Anderson's yard. She's the neighbor on the other side of my house, and she isn't so nice. In fact, she made it a point to tell me that I wasn't keeping up my yard and that made her place look bad.

I shuffle down the hall. When I get to the front door, I pause. It sounds like someone's on the porch. Low voices reach me through the door. *Is someone here? A neighbor who needs help? Chance?*

I jump, startled, when a knock comes, sounding like thunder. I stand frozen to the spot for a few seconds, and when it is repeated, I move to the door.

Peering through the window, I see two dim shapes on my front porch. One is rather tall and the other is shorter. They are slight of build. Two boys. They are looking down, and the hoods on their jackets shade their faces. My first impulse is to open the door and ask what they need, but as I grip the doorknob, I stop.

Don't open the door. It sounds like Dad's voice in my head. I almost slap myself. *No, of course, I can't open it.* Has country living made me forget everything I've learned?

"Yes?" I clear my throat. Calling out louder, I say, "Who is it?"

The answer comes back immediately. "We need help. Our car broke down out on the road. We need to borrow a phone or get a jump. It might be the battery."

I'm watching the boy as he speaks. Neither of them lifts their heads. Don't most young adults have cell phones? There's something going on here. It's scaring me.

"Okay, I'll see if I have a jumper cable around. Be right back."

There's a land line into the house. I lift the receiver. It's dead. Shivers tickle my neck and race down my arms.

They've found me. But why would they send two boys? Maybe because no one would turn away a couple of kids in need. I glance out into the night. Are others of the gang out there? Or are these boys trained killers like the one Chance faced at the border?

I return to the door, still in the dark. "Sorry, I can't find one." I turn on the lamp in the living room and lift the little curtain on the window of the door with the hand that is holding the Glock. "Don't you have a phone?"

"The batteries are dead. Can't we come in? It's cold out here." The boy lifts his head.

I make sure he sees the gun. "Just give me a minute. I'll call the tow truck. Wait right there, okay? I'll be back."

I dash to the bedroom, get my cell phone, which I keep beside the bed, and punch in 911. "I've got two suspicious young men on my porch. It looks like they are preparing to enter my house," I report breathlessly.

The female voice that answers sounds tired. "Address, ma'am?"

"1657 S. Deer Trail Road." I hear a low conversation from outside. The boys have moved off the porch, but they are not leaving my property. "Please hurry. I think they are planning to enter."

"All right, ma'am. Hang on. I'll call the sheriff."

I know the sheriff in this county, and I'm guessing it would take a bomb to get him up in the middle of the night to investigate this kind of call. I don't have a bomb, and I'm short on time and patience.

Lifting the curtain in the bedroom, I see them. The taller of the two is now carrying a rifle. A semi-automatic rifle. I clutch the phone as if it's a lifeline.

"Ma'am," I say breathlessly. "They have a weapon. I can't tell for sure from here, but I think it's a semi-automatic rifle."

She perks up. Her voice is urgent as she says, "Stay inside. We'll get some officers out there right away. Don't hang up."

I want to tell her that my enemies are not very squeamish about killing people. Including me. Especially me. What seems like hours later, but is probably only a few minutes, she comes back.

"Are you with me, Gina?"

"Yes, ma'am."

"Okay. The officers are on their way. I'll stay with you until the officers come."

I take a deep breath, telling myself that I should remain calm, that I should sound professional, yet my nerves are starting to give way.

"Tell them that if these guys come in my house, I've got a shotgun aimed at the front door, and I'm prepared to use it. If the officers don't want to deal with the kind of mess that's going to cause, they better hurry up." I hang onto the phone, hoping my batteries won't die.

Dashing to the front door, I see that the boys are gone. But where are they? Have they sneaked around to the back door? Will other assailants descend on the house and break in? Old farmhouses are easy to break into. It would only take a minute to jimmy the fragile lock on the back door.

I decide that I should get to a safe room. The bedroom is ideal, as it has a window, a door that can be locked, and I have my cell phone. Sprinting to the room, I lock the doors, but I don't turn on the light. I yank on my jeans and a t-shirt, pull on my socks and tie my shoes. Then I open the window and toss out my car keys that I keep in my purse. Re-lock the window.

A siren shrieks the night awake, coming down the road like they're on the tail of a gang of terrorists. Nice. It gives the right amount of time for the assailants to get away. Where do these officers get their training? From a cereal box?

Dispatch, the lady who has never left me, connects me to the officers. I tell them which is my bedroom window, and they come around and get my keys. They enter the house. I meet them in the living room with my flashlight in one hand and my rifle in the other, just in case it's the boys and not the officers.

The deputies find nothing. They take notes, and my statement, and after assuring me that they will investigate it further, they take their leave.

Fully clothed, I lay on top of my bed and close my eyes, holding my Glock on my stomach.

Sleep? Yeah, right.

Chapter 9

A Midnight Ride

Northport, June 5th

Chance rolled out of bed, wondering if he should go to church or ride into the place where Dusty was shot last night.

He had to work tomorrow, and if he was going to that retreat, he'd have a lot to do in the next couple of days. The camp started Wednesday. If he didn't go today, he wouldn't go at all.

Besides, the trail would get cold — any clues that lay hidden in the forest paths would soon be gone. He wouldn't have a chance to search when he was working. In fact, he suspected that they would keep him off the patrol tomorrow. He'd probably be given a desk job, which he hated.

He decided to take Santiago, his Morab gelding. The horse, a combination of Morgan and Arab, was a dark bay with black mane and tail. He was fast when he wanted to be, and he was trail savvy, keeping his head even during lightning storms and other situations that would make most horses go wild.

After a shower and breakfast, he loaded his gear into his pickup. Santiago greeted him with a low nicker and seemed eager to go. He loaded him in the trailer and headed out.

On the way through Colville, he stopped at the Border Patrol office. He wanted to find out if McClurry had a take on the incident last night. But McClurry wasn't on duty.

To his surprise, it was the PAIC (Patrol Agent in Charge) himself, Alfred DeMoss, who was in the front office. He looked up from a desk when Chance entered.

"What're you doing here?" DeMoss stared at Chance with lowered brows. "Isn't this your day off, Marshal?" He was an older man with white hair and sharp blue eyes. His weathered face showed his many years on the line before he rose to the senior position he now held.

"Yes, sir, it is." Chance took off his hat and ran his fingers through his hair, glancing around the office, hoping he'd spot a friendly face. But, of course, no one else was there.

"I wanted to find out if you have any information on the incident we had last night. Have they apprehended the woman and boy who came across the line illegally? I'm ridin' in to where Dusty was shot to see if I can find any clues."

DeMoss stood and paced toward the front. He carried his body with the grace of a hunting tiger. "For what reason, Marshal? Haven't you done enough harm?"

"I don't believe I've done any harm, sir. I'm as torn up about Dusty as anyone. But I'd like to get a line on those smugglers. Did you catch them?"

"We aren't releasing any information about that right now." DeMoss turned and poured himself a cup of coffee from the pot by the wall. "I'd suggest you keep a low profile, Marshal, and let others take care of it. The sheriff went in with some of his deputies this morning in a chopper. If there's anything to find, they will find it."

"I know that, sir, but I'd like to have a look around myself."

DeMoss strode to the hallway leading to the offices that the upper echelon agents occupied. Before disappearing, he turned and pierced Chance with a rapier glance. "No one can stop you from riding in there, but my advice is to stay away. If you're smart, you'll listen to me."

"Okay. Thank you, sir. Have a good day." He left the office without DeMoss replying. In the last instant before the door shut, Chance thought he saw the man step back and reach for the phone.

Who is he calling? Chance jumped in his truck, thinking it over. He couldn't believe they wouldn't tell him if they'd caught the perpetrators who'd shot his partner. Why was it being handled with a cloak of secrecy? Were they trying to hush it up?

He had the right to ride in the national forest as much as anyone. So what if his trail led to the meadow where Dusty was shot?

A sour taste chewed in his stomach. He felt he had to bring the people who were responsible for shooting his partner to justice, and he felt in his bones that if he didn't, the whole ordeal would be swept under the rug and forgotten. It would be hushed up to avoid a lot of bigwigs nosing around and making reports to congress, limiting their ability to do their job. Maybe it would feed the lax immigration laws already in the works.

He headed north again.

After filling up at a gas station in Kettle Falls and grabbing a sandwich at Subway, he drove without stopping to the Patterson border station and pulled in behind the building. He unloaded Santiago, tightened the cinch, and started out.

The day was muggy with clouds building up on the horizon in great white heaps. Flies buzzed his head and bit Santiago. Crows cawed at him in their strange, coarse language, but other than that, the forest was as silent as a tomb. In his backpack, he carried food and water, survival items, and evidence envelopes. He also had a flashlight, tweezers and a pen. And he had his 30.06 rifle.

It took a couple of hours to reach the meadow. He dismounted and tied Santiago to a slender birch, about the same place he'd tied the mustangs that night. He ate an apple and fed one to Santiago. Shouldering his backpack and picking up the rifle, he looked around.

He noted the circle of fire where he'd kept Dusty warm. Just to the north, along the path, he might find more evidence. The air was still as he inched his way along the dim path at the place where he figured the woman and boy emerged from the forest.

Brushing back limbs from bushes in the path, he bent over to investigate the ground carefully.

Nothing. But there had to be something. Thunder rumbled from black clouds. The sun disappeared, and the wind picked up, bringing with it a sprinkling of rain.

He worked his way north along the trail, thinking they had to have stopped to eat or drink, and maybe they dropped something. Isn't that how it works in mystery books? *Something. Anything. Please, God. Anything.* The words became a chant. A prayer. But it didn't work.

There was nothing.

He straightened his aching back and rested on a big rock. The rain began, first with a pitter-pat on the bushes around him, then it increased. Soon he sat in a downpour.

A rumble of thunder boomed overhead. He had to get back to Santiago. Casting one last glance at the trail that was swiftly turning into mud, he caught the faintest tinge of white amidst brown leaves about three feet from where he sat.

White. He scrambled off the rock and fell to his knees, mindless of the mud. With his tweezers, he withdrew a card from under a moldy leaf. It was a business card from a motel, the Rambling Inn. Bringing it closer, he read the smaller print, *63 Main Street, Trail, British Columbia.* Under the address was a phone number. A tiny picture of the motel decorated the top right corner.

Flipping the card over while he protected it from the rain with his hand, he saw faint pen marks. *7pm meet ____nk, deliver goods.*

He slipped the card in an envelope and looked for more. Yes, a cigarette butt lay nearby. He lifted it with the tweezers and deposited it in the same envelope. On the front, he wrote the date and signed his name.

Further searching produced nothing else. There were footprints, but they were too dim to take a cast, and besides, the rain was washing them out swiftly. In another place not far from the initial find, he discovered a plastic bag. This, too, he lifted from the ground and placed in another envelope. He stuffed the envelopes into a plastic bag and placed them in his backpack.

Rain fell in sheets as the storm grew closer. Lightning and thunder cracked together. He ran back along the path, the rain pelting him, thinking that his position under the trees was not a good one. He had to get out of there.

He worried now about the horse, for the wind and rain and lightning increased each moment. Trees swayed dangerously and shed limbs all around him.

Hurrying faster than he should, he stumbled once and fell to his knees. Pain shot up his right leg. He staggered to his feet and found he'd fallen on a stone. He rubbed his knee but that did little good. After a few seconds, he found he could walk on it.

Good. Nothing seriously damaged, then.

He arrived at the place where he'd tethered the horse and found him gone! Wiping his face of the rain, he found the bush where he'd tied the rope. No rope, but a branch had been ripped off. The horse was out there somewhere with a dragging lead line. *Great!*

In a lull of wind and thunder, he called, "Santi!" He listened and called again but heard nothing. The ground was soggy, and in a few places, he could make out hoof prints, but it was getting darker, and soon he wouldn't be able to see, especially under the trees.

The horse had gone south along the meadow. He followed the trail as the storm moved on, and the wind lifted the branches of the trees as if waving good-bye. The clouds broke overhead and gave him a little more light.

He was tired, wet, and cold. Besides that, his knee kept giving out on him. He almost tumbled to the ground several times. He called until his throat was sore and tried to follow the prints in the mud. An hour later, he saw Santiago standing with his head down along a forest path just off the meadow.

The rope had caught on a tangle of bushes near the path.

Chance went up to him, speaking softly so as not to frighten him. "You look about as done in as I am, fella," he said, yanking the lead line from the brush. "You wanta go home?"

The saddle hung askew. He straightened it and tightened the cinch. Chance mounted and rode back to the meadow. It would be almost ten o'clock by the time he got to the pickup, but he didn't want to spend the night in the woods with a wounded knee, a tired horse, and no food.

When he got back to the parking lot, he put Santiago in the trailer and headed south, turning up the heater. What should he do now? He might have some solid leads, but would the department allow him to follow them?

Should he call Dad? The senator had connections and could get him information. Surely, he would help if he knew what happened.

He shook his head. Appealing for help from his father sent cold shivers down his back. When was the last time Josh Marshal paid him any attention? He wouldn't even answer his calls or texts.

He stopped for a bite to eat at Zips in Chewelah, then continued out Cottonwood Drive to his place. He wondered if he would get into trouble for the ride. His supervisors at work had given him a strong message that he should quietly withdraw, disappear for a time, and not concern himself with the investigation. It wasn't his problem. What would they do if he didn't?

He sighed. He was getting in way over his head. He had to do something to help Dusty, but what? He had some evidence in his backpack, but he needed time to follow up on it. Maybe he should give Gina a call. She could help. If she had time.

As he pulled into his driveway, he rubbed his head and tried to pray, but the prayer got lost when he looked up. In his headlights, a column of black smoke billowed above the trees.

Chapter 10

Foul Play

The senator slicked back his dark hair and smiled.

He sat in his favorite red-padded lawn chair, and leaned back, taking in the scene. From his perch high above the Columbia River, he viewed his kingdom.

While he called this place a cabin, it was actually a large, beautiful home. It was all his – everything he could see and more – seventy-five acres of prime river frontage and fertile fields of hay and barley. His pet project, the school, lay behind him on a plateau of land above the river.

He started the school and farm as a tax write-off. It housed at risk young people of all ages from Asia, Mexico, Central America, and the United States.

The young people who came to his organization learned to work and tend gardens, cook, and make things in the shop. He believed that hard work never hurt anyone, least of all troubled young people.

His phone buzzed. He took it from his pocket and flipped through his messages. Nothing to answer immediately, it seemed. All those people who hung on his every word and anticipated his every need could wait.

He navigated to his webpage. Everything looked good. In a short while, he'd have all the details of this newest venture sewn up neatly. He leaned back in his chair with the warm summer sun on his face. It was wonderful to be away from the hustle of his office and home. His wife, Kathy, was busy with her committees and church work. Thank God for that.

Her pre-occupation with her own concerns gave him a chance to come here with the newest interest in life – a girl named Patti Jo.

He'd met her at a restaurant in Seattle and lured her into a relationship with him. It was fun and exciting, yet he couldn't allow it to leak to the press or to his wife, for she held more than half the purse strings in the family.

He liked to think of his ranch and school here in the remote corner of Washington as a way to salvage lives, to help children and young adults. Boys who'd been in the gangs and were in trouble with the law. Girls who were bound to be caught in the deadly trap of human trafficking.

He'd thought up a cool name for his new organization. Forward Guard for the People. His mission statement was even better. *Reaching out to those in need, offering a new start, a helping hand, and a loving heart for all peoples, races, and cultures in our world.*

It sounded compassionate and purposeful. It was, in fact, his short cut to power and prestige which lay before him like a road map.

***

"Get the shipment inside. Now!" A tall, broad-shouldered man, known by some as Tank, bellowed the command. He stood with feet apart, his head held forward, his hands on his hips. He carried two hundred pounds of solid weight. In his right hand, he held a thirty-aught-six rifle like it was a toy. In his left, he wielded a whip.

The Columbia River flowed smoothly past the pebbly beach where a houseboat was tied.

Ten girls, all from Thailand, stood beside the van, so silent and still they seemed carved from dark brown stone. Their ages ranged from thirteen to twenty. They waited docilely until two women emerged from the double doors of the big lodge-style building, corralled them and herded them through the doorway.

When Tank entered the big room inside the lodge, the girls sat hunched together at round tables in the dining room. They were about as talkative as a roomful of skeletons.

He stomped to the kitchen and addressed an older woman. "Hey, you! Bessie! Get them girls over to the cabin, you hear? I don't want them in view any longer than they have to be. We gotta move 'em out fast."

She lifted her chin and stared at him. "They have to eat or they won't be any good for your buyers. We'll get them over to their quarters soon enough. You just sit out there and keep nosey people from coming in. Think you have enough brains to do that?"

He got a cup of coffee and slurped it. "I'm the one who gives the orders around here." But his tone had softened. He tossed her the whip. "Here. Use this on 'em. It's what they understand more'n anything."

She caught it neatly and laid it on the table. "Yeah, I know how much you like the whip." Tucking a strand of gray hair behind her ear, she nodded to another other woman. "Get them biscuits and follow me." She lifted a pan of sausage gravy and headed to the counter.

Shu, the oldest of the girls at the round table, leaned toward one of the other girls and whispered to her in Thai. "Be of good cheer, Le. I will not let them hurt you. This man is loud, and he is mean, but we are going to a place where we can work and make money. Then we can send it to Mama and Papa." She nodded several times as if to convince herself.

"But why do they ..."

"Shut up, girls!" Bessie yelled at them. "Come." She motioned toward the counter. "Eat. You will need it."

They did not understand her, but they knew her meaning. Slowly they stood and filled their plates with the hot food. Some of the younger ones even bowed and thanked her in their language.

She did not wait to hear them or to respond. With a flounce of her apron, she returned to the kitchen and began washing up.

Outside, Tank sat at a bench alongside the building and got comfortable, leaning his rifle against the log wall of the lodge. Another man approached. He limped slightly, his red face outlined with a halo of white hair. Slowly he mounted the steps and sat beside Tank. He rolled a cigarette.

After taking several puffs, he said, "The shipment is hot, huh?"

Tank grunted, adjusting his wad of chewing tobacco behind his lower lip. "You heard that the feds are on our trail? Some trouble down on the river. Cops swarming the place. But we'll wait it out. They won't bother us. The boss has 'em in his hip pocket." He laughed.

The old man took a puff of his cigarette. "You got everything set for the big shindig?"

"I think that's going all right. A few glitches to take care of. That's all."

***

Chewelah, June 5

One of those glitches gripped the steering wheel in shock as he approached his house.

The barn's on fire! Slamming on the brakes, Chance stopped in front of the corral gate and leaped from the cab. As he landed, he dug his phone from his pocket and punched 911.

"What is your emergency?" A curt woman's voice answered the ring.

He responded with his name, address and the fact that his barn was on fire.

"We'll have a ..."

He didn't wait to hear the rest of what she said.

Vaulting the gate, he dashed to the barn where smoke billowed in a sickening column against the dark sky, and flashes of fire climbed from the high windows. He'd left his horses, Cyndi and Cheyenne, in the pasture, yet if someone wanted to really hurt him, they could have put them in the barn and closed the door.

A quick glance told him there were no horses outside. He clenched his teeth and approached the building. That's when he

65

heard them screaming. Yes, they'd been put in the barn. He opened the big double doors. Smoke poured out. He coughed.

Someone had put a match to the hay in the back, but it was baled, not loose, so it would take some time to really get going.

There was a flash and roar of fire and a cloud of smoke coming from the top, where they stored the hay that was left from last year. The fire there would be more dangerous because it would cause the roof to cave in and trap the horses inside, away from him, away from escape.

He drew his kerchief over his nose and plunged into the darkness, flashlight in hand. He shone it around and located the horses. They were huddled toward the back, eyes rolling, stamping their feet, already panicked. They wouldn't come out on their own.

He whipped off his shirt and cautiously approached Cheyenne, the big black. Cheyenne was the leader, the boss. Maybe Cyndi would follow his lead.

The horse was edgy and tossed his head as Chance approached. Choking on the smoke, eyes burning, Chance tried to ease the gelding's panic with low words. He had to hurry because he had to make another trip inside for his mare, Cyndi.

"C'mon, boy. You know me. Steady. Whoa." Calming words didn't come easily when his pulses were racing, and it was difficult to see or breathe. Yet he got up to the horse and tied the shirt around his eyes. Grabbing the loose ends tightly under the gelding's neck, he tried to turned him. The horse refused to budge.

Wham! A piece of the roof landed five feet away. The horse reared and screamed, but Chance kept his hold, rising up with him, coming down on the boards. Once again on his feet, he tugged harder, hoping the shirt wouldn't tear.

"Cheyenne! We gotta get out of here!" Finally, the horse moved with him.

Chance started down the length of the barn, coughing, hoping more burning debris didn't land beside them or in front of them. He was blinded by smoke and blistered with heat. It was too far. His breath came in gasps, and his legs felt like they were going to collapse. He would die in here with his horses.

Tears streamed from his eyes as he took two more steps, leading the reluctant horse. Cheyenne didn't like being blinded. He reared again and tried to go back. More of the ceiling fell with a crash.

As he drew close to the doorway, a figure emerged through the smoke. A muffled yell. The man was tall and wide-shouldered. As he came closer, Chance still couldn't make out who it was.

Chance motioned toward the mare at the back. "There's another one in there! Get your shirt off and tie it around her eyes! Then follow me!"

Not waiting to see if the man obeyed, Chance yanked harder on the shirt around Cheyenne's head. The horse was quivering with fright, pressing hard against him as if for support, but he didn't scream or rear again. Chance emerged from the building.

Outside, he leaned over, coughing and crying. About twenty paces into the barnyard, he let Cheyenne loose with a slap on his rear. The horse took off like a startled rabbit.

Chance turned and dashed to the doorway of the barn. Yes, the man was coming, leading the mare. It wasn't long before the horse and man burst from the depths of the smoke and fire. He released her and slapped her rump. She leaped outside as a spasm of coughing racked the man's throat.

Chance laid his hand on his back. "Thank you, my friend." He still had no idea who it was.

The man straightened, wiping his eyes. It was Pole. Larry Polluck, Chance's neighbor. Everyone called him Pole. He was a long-time resident of the area.

"I ... was drivin' by and saw the fire. Thought ... you could use some help."

"I sure appreciate it, buddy. Would've lost the mare, for sure. Hey, go over to the house and get a drink. That cough is bad."

Pole shook his head. He was older, maybe in his sixties, with a grizzled beard and friendly blue eyes. "No. We gotta git water on that fire or you'll lose more'n your barn. It'll spread. C'mon. Where's your garden hose?"

Chance showed him where the hose was and got Santiago out of the trailer, releasing him into the pasture. The horse ran to the far end of the pasture where the other two stood.

A fire engine arrived, its sirens blasting holes in the night, its lights carving out weird patterns of red on the trees. Four firemen in full gear jumped off the truck. It didn't take them long to unwind the hoses and begin fighting the fire.

"How'd it start?" Pole asked, wiping his face as they stood outside for a breather. His white t-shirt was blackened with smoke and sweat.

Chance shrugged. "Don't know. Just drove in and saw it burning. I think someone set it because the horses were inside. I'd left them out."

Pole gave him a startled glance like he was thinking *who would do that*, but he didn't say anything. Instead, he jumped in and helped the firemen. Chance found work, too, and for a solid hour, they battled the blaze. When it was finished, they stared at the blackened building that had once been a barn while a police car pulled into the driveway.

Stevens County Sheriff, Bruce Roberts, got out and approached them. His deputy came behind him. They watched the firemen mopping up the last of the flames.

"Howdy," Chance said, extending his hand.

Sheriff Roberts shook it. "How'd it start, Chance?"

Chance told him what happened. The sheriff asked him to come to the office and file a report on it in the morning. With a nod to Pole, the two men got in their car and drove away.

"Well, we saved the horses," Chance said to the fire chief, Calvin Bryson. "That's a blessing." He was thinking of the tack he'd lost, but in comparison to the lives of his horses, it was nothing.

Bryson removed his helmet and swiped his forehead. "Yes. At least they were saved." He glanced at Chance. "Did I hear you say you suspect it was foul play?"

"Yes, sir. I was out, riding. I'd left the other horses in the pasture. They couldn't have gotten in the barn and closed the door by themselves. Somebody did that, because when I got here, they were trapped inside and that fire was going."

Mr. Bryson nodded curtly. "Stay away from the barn. We'll have an investigator come out tomorrow morning. Glad you're safe. It was a fool thing to do, running back in that burning building." He pierced Chance with a brittle glare and took another drink. "Your life is more valuable than your livestock."

"I know that, sir. But my horses are more than livestock to me."

"Just sayin'," the man concluded.

He and the others wrapped up the hose and climbed in the truck. Pole left, too, saying he could spare some hay for the winter if Chance needed it. Chance thanked him again and waved as he pulled out of the drive.

Back in the house, shower done, clothes in the wash, and supper cooking in the microwave, the jitters started and didn't want to stop. He thought he was impervious to danger, that there wasn't much that could rattle him, but he was wrong. He poured himself a strong cup of coffee and wondered where he should go from here.

What would stop them from coming and trying again? Maybe next time it would be the house. With him in it. He didn't doubt a second that it was the same bunch of crooks who were down on the river the other day. They'd gotten his license plate number. Traced him here. And he couldn't do anything about it.

He stood and paced to the window, staring out into the darkness, wondering if they were out there, watching the house. Laughing because they'd torched his barn. Plotting how they'd kill him.

He went outside. The stars were bright. Smoke hung on the air and burned his nose. He went down to the fence and crawled through it. The horses stood over by the creek under the big elm tree where they liked to sleep.

He called to them softly. They shifted their feet in the dry grass.

"Hey, guys. You okay?"

Cheyenne lifted his head and snorted. Not like he was mad, but maybe a little upset. Chance didn't blame him. He patted all three and talked to them, more to reassure himself than to calm them. Cyndi nuzzled his hand, looking for a treat.

"Sorry, girl. I forgot. I'll bring you something tomorrow. Okay?"

With a final pat, he headed back up to the house, but stopped dead in his tracks when he caught the sound of something in the brush not far away to his right. He wished he'd brought his gun as he stood there, shivers running up and down his spine, waiting to see what it was.

Maybe it was a small animal or a deer getting ready to venture out and do a bit of browsing. He turned and went back to the house, still jittery.

Just as he opened the door, he thought he heard a board squeak. He froze. Waited. Were they inside the house now? With a gun pointing from behind that half-closed door that led to his bedroom?

Chapter 11

The Girl on the Sidewalk

June 6th

The storm has left my front and back yards a mess. I groan as I head out to feed and water the horses. The fallen limbs and leaves will take hours to clean up. Well, it will have to wait. I don't have time today.

At the Spokane Police Department, which is housed in a nondescript block building on Mallon Avenue, downtown Spokane, I show my ID to the guy at the guard booth and drive into the parking garage under the building.

I'm early, as I want to read the information feed from my computer. I also wanted to get some paperwork done.

My office is painted drab green. I'd like to repaint it bright blue or a dark red, but I doubt if they'd let me. With a cup of coffee in my hand, I boot up the computer and check reports.

Will I find something on the police log about the shooting up on the Pend Oreille River yesterday? Or will I have to check with the Spokane Violent Crime Gang Enforcement Team?

The team consists of SPU officers, Spokane County sheriffs, officers from Washington State Patrol, the U.S. Border Patrol, and the F.B.I. Clicking over to their site, I find nothing. Next, I check the reports coming from Ferry County and see a brief memo from the sheriff, Gary Stevenson.

"Shooting incident on Pend Oreille River north of Boundary Dam. Christian Marshal, who made the report, stated that several male assailants shot at him and his companion, Gina Lindsey, while on the bank of the Columbia River north of Kettle Falls. The assailants followed Marshal and Lindsey to their car that was parked above the highway. Gina Lindsey suffered a wound to her upper left shoulder, and Marshal reported that they shot out his front and rear windshield of his pickup. I will send an officer to interview both Lindsey and Marshal and to look at the pickup. Investigation at the alleged shooting site showed nothing. Officers found no bullet casings, footprints or any other indication of illegal activity on the riverbank. Suspect it was a shooting accident."

That was it. Signed and dated by the sheriff. I lean back and rub my forehead. It would be forgotten in the stack of cases that the officers in the small police stations have to deal with daily. Most sheriff offices are woefully under-staffed.

After I debrief my team on our assignments for the day, I return to my office and settle into my chair, ready to work. But I don't have long to get comfortable. Mike Rudolph, an officer on my team, taps on my door and pokes his head in.

"You ready to go, Cap?" He gives me a cocky grin.

"Oh, yeah. The time got away from me."

We're scheduled to check out several houses that have come up for surveillance. I gather my camera and backpack and follow him to an unmarked police car.

It doesn't take us long to get from downtown to North Walnut Street, just off Broadway. It's a drab affair, two-story, needing a paint job. The yard has no grass, only weeds. A wooden fence is about to topple down along the north side. There's graffiti painted on the side of the house.

We cruise by in our unmarked vehicle, turn the corner and make another pass from the back. There's a derelict car in the backyard, weeds as high as a man's head, and other junk lying around.

Several small girls are playing in the back. A young boy, maybe about thirteen, approaches from the sidewalk with a skateboard under his arm.

"What kind of a place is that?"

Mike shakes his head. "It's a group home. It's run by a religious group. It's all legit, funded by grants from the government. We've checked out the reports from the agencies – DEA, FBI, and CPS. They've gone through it with a fine-toothed comb. The place is clean." He sounds disappointed.

Turning onto Maple, he heads north.

I pull out my phone and show him an address. "Let's go over to this place that I noticed on the reports this morning. Sounds interesting. It's called Forward Guard for Youth. That name rings a bell, but I can't place it. Do you know anything about the organization?"

He sighs. "It's clean, as far as we can tell. They run a ranch of some sort up north out of Chewelah. A survival camp. Military types."

"Ah! That's it. My friend got a brochure about that place just the other day. He says it's about weapons and fighting. I was wondering about it, but you say it checked out okay?"

"As far as we went with it." He turns right onto West Gardner Street. "Couldn't go very far. Was blocked by something. Figure it's a political set up. Or someone with a lot of money."

I'm watching the house numbers, a habit I've gotten into since I've done a lot of surveillance work. The houses along here were probably built in the 50's and 60's during one of Spokane's growth spurts. They are two-story with wide porches, deep lawns, and big trees. I suppose they were grand then, but now they're weatherworn and have the look of neglect.

At number 2532, a young girl, maybe thirteen or fourteen, walks through the weedy lawn toward the street. Her long blonde hair hangs in limp strands down in front of her face. She meanders from side to side like she's on drugs or can't decide what to do.

"Stop the car." As we pass the house, I swivel my head to study the house.

"Is that the one?"

"Yup." I don't even glance at Mike. I'm busy taking pictures. He obediently pulls over to the side of the street. A couple of big maple trees line the street, and a tall lilac bush has grown over the sidewalk.

I don't want anyone to see my face in case there's someone peering out the window of the house, so I pull on my jacket and yank up the hood.

"Okay. Stay here. I'll be right back."

"You going back there? Are you sure?" He shoots me a puzzled look. "You want backup?" He unfastens his seat belt.

"No. I gotta do this alone, or I'll spook that girl. Didn't you see her?

"Of course, I saw her." He looks out the side window. "All right. Signal if you need help."

As I step out on the sidewalk, only a part of the brown house with the yellow lawn is visible through the thick lilac bush. *Good.* I couldn't have found a better place to park if I'd done it myself. Mike knows his business.

I straighten my shoulders and make sure my revolver is in its holster under my arm. But I don't want to use it.

After grabbing a business card from my bag, I stroll down the sidewalk, not looking directly at the girl but casting my glance around at the other houses. She's on the sidewalk now and has taken a few tentative steps toward me.

It's only a half a block to where she stands, but it seems a long stretch of no-man's land between us. She's clad in shorts and a long, over-sized green plaid shirt that's unbuttoned. Underneath that, she wears a black cami undershirt. Flip flops on her feet. Nothing on her head. Hands are empty. No backpack.

She looks up.

My heart is nearly torn from my chest by what I see on her face and in her eyes. Her face is a twisted mask of torment, and there's something in her eyes that freezes my soul. It's the look of one who's being tortured almost beyond endurance. Her shoulders are hunched like she's unconsciously warding off a blow, yet the pain is inside and can't be warded off.

She stumbles, and I reach to catch her. But she rights herself and takes another step. I'm guessing they haven't used her yet as a hooker, but they've taught her some grim lessons about obedience and life on the street.

"Hello," I say and pause before we pass each other.

She doesn't respond. Moving past me, she continues her shuffling gait, her eyes averted. A sob tears at her throat. She lowers her eyes as shame washes over her face.

I step back and bring myself into her line of vision, almost close enough to touch her. "I ... uh, I'm looking for a house, number 2541. Do you know which one it is?" We're face to face now.

Still she says nothing.

I reach for her arm. "Let me help you. My car is right there. Get in. I can get you out of here. Please."

She stares at me, not yanking from my touch as I'd expected. "No. Um ... I can't. I have to ... uh, no, I can't." Another sob tears at her throat. She pulls away and turns back.

A woman's voice calls from the house. "Susie! Susie! Where are you, honey? Lunch is ready!"

I shake the girl's hand like we've met and are saying good-bye. "It was nice meeting you, Susie."

She tears away from me, a spitting kitten, afraid of everything. "That's not my name," she spits out. "It's Sanora. They call me that because ... "

I force my card into her hand. "Here's my card, Sanora. Call me."

She tucks it into a pocket in her shorts and turns back to the house, indecision written on her face, her steps lagging as if her mind is telling her to flee, yet her body is urging her to stay.

The woman is now striding down the walk toward us.

Sanora gives me a glance over her shoulder. "Thanks."

It was a whisper. Hope flickers in her eyes. The woman grabs her arm and pulls her back to the house. As they clomp up the stairs, the woman rakes me with a sharp, piercing glare. Sanora's shoulders slump as she allows herself to be shoved inside.

I climb in the car, wondering what kind of punishment the girl will get for her few moments of freedom They'll beat her, and they'll tighten security. She won't get a second chance. *Oh, God!* Why wouldn't she jump in the car? It was only a few feet away!

But she hadn't. Maybe they'd threatened to harm her family. I clench my fists so much my nails dig into my palms. I'm barely aware of the pain as I tell Mike what happened. I'm not supposed to get emotionally involved with all the cases I deal with daily, yet I can't help it.

"Huh. Figured as much," he says in a grunt as we turn onto Maple and head back downtown. He clenches the steering wheel. I can sense he'd like to tear those people who run that place from limb to limb. "We can have officers there in a few minutes. We'll shut them down." He reaches for the radio.

"It's no use," I say, staring out at Spokane River as we cross it. "They'll clear out. Probably doing it right now. The officers can't get inside without a warrant, and by the time we get one, they'll have disappeared."

He makes the call anyway, dumps me off at headquarters, and drives uptown. I return to my office and sit down at the computer. I check out the organization, *Forward Guard for Youth.* The web page portrays what looks like a summer camping program. It looks legitimate.

I can't get the girl's face from my mind. *Sanora.* A strange name. How would it feel to be trapped like that? To lose not only your family, but your identity and your freedom all at once?

The door opens suddenly and Police Chief Gerald Smithers enters the room without knocking. He never does that.

I look up and say, "Hello, Chief. Why don't you come in?"

He doesn't look at me. Pacing to the window, he gazes outside. Before he utters a word, I know something bad has happened. But there's no way to prepare myself for the shock of his next words.

Chapter 12

Seattle City Lights

Boundary Dam, June 6th

Chance made one phone call before he hit the sack that night. He speed-dialed Gina, and when she didn't answer, he left a message.

"Hi, Gina. I had something bad happen tonight. I can't tell you this way. Everything's okay now but it was touch and go for awhile. Call me when you can. I know you're probably in bed and won't get this until you have a break tomorrow at work, but please call. I need to talk to you."

He hoped he didn't sound too distressed, but his nerves hadn't stopped jumping. All he could think about was getting out of there – take the horses to a safe place and find one for himself. But where would that be? Would they shoot his horses next or set fire to the house?

It took awhile and some prayer before he drifted off to sleep. He awoke with a jerk the next morning to his phone ringing. He thought it was Gina and was surprised instead to hear his dad's voice on the line.

"Hi, Chris! Are you up for a little adventure with your old Dad?"

Chance smothered a yawn and set his feet on the floor. "Hi, Dad. This is a surprise. What's up?"

"Well, I'm here in Spokane, flew in last night, and want to take a look at Boundary Dam. Have you been up that way? I understand it's north of Chewelah."

Chance shook the sleepiness from his head. He stood and stretched, glancing out the window at his charred barn. "Well, north of Newport. Why do you want to go up there?" He'd heard about the dam on the Pend Oreille River near Metaline Falls, but he'd never been there and couldn't fathom his father's sudden desire to see it.

"Business. I'm on a senate committee, and we're looking into the dams in the state, which ones could be breached. Hey, do you have a restaurant in Chewelah that serves breakfast?"

Chance grinned. "Uh, yeah. It's not fancy. Zip's. Right on 395 as you come through town. It's a fast food place, but they serve a decent breakfast."

"All right. Sounds good. Meet me there in about an hour, okay?"

"Okay. Hey, Dad, I ..." But his father had disconnected.

What he hadn't been able to say was that he was glad his dad had called, that there were lots of things he wanted to talk about. But of course, Josh Marshal was too busy to hear him out. Like always.

After a quick shower, he checked on the horses and gave them some grain. They seemed uneasy, probably because of the smell coming from the burned barn. "You guys will be all right until I can figure out something," he said, patting Santiago. "Okay?"

Santiago snorted and tossed his head. Chance took that as a *yes* and headed back to the house, stopping to see the damage done to the barn. He had to submit a report to the insurance company with pictures. Maybe he should call before he left for the camp.

He was just getting in the rig when his phone jangled its little tune. It was Gina. He said, "Hi! Whatcha doing these days?"

"Hey, Chance. What's going on?" Her voice sounded wary, tight. Was it from worry? Or had something happened to her?

"Are you all right?" He slapped on his seat belt and turned the ignition. He had to drive and talk, which was against the law in the state of Washington, but he doubted if any cops were patrolling Cottonwood Drive this early in the morning.

"Tired is all. Tell me what happened. I don't have long."

He knew she wasn't really okay, but he didn't press her. "Well, I went up to the place where Dusty got shot, and I found some things the cops missed. It started raining, and I was late getting back. It was dark when I pulled into the place, and I saw light coming from the barn. And smoke billowing up. It was on fire."

She gasped. "Oh, no!"

"The horses were locked inside. I'd left them out, of course. I ran over there and got Cheyenne out first, but I couldn't get Cyndi. A neighbor came by, and he helped me. We got all of them, thank God. Santiago was in the trailer. The fire department arrived and put it out, but there's quite a bit of damage." He paused and shifted down when he got to Flowery Trail.

"Someone set it?"

"No question about that. The fire chief said he'd send a detective to take a look around. I'm a little uneasy about the horses, though. I'd like to take them somewhere else."

"You wanna bring them over to my place?" She was eating breakfast at work. He heard the crackle of paper and the slurp of a drink.

"I thought of that, but you've been too busy to worry about them. I think Pole will take them. What's going on with you?"

"I had some excitement here last night, Chance. Two boys showed up. I was suspicious of them, and even more so when I discovered the land line to the house was cut. I wouldn't let them in and called the sheriff. They left after awhile. So, I guess they've found us."

He turned north on 395 in Chewelah. "I guess so. Hey, my dad is here. We're going over to Boundary Dam. I don't get to be with him very often, so I thought I'd better tag along like a good son. You take care. Will you call me if you're in over your head?"

"Yeah, I'll do that, Chance. I gotta go. Call me before you head over to that camp thing."

"Okay. I have some evidence I found that I want you to see." He pulled into Zip's and parked. "Can we meet somewhere tomorrow?"

"When are you going to the camp?"

"Wednesday. Call me tomorrow, okay?"

"Okay. Take lots of pictures of the dam. I've always wanted to see it."

"I'll do that." He disconnected and climbed out of the vehicle just as a dark blue Lexis SUV pulled into the parking lot and stopped.

A man stepped out. He wore sun glasses and was dressed in khaki shorts, a red dress shirt, tucked in, and a baseball cap with Mariners printed on the top.

He lifted his sun glasses and set them on the baseball cap as he marched across the lot. "Hi, Chris! It's good to see you!" Josh Marshal slapped Chance on the back and grinned.

"Hi, Dad. It's good to see you, too. This is a surprise. I can't spend all day with you. Are your people with you? Your senate committee?"

Josh laughed liked Chance told a huge joke. "No, we're meeting in Spokane later. C'mon, I'm starved. You have to work?" He opened the door to the restaurant, stepping back so Chance could go first.

"Yeah, I'm afraid so. Dirty job. Someone's got to do it." He grinned at his feeble joke, but his father was too busy studying the menu above the counter to notice.

A young girl greeted them with a big smile. "You make your order here, and I'll bring your meal to you," she said.

They made their choices, got their coffee and went to sit in one of the booths. Chance reflected that his father looked strangely out of place here.

Josh leaned forward. "Well, I don't think this will take very long. I've got a ... situation going on and wanted to check out the dam. Heard a lot about it."

"A situation?" Chance pulled out a napkin and folded it like a paper airplane. "What's going on?"

Josh waved his hand. "Oh, it's nothing to be alarmed about. Just some warning signs that I wanted to debunk. I suspect it's a false alarm."

The meal came. Chance wanted to pump the information from Dad about the dam, but Josh changed the subject and was now waxing eloquent about a big highway project he'd gotten passed through the senate.

Chance bowed his head briefly, said a quick prayer, and began eating.

"So, how's work going, son? I heard you had a problem the other night. Want to tell me about it?"

Around mouthfuls, Chance said, "My partner was shot by someone coming over the border illegally. It was bad, but I think he'll make it. They're doing an investigation. I think they're trying to keep it quiet. What did you hear?"

Josh shrugged. "Oh. Nothing much. Just that there was a shooting. You okay? Need a break? You could come on over and stay with us for a couple of weeks."

"No, thanks. I'm going to be gone a week, to a camp where they train in martial arts and weapons and night patrol. It's right up here in the mountains. That's for five days. Then I have other things to do."

They finished breakfast, and Chance got in Dad's Lexis, leaving his truck parked beneath one of the big cottonwood trees that grew by the creek near the drive-in. It didn't take them long to drive over Flowery Trail, and head north on Highway 2 toward the Canadian border.

The dam was located fifteen miles off the highway up in the mountains. From the map the elder Marshal provided, Chance noticed it was five miles south of the border. Crawford State Park which included Gardner Cave was smack dab on it, or very near it, maybe only a few hundred feet away.

Josh seemed uninterested in these details. He chatted with Chance, but mostly took phone calls while he drove. They turned off the main highway and climbed a hill, winding higher out of the valley where the Pend Oreille River flowed on its way north.

There were only two cars in the upper parking lot when they arrived. Josh stopped at a guard shack. A young man in uniform appeared and told them to proceed down the hill. Chance noted he didn't carry a gun.

"Someone will meet you down there," the young man said with a smile. "You can take the tour, if you want to, or just admire the view. Have a good day."

"Nice fellow," Josh commented as they turned down the hill and proceeded to the lower parking lot.

"Not much security," Chance said.

The dam curved across the canyon. There was a flow of water coming over the dam, but not much. A big, round tunnel mouth opened at the bottom of the cliff they faced, large enough to accommodate several good-sized semis stacked on top of one another.

"That's where we go for the tour," Josh said, taking in the surroundings immediately. "And there's my crew." He nodded to two men who got out of a red pickup and walked over. Josh introduced them to Chance as Bill and Mike. Chance wondered if they were body guards.

"Here comes our guide," Chance said after he shook hands with the two men.

A girl with her hair in a pony tail approached the car and smiled. "Hello, folks! Would you like to go on the tour?" She wore a blue uniform that fit her slender figure nicely. On her left sleeve and over the front pocket were the words, "Seattle City Lights."

"Yes, ma'am," Josh said, flashing his wide grin. "Can we go right now?"

She nodded. "There's no one else coming. This way, please."

She wore a two-way radio and carried a flashlight. As they approached the opening in the cliff, a young man joined them, wearing the same blue uniform.

Chance bent his head back and looked up the face of the rock cliff above them. Huge transmission poles carried electrical lines straight up the cliff, and across the state, all the way to Seattle. The sheer genius of the engineering job took his break away.

He was in for more surprises as they followed their guide and her side-kick into the long, curving tunnels underneath the mountain.

Boundary Dam, he discovered, provided forty percent of the electricity for Seattle. It was carved from underneath the mountain and housed huge electrical generators that sat in a neat row in a long room.

In the visitor's room, he gazed through large windows to view the generators below, humming away, vibrating the whole mountain.

When they finished the tour, and Josh told his friends he'd see them in Spokane, they drove through Metaline and north to a small road that wound up a mountain and came out on the opposite cliff from the dam. An observation shelter stood there with more information about the dam.

Chance and his dad inspected the view from the building, then walked down a paved path that led to a deck below, facing the dam. Here Chance found three free-standing binoculars.

"This is quite a project," Josh commented as he finished looking through one of the devices. "It's one of the best kept secrets around. Who would think that this dam would provide that much electricity to the city of Seattle?"

"Yeah." Chance took his turn at the binoculars and studied the dam's layout carefully. A thought had been tugging at the back of his mind. What would hinder someone, say terrorists, from blowing the dam and disrupting the city of Seattle?

But why would anyone want to do that?

Josh brushed his hand through his spiked blond hair. He was ready to go. "You seen enough? I have to get back to Spokane."

Chance nodded, taking one last look upriver through the binoculars. Suddenly something caught his eye. He stared.

Something was on the riverbank, just north of the dam. It was in the bushes and glinted silver in the sunlight. He peered at it a bit longer.

It was the prow of a metal boat, stuck in the brush. While he was looking intently at the boat, he noticed movement. Swinging towards the river, he saw another boat approaching. Several men were in it, but he couldn't see their faces.

"Come on, Chris! We have to go!" Dad's words echoed against the wooded cliff.

The people in the boat beached it and stepped up on the shore. Try as he would, he could not see their faces. They seemed to be carrying things onshore. Drugs? He couldn't see anything else, and Dad was already out of sight.

He left his post and bounded up the trail, still puzzling over it. Someone was up to something, and he suspected it was for no good.

As he joined his father on the path, he said, "Security is lax here. Have you noticed? What's stopping someone from blowing up the dam?"

Josh looked over at him with surprise in his blue eyes. "Blowing up the dam? Why would anyone do that?"

"I don't know. Disrupt the city. Take out the power. You can do a lot of damage without lights or power. Maybe some terrorist cell group?"

Josh snorted as he unlocked his vehicle. "Sounds like a corny movie plot to me. I can think of more volatile targets. Hey, you up for some grub? Is there a place around here where we can get something to eat?"

Chance laughed. "I don't think so. The closest town is Ione, and I don't think they have anything much there except a grocery store. We'll have to wait until we get to Chewelah, Dad."

As they traveled back over the pass on Flowery Trail, past the ski resort, and down into town, Chance knew he'd seen something important, and something dangerous. It sent chills up his neck and twisted his stomach.

Adding it all up, it meant something big was about to happen, and the worst of it was that he could do nothing to stop it.

Chapter 13

Niagara Tightrope

June 6th

Police Chief Smithers' sandy-blond hair, which he usually wears combed flat on his head, stands straight up – it looks like he's stuck his finger in a light socket. His shoulders are ramrod straight, and his piercing blue eyes seem to see right through me. He's not smiling as he leans over my desk with his nose about three inches from mine.

Without preamble, he says, "Lindsey, you're finished here."

I stare at him. We lock eyes. I notice his are blue-gray, more gray than blue, I decide, and they have little flecks of gold in them. Interesting. I'm the first to look away.

"You're joking, right?" I push back my chair to give myself more personal space.

He straightens and folds his arms across his chest. He never jokes. "Let me put it more succinctly. You're fired. What do you say to that?"

I lean back and decide to call his bluff. He can't mean this.

"Well, sir, I have a lot to say. I'll write a letter to the commissioner first, and I'll send off one to my senator. Then I'll write one to the governor. We've met, you know." I glare at him. "Why have you come to this decision? Maybe I need to call Human Resources."

He chuckles and unfolds his arms, gazing at a picture I have on the wall of my horse, Gypsy. "Well, I can save you a lot of time and paper. We might need you back with us after awhile. You see, we're in kind of a predicament. We have a ... situation and it's

85

dangerous. It's also out of our jurisdiction. We've called in the heavy weights."

Turning, he stares at me as if I were the culprit of this monster he's describing. "But first I need to know. What were you doing on Friday?"

"After I tell you, are you going to fire me?"

He strolls over to my window and opens the blinds. "Well, more or less." I hear a smile in his voice. "Tell me what happened at the river. I want to hear it from you."

"I was going to send you a report. I thought the Ferry County sheriff would contact you."

"They're rather slow, and I'm running out of patience." He marches to the front of my desk and taps it impatiently with his index finger.

I want to get to the point of this meeting. His first words sucked the spit out of me, as Dad said all the time. I ruffle my hair. "I suppose you've heard the facts already." I give him the basics of what happened on the river and add what occurred last night when the two boys visited me.

"Why do you suppose they came?" He paces to the chair in front of the desk, but he doesn't sit down.

I straighten Gypsy's picture. "To finish off what they started up there on the river. No question in my mind at all."

"You think the two incidents are connected."

"Yes, I do."

He nods and sits down, letting out his breath like he'd been holding it in. "Well, sorry to startle you like that, but I had to know, and I had to scare the dickens out of you so you wouldn't cover it up." He holds up his hand to block my protest. "Not that I think you would. But I know you by now, Gina, and you downplay the danger you're in. You try to handle things yourself. Am I correct?" He gives me the benefit of a sharp-eyed glare.

"Well, not always."

"We've sent an investigative team to the river to search for evidence, but I doubt if we'll get anything."

"No, I don't suppose so," I say. "It's something big, isn't it?"

"We don't know the extent of it yet, but it feels big. We've known about it for some time. Just haven't been able to get a lead on it."

I plunk down in my desk chair. "Oh. There's something else you won't find on your regular channels, but maybe you've heard about it. My friend, Chance Marshal, is a border guard. He and his partner were patrolling last night, and they got shot at by someone coming across the border illegally. Wounded his partner. The two perps got away. Interesting, huh?" I was going to say scary, but I don't think he finds anything scary.

"Is his partner going to make it?"

"Yeah, thank heavens. I don't know if that's connected with what went on by the river. What do you have, and why do you say I'm terminated here?"

He brushes his hand through his hair, smoothing it down. "There's an organization operating up by Colville somewhere. We've gotten some of their victims down here in the city, and they funnel people up there from Spokane. This is sensitive, Gina. One false move and everything goes *poof!* in our faces. If we make accusations before we have the facts nailed down, we could all be prosecuted."

"Sounds like there's someone behind it who has money."

He doesn't answer, only moves to the window again and stares outside.

I wish he would get to the point. "Where do I come in, sir?"

"We want you to go undercover with the FBI. You don't have to accept the assignment, but that's what I came to talk to you about. Maybe you could get in when others could not."

"Okay." I shove back from my desk. I'm so jittery, I can't sit still. Rising, I join him at the window, fiddling with the strings that lower the blinds. "Will I keep my job here?"

He nods. "They're borrowing you. I've talked to them, and you are to report to an ... Agent DeLaney." He hands me a slip of paper. "Today at one-thirty."

I take it and set it on the desk, my heart thumping, unable to speak.

He moves toward the door. "Well? What are you going to do? Either way, I won't be upset. If you decide against it, you can stay here. This conversation will have never happened."

I nod. "That's fair enough. What will it ... involve? Or do you know?"

He shrugs. "I have no idea. Where you go and what you do is not my call. We suspect they have a business cover north of Colville, maybe around Kettle Falls. Near the border." He moves to the door. "Well, let me know what you decide."

I take a deep breath and move around the desk to stand in front of him.

"I'll tell you right now, sir. I'll do it. It feels ... right, if you know what I mean. I'm pleased that you consider me qualified. Can I get some things in order first?"

For some crazy reason, I hold out my hand. My insides are all quivery like I'm standing on a tightrope strung across Niagara Falls.

He shakes my hand and favors with me a rare smile. "Good for you, Gina. That's up to the agent at the FBI that you'll be working with. Good luck. You'll need it."

"I wish you hadn't said that, sir. Thanks."

After he's gone, I sit at my desk, staring into space, trying to assimilate what just happened. Going undercover with the FBI is a big deal, and I'd agreed to it readily. You don't do something like that without a lot of preparation, thought, and prayer. Without a lot of fear, usually.

What will it mean? Total undercover or light? Total undercover means you disappear from your friends, your home, your work. You take on a new identity and become another person.

Yet I'd accepted it all, a blank check, without much thought. *Why? Am I trying to prove myself? Still wanting to become the cop that Dad would be proud of?* No, there's something else, and when I think about the girl called Sanora, I find the answer.

I look at my hands. They're shaking. I rise to pace the office, a red haze filling my vision. It started when I saw Sanora and know what kind of life she's heading for, and it grew when I realized they would escape and she would be lost to me, that I can do nothing to save her.

This isn't the kind of anger that makes you go off on a screaming tirade, or fling things around, or attack people. It's not about me.

Who are the people who think they can kill, maim and destroy the lives of little children, young girls and boys? Who are the people who profit at the expense of girls and women for money?

I glance at my watch. I don't have time to think about what I've done. I have time for a quick bite of lunch and a drive over to the FBI office where I'll meet Agent... I look at the piece of paper Chief Smithers gave me... DeLaney.

I clean off my desk, shut down the computer, and pick up my car keys. Shouldering my backpack, I lock the office door. My knees are weak. I feel like a person who is about to dive off a fifty-foot cliff into the water.

Well, here it goes. *God, help me!*

Chapter 14

I'm Ready!

The girl digs through a pile of old blankets in a drawer and at the bottom, retrieves a blue notebook. Finding a stub of a pencil, she goes into her closet, sits on the floor, and begins to write.

It's been a long time since I've written, but things got really weird there for a while, and I didn't have time. I'm now living at a farm somewhere, don't know where for sure, in a dorm with other girls. I like this better than Spokane because we're outdoors a lot and the air is clearer, but they keep us locked in and we don't have much free time.

Even though I know this is risky, I'm going to write about what's happened to me. I can't keep it bottled up inside any longer.

A couple of weeks ago, when I was still in that house in Spokane, on West Gardner Street, I got outside one morning. I think someone left the front door unlocked by mistake. I wandered down the front sidewalk, kind of in a daze. I think they give us drugs to make us do what they tell us to do.

I say "us" because I soon found out that there are six other girls here, some older and some younger than me. While the older girls go out at night, my job is to help in the kitchen and clean the house. I know that unless I can somehow get away from here, I will never see my mother and family again, and that I will be used like the older girls are.

Anyway, I got out that morning and strolled down the sidewalk. I thought I was going to get away and couldn't believe my good luck.

Before I got to the end of the walk, this lady comes toward me. I'd seen a black car pull into the curb a little way down the street and park behind a big bush. The woman got out, threw up the hood of her jacket over her head, and walked toward me. She was craning her neck, looking up and down the street, like she was trying to see into the houses or something.

As I got to the sidewalk, she came up to me and said she's looking for a house. I told her I didn't know and wished she would go away because the woman inside who is in charge of us, Margo, would hear us talking and look out the window and my chance to escape would be gone.

I stumbled and the woman reached for me, but I got my feet under me, and I was going to go past her, when she said, "I want to help you," or something like that, and, "Get in my car. It's parked up there."

Yeah, right. Like I would do that without knowing her or where she was taking me. I got in this mess because I got into Jim's car that night. My mind was real foggy, and I couldn't understand what she wanted me to do. So, I just stared at her, sort of frozen.

That's where I went wrong. Because now I think that lady could have helped me. She had kind eyes. She gave me her card. I tucked it in my pocket, but of course I got rid of it. Not before memorizing her name and phone number, though.

I can still see that fancy lettering on the off-white card. Gina Lindsey, SPD Police Officer, Staff Sergeant, SIU (whatever those letters mean), 509-680-5324. She was a police officer! Maybe she carried a gun. I'm groaning inside as I write this because I know I blew my chance.

I can't let them hurt Mom and the little kids, like they threaten to do. They tell us that someday we can earn money and send it to our families to help them out, and when we get a little more experienced, we can get more pay.

Anyway, Margo came outside and took me back in. She had a gun concealed in her apron. And she will use it. Even in front of that lady! I seen Jim shoot a boy and drag his body away just because he refused to do what they wanted for a filming session.

She gave me a whipping for my escape. My back was sore for awhile, but it wasn't as bad as what I used to get from Mom's boyfriends.

Soon after that, we left the house. They are always ready to move, so it didn't take very long. Before we got going, the cops came to the door. Birdie, the other woman who guards us girls, answered it. She's younger than Margo. Standing in front of the door and barring it with her body, she refused them entrance and said they needed to get a court order.

After the cops left, they got us ready to go. We loaded up things in two vans and a pickup and drove away about an hour later. I remember Margo gave us some pop in glasses, and I think they drugged us, because before we left Spokane, we were asleep.

I remember trying to stay awake because it might be important to know where we were going, but I couldn't.

When I awoke, we'd already arrived here. Like I said, it's a farm with two big houses for dormitories. They really do farm. We have to go out and weed in the gardens all the time. And it's near a river.

My job is to help in the kitchen, learning to cook. I don't mind that so much as not being able to see Mom and to be free.

My only hope is that I can escape. But I don't see how that's going to happen. I remind myself of that woman's name and phone number, but I don't ever get a chance to use the phone.

The bell just went off for supper. I pray to God every day that I'll have another chance to escape.

For now, I've decided to keep low and try to do exactly what they tell me to do. My plan is to wait and watch for my chance. When it comes, I'll be ready.

Oh, yeah.

Chapter 15

Enter Angela Brubaker

June 6th

"Take a seat, Miss Lindsey. Agent DeLaney will speak with you in a few minutes." The secretary at the desk doesn't smile. She only gives me the merest of nods.

Of course, they'd seen me arrive. Knew me by sight. It always surprises and amuses me that they seem to know everything. I sit obediently in the dentist-style waiting room.

No magazines, though. What would they have? I imagine the titles – Life and Crime Through the Eyes of An FBI Agent. Or How to Eliminate Your Problems the Easy Way – Kill Everyone.

The FBI offices in Spokane are located in an apartment complex near the Spokane River on West Boone. I check my phone for messages and lean back in the chair, thinking about what was going to happen next. I try to shove aside my fears, doubts, and concerns that yammer at my subconscious like naughty children, but I can't do anything about the queasy feeling in the pit of my stomach. It's there to stay.

I'd only gotten comfortable, as much as one can in such a place, when the secretary asks me to follow her down the corridor to an office.

Agent DeLaney rises from behind his desk and grips my hand. "It is good to see you, Miss Lindsey. Please take a seat."

I obey him wordlessly, allowing him to take the lead.

He's a seasoned warrior, an agent past his prime. Yet I feel at ease with him immediately, for he reminds me of my dad. Even though his hair is graying, and he uses glasses to read, he misses nothing in the glance he gives me before studying the papers on his desk.

"I see you've been stirring up a hornet's nest," he says with a flicker of a smile. "Trying to get yourself killed?"

"Have you been up there?" I lean forward, hoping he'll have some information.

"Yes, but we didn't find much. The sheriff had already taken casts of the tire prints. They collected some cigarette butts and a lot of rifle shells. But no fingerprints. Nothing solid." He leans back and gives me the benefit of his direct gaze. "What do you figure, Miss Lindsey? Any ideas?"

His candid approach unnerves me. I shrug, keeping my body still. "I honestly don't know, sir. The only thing I can think is what I told Smithers. I was interrupting something, maybe a shipment, and they thought I'd seen too much. I didn't actually notice anything until that man started shooting at me."

He nods. I'm sure he's read my statement. "Can you identify either of the two men?"

"Well, I can't identify the one who began shooting from cover. The other one, I only saw part of his face under his hat. Maybe I can identify him. You have some mug shots you want me to look at?"

He shakes his head, fiddles with a pen. "No. For now, let's concentrate on locating their headquarters." He lifts his eyes and smiles. "Oh. By the way, welcome to the team, Lindsey."

"Thank you, sir. It is a privilege to work with you."

He rifles through the papers. "You'll be given a dossier of the pertinent facts. For now, I want to discuss your immediate assignment with us. You will be working light under-cover. You know what I mean?"

I nod. Light under-cover means you live elsewhere, making contact with those you suspect, nosing around for information.

Heavy under-cover means you change your identity and get into the organization.

He continues in a calm voice. "At this point, this is light. We'd like you to go up to Colville and look around. You don't have to change your residence. You can say you're from out of town, looking for a job." He glances up. "You don't mind dying your hair, do you?"

I chuckle and ease back in my chair. "None whatsoever. I've done it before. What color do you prefer?" I'm smiling, too, but it's a cautious smile as I don't want him to think I'm unprofessional.

He laughs outright and stands. Moving to the printer, he retrieves some pages from it. "Here you go. Read and study them before you leave, then return them, and I'll shred them." He hands me the dossier. "I don't care what color you dye your hair. Just make it so you aren't recognizable. In that file, you'll also find the particulars of your new identity. Memorize it, okay? I hear you have a talent for that."

"Yes, sir. When do you want me to start?"

"As soon as you can. I don't have to remind you to keep quiet about what you're doing, do I? Not a word to anyone, not even your mother or your boyfriend."

I stare at him. "Absolutely, sir. So, it *is* heavy. "You want me to drop out of my present life, change my appearance, and infiltrate."

He holds the door open for me. "We won't go in until we know where they're located. You're not officially under-cover. Not by the books. But, yes, essentially that is the kind of work you are going to be doing for us. You'll find all the information you need in the dossier I printed out for you. I'll get your IDs to you in a couple of days. And I want reports."

I groan as he shuts the door on any further questions. But at least he didn't slam it.

The secretary directs me to a conference room down the hall. Comfortable leather chairs circle a large oblong table. There are two computers on desks along the wall. A whiteboard, probably interactive with electronics, is on the wall and a wastebasket sits beside the table. There's probably a security camera whirring silently somewhere in the room.

I study the printed material. They're after an organization that includes the production and sale of illegal drugs, human trafficking, prostitution, and racketeering. I shake my head. There's someone big with a lot of money and power at the head of this monster.

One branch they'd been able to trace is located north of Spokane. The name of the small town, Kettle Falls, comes up repeatedly in the reports. The organization could be masquerading as a church or a church-affiliated ministry. Or a charity of some sort. There are several leads, some located in Colville, some in Kettle Falls and the area, that are duly recorded with names and addresses.

I sigh as I set aside the pages. It doesn't seem like much to go on. Is this organization also smuggling drugs and people across the Canadian border? I make a mental note to collaborate with Chance tonight when I get home. He should be home.

I take a look at what most concerns me most − my new identity. I'm going to be Angela Brubaker. Oh, Lord. Where do they get these names?

My age is the same, 25, and my hair color is blonde. Oh, great. I hate blonde! I'm from Billings, Montana, and I've been divorced. My husband's name was Jim McDowell. He left me for another woman, but I'd filed a police report on his abuse, so I guess I'm not too upset that he left me.

I have no children. My education includes Montana State University of Billings and post graduate studies at the University of Colorado in Denver, emerging with a BA in Sociology and a MA in Accounting. After memorizing the rest of my life history, I return the papers to Agent DeLaney. He gives me a secure cell phone and tells me his number is the only one on it.

There. I'm done. With my mind on the thousand and one things I have to do, I drive out of the city and head north on Highway 395. I wonder if Chance will call.

I can't tell him about my new assignment or that I won't be around much for the next several weeks. Of course, if he goes to that camp, he won't be here, either.

Turning onto my road, I pass the sheriff's car going the opposite way. He gives me a nod. I'm glad to see he's been down by my house. The horses are over by the barn, which is strange. Usually they're out in the pasture or under the big trees in the back, if it's hot.

I pull into the garage and notice that the blinds are up on the living room windows. I leave them down to keep out the hot afternoon sun. Did I forget this morning? Or is someone in there?

Slowly I climb out of the pickup, gripping my rifle that I keep on the window rack behind the seat. With it in my hands, held waist-high, and my finger on the trigger, I creep across the cement floor to the door that leads to the house. Six steps. There haven't been any other sounds – no squeaks, scratches or branches moving. No clothes brushing against the gate. Someone is being extremely cautious.

I peer outside. The kitchen door and the screen are both shut, but there are big bushes beside it. Someone could be hiding behind one of those. I can't see the length of the garage where tires, the garbage can, and other junk is piled. That would be handy hiding places for an assailant.

Stepping out on the cracked sidewalk, I pause, glancing left and right, gripping my gun like it's my lifeline. My heart pounds hard in my ears. My world shrinks to listening for the slightest sound, even the intake of breath. The sun reflects from an old milk can by the door, a fly buzzes around my face, and a crow caws from the big pine in my back yard.

Sweat dribbles down the side of my head. I ignore it. A footstep crunches on the gravel. I lean forward cautiously, gripping the rifle. Someone emerges from the stack of wood beside the garage.

Chapter 16

Power Source

June 6th

I curl my finger around the trigger. This is it. I'm ready for them. A figure appears from the side of the garage. I hesitate. The form is wrong. It's not a man or even a boy.

A woman closes the distance rapidly. She laughs and holds out her hands. "Gina! It's me, honey!"

I stagger back, glad there's the garage wall behind me, or I would have fallen. It's Bobbi! "What are you doing here?" My tone is harsh.

She envelops me, rifle and all, in a bear hug. I step back and set the rifle down, wiping my face because tears flood my eyes. She thinks I'm crying for joy. But I'm not. I'm crying from shock.

"Bobbi! I... can't believe you're here. Where... how...." I draw a breath as the realization of what I'd nearly done sweeps over me. "I nearly... don't you know you shouldn't startle a police officer like that?" I turn away.

"What's going on? Do you like my surprise? How are you doing? I want to know everything. Let's go inside. No use standing out here."

I return to the pickup where I lock the door.

She follows me. "Oh, honey! It's so good to see you! Give me another hug! I can't take my eyes from you. Are you all right? Why the gun, sweetie? Did you expect a ... burglar or something?" She chuckles as I give her another hug.

"Just being careful, Bobbi. How did you get here? I still can't believe it. I was going to call you, but I got busy and forgot. And here you are!" I hope my voice doesn't register the anger that's swelling inside me, bringing with it the shakes of after-shock.

She's been inside. The blinds are drawn, her purse sits on the table, and a sweater is flung over the back of a chair. She says she parked behind the barn to surprise me, and when I didn't come, she got in the house by crawling in a window.

I don't tell her that she almost got more than she bargained for as a reward for her trouble and make a mental note that I'll have to improve my security system.

She explains that she'd heard something wrong in my tone last night and thought I might need help. She'd driven to Billings, gotten the first flight to Spokane, rented a car, and here she was.

As I start a pot of coffee, she gazes around the kitchen. "You've fixed things up nice since I was here last fall, You could organize your kitchen a little better. I couldn't find the coffee anywhere."

"I know. It's just that I work so much, I can't take time for that sort of thing." I wipe my hands on a towel and attempt a smile.

"This room could stand a new coat of paint, too. And the bathroom needs an overhaul. Hey, why don't we do it together? What color do you like?"

I put away the groceries I'd gotten in Deer Park. "I ... uh, well, we can talk about that later, Bobbi. Have you had supper?"

When she says no, I pull out some hamburger and thaw it in the microwave. She takes over, saying she makes a delicious spaghetti sauce. I tell her to go ahead while I change and get a quick shower.

When we've eaten and cleaned up the kitchen, I take her out to show her the horses. She admires them, and as we stroll back to the house, she tells me how I can fix up things in the barn, and what to do about the nagging cough that plagues Pecos Bill.

We look at the garden and end up sitting in the back yard on the two plastic lawn chairs, sipping our drinks. I'd made her a banana and strawberry smoothie and me a strawberry margarita. I thought they were really good, but she didn't think to compliment me.

My back yard is a mess. It needs to be mowed and trimmed, and there's fallen limbs on the grass from the big wind storm the other night. The garden, a little patch in the corner, needs weeding. So do my flower beds.

She looks around and says, "It looks nice, honey. You've done a great job. Would you like me to help you with the weeding?" She grins. "It helps me get rid of my stress."

I think about her immaculate garden and yard. A weed wouldn't dare to show its head there. I sigh, wishing she hadn't come. With everything else on my mind, I don't need this.

"Help yourself, Aunt Bobbi," I reply. "Feel free. Whatever you want to do. I'm going to be busy, so ... "

"Busy? What's going on? I heard something in your voice. That's why I came."

I can't believe she would come all this way because she heard anxiety in my voice. I watch the hummingbirds that come to my feeder, wondering if I'd made the right kind of sugar water for them.

Waving away her concern, I attempt a light tone. "Oh, it's just my job. I have a lot of things on my mind. It could have been any number of situations we're dealing with right now." I stand and yank some weeds from the flower bed nearby. "Really. It's nothing."

"Nothing?" She eyes me speculatively. She's not buying it.

I straighten and look at her directly. "Nothing that you can help with. I can handle it. And you know I've learned to pray, and so God is on my side now. That should count for something."

She isn't smiling. Worry deepens the furrows in her brow. She's always been this way – she wants to know each detail of my life, and she uses that information to control me.

She shakes her head. "Somehow that doesn't relieve my mind, Gina. You been going to church, honey?"

"I go with Chance when we can." I brush off my hands. "Well, let's go inside. The mosquitoes are getting bad. How long are you staying?"

She gives me another one of those sideways looks. "I don't know. Surely you can use help around here. What's your schedule like? Maybe we can do something fun. Like go over to the lake. You know a place we could rent on the lake? I'll pay."

"That sounds nice, but I'm not sure if I can get time off." I lead the way inside and rinse out our glasses before putting them in the dishwasher.

"Oh, that's not the way to load the glasses, honey," she says, rearranging them.

I grit my teeth. "Look, Bobbi, I'm not sure about my schedule. I'm afraid we're busy right now. Maybe on the weekend..."

"Oh, I'm sure they'll let you have some time off. For something like this."

"Well, I'll see." How can I keep her occupied? The lake might be a good idea. If I can get her over there, I can get away to work on the assignment in Colville.

I have an appointment at the beauty salon in Deer Park tomorrow to have my hair cut and dyed. I'll have to change my appearance in other ways, too. Sometimes it's very subtle, like your eyebrows reshaped, or pads of cotton in your cheeks, or dummy glasses. Or different clothes.

As Bobbi gets settled in the guest room, I wonder if I should call Smithers and postpone my assignment with the FBI. No! What about Sanora and girls and boys like her? How many will be taken by this gang of thugs while I sit around and entertain my aunt?

As we get ready for bed, I decide to level with her.

"Bobbi, I have to work this week. It's a very significant investigation that I've been assigned. It might take quite a bit of time, but when I'm finished, I'll take the weekend off, and we can do something fun."

"How long will it take?"

"I don't know. A week. Maybe more."

She nods, pulling her sweater around her chest like she's suddenly cold. "Well, I guess that's the way it will have to be. I don't mind you working, honey. I can find things to do around here."

I show her where the towels are in the guest bathroom and tell her good night. Then I check the horses.

It's a warm evening with no wind. The stars are out in a dark velvet sky and crickets over by the creek tune up their fiddles for the concert that evening. I feed Gypsy pieces of an apple and kiss her nose. Pecos Bill comes over and wants some attention, too. I rub his neck and tell him he's handsome and a good horse.

While Bobbi's getting ready for bed, rustling around in her room like a cat about to have kittens, I shut and lock both doors and make sure the windows are down and fastened tightly. Then I turn on the air conditioner and start packing. I might need to spend several nights away from home, so I throw in all the necessities of life, even a first aid kit and my camera.

As I get ready for bed, I think about Chance and hope things have settled down for him. He was supposed to work today. I wonder if he got put on leave like he said he might. I remember to pray for his partner, Dusty.

I set the alarm for 5:30am, and lay back on the pillows. I feel bad that I can't take time off from work for Bobbi, but I have to do this assignment.

I have to find the people who are stealing girls and enslaving them. But is there more to it? Does the trail lead deeper into danger than I think?

As always, I end the day with a prayer for my mother. I'd started it when she left us when I was five, and I'd kept it up, even when I said I didn't believe in God. I feel like if could only find her, my life would be complete and happy. If only I could see her, look into her eyes, talk to her.

But I can't. She's gone from my life, and I don't think I will ever find her.

A single tear finds its way down the side of my face. Turning over to my side, I drift into an uneasy sleep.

Chapter 17

Leave of Absence

June 7th, Chewelah

The place was quiet when Chance arrived home. The horses stood down by the creek under the big box elder tree. He made a circuit of the barn and pasture, assuring himself that everything was okay. Since the fire, he'd felt like someone was watching the place, but so far no one had made a move, and he hadn't seen any cars or vehicles parked around.

How much did they know about him? Probably everything. It wasn't a happy feeling to be the target in someone's sights.

He called the auto body shop in Chewelah and took his pickup down to the shop. After Charlie, one of the guys in the shop, took him home, he poured himself an iced tea and sat on the swing in his back yard.

He sent a text to Gina. "Home until 7pm. Call when you get off work, okay? Need to meet you somewhere."

He didn't expect an answer because he figured she'd still be at work. But, to his surprise, her answer came back almost immediately. "Off work. Aunt Bobbi is here. Don't know why. Where do you want to meet? I can drive to Loon Lake."

He shot an answer back. "Ok. Where?"

"Pizza and ice cream place on the corner by the light. Half hour?"

"OK. See you." She included a thumb's up icon.

He looked at his watch. Well, he'd better get going. He gathered his backpack and got into his old pickup, the 1997 Ford. It was dented, and the windshield was cracked, but it ran well.

Gina looked a little distracted, maybe even distraught, when he pulled up beside the ice cream place and parked. She was sitting in the shade at a white plastic picnic table. Her red hair was blowing in the wind. She stood when he got out of the truck.

"Hi, sweetie!" He liked calling her endearing names because he knew she hated it. "How are you doing?"

She removed her glasses and frowned. "Hey, I like your new wheels. Going with the antique look?"

He grinned. "Have to. Getting a new windshield in the Silverado. What's going on?"

"How can you always tell? Well, besides a lot of other interesting things, Bobbi's here." She shot him a glance. "How about you?"

He noted the tight way she said it and her disgruntled glance. He shrugged. "I've had better days."

"How'd your trip with your dad go? I was surprised he came." She led the way to the window of the ice cream shop.

"He said he had to attend a meeting in Spokane and wanted to see Boundary Dam."

"How was that?"

Before he could answer, the girl appeared at the window and took their order. Gina got a caramel chocolate cone that would have sufficed King Kong. and he got a huckleberry shake. They returned to the table.

Chance enjoyed a gulp of the shake. "The dam was something to see. Maybe we can go over there sometime. Did you know it provides power to Seattle? They have this guy in a guard shack who comes out and gives directions. Maybe he had a gun, but I didn't see one. We took the tour of the dam. After that, we drove to the overlook on the opposite side of the river. I used the binoculars they have there, and after I'd studied the dam, I noticed a boat on the bank beside the river. Then, while I was watching, another boat came downriver and some men got out of it." He paused to take another slurp of his drink.

"Did you see their faces? Were they unloading anything?"

He shook his head. "No. They had boxes of stuff they were unloading, but Dad wanted to get going, so I couldn't watch. I called the border patrol station over there and they said they'd do a patrol on that place." He paused. "Something's going on, Gina. I don't like it."

"Me, neither." Gina looked around and leaned closer to him. "I'm not supposed to tell anyone, but I know you won't repeat it. I'm on a special assignment with the FBI. Starting tomorrow, I'm working up around Colville. We're looking for their headquarters."

"Whose?"

She shrugged. "I don't know. They didn't tell me. It's a gang who uses a cover organization for human trafficking and drugs. And I don't know what to do about Bobbi. She wants me to go places, have fun. What should I do, Chance? Just leave her and rent an apartment in Colville?"

"You can't do that. I'd tell her that you have extra work to do and that you'll be gone a lot. If she doesn't like it, she can go home."

Gina leaned her head on her hand as she finished the last of her ice cream. "You don't know Bobbi. She wants to know everything about me. She's always been that way. But I can't let her do it to me."

"Well, that's something I guess you'll have to work out with her. I'd suggest you level with her, though. Tell her you have to work."

She sighed. "Where's the evidence you mentioned?"

He retrieved it from the truck. "It's a business card from a motel in Trail, BC, a cigarette stub, and a plastic bag. Might be some prints on them. Can you run it through the lab?"

She nodded and took the packet of envelopes. "Sure. I'll see what I can do." She stood. "Are you bringing your horses over to my place?"

"I guess I'll leave them home. Could you go by and check on them? I'll have Pole, my neighbor, feed them, but I'd like to think that you were watching them, too."

"Well, when I'm home I can do that. When will I see you again?" When she looked up at him, her expression stopped his heart. It was a fleeting glimpse into her soul that revealed a broken heart from an ache that couldn't be put into words.

He walked with her to her car. "Call me when you can. I'm leaving first thing in the morning for that camp. I catch the bus at 10am."

"Where is it?"

"It's out Sand Canyon road, north of Chewelah. Up in the mountains. Very remote."

It was small talk. They did it all the time to delay saying good-bye. Yet this time, he sensed she was worrying over something. She didn't want to leave him.

She stopped and turned to him. "I checked for that organization, Forward Guard, online, but couldn't find anything on it. I wish you wouldn't go. I ... have a bad feeling about it, Chance. Something isn't right there."

"Oh, I think it's okay. It might be tough, like in the military. I'll be all right. I can't call you, though. They don't allow cell phones or other electronics."

She tossed her head. "That's just stupid! What do they think they're doing? Handling classified state secrets? You can't call? But I imagine you'll find a way to call me, anyway. Right?" She grinned up at him with her best pleading look.

He laughed. "I don't think so. Don't worry. I can take care of myself. It's probably a bunch of guys who are playing at being military."

"Have you checked this out, Chance? Are they legit?"

"Well, my boss gave me the brochure. I don't think he'd suggest it if it wasn't okay. The flyer said the food is good." He grinned at her. "I'm more worried about you. Are you going to be okay? I mean, with all the stuff that's been going on?"

"I'll be fine. You know me." She laughed and tipped her head the way she did when she's pleased. He smiled and wanted to kiss her, but he didn't. He gave her a one-armed hug and opened the pickup door for her.

"Be careful. I don't want to lose you." He admired the way her green eyes glinted with unshed tears, and the way sunlight danced in her red-gold hair.

"You won't, Chance. See you in later." With a nod, she climbed in the pickup and drove off.

He watched until she pulled out, then he drove north on 395, heading for Chewelah. He had time to grab a bite to eat, pack his lunch, and drive up to Colville for work. He wondered how he could investigate the shooting incident. So far, he had accumulated lot of questions and no answers.

He gritted his teeth. When he got back from the camp, he was going to get to the root of this.

At the Border Patrol in Colville, he strode past the front desk and went down the hall in search of his boss. He stopped at Agent in Charge, Stuart McClurry's, office. McClurry lifted his head from a cluttered desk and grunted when he saw who it was.

"Oh. It's you. How're you doin', Marshal? Heard you went up on the line the other night."

"Oh, it was nothing. I just had to satisfy my curiosity. Can't I ride where I want when I want on my time off?"

Stuart shook his head. He was a seasoned line agent, injured from a nasty fall from a horse and given a desk job. His first love was patrolling the line. He ran his hand through his short, gray hair and shoved back from his desk.

"Darn it, Marshal, I know you're talking the truth, and I see your point. But we can't have maverick agents going off on their own after a hint of trouble." He held up his hand. "Let me have my say. I know your partner got shot, almost killed, but you have to focus on your job here. Your job is to patrol the border. If you find trouble up there, you deal with it and report it to us. As far as tracking down a gang of smugglers or whatever they are, you'd do better to let the pros handle that kind of job."

"But, sir, what happened to Dusty —"

"I know." A hint of a smile came to his mouth. But his eyes were stern. "I know you want to bring those people to justice, but you aren't a cop anymore. You have to let it go. Call the FBI. Get them on it and leave it there. I like you, Chance. But I have to warn you in the plainest language I can find that if you try to go after these guys, your job here will be in question. Do you understand?"

Chance nodded. "Yes, sir. Guess I'll get Dynamite ready."

McClurry gave him a last look as if he knew he hadn't convinced Chance, then got on his jacket. "I'm finished for the day. See you when you get back, Marshal."

Chance clocked in and exchanged a few words with the night secretary. Then he got a cup of coffee and went to the horse barn. On his locker, he found a note taped.

"Memo to Chance Marshal: your shift was changed. You are not on duty to night. Please check with AIC." It was signed Roger Whitley, Field Operating Supervisor.

Chance studied the note, his heart sinking to his toes. He had the urge to shred the paper. Everything in his being demanded that he saddle Dynamite and go for his patrol. But he couldn't.

Determined to find the reason for the change, he returned to the office building and charged down the hallway to Whitley's office. But the man had already left. McClurry must not have known about this, or he would have said something.

The Deputy Patrol In Charge had left, but he finally found the door open at the end of the hallway, the office of the Patrol Agent in Charge, boss of the department, Alfred DeMoss. His secretary was not there. The PAIC was putting on his suit coat and picking up his briefcase when Chance knocked on the door.

"Yes? Come in, please."

DeMoss was an older man with white hair and sharp blue eyes. His weathered face showed his many years on the line before he rose to the senior position he now held. That face now held mild surprise when he saw Chance. It wasn't often that one of the line agents penetrated past his dragon of a secretary and appeared at his office door.

"Good evening, sir," Chance said, standing straight and looking the man squarely in the eyes. "I'm sorry to bother you, but I have something urgent to discuss with you."

DeMoss smiled grimly. "I suppose it can't wait for morning, and let me guess, my subordinates have all left. You worked your way down the hall, didn't you?"

Chance lifted the note. "Yes, sir. I found this on my locker. It's from the FOS, from Whitley. I'm wondering why my schedule has been changed. Am I on leave, sir? One day early?"

DeMoss didn't take the note, merely glanced at it. "Oh. That. You just got a holiday. With pay. What're you griping about? Most guys would be happy about it. Go find a bar and a pretty girl. When you get back, we'll put you up on the line again."

There was a sharp note of impatience in his voice like he didn't want to waste his time on such menial matters.

Chance nodded and turned. "I'm sorry to bother you with it, but it seems strange to me. This doesn't have anything to do with my ride up on the line the other night, does it?"

"What ride?" DeMoss stepped forward, almost threatening, his left hand rested on his hip.

"I thought maybe Whitley told you. Well, if you don't know, I won't bother you with the details."

"Good. We'll call you when we have you scheduled again. Good night." The barest of nods told him the interview was finished.

"Good night, sir. Thanks."

Wondering what he was thanking the man for, he fled down the hall as if being chased by dogs and men with guns. One thing was clear – DeMoss wanted the whole issue of Dusty's injury on the line hushed up.

Chance unlocked his pickup and got in. Sitting the darkened parking lot, he stared straight ahead. DeMoss exited the building and got in his BMW, talking on his cell phone, not glancing toward Chance's pickup. Chance saw his face for an instant when the man sped past. The man was furious.

Letting out a long breath, Chance drove from the parking lot. Where did this leave him? Maybe he should call Dad. But not tonight. He was in that meeting in Spokane. He turned up the heater and pulled out onto Highway 395, heading south.

It all came down to this – he was at the end of the road. He could pack it in, he supposed, and move to Seattle. His dad could find him a job. But what about Gina? How could he leave her?

He took a deep breath of piney mountain air and glanced at the sky where a crescent moon topped the trees on the mountain. *Let it go and let God.* The old saying drifted through his mind.

Okay. Starting tomorrow morning, he would focus on learning all he could at the retreat, and when he came back, he would help Gina solve her mystery. Maybe they could go up to Trail and visit that place north of Kettle Falls again.

He pulled into his lane and drove up to the house. It looked peaceful, but he was suddenly aware that he'd left the gate closed. It was open now. *Was someone here?*

Carefully he reached behind the seat and lifted his loaded rifle from the rack on the window. Opening the door, he listened to the night sounds. How long could he go on this way?

As he set his feet on the gravel and slammed the truck door, he knew how he could endure. By God's grace alone.

So be it, God. By Your grace I will survive this. Now. Be. With. Gina.

Chapter 18

A Black Suburban

June 7th

Someone is watching me.

I've been trained to be sensitive to my surroundings, and I've learned to trust my gut feelings. As I trudge through the wet grass to feed the horses in the early morning, I know I'm not alone.

I'm wearing my faded plaid jacket, holey jeans, and rubber mucking-out boots. The sun is about ten minutes from rising. It glows on the horizon while a heavy layer of fog shrouds the mountains. There's not a breath of wind.

I call to the horses, and they whinny in response. They're in the barn. Thudding hoof beats herald their appearance at the door. Ears pricked, they look my way. But then something in the brush up by the road catches their attention. Gypsy Rose shakes her head. Pecos Bill looks at her like he's wondering what's wrong with her.

I glance that way, but I see nothing. Chills race down my spine. I wish I'd brought my rifle out with me.

"C'mon, girl, there's nothing there. It's just a deer." I call to her as I climb through the fence.

She bobs her head as she approaches me, anxious for her grain. I fill both their pans and check the water. Pump is working fine. But the pump in my chest is not doing so fine – it's pounding like a booming drum in my ears.

Back inside the house, I gather my backpack and phone. A board creaks behind me. Whirling, I turn.

Bobbi stumbles down the hall, rubbing sleep from her eyes. "Where you goin', honey? It's a little early for work, isn't it?"

I shake my head and place my lunch in the pack. "I have to go into work this morning and get some things done. I thought you were going to sleep in."

"I slept in yesterday." She glares at me as if I'm crazy to think she'd sleep in two mornings in a row. "I hardly saw you yesterday. I was hoping we could do something, like go to the garage sales, or shopping in Spokane. I don't get to a big city very often, you know."

She pours herself a cup of coffee and shuffles to a chair at the kitchen table where she plops down. "What's going on?"

I sigh and set the backpack down. "There's something that's come up at work. I'm going to have to be gone quite a bit in the next couple of days. It's kind of an ... emergency. You sure you want to stay? I won't have much time to spend with you."

She thinks about this. "Well, if you want me to, I guess I can find some things to do around here." A smile of hope flickers over her face, a vulnerable, frightened glance like she's afraid I'll reject her offer. "Got some jobs for me? I'm pretty handy, you know."

"Of course, I want you!" I give her a quick hug, pleased she's willing to accept my situation. "You can do lots. Go wild. Fix up the old place and work all you want. I should be home every evening around five or six." I head for the door. "I have to get going. See you tonight. You okay? Know where the stores are?"

"I can find my way around." She turns away from me, waving me away gruffly. "Go save the world, honey. You're going to be late."

By the time I pull out of the driveway, the sun has climbed over the top of Mt. Spokane, casting long golden rays into a robin's egg blue sky. A few clouds dot the sky in the west and breezes stir the pines. I glance in my rearview mirror as I come to a stop at Highway 395. No one tailing me so far. That's good.

Finding an opening in the traffic, I turn south toward Spokane, flipping on the radio. It's then that I see a black vehicle that keeps a tidy distance behind me, maintaining the same speed. I can't tell if it's a pickup or a van. *Hmm. Not good.* But what can I do about it? Exactly nothing.

A white pickup comes up on my rear and sticks with me for a while, but after we get into traffic on North Division street, he heads off towards the Fred Meyer store. The black vehicle has vanished, too.

As I make my way downtown, I get busy with lights and traffic and forget to check my mirror. But just to be careful, I turn off Division and take some side streets, then double back, driving through an Espresso stand.

I drive past the SPD office building. I don't drive past the security gate and down into the lot but pull over and park beside the sidewalk. While I'm watching the cars who drive past, I notice a black suburban with tinted windows, parked down the street. It crawls forward.

I'm curious, so I get out from my vehicle and study the houses as if I'm searching for an address.

That's when they open fire on me. I hit the pavement and roll under the pickup, coming out on the far side, drawing my gun as I peer through the broken windows. I hadn't expected that kind of brazen attack, not right in front of the police department. Another round of bullets comes at me. The guard in the shack half-way down the block emerges from his booth, talking furiously on his radio, then he fires at them.

The suburban screeches away and is gone.

I expect the place to come alive – officers pouring from both doors, sirens sounding, dogs barking, shots fired after the fleeing car. But nothing happens except that the guard from the shack runs towards me with his gun held at his waist.

A deathly silence falls on the busy street like everyone, even the birds, are holding their breath. My heart is hammering in my ears so hard I think a drum band is on its way down the street, and my mouth is as dry as the backside of a desert. I sag against the pickup and groan. So much for my windshield.

Where is everyone?

"Are you all right, miss?" The guard, an older man who allows me entrance every morning, arrives out of breath. "I called in the alert. Oh, it's you, Miss Lindsey." He tips his hat and summons a smile.

"I'm okay," I say. "Thanks for giving me back-up."

Two officers emerge from the building, gripping semi-automatic weapons. They come toward us. The guard returns to his shack, stopping to exchange a comment with the tallest of the two.

I meet the officers halfway to the SPD lot.

"What's going on?" The taller one stops to talk while the other one searches the lot. His snappy blue eyes study me from head to toe. He's checking out my weapon.

"There was a car over there," I motion to the street. "Parked down the street. When I stepped out of my car, over there," I point to it, "they pulled forward and started shooting at me with semi-automatic rifles. I dove under the pickup and returned some shots. The guard will confirm my story."

I'm not in uniform, and although they must have seen me around in the office, they're playing it cool. The tall officer stares at me like he doesn't comprehend. I prod his memory. "I'm Gina Lindsey. I'm with the SIU."

He nods and looks over at the other officer who is prowling around the area like the assailants are going to come back to continue the attack. "It's okay, Stevens. Let's go in."

"Yes, sir."

The officer glances at me. "Come in and make a report."

"I'm supposed to be at another location. I was just passing by and decided to stop. Those guys were waiting for me."

"This won't take long."

I follow him to the front office. There I fill out the required paperwork and sign my name to about a dozen papers. Chief Smithers comes in while I'm at it. I tell him what happened.

He rubs his head like I've given him a headache. "Wish I hadn't loaned you to the FBI. I'm afraid this is bigger than what we thought."

I finish the paperwork. "I'll be okay. The FBI knows how to protect their agents." I say it with a straight face, hoping he won't challenge me on it. Of course, they lose their people occasionally, but we don't hear about it.

He nods. "Why don't you ride over in a patrol car, and I'll see to it that your pickup is fixed." He orders a car, and a young officer drives me over to the FBI office.

I'll let DeLaney know that my car is at SPD. He'll do something with it until I'm finished with the assignment. Or until it's finished me.

I grasp my bag and start for the door. There. Goodbye, Gina Lindsey. I'm going in as Gina Lindsey and coming out Angela Brubaker.

The FBI will issue me a different car, new ID cards, new everything. It's strange. For most of my life, I searched for the real me, always afraid to face what I would find in my heart, afraid of what others would think if they knew me. I've hidden behind my work, my appearance, my skills, my job.

Now I have to pretend to be someone else, much like an actor on a stage. I can become Angela Brubacker, but I'll hate every moment of it.

Stepping inside the glass doors, I find myself in front of a bullet proof glass window that is protecting the receptionist who sits at a desk. She's in her mid-forties, tightly curled red hair, glasses. She speaks through a round speaker unit on the window.

"Yes? How may I help you?"

I show my ID. "Officer Gina Lindsey from SPD, on assignment with Agent DeLaney."

She nods, types something on her keyboard, studies the screen, then glances at me. "Very well, Miss Lindsey. Agent DeLaney will see you now. I'll open the door." She presses a button.

DeLaney glances up from jumbled piles of paperwork on his desk and smiles. After finishing a phone conversation, he shoves back his chair.

"Good morning, Angela. Are you ready for this assignment?"

"As ready as I'll ever be, sir."

He hands me a manila envelope. "Here's your new ID and car keys. You'll find the car in the garage below. I assume you know what to do to change your appearance. "

"Yes, sir. I have an appointment at the beauty parlor this morning."

He nods. "That's great. You can leave all your personal items with me." He holds out his hand while I fish my wallet from my pack. "Stop in at the make-up department and they'll give you a packet that will come in handy. In the envelope, you'll find a credit card, some cash, and an apartment key in Colville with the rent paid for a month. Anything else?"

"Do I have back-up?" I pull out the driver's license and take a look at the photo. It's me with curly blond hair and glasses. Cute.

"Yes. They will make themselves known to you."

"How do I contact you?"

"Through the agent." He puts on a pair of glasses and picks up a file folder.

I stand. "Oh, by the way, I have a friend who is a border guard. While he and his partner were on a patrol the other night, they were shot at. His partner nearly died. The border guard isn't investigating it. They reported it to the sheriff in Ferry county. My friend went back to the place where they were shot at last night and found some things dropped on the ground. Do you want them?"

I dig in my backpack and pull out the evidence envelope Chance gave me.

He comes from behind his desk and takes them. "You think this might tie in with the organization we're looking for?"

I shrug. "I don't know, but I thought you'd like to have it. There's a card in there from a motel in Trail, BC that might bear looking into."

He nods. "We'll check it out. Thanks. Agent Roberts will show you to the garage."

Lugging my backpack, the only item I'm allowed from my old life, I follow Roberts to the garage below ground where he gives me the keys to a cream colored Toyota Camry, a car about eight years old. Its front fender is dented, the windshield pitted, seats are cigarette burned. I thank him and stow my belongings inside.

After winding through the streets and hopping on Division street, I start north on Highway 395. I glance at my watch. Just in time for my appointment at the beauty parlor.

Two hours later, I exit the place, my hair cut, dyed blond, and permed. Now I have to get some really ugly clothes and pad my cheeks with cotton.

I find the clothes at a second hand store, then stop at a grocery store. I purchase a roasted chicken, a potato salad, some apples, and a cake. This ought to satisfy Bobbi, but I'm still not sure what to tell her about my changed appearance.

She's going to have to know.

Bobbi is full of questions when I walk in the house fifteen minutes later, carrying supper.

"Oh, my land, Gina! Is this you? I thought ..." She eyes me speculatively. I can see the truth dawning in her eyes. "You're on ... an assignment, aren't you? Going undercover? I read detective books, you know."

"Not going. Gone." My tone is dry, just short of mocking. "But you aren't supposed to know, so don't tell anyone, not even Uncle Elton or your friends on Facebook." I deposit the food on the counter, hating the smell of the perm and my new look. "Why don't you get things heated and the table set? I'll get a shower and be right back. Maybe we can take in a movie tonight if you want."

Supper is a great success even if I didn't cook it. She talks about painting the kitchen, and we drive to Deer Park and check

117

out a paint store. After choosing a color, we decide not to go to a movie but to watch something at home.

It feels good to be myself again, but I am dreading tomorrow. I memorized the name and address of the motel in Trail and think maybe if I have time, I'll take a drive up there.

The next morning, Bobbi isn't up when I get ready to leave, so I leave her a note. It's 8am by the time I've dressed in my Angela Brubaker costume and head out in my little tan Toyota.

Thirteen miles north of Chewelah, I hear a sharp *bang!* and wrestle with the steering for a few jar-clenching seconds before finding a wide spot in the narrow highway and pull over to a stop. Before I get the vehicle parked, I know it's a tire. Front right. *Great.*

I find I'm correct. I'm sitting across from a vegetable and fruit stand. The sign says they also sell antiques. It doesn't look threatening, but who knows? Maybe there's a spy in there. I'd like to take a look inside, but I decide against it. *Stick to the job, Angela!*

Buffeted by semis and other vehicles that pass on the highway, I dig in the trunk for the spare tire. *Hmm.* Surely, it's in here somewhere. After scratching my head for a while, I ask the information lady on my phone how to change a tire in a 2006 Toyota Camry and watch a You Tube video. *Aha!* Lifting the carpet in the trunk, I find the hidden cavity and go to work.

A car stops behind me. I'm thankful I have my pistol in my jacket pocket. Tossing a glance over my shoulder, I see it's a young man, maybe about my age. He gets out and comes toward me. He's wearing jeans, a tucked in dress shirt, a Cowboys cap, and tennis shoes.

But the thing that sets my nerves jangling like a hundred irritated cats is the vehicle he's driving, parked snug behind my Toyota.

Suburban. Black. Tinted windows.

Chapter 19

You're In the Army Now

Forward Guard Camp, Chewelah, June 8th

Chance arrived early for the pick-up. He and Pole waited in the Safeway parking lot, sitting in the cab of his neighbor's truck. The man was a good partner to have in this sort of circumstance because he was never without a story, and he could tell them well.

Right on the dot, at 10am, an unmarked blue bus pulled into the lot and stopped.

Chance turned to Pole. "This is it. Guess I'd better get my stuff. Gosh, I feel like a school kid."

Pole laughed. "You don't look much like one. Take care, my friend. See you in five days. I'll watch your place for you."

Chance grabbed his duffle bag from the back. "Thanks! See you."

The driver of the bus opened the door.

"Good morning," Chance said pleasantly as he chose a seat toward the front.

The driver grunted something in reply as he put the bus in gear and pulled out onto the highway. Chance glanced at the other occupants. Two women. Five men. He nodded to them. "Howdy, folks."

They didn't meet his eyes or answer his greeting but stared moodily out the window. Strange. He plunked down and adjusted his bag at his feet. These guys are going to be fun to be around for a week. But maybe they were all as uneasy about this as he was.

Sand Canyon road curved up a hill and went past a golf course. Then it followed a narrow valley, winding past large farms and fields. Chance fought fatigue that dragged on his senses like a ten-ton weight. He'd slept only a little last night as he was still on edge, watching for another attack.

The sun climbed the vast dome of sapphire sky as they journeyed up into the mountains. The road turned to gravel and narrowed, following a stream that wound through meadows and forests. It was close to noon when the bus pulled into an unmarked driveway that headed off to the right.

After about a mile, the driver stopped at a guard shack and an electric gate. On both sides of the shack, a ten-foot chain link fence bordered the property, topped with electric wire. A sign on the white guard shack read in big black letters, "Private. No Trespassing."

A uniformed guard stepped from the building. He was carrying a semi-automatic rifle. He boarded the bus with a short nod to the driver and said, "Please produce the confirmation paper you received. I will come down the aisle and check each one."

He studied each document, making a precise notation on his clip board and went to the next person. It didn't take long. Then he jumped down the steps to the ground, entered the shack and pressed a button that raised the gate. The bus ground through its gears and lumbered past the gate.

The fence stretched away on each side, dotted here and there with guard towers. It seemed they were taking this security thing way too far. Why the fence? The uniformed guard?

A prickly feeling of danger crawled up Chance's spine, but he shook it away and watched out the front window as the narrow dirt road wound up a hill, descended into a valley, and crossed a quaint bridge.

They passed under a sign that spanned the driveway with a sign hanging in the middle. *Last Gulch Ranch*, it read, and sported a cow's skull.

The bus stopped in front of a log-built lodge. It had a wide porch that spanned the outside, a stone chimney, and plenty of picture windows. Several small cabins ranged in a row beyond the lodge, and a huge Quonset-shaped equipment building sat at the far side of a square of open ground. As he watched, a group of men approached in straight lines and began drilling, marching in cadence to the call of an officer. They wore black uniforms.

"Enter ye into the dwellings of the dead," Chance said softly, recalling something from high school literature.

He gathered his duffle bag and waited for the driver to open the door.

A man stepped out on the porch of the lodge and descended the front steps. He had dark hair tinged with gray, wide shoulders and the posture of a person who had spent his life in the military. There was a slight limp to his gait. He was clad in black jeans with a large silver buckle on his belt, a black shirt with a logo on the right pocket, and a black cowboy hat that seemed strangely out of place. Chance noticed with rather a shock that he wore a revolver in a holster on his belt.

The man smiled expansively as he marched down the steps. "Howdy, folks! Welcome to our little piece of paradise, Last Gulch Ranch. My name is Captain Grant. Come on in. We've been expecting you." His voice held a western twang, yet his eyes were cold and calculating as if he was already ticking up the points in their favor or disfavor.

Grant greeted each one and asked where they came from, his large hand outstretched.

Chance, the first one in the line, nodded and smiled, taking his hand. "Chance Marshal, sir. Chewelah. Good to be here."

As they filed past, each of the others responded in the same way, some of them rather sullenly as if this routine was below their dignity. Chance caught a couple of their names and home cities and was surprised at how far some of them had come. One fellow was from Korea and another from Taiwan! One woman had arrived from Ontario, Canada, and the other hailed from Montana.

A man who sat at a table filled with literature greeted them inside the open-beamed room. He, too, was dressed in black. The logo, embroidered on his shirt, read *Forward Guard* and displayed two swords crossed over a globe.

When he was registered, Chance wandered over to the dining room where a fire crackled in a large fireplace. He got a cup of coffee from the urn on the counter and gazed at the room. Who would have thought that something like this was up in the mountains beyond Chewelah? There was a lot of money sunk into this set-up, and he guessed he hadn't seen half of the ranch.

Grant marshaled them to the area below a stairway and motioned upwards. "You'll find your names on the door of your room. You will be bunking with one person. There are bathrooms at the end of the hall." He checked his watch. "Lunch will be served in half an hour. Report at the fireplace at 1400 hours. Everyone hasn't arrived yet. Some of them will come in later this evening, but we will have an informational meeting for those of you who have arrived first."

He nodded once as if satisfied that he'd delivered his message and left.

Chance climbed the stairs to the second level and discovered there was a third floor to the building. He guessed there were offices on that floor. He found his room, third on the right. It was sparsely furnished. Two beds stood on opposite walls, the blankets folded with Army regulation corners.

A night stand of plain yellow wood was placed between the beds and a chest of drawers squatted on the far wall below a faded ranch photo. Besides that, there a closet with some hangers, a braided oval rug, and a washstand and sink with a counter and two drawers.

The sign on the door identified his room-mate as Caleb Ostranger.

He carried his bag to the bed. As he unpacked, he wondered where the surveillance camera was hidden, for he was sure there would be one in every room. He looked at his watch. Time to go. There were no locks on the doors, but since he'd been instructed to leave behind electronics and anything else of value, he figured that was okay.

Lunch was prepared by the time he went downstairs, and the food was all that it had been advertised in the brochure he'd received. He helped himself to the sandwich bar, the salad bar, and to the desserts. Carrying his plate to a round table, he hoped to get to know some of his fellow retreaters, but the others merely grunted replies to his questions. He finally gave up and concentrated on the food.

At 1400 hours, Chance joined the group as they went outside to a small cabin. He found it was set up as a classroom, the desks positioned into neat rows. Three men in uniforms stood ramrod straight at the front. No one looked in his direction when he entered and sat toward the back.

Grant began the meeting. "Welcome to Forward Guard Weapon's Retreat." He turned to the other two men who stood beside him. "I'd like to introduce the men who will be teaching the classes this week, Staff Sergeant Brooks and Lieutenant Rodgers. There isn't much about weaponry that Brooks hasn't handled, made or studied. Rodgers will be leading you on several field excursions. You will be tested to the limits of your physical endurance, and when you are so tired you want to drop, you will have to answer questions correctly and stay awake long enough to fill out reports." He did not smile as he looked at each participant. "Have fun."

Chance almost laughed but checked it in time. There wasn't even a glimmer of a smile on anyone's face.

Grant handed out folders to each participant, which turned out to be printed class notes. He explained that they would be teamed up to do maneuvers and war games.

"This isn't kindergarten, people," he said, returning to the front, "so we won't beat around the bush. We expect instant obedience to commands. For the duration of your time here, you figure you are in the army. Anyone who lags behind or questions authority will be given the appropriate discipline. I assure you that you don't want to go there."

Chance groaned. What had he gotten himself into? It sounded more like boot camp for the Marines rather than an interesting week learning about weapons and martial arts fighting techniques. He sighed.

It was only five days. What could go wrong in that length of time? As he gathered the material and followed behind the others as they filed out, the answer came to him.

Plenty!

Chapter 20

Call Me If You're Dying

Deer Park, June 8th

Bobbi awoke with a headache. As she rose and stumbled to the bathroom, she swore the throbbing in her head could have moved Mt. Everest. She didn't know why these migraines hit her but guessed it had something to do with stress. Or allergies.

She threw a robe over her pajamas and, in a fog of pain, made it to the kitchen. It was spotlessly clean. The coffee pot was full and hot. *Bless Gina!* When she went to get a mug from the cupboard, she saw a note on the counter. She picked it up and after blinking several times, read it.

"Bobbi, sorry I have to take off without talking to you, but I have to get going pretty early. I'll call when I can. I ran out of time, so could you feed the horses and make sure their water is coming in? Sometimes the pump gets jammed. You'll find their grain in the tack room in the barn. Half a coffee can to each. See you tonight. Have a good day. Gina."

There were some muffins in the refrigerator, so she warmed one in the microwave, poured herself a glass of orange juice, and sat at the counter to eat, hoping she could keep it down. After that, she took two Excedrin.

Maybe if she caught this in the bud, it would be gone by the time Gina got home.

Sometime later, she awoke to the sound of pounding. Was it Elton putting the new porch on the house? Or the guys down at the barn, fixing the roof? She rolled over and opened her eyes. No. She was in a strange bedroom. Sunlight flooded the room from an open window, and a light breeze lifted gauzy curtains.

The pounding went on, relentlessly.

Suddenly she remembered. She was at Gina's. The noise came from the front of the house. *Someone was at the door!* She sat up, brushed back her hair, and reached for her robe.

Tying it on, she shuffled out to the hall. The knocking came sporadically as if the person was getting tired of beating on the door. She'd left her car behind the barn, being too lazy to move it to the front. They would think no one was home.

Hurrying to the living room, she peered out the little window on the front door. Two women, gripping briefcases, stood on the front porch. One held a pamphlet in her right hand. Both were middle-aged, rather dumpy, with sincere looks on their faces.

Bobbi put her hand on the doorknob, thinking how she must appear. Thankfully, the headache had diminished to a dull throb, but she felt like a rubber mat that had been trampled on by elephants.

The ladies were not going to give up. After speaking to one another, the one closest to the door knocked again.

She was glad they hadn't seen her. She sighed. *I guess I'd better answer the door so they'll leave.* Just as she started to turn the lock, something rubbed on her leg.

She jumped back, looking down. *Oh. It's the darn cat* – Ricki, she thought his name was. She took a deep breath and gripped the door handle again.

Suddenly she remembered what Gina told her last night, how she'd been shot at on the river up north, and after she'd gotten home, two boys had come to the house, wanting help. But she wouldn't let them in. Two boys. Now two women.

She released the knob like she was touching molten lead. Should she holler at them to leave? Or should she get into a "safe" room like Gina told her to do? Holding her breath, she went to the big window in the living room and, lifting a corner of the curtain, watched them.

They talked to one another quietly, and with a shake of their heads, they descended the steps. She let out her breath. Maybe she'd been wrong. Maybe they were exactly as they seemed to be. Yet she'd seen no car. Had they left it out on the road? Strange.

Bobbi lost sight of them as they walked down the driveway. They didn't seem intent on getting inside. Or breaking in from the back.

Thinking she'd been wrong to be afraid, she got a shower and dressed. Feeling a little better, she made her way to the kitchen, poured herself another cup of coffee and toasted a piece of bread. When she finished, she rinsed out her cup and tied on her shoes.

The horses probably thought they'd been forgotten.

She locked the back door and put the key in her pocket. Then, crawling through the fence, she saw the horses standing by the barn. The mare, Gypsy, nickered anxiously.

"It's okay, girl," Bobbi said to her, approaching carefully so as not to startle her. "I'm not your mama, but you know me, and I'll give you some oats. Okay?"

By this time, she was near enough to hold out her hand. Gypsy came forward, sniffed her, and tossed her head as if to say, "I don't care about your hand. Just give me my breakfast."

Pecos Bill came over to investigate. She petted him, too. She gave them both their oats, and while they were eating, she inspected the water trough and found the water was coming in without hindrance.

Brushing off her hands, she went out the corral gate and cut through the garage to get to the back door of the house. It was there that she stopped in mid-step. Low voices reached her. Tiptoeing through the garage, she peered out the door.

The two women had returned and were peering in the little window on the back door. Now they were accompanied by a man. They'd discarded their briefcases and literature. The man began working on the lock.

They're trying to break in! She put her hand on her chest and told herself to breathe, then checked her pockets. No phone. Looking around for a weapon, she picked up a shovel that was leaning by the wall.

With a prayer and shaking knees, she advanced outside with the shovel in both hands. Conversationally she said, "How can I help you?"

All three jumped and turned. She gripped the wooden handle tighter. Now was the moment. Would they run – or attack? She was more worried about the man than the two women.

Without glancing at each other, they bolted from the small porch and dashed around the house. She ran after them, but they had vanished. She sprinted to the driveway. They were in full stride, racing toward the road.

She sighed and leaned against the porch post, lowering the shovel. Her head was dizzy. Going back around the house, she unlocked the door, went inside, and dialed Gina's number. She didn't pick up.

Bobbi left a message. "I've had quite a morning. Two women and a man tried to break into the house. I guess they didn't think you were home. They ran off when they saw me. I'm okay, but ... well, a little shook. Give me a call when you can. Would appreciate hearing your voice."

She dialed 911. After one ring, a woman answered. "What is your emergency?"

When she related what happened and where she was, the lady on the line said an officer would be out there in a little while.

Expelling her breath, she set down the phone, wondering how long a *little while* would be. A few minutes? An hour? *Shucks. The bad guys could kidnap me and take me to the next county by then.*

When a car pulled into the drive about a half an hour later, she glanced at her watch. Thirty-five minutes. An officer got out, came up to the steps, and introduced himself as Officer Ward.

"What's your complaint, ma'am?" He shifted uneasily.

She was surprised he was alone. Maybe they were short-staffed today.

"Two women came to the door." She stuffed her hands in her pockets. "I thought they were pushing their religion, so I didn't answer the door." She continued with her tale, ending with how a man joined them and how they had tried to enter the house.

The officer nodded. He hadn't been taking notes. "Same two women you saw the first time, ma'am?"

"Yes, sir. Same ones, only they'd dumped their literature. They were surprised to see me and took off. I haven't seen them since, but I thought I'd better report it."

"Can you give me a description?"

"Well, they wore dresses. Both about the same age as me. The man was dark, like maybe Mexican or something." She shrugged. "Can't remember much more. Just looked like ordinary women to me." She removed her hands from her pockets and brushed back her hair, wishing he would sound sympathetic.

He nodded again and glanced around. "May I take a look at the back door?"

"Of course. Follow me."

She showed it to him. He examined it and inspected the ground. When he straightened, he said, "There were some boys here two nights ago. Reported by Gina Lindsey. Is she here?"

"No. She had to go to work. I'm Bobbi Lindsey, her aunt. I'm visiting from Montana."

He gave her a sharp, quizzical glance. "Very well, ma'am. We'll look into this. Thank you." With a curt nod, he turned and marched away.

Bobbi went into the kitchen and picked up her phone. No return call from Gina. She called Elton, but he didn't answer. He was probably out fixing the fence or feeding cattle.

Her knees felt weak. Should she go ... do something? Shop in Spokane? Get something to eat in Deer Park? *No.* The headache was back, worse than before.

She felt like she was going to throw up. She lay down on the couch and covered herself with Gina's afghan – the one she'd saved that had belonged to her mom.

Loneliness like she'd never known before invaded her heart.

She couldn't weep – the pain when too deep for that. It was an old wound, one she was familiar with, but she thought she'd put it to rest a long time ago. But there it was, rearing its ugly head, searing her consciousness like a hot coal, tormenting her soul with *what ifs*, ten times worse than she'd ever known it before.

She rolled over and faced the back of the couch, trying to shove away the ache.

Had something happened to Gina? What would she do if Gina was killed, like her dad ... *no, I can't think like that.*

Tears trickled down her cheeks. She didn't brush them off. *Should I go home?* But the horses and the cats needed feeding, and she couldn't abandon them until she heard from Gina. Should she call her work number? *No.*

She remembered what Gina said when she gave her the number. "Don't use this, Aunt Bobbi, not unless it's an emergency. I mean a real one, like if you're dying or something. Of course, if you're that bad off, you probably couldn't call me anyway." She laughed like it was a joke.

Bobbi pulled the blanket up to her chin and rolled over. Well, this situation was getting to be about that dire. Not that *she* was dying, but maybe Gina was in trouble. Real trouble.

She sighed. There was nothing she could do about it. Nothing anyone could do. She couldn't even pray. As the pain pills began to kick in, she closed her eyes and drifted off to sleep.

Chapter 21

On the Right Trail

June 9th

A black suburban with tinted windows is parked behind my Toyota along the highway, and a man is approaching me. He isn't carrying any weapons that I can see, and he's clean and well dressed.

But is he as harmless as he seems? His vehicle is like the one that was used by the assailants who shot at me in front of the police office this morning, yet there must be hundreds of black suburbans.

The jack is in place on the fender of the Toyota, and I'm working the handle but not getting very far with it. As he draws near, I say, "Hi. Nice day, huh."

He laughs. "Yeah. Here, let me do that."

I relinquish the handle and rub my hands, remembering I don't look like Gina Lindsey anymore, and that I should probably be tough, since I'm dressed in jeans, boots, a plaid shirt and a wide-brimmed hat. Like a person who might scale Mt. Everest. Or at least be able to shoot a coyote and skin him.

I pick up the lug wrench and start to work on the nuts of the damaged tire.

"Leave that for me, Miss ... " He glances at me, and I see in that look what he thinks of me. Blonde, funny clothes, heavy shoes. Glasses.

"Angela. I can do it. Honest."

He grins and holds out his hand. "Jerry."

We shake. He changes the tire while I watch.

When he's finished, he dusts off his hands and straightens. "You shouldn't go over forty-five on that donut tire, Angela. Take her straight to Les Schwab in town on the main drag. They'll fix it for you."

"Thanks." We exchange another smile.

He looks at me like he wants to ask something more. My phone number? I chuckle. *Yeah, right.*

"Do you ... live in Colville?"

I nod. "Just moved there. Looking for a job."

"Great." He turns away and points his feet toward his car — signaling that he wants to leave by body language. Yet his words belie his body posture and whenever that happens, I take notice.

"Hey, how about if I follow you in? I'll introduce you to the guys at the tire store. I work there."

I don't want him following me anywhere. He's not wearing a white Les Schwab shirt, and his fingernails are clean, too. But what can I do?

"Okay. Thanks."

He trudges back to his car.

We limp into town. I pull into the Les Schwab store. Two guys wearing jeans and white shirts run out and take my car. They seem to know Jerry. He goes inside, and I follow him. Sure enough, he walks up to the counter, and leaning his elbows on it, talks with them like he owns the store. But he doesn't go to the office.

I sit down as they fix the tire. Jerry disappears. When the tire is fixed, they call my name. I have to remember it's Angela now. Jerry comes from the back. He still isn't wearing the Les Schwab shirt.

As I pay and get the keys, Jerry turns to me and winks. "Nice meeting you, Angela. Hey, do you want to go for coffee?"

I'm surprised. "Uh, some other time, Jerry. I'm trying to get settled. Nice meeting you, too."

He grins, but I see anger in his eyes. He doesn't like it that I've refused him. "Well, come by another time, then." He whips out a business card. "Here's my card. Phone number. If you need anything, I'll help. Show you around."

"Oh, okay." I take the card. "Thanks, Jerry."

I tuck the card in my purse and turn to the door, taking a deep breath when he doesn't follow me.

The little town of Colville dozes in the late afternoon sun. It doesn't have much to offer after living in Spokane for several years, but I'm not here to enjoy the shopping. The highway through town is busy and boasts of several restaurants, a bank, and an assortment of other small shops.

I check my phone for the map of Colville when I get in the car to find the apartment that the FBI rented for me. I won't be living there, but it will be handy to have in case I need to recoup and rest. It's on 6th street, a block off Main Street. When the main drag turns left, I head up a hill and turn right. Down a block. Corner of 6th and Oak. There it is.

It sits on the corner in a faded coat of green paint with a sign outside that reads Hillside Apartments. Red geraniums brighten the planter by the sign. I find number ten and discover it's on the first floor.

The apartment is clean, bright and smells nice. It has a living and dining room area, a kitchenette with a small table, and one bedroom.

I find a few things I need, like sheets and dish towels, at a Habitat for Humanity second-hand store Highway 395 only three blocks away. After I make my purchases, I return to the apartment and get it set up.

As I don't officially start this assignment until tomorrow, I feel like I have some time to investigate the evidence that Chance gave me. Trail, B.C. is not far. So, armed with snacks, water, my passport, and my phone, I head north to the border.

I'm traveling the same road that Chance and I drove that day I was shot. In fact, I note the very place where we turned to drive off the highway, and I'm pretty sure I see where I went down on the river to eat lunch that day because there are the white rock cliffs and the tall pine.

I cross the border about 2pm and drive another fifty miles, winding along a river, through heavy forests of pine and fire. This is mining and logging country. I don't see any houses until I get near the city of Trail. It sprawls along the Columbia River, a thriving center below towering mountains. In the past, it made its' mark on Canada as a gold and copper mining town.

There's a beautiful bridge spanning the river. As soon as I cross it, I'm downtown. I find the address of the Rambling Inn motel. *563 Main Street.* It isn't hard to find. I pull into the driveway and locate the office between two over-grown shrubs. The rooms are strung out in a row, maybe twenty in all. The motel needs a coat of paint and a good maintenance guy.

An Asian woman lifts her head as I enter the office.

"Hello," I say, smiling. "I'd like a room for the night. What are your rates?"

She gives me a once-over look and studies her computer screen. "We have ... one room, queen bed, no smoking. Eighty-nine dollals and fifty-two cents. You want just one night?"

I nod. "That sounds good." I slide the money over the counter. She prints out the information and has me sign my name. I sign Linda Downing and give a fake address and license plate number. She hands me the key.

"You stay in Room 12, down side of building here," she points to the left. "Thank you." She bobs her head but doesn't smile.

"Thank you. It's really nice here. Have you lived here a long time?"

"Not long time. Thank you." She gives me a sharp glance from her dark eyes like she doesn't want me bothering her anymore or asking personal questions. To avoid that, I suppose, she disappears into a back room. Not the friendliest sort, but that's not a crime.

I gather my backpack and glance around the small lobby. There's a coffee pot on the counter with Styrofoam cups, an information rack beside a couple of rickety plastic chairs, and the smell of old coffee and mildew.

Everything in my room is old and faded. I sit on the bed. Turn on the TV and turn it off. Get up and wander to the window, lifting the curtain. The sun is setting behind the mountains, leaving pink and purple on the clouds above them. I want to go for a walk, but something tells me to sit tight.

And so, I do.

It isn't long before I hear the *rumble, rumble* of a cart being pushed along the walk by the rooms. I step outside the room. The cart approaches. It looks like it's self-propelled, but then I see the dark head of a tiny person pushing it. Stepping aside hurriedly, I barely avoid being mowed down.

When the girl behind the cart sees me, she is horrified. Throwing her hand over her mouth, she exclaims, "Oh, vely, vely solly, miss. I did not mean to bump you!"

Her English is not good, but as least she can speak it. I sense she hasn't been in Canada for long.

I laugh and put a hand on the cart. "No. You did not run me over. Hello. My name is Jane. What is yours?"

She looks down at the sidewalk, suddenly shy. Then, shaking her head, she says, "I not care. I speak to you. I am Tam." She grabs my hand as we make eye contact.

"You have just come from ... from Korea?"

"No. From Thailand. My sister come, too. We work. To send money back home. Where you from, missy?"

"I'm from Washington." I motion to the south. "Not far. Can I talk to you? Visit?"

She shakes her head. She understands more than she can speak. "Vely busy, missy Jane. Thank you for coming. Thank you. I have to work now. Goodbye." She pushes her cart down the walk.

"Oh, wait. I would like your picture to remember my trip to Canada. Please wait." I hurry inside the room and come out with my phone. She doesn't want her picture taken, I can see, and ducks down behind the cart. But I get a couple of good ones.

I'm thinking I'll follow her and help with her work and maybe get a chance to ask where she lives, when the woman from the office comes out. Her face is twisted into an angry mask, and she rests her fists on her hips.

Her voice is raw with rage. "Get busy, you girl! How many times do I say you do not speak to guests? You are in big trouble! Get back to work! Now!" Having vented her anger, she turned hastily and re-entered the office.

Well, so much for talking anymore to Tam!

I return to the room and sit on the bed, my nerves tingling. I need to find out more. I leave the room and creep along the sidewalk. There aren't many other guests. Not yet. I enter the office, taking care not to jingle the little bell above the door. The woman is not at the counter. I hear her voice coming from the back room.

"Yes. Yes. Just now. She talked to the girl. Took her picture. Yes. I wait."

I've heard enough. She'd seen me talking to Tam and is reporting to her boss. I want the woman's picture, but I realize I'm not going to get it. I figure I have a window of about two minutes to clear out. When I exit the door, I don't care if the bell rings.

No one is on my tail as I drive downtown, stopping at a Tim Horton's for a cup of soup and a doughnut. It takes me three hours to get back to Colville. I'm exhausted, so I decide to drive home for the night. I'll feel more comfortable in my own bed.

Bobbi's glad to see me when I enter the house. We eat at the Mexican restaurant in Deer Park and afterwards watch an old movie. Before I go to bed, I walk out under the stars and tell the horses hello and good-bye. I don't know when I'll be back.

The next morning, I drive north of Kettle Falls and check out the place on the Columbia River that I'd seen the night before, the River Valley Farm and Bible Camp. It's a produce farm and resident camp for children.

It doesn't take more than forty-five minutes from Colville to drive to the camp. After a bit of back-tracking, I find the driveway to the right of the road and turn down a steep hill toward the river.

From what I can figure, this is about ten miles south of the place where I was attacked.

My heart pounds heavily in my ears as I drive underneath a sign that proclaims their name. Is this it? Could I be so lucky as to stumble on the right place first stop?

Beside the driveway, a smaller sign advertises tomatoes, peppers, potatoes, and corn for sale in season. There's a big garden area to my left as the ground levels off, surrounded by a six-foot chain link fence. A lady is working in it. She doesn't look up as I drive by.

I proceed to a log building that must be the main meeting place and maybe the dining room. Beyond this, other structures and a few vehicles are scattered among the trees. There doesn't seem to be anyone around except the lady in the garden.

I park the car in front of the log house. Two dogs come out from the shade, both hounds. They don't bark. Stepping out of the car, I hesitate when one of the dogs lifts its muzzle and howls loudly. But then it comes right up to me with tail wagging. The other dog follows.

A man emerges from the log house, jumps down the steps and walks briskly over to me. He's maybe in his sixties and wears a long-sleeved plaid shirt, jeans with suspenders, and a baseball cap. "Yes? May I help you?"

"Oh, hi. My name is Angela Brubaker. I'd like some information about the ranch and camp here."

"Oh, yes. Billy Sunday, ma'am. Pleased to meet you." He grins and pumps my hand. His face has a two-day stubble on it, and he's missing several teeth.

I'm stunned. "Billy Sunday? Wasn't there a famous evangelist by that name? Are you related to him?"

He laughs, revealing gaps in his upper teeth. "Yeah. I took it when I got saved, cuz I shore do admire Billy Sunday. Thought it would be a good one."

I nod. "Yes, it is." Not too original, though. I knew about Billy Sunday because Dad read a book on his life and ministry and shoved it under my nose like he thought it would reform me.

"Well, Mr. Sunday, I'm a writer from Farm and Country magazine and we're doing a series of articles about small businesses in this part of the country. Do you have time to allow me to walk around, take some pictures, and ask you some questions?" From my pack, I pull out my clipboard and camera.

He beams. "That sounds like a wonderful idea. We haven't started camp yet, so I got all the time in the world. That is, unless my wife hollers at me to do somethin'."

Billy takes me on a tour of the place, past a big shop building, a barn, a little church that must have been a small house at one time, and guest cabins. The place used to be a guest ranch, Billy told me.

When I draw his attention to a bigger building toward the back, he shrugs.

"Used to be a lodge of some sort. Was in need of some major repairs when we bought the place, and we haven't fixed it up yet. When we get the kids we want to help, we'll probably get that done and use it for a dormitory."

I want to go back there and investigate it, but he wheels away and starts toward the front of the property again.

"When are you getting the children?"

He shrugs again. "Don't know. We've applied for the license, but the darn government is so slow. We also need some help with them, like dorm moms." He gives me a direct stare. "Hey, are you interested, missy? You'd be good with the kids."

I choke and clear my throat. The thought of being a dorm mom leaves me with cold chills. "I don't think so, Mr. Sunday."

He wants to take me to see his farm equipment, but that involves going inside a big machine shed, and I'm not doing that.

This place has all the requirements I've been looking for in the organization that is involved in human trafficking, but I can't see Billy Sunday as the boss of it. He could be the front guy, the manager, though.

After thanking him for his time, I drive up the hill to the road.

I glance in the rear view mirror as I drive south along the Flat Creek/Northport Road. My heart stops. There's a dark blue pickup behind me, keeping close but not passing. I pull into a driveway wait until it's gone past. Then, breathing deeply, I head south again.

I pass the place where Chance and I had driven off the road to find a hunting spot that day. On a whim, I pull over at a wide spot in the road and stop. Maybe I should search the river bank where I was shot. I have time and there might be something that the sheriff missed.

It's three pm when I loop my camera and binoculars around my neck and strap on my shoulder holster. I slide down a steep bank off the road, angling toward the river.

It was as I remembered it. Dense brush, the smell of pines, the sound of the river lapping against the beach as I draw closer to the spot. I advance carefully, listening, my Glock in hand.

It's deserted. I don't break from the cover of bushes but stand on the top of the bluff, gazing over a broad expanse of river, inhaling deeply of the smell of the water.

Below me to the right, I see where I sat that day, eating my lunch. They took my pack. The beach is rough pebbles and drift wood, nothing else. I climb to a higher perch. From this vantage point, I can see a little-used track that threads its way through the bushes from the highway down to the beach.

My attention is drawn to the river when the *put-put* of a motorboat draws close to the shore. I step back into the bushes, making sure I can still see the beach. At the same time, a car motor starts up. It's parked on that little road. *Yes.* Now I see it. It's a green van. Older model.

I whip out my camera, set the zoom, and take a bunch of pictures as it backs slowly toward the river. I'm not in the right position to get a view of the license plate. *Darn!*

No one gets out of the van. A small houseboat edges to the bank. I want a picture of the man who's driving it, but he's behind glass in the pilot's seat, and the setting sun blinds me as it reflects off the window. I snap several pictures of the boat, moving out a little further on the bank to get a good shot.

Pulses racing, sweat beading my forehead, I steady my hand and continue shooting while the boat docks. A young man appears from inside and jumps into the water, pulling the boat up further as it rocks with the waves it generated. He's wearing jeans, a white t-shirt and a red cap. I can't get a good view of his face. Maybe the zoom lens on my camera will get it.

When the driver of the van steps out, he's on the far side away from me. I can only see his feet and the top of his head. He opens the side door on the van and waits. There are a few words shouted back and forth, but I'm too far away to catch them.

The fellow with the red cap is waiting by the boat, still standing in the water. People begin emerging from the covered portion of the boat. They are huddled shapes, very small, covered with black cloth from head to toe. The first is a woman. I can tell because of her form and the way she moves. The young man in the water grabs her hand and helps her to the beach.

I train my camera lens on them and catch a glimpse of the girl's face. Why are they beaching here? Six people follow the first woman. I take pictures of all of them, yet I can't catch their faces. Then one of them, a young man, allows his hood to fall back. He's Asian.

The first one, the woman, stands on the shore as the rest arrive in a huddle. She drops her hood and turns toward me. Through the zoom, I study her face. It's Tam, the woman I met in Canada yesterday!

I snap more pictures, not certain I caught her, as she dips her head and turns away from me. A man who jumps from the boat hustles the group to the van. Are these people victims of human trafficking that have been brought from Canada?

I really want a clear shot of the license plate on the van, but it seems they are about ready to leave. Edging along the top of the cliff, I try to get into a position directly in front of the vehicle.

Suddenly the ground beneath my feet gives way. I'm sliding down amidst dirt, rocks and other debris toward the shore, in plain view of the gang of crooks, holding my camera up so it won't get damaged. At the bottom, I lay still.

My foot is twisted underneath me. When I move it, pain shoots up my ankle. *Oh, great.* I won't be able to do a hundred-yard dash if I've injured it.

A man yells. They've seen me.

Chapter 22

Escape!

The girl goes into the bathroom, locks the stall door, and draws out from under her shirt a tattered blue notebook. With the pen in her hand, she begins to write.

We're getting more time to ourselves these days. They say we have to do school work in the fall. Funny. Who would think a prison would have a school?

I've gotten to know some of the other kids. At first, they kept their distance from me and didn't talk because I think they're a little leery of anyone new. Maybe I'm a threat to them, although I can't see how that could be since I'm such a nobody.

Everyone is against everyone else here because you have to look out for yourself. Those that are in favor with the bosses get special treats, new clothes, and they get out of the worst chores.

So, there's a lot of competition. I wish we could all pull together, and maybe we'd come up with a way to escape. Or a way to contact the police.

The oldest girl here (I think) is Kathleen. She and her sister, Julia, have been here the longest. I'm surprised they haven't been moved on, because that's what happens to the kids – they come, get trained, do some work, then they are placed. What that means, I don't know. I've seen big cars come and meet with Mr. Sargent. Then they take one or more of the kids away.

I think they buy them.

There are Asian girls here, too. They don't teach them English. I don't see them much because they keep them separated from the rest of us like they don't want them learning English.

Anyway, back to Kathleen. She's real pretty with long, dark hair and big brown eyes and a nice figure. She and her sister are from Vancouver, British Columbia, but that's a secret, as she's supposed to tell people she's from LA.

Julia has dark hair, too, but it's cut short. She has like the greenest eyes I've ever seen. I call her Cat Eyes, and I think she likes that because she <u>loves</u> cats. I got to know them because their room is next to mine. My roomie's name is Rita, and she's 15. I hear Kathleen and Julia talking after lights out.

Kathleen told me what happened the day they were kidnapped. They'd gone on a picnic with some of their friends and were at this park. They went across the park to the restroom. There was a van with tinted windows parked near the building. This guy jumped out just as they passed it and shoved them inside. Someone pressed something wet around their mouths, and they passed out.

They were taken in the van to a town in British Columbia, she didn't know where, but it was near the river. Then they were put on a small boat and taken down the river into the US. Someone picked them up and brought them here.

Kathleen said if she'd known what they intended to do to them, she would have fought until she died. That was two years ago, so Julia was stolen when she was only eleven. They were in a foster home since their mom was on drugs and couldn't take care of them. So the police never investigated their case much.

Anyway, I think Julia is going crazy. Kathleen tries to help her and covers for her mistakes, but Julia scares me. And it's getting worse. She's tried several times to kill herself.

Once she took a handful of pills, but she just got sick, and they took her to the ER and had her stomach pumped. Then another time she tried to hang herself, but luckily someone came in the room. After that, she was in a room they put the kids in if we cause trouble. It's below the main lodge. Solitary, we call it. She was down there for a while. She's never tried to do that again.

Last night, Julia crawled out of bed and was mumbling to herself and swaying around. It was spooky. I woke up and thought she was sleep walking. But she was wide awake and was staring at me like I was a monster. She was shaking all over.

Then, with a muffled shriek, she lunged at me, grabbed me around the neck and started to strangle me! I screamed (as much as I could) while I was kicking her in the stomach.

My head was going fuzzy when Kathleen woke up and got her off me. The matron, Delphine (we call her the Delph), didn't come as we hadn't made that much noise. Kathleen took Julia to the bathroom. They were gone a long time. Then they came back and Julia seemed calmer. They got in bed and everything got quiet again.

But it took me a long time to get back to sleep!

Kathleen and I had to go feed the chickens. On the way to the chicken coop, she told me that she was worried about Julia, and that she had to find a way to get her out of there. I was surprised because that was the first time anyone had said anything about escaping. Most of the kids go around with dull eyes and slumped shoulders and act like they don't care anymore.

I told her that I wanted out, too. She nodded but didn't say anything more because right then one of the other matrons, a woman named Tiffany, came up from the creek and joined us.

In the morning, they teach the girls things like cooking, housekeeping, serving a meal, and cleaning. The boys are taught mechanics, woodworking, construction work, and things like that. Then we have to do our chores, and after that, there's garden and farm work.

After supper, the older girls leave for town. I'm pretty sure I know what they do, but no one talks about it.

I pray for my Mom and for Jamie and Bonnie every night. I also pray He will help me get out, but He doesn't seem to hear me.

In the meantime, I'm going to watch for a chance to get out of here. It's not right what they're doing to us. I want out of this place and this life, and I'm going to fight for it, or die trying.

Chapter 23

Ramone

Forward Guard Retreat, June 9th

Chance shifted and wondered how long this session would take. What he wanted was a run, a shower, and a soft bed. But he wasn't going to get any of it in the near future from the looks of things. He sat at a desk in a small log cabin that had been turned into a classroom, trying to concentrate on Captain Grant's lecture.

He glanced at his watch for the tenth time. *4:45pm.* Another busload came in during the break, and he met his room-mate, Caleb Ostranger. Caleb was a strange person, very small, with cold, blue eyes, crew cut blonde hair, and a chip on his shoulder.

Chance sat up straighter. Grant was closing the meeting.

"We will have supper and meet back here at 1900 hours. That is all." With a smart salute, he left the cabin.

Chance fell into step with Caleb as they made their way to the dining room. "Nice day, isn't it?" He glanced sideways at the man.

Caleb regarded him like a king would an impoverished commoner. "You are so totally out of it."

There wasn't much to say to that. Chance got in line for the meal. He glanced back. The Korean fellow, Hyun, stood behind him, talking to a girl behind him, the one from India. Hyun's low chuckle caught his attention.

"I know," the man said in an undertone. "It will be interesting to see who it is. Are you ready for it, Rasha? I hear you've signed up for the big hunt."

Chance did not turn. He inched forward in the line.

Her reply was so low he almost missed it. "Yes. I am ready. It will be worth the extra money. I would like to take your workshop on martial arts."

The Korean nodded. "Yes. It will be good."

After Chance filled his plate with fried chicken, mashed potatoes, salad, rolls, and picked up a small plate of cherry pie, he sat across from Caleb in the dining room. He was unnerved when he looked up and found the man's cold, blue eyes staring at him.

"Howdy," Chance said. "The grub's good here, anyway. Where are you from?"

Caleb finished a bite of chicken before answering. "Seattle."

"Oh. I'm from Chewelah. Didn't have too far to come. Have you been here before? I mean, it looks like you know Grant and the lay-out here." He tried a chuckle, but the other man didn't even twitch a smile.

Caleb wiped his mouth with a napkin and grunted, not meeting Chance's eyes. "No. I have never been here."

Chance sipped his coffee. Keeping up a conversation with Caleb was like slogging through the mud. "Nice place they have here. What line of work are you in? I'm a border guard. Not much pay, but it's great work."

"I work for Microsoft. Now. I'd like to get some work done, if you don't mind." Ostranger pulled a tablet from a briefcase and set it on the table.

Chance carried his tray to another place and finished his meal, stealing glances at his room-mate. Caleb's blonde hair was cut so short it almost looked as if he'd shaved his head. His clothes looked new and were impeccably clean and pressed. He wore a medallion of some sort around his neck on a leather thong. His boots were black and shiny.

Shaking his head, Chance dumped his garbage and dishes in the kitchen. This retreat was definitely short on social graces. He looked around for anyone else to chat with, but they were all busy with their food, and no one was talking much. So far, the only attractive thing about the week was the food.

Fifteen minutes later, they assembled once again in the log cabin that was a classroom. Now it seemed that everyone was present.

Chance endured another two hours of lectures. At last, Grant sat on a desk at the front of the room and said, "Very well. That is all for tonight, people. We will reconvene tomorrow morning at 0700 hours. Rodgers will assign you to your teams. We will have competitions, and the team that wins will be rewarded." He saluted and stepped back, still eyeing them with the attitude of a hawk about to pounce on the unwary mouse.

Rodgers read from a clipboard. He announced that Chance's partner was Rasha Sarkis from India.

"Canada, sir," she spoke up sharply. "We moved to Vancouver a month ago."

Chance glanced over at her and smiled, but she scowled in return and cast him a disdainful look down her long nose.

He studied her. Late twenties, works out, probably as tough as steel. Her smooth, flawless skin and slender body would be acceptable on the cover of Glamour, but she never smiled and carried about her the attitude of an offended deity. She was pretty, no doubt about that, but falling in love with her would be like having a relationship with a hungry leopard.

At the end of the class, she moved to the back of the room, and he followed her. "So, Rasha, how do you like this part of the country?"

She stared at him like he'd lost his mind. "Does it matter if I like or not? Why do you ask such inane question?" She had an accent but spoke nearly perfect English.

"Well, I guess it doesn't, really. I was just trying to be friendly."

"Well, I don't have time for friendly. Let me tell you something else. You better be ready to kick ass tomorrow because if you don't, and we fall behind in anything, I'll bust your head wide open and have your brains for lunch. Got me?"

He stared at her. "Shore, ma'am. I gotcha. Hey, this is gonna be real fun, Rasha the Tasha. Your middle name ain't Lara, is it?"

147

He grinned, hoping she would have a spark of humanity in her somewhere.

She whirled and stomped out of the room. He winced. Big mistake. *Note to self: don't joke with Mama Tiger.*

As he stood watching her leave, someone boomed a laugh. It sounded so strange with this somber group that he looked up and found the laugh came from the Mexican in the group, a man named Ramone from Los Angeles. He was tall, broad-shouldered, and his dark hair was held in a pony tail. Chance remembered seeing him at dinner, shoveling food into his mouth faster than he talked, which was quite a feat.

That evening, they were taken on a tour of the ranch and shown the weapons they would be learning to use, including an assortment of mini-submachine guns made in Israel. The last item on the tour was the pride and joy of the outfit, a mounted M61, 20mm Vulcan Gatling gun, and a Light Towed Howitzer, sitting austerely on its carriage.

Chance couldn't figure how the organization obtained the Howitzer, but most of the students were drooling to fire it. It took five men to do so, and cost $1200 a round, so he figured it wouldn't be used much. Still, it was an amazing gun. The sound of it would be awesome.

He was standing on the far side of the gun, studying it, when he heard a low voice. It was Caleb, his room-mate, speaking to Grant.

"Too bad we can't use this on our hunt," Caleb said.

Grant grunted. "It wouldn't be useful for moving targets." There was a pause. He continued with a chuckle, "And I intend to see that they're moving. It's more ... interesting that way."

Ostranger barked a laugh in response as the two walked away.

On the way back to his room, Chance rubbed his chin, thinking. Twice now he'd heard someone talking about a special hunt. Now they spoke of moving targets. Did they have game here? Like elk or moose? He hadn't seen any, but then he hadn't been around the whole ranch.

In the dining room, he got a cup of coffee and went over to the fireplace where a fire burned. Ramone followed him there.

"What do ya think about this place?" Ramone said as he slurped his drink. "For myself, I'd prefer if they served up a mug of beer."

Chance chuckled. "Yeah. So, you're from LA? Like it there?"

"Sure. It's okay, but I like getting out of the city, too. Like this." He stretched. "You from Washington? You like apples?" He flashed Chance a white-toothed grin.

"Well, I'm not originally from Washington. I was brought up in Colorado." When the conversation lagged, Chance figured he would risk some questions. "Hey, what do you figure about this place? Does it seem a little off-beat to you?"

The man stepped closer and pulled a phone from his pocket. "Take a look at this." He leaned closer and turned to the fire.

"I didn't think you were supposed to have phones here." Chance peered at the phone, curious to see what the man would show him. A picture of a wife? Daughter?

Ramone chuckled. "Let's say I'm a rebel."

Chance gazed at the phone. It was a picture of Grant. He was wearing a prison uniform. "Really! When was this?"

"Back in the '90s." He turned it off, lowering his voice. "They got the place bugged, and every move you make is on a TV screen somewhere." He glanced up. A camera lens protruded from the underside of a moose's head mounted above the fireplace. They were not in its range, and the sound of the fire would mask their conversation.

Ramone was not smiling. "I figure this a bad set-up, but I can't figure it. What's the deal?"

"I don't know. I heard someone talking about a special hunt. Some of them paid extra money to be in on it. Do you know what that's about?"

Ramone shook his head. "Nope."

"So, what're you going to do? Leave?"

Ramone shrugged. "Ride it out, I guess. How about you? Gonna take off?" He snorted. "As if you could. They got you, and they ain't gonna let you go. Have you seen that fence? It goes around the whole place."

Chance nodded. It seemed unreal. Some of the people were in the know, others were not. As he considered the situation, it felt like ants crawled up his jeans.

He shook his head. "I'll wait and see. At least I know I have a brother here." He looked at the cross hanging on Ramone's neck. "I'm a Christian, too."

Ramone smiled, stowed away the phone, and turned back to face the room. "I figure a cross will ward off evil spirits." He looked upward and said in a louder voice, "Yup, I like nothin' better than a big fire. Well, I gotta git my sleep, cowboy, or I won't be good for nothin' tomorrow. See ya around, *amigo.*"

Chance nodded. "*Nos vemos más tarde, senor.*" He smiled to see surprise in Ramone's eyes. "I speak Spanish, too. Grew up in Columbia. Good night."

The next morning, it was still dark when a bell clanged somewhere, and Chance rolled over with a groan. There were voices in the hallway and footsteps. Some of the men were already up. He stared at the luminous dial on his watch. *5am.*

Grabbing his towel and soap, he headed down the hall, hoping the showers weren't busy. He showered and shaved. Back in his room, he found that Caleb Ostranger was gone. His bed was neatly made, and his things were arranged with military precision on his side of the desk.

The smell of freshly brewed coffee drew Chance to the dining room, and after filling a cup, he went through the breakfast line. During the meal, Captain Rodgers, dressed in fatigues that were creased to a fine point, addressed them.

"At zero-seven hundred hours we will meet in the classroom," he said, pointing out the window. "Promptly." He glared at them as if they were going to complain. "Exercises will begin at ten hundred hours at the practice field. You will be given instructions at that time. That is all." With a smart salute, he turned and marched away.

Chance wondered why he hurried off. Had the President called? Was he going to go prepare their torture chambers?

After finishing his bacon and eggs, Chance started on the muffin, figuring he'd better power eat if he was going to survive. He sat across from Rasha, his partner in the war games. She didn't meet his eyes and seemed annoyed that she had to team up with him.

She rebuffed his weak attempts at small talk, and after a short while, she left without a word. He noticed she went outside. For a run? Maybe to fire off the Howitzer by herself?

When the bell rang, he retrieved his backpack and stepped outside. Dawn was breaking over the treetops. The sky was clear, and birds twittered from their nests in the eaves. As he made his way to the classroom, he chided himself that he hadn't prayed or had his devotions, although he'd had little time. He sensed he was going to need divine wisdom and strength this day.

The men and women gathered silently, almost sullenly, and took their seats. No one spoke. No one looked around. There were no smiles, no jokes, no greetings. He puzzled about the mood. It was almost as if they knew something he did not. Had he stumbled into something sinister? A cold chill crept into up his back.

He sat next to Caleb who gave him a quick look from his pale blue eyes and inched incrementally away from him.

"Nice day," Chance said.

Caleb stared straight ahead and made no comment whatever.

"Why did you come?" Chance probed.

The answer came in a harsh voice. "I love guns, and I love to shoot them. Anything else you want to know?"

Chance shrugged. "No, I guess not."

A two-hour session on guns, weapons and killing that would have made any Al Qaeda training camp proud filled the morning. Chance took notes and kept his head low, watching the others, but getting no signal from anyone, not even Ramone.

After a quick lunch, they filed out to the firing range. Grant led them to the Howitzer. Ten smartly uniformed men marched from a barracks that stood some distance from the main ranch buildings.

The soldiers, for so they seemed in their black uniforms, came to the front near the Howitzer and went through a complicated routine of firing it, destroying an old car that sat at the far end of the meadow. The range for the gun was 15 miles, so they had no trouble at all to blast a car that stood only about a half a mile away.

The sound of it echoed in Chance's ears long after it was gone. *Quite a gun. Glad I'm not the one they're firing it at!*

After that, the trainees were paired up with their partners and given instructions on participating in a war game that involved running, searching, hiding, and shooting their weapons at the other teams. Their weapons, of course, were only paint guns, yet as he ran, dodged, hid and attacked over the rough terrain, Chance sensed this was something much more than a game for his partner and for many of the other retreaters.

If a person was hit, they dropped out of the game. The last pair left standing was declared the winner, and each team got points. At the end of the week, there was an awards ceremony.

Rasha led him to a swampy area. Chance wondered if she did it deliberately because she chuckled when he fell in the mud. She seemed to know her way about, and he wanted to ask her why, but he was too busy keeping up with her to say anything at all. He had to watch for exposed roots to avoid a nasty fall.

The countryside seemed dry, even this early in the season. The woods hadn't gotten much snow cover last winter to help through the long, hot summer months, and now it was like tinder, ready to explode into flames at the least spark.

Chance thought he and Rasha did well, but as the sun dipped lower to the horizon, they were both shot and killed. It was Dale Walters who shot the killing blow. He was paired with Hyun Su Nguyen, the Korean. Hyun Su taught martial arts. He was another one that Chance knew would not hesitate to kill for real. Hyun Su shot Rasha because she'd allowed herself a moment to enjoy Chance's fall.

Rasha dusted off her jeans and regained her feet, for the shot knocked her down. Dale Walters and Hyun Su gave each other high-fives and marched up to them to take their numbers.

She handed over her card, and said quietly, "I'm getting a new partner." She was dead serious. Her tone and look sent chills down Chance's spine, but he tried to be jovial and make the best of it.

"Well, hey. At least we came in second. That's pretty good."

She didn't give any indication that she heard him. Hefting her gun under her arm, she stomped to the staging area.

Rodgers strutted to the front of the assembled group. They were all filthy and sweaty. "I am not impressed. You did not do well. Before this week is out, you will learn to fight and to kill, and to enjoy it. You will learn to run until you drop. Then you will run some more. To pay for your poor performance, you will put on your backpacks now. We will encircle the entire acreage. Five hundred square acres. Grant will lead in the jeep. Keep up the pace, people. Anyone who falls behind will be disciplined."

He paused as Chance and the others looped on their backpacks. Chance noted that his was heavy and saw the surprise in the others' eyes as they discovered the same thing. They were loaded with rocks. His heart sank when they started out, for he was already exhausted.

Rasha shot him a triumphant look as if she expected him to faint or do something stupid. But he only nodded to her and managed a weak smile. There were a few groans and mutters, but everyone seemed to be resigned to the run.

Everyone except Jacqueline, the girl from Canada. Her face was puffy red, she was panting heavily, and sweat drenched her shirt. She was a little overweight and had struggled all morning trying to keep up with the others.

"I ask to be excused, sir," she said. "I can't do it."

Rodgers marched over and frowned down at her where she sat on a stump. "You will do it, or you will feel the lash of this whip."

153

He carried a long whip that he liked to snap at the heels of the men.

"I'm ... I'm sorry, sir," she replied. "I'm too tired. Can't I rest a bit?"

Rodgers nodded to two of his officers. They grabbed her by the arms and made her stand. She cried out. "No, really! I'm sick! Why don't you listen to me?"

This can't be happening, Chance thought as his stomach churned.

They held her upright. Rodgers looked around. "You!" He pointed to Ramone. "Give her the lashes. Ten ought to do it." The woman cried out and wept, but they yanked up her shirt on her back.

Ramone stood straighter. "I don't believe my eyes or my ears," he said. "This isn't right. Let that poor woman go. She needs to rest."

Rodgers glared at him. "Are you refusing to obey a direct command?"

"Yes, sir," came the stubborn reply. "Let me take them lashes. She don't deserve it, and this ain't right. We paid good money to come here, and she don't need to be whipped like that. It's against the law. I aim to call the police."

Rodgers grinned as if satisfied by this response and was hoping for it. "We are the law here, and you can't call the police. I thought it might take longer to break your spirit, Sebastian. Anyone else want to say their piece and support this man?" He cast a challenging look at each participant.

Chance bit back the comment he was about to make. Rodgers glared at him as if he hoped he would say it.

"Very well. Sebastian has earned a night in detention." He nodded to his men, five of them, who marched to Ramone and grabbed his arms. They escorted him toward the Lodge. Ramone did not fight them.

The woman was not whipped, but she was also taken into custody.

Rodgers shouted, "Let's go! No dawdling now! Run!"

He leaped in the jeep. Chance noted that some of the uniformed soldiers followed in another jeep behind the group. They kept up a grueling pace over a bumpy trail that wound in and out of scrub cedars, down across a stream, up steep-sided gullies, and on around the place, following the chain link fence. Chance wondered if he could do it and found he could. From somewhere deep inside, the strength welled up inside him. But it was torture.

In fact, he wondered if Ramone had not chosen the better part of the deal. After about twenty minutes, he stopped and vomited the meager remains of his lunch into a bush. But he was not allowed to rest. The men in the jeep behind prodded him on with shouts.

He knew if he tarried, they would jump out and kick him as he'd seen them do to the girl, Jacqueline. They arrived back at the Lodge, drenched in sweat, just as the supper bell rang.

"You have ten minutes to clean up," Rodgers said. "Then report to the dining room. After our meal, at 1900 hours, you will assemble in the classroom. Dismissed."

No one spoke as Chance joined the others in a stampede for the Lodge. Yet he noticed that his roommate, Caleb, was not among those who hurried to find relief and rest. Looking back over his shoulder, he saw the man conferring with Rodgers.

Not caring to find out what they were saying, Chance went to his room and washed his face and hands. Then he sat on the bed and pried off his boots. His feet were red and swollen. He rubbed them and put his socks back on. Another bell rang. His muscles were tightening even in the few minutes he'd been sitting on the bed. What would it be like tomorrow? He'd be sore, yet he bet they'd be at it again in the morning.

More classes, more weapons, more grueling "games," more runs. And those who complained or couldn't keep up would join Ramone in the jail, wherever that was.

155

He tied on his shoes and hefted himself from the bed. Then he made his way to the dining room, coming last in line. He filled his plate, got a cup of coffee, and sat at the long table.

This time, he was across from Richard de Fouche, a computer geek from Vancouver, B.C. Richard was slender and short, wore glasses, and had given a demonstration on throwing knives. He had difficulty keeping up with the group on the run, but now he seemed happy and was eating like an elephant.

"I think I'm going to be a little stiff tomorrow from that run," Chance said. "How about you? You doing okay?"

Richard glared at him through the thick lenses. "I'm fine. A little tired, but that's what we're here for. To test ourselves. And to learn. I'm not complaining." His look was challenging.

Chance sighed. So much for trying to make friends. "Yeah."

The group was quiet during the after-dinner lecture. Ramone was not present. Chance wondered where they were keeping him. With cameras everywhere, how could he find out?

After the lecture, he went to the Lodge and got a cup of coffee in the dining room.

Larry Kenyon, Rod Osbert and the Korean, Hyun Su, sat at a table playing cards. Rasha was curled into a big chair by the fireplace reading a book. There was no sign of Rodgers, Grant, or anyone else in command.

It was nearly dark outside, that time of the evening when the sun was gone behind the low hills, yet the colors in the sky had not faded. A mourning dove cooed as he stepped out on the porch. He took a deep breath and walked the length of the deck, meandering along it, taking his time, looking around.

A door slammed. The sound directed his attention to a small cabin set back in the woods away from the other buildings. There were two small cabins back there. Someone approached from that direction. Is that where they kept Ramone?

It wouldn't be long before they would be rounded up like school children and told to go to bed. Lights out promptly at 2100 hours.

All rooms checked to make sure each person was where they should be. If he was going to do anything, he had to do it now.

Hoping to avoid the nearest camera, he stepped off the porch and slid behind a big laurel bush that stood beside the step. From there, he stepped without haste toward the classroom and walked across the open square between the buildings. On the far side of that, he hid in the shadows and made his way to another large building that looked like an equipment building.

Still without haste, he moved with quiet precision to the small log cabin he'd spotted and squashed his body in its shadow. The one window was open a crack. He inched toward it and tapped on the glass. "Ramone? You in there?"

There was a rustling sound. The window squeaked open another inch. Ramone's voice came indistinctly like he was speaking through a cloth. "That you, Chance?"

"Yeah, man. What's going on?"

"Whipped the daylights outta me. I'm tied up. Can't get out." There was quiet desperation in his voice.

Chance mopped his brow. "For how long, buddy?"

"Don't know. Hey, you better git goin'. It don't matter about me. Jest git outta here, do you hear? This place is some kind of ..."

He didn't finish. Chance risked a quick glance through the dirty window. Someone had come in from the front room. A big man. He slugged Ramone in the face.

Chance ducked down. He sprinted to a cover of bushes that grew nearby. From there, he made it to the shadow of the equipment shed. No one was pursuing him.

The bell sounded for lights out. Wiping his face, he hunkered down by the building, the cold seeping through his jeans. His stomach turned like he would be sick.

He had to escape this place, but he couldn't leave Ramone. If it was the last thing he ever did, he had to free Ramone and get out.

He shook his head. It was not possible. He'd seen the fence. He'd seen their guns. Grant and his men were ruthless killers.

Nevertheless, he had to try, and he had to do it now.

Chapter 24

Crime Scene Investigation

June 9

I'm lying at the bottom of a shale cliff, covered with dirt and debris, and my ankle is killing me. I have to get up and run, but I can't. Something tells me to lie low and be as quiet as I can.

"What was that?" A man's sharp voice nearby echoes off the cliff.

Footsteps approach. I'm behind a scruffy bush. Curling my feet closer to my body, I hold my breath as the steps draw nearer. Nearer. Surely, he can see me. I hold my breath.

After a pause, he says, "Nothing. Must have been a rock slide."

Someone else says, "Come on back. We've got to get out of here."

The steps recede. I allow myself to breathe again. Lifting myself up on an elbow, I peer through the bushes. The guy who was holding the rope to the boat leaps onboard as the motor accelerates. The boat moves out into the current.

A sliding door on the van crashes shut, and the van drives up the bank.

I wait. Did they leave someone behind? I don't see anyone, and there's no undergrowth near the boat landing. When I'm sure I'm alone, I scramble to my feet and dust myself off, checking to making sure my camera is okay.

Pain from my ankle twists my stomach as I trudge up the hill and get in my car. My shoulder hurts, too. The gunshot wound has barely started to heal, and when I wrench it, it tells me. I comb out my hair and wash off my hands in the little bit of water in my bottle. Well, at least I have some pictures I can share with Agent DeLaney.

I drive back into Colville and pull into the Safeway parking lot. I can't call Bobbi on the cell phone I was given by Agent DeLaney, and I left mine with the FBI. Inside the store, a clerk at the customer service counter allows me to use the store phone. Bobbi answers on the second ring and sounds out of breath like she was running.

"Hi, Bobbi. This is Gina."

"Oh, hi, sweetie. I was wondering when you're coming home."

"I wanted to tell you I probably can't make it tonight. I got an apartment, so I'm okay, but I wanted you to know so you wouldn't worry. How are things there?"

"Oh, I don't feel very good. I had one of my bad headaches. There was two women who came and knocked on the door. I didn't answer. A little later, I went out to feed the horses, and they had come back with a man, and they was trying to get into the back door. Lucky I locked it."

"What did you do?"

She chuckles, a forced laugh like she doesn't really think it's funny. "I grabbed a shovel from the garage and scared 'em off. Then I called the sheriff. A deputy came out. He questioned me and looked around, but I don't think he took it too seriously."

"Maybe I should come home."

"No, no, dear. It's okay. I've got things under control, and my headache's gone. I always feel awful for a day or two afterwards, though. No, you stay up there. You need your rest. I can always call Chance if I need help."

"Uh, I hate to tell you this, but Chance is gone, Aunt Bobbi. He's at a weapons and gun retreat out of Chewelah."

There's a pause. "Oh. Well, I'll be fine, Gina. Just call me once in a while to let me know you're still alive."

I laugh. "Will do, Aunt Bobbi. Bye!"

In the apartment, I make the bed and put the groceries I'd purchased in the little fridge. It isn't much, just some milk, yogurt, cheese and eggs. I'm too hot and tired to cook tonight, so I drive down to a Mexican restaurant I'd spotted on Main Street.

When I'm finished the meal, I return to the apartment and call Agent DeLaney. He doesn't answer, so I leave a message and download all the pictures I've taken to his private email. Then I curl up on the couch with my iPad and scroll Facebook.

I'm just thinking that I'll hit the sack when someone knocks on my door. It's a little past ten o'clock. *Who would visit at this hour?*

There's only one answer, and I don't like it. *Jerry.* If that's his real name. The knock comes again. I'm glad I have only one small lamp on – maybe the light isn't showing through the blinds. It may seem like I've gone to bed. If it's the gang who have been following me, a light won't deter them.

I get to the window and lift the curtain a fraction of an inch. Yes, a man is standing on my doorstep. It's Jerry. He's looking away like you do if you think someone might be watching you. I catch the faint sound of whistling. One hand is in his pocket.

He turns. Knocks again, this time a little louder. I know that if I could see down the block, I'd probably spy the black suburban, and also a couple of guys, watching the front and back entrances. Armed to the teeth. Ready to kill.

I grab my backpack and stuff in all the ammo I own, along with my camera, iPad, and wallet. I place my Glock firmly in my shoulder holster. I don't wear Angela's padding or her make-up. Does it really matter now? Jerry, who tailed me from Spokane, doesn't care what my name is. He's followed me to the apartment, and now he and his buddies are going to eliminate me.

If I was allowed to swear, I'd do a fair amount of it right now. My anger, however, is turned inward. How could I have been so careless as to lead them here?

I glance out the window to the pocket-sized lawn and consider my options. If they're watching the building, this will be interesting.

I edge open the sliding glass door that leads to a small patio in the back yard and step outside. I wait. Listen.

A siren wails down on Highway 395. Someone's radio is playing country music. A dog is barking. From someone's TV, the theme song from CSI provides the background music I need.

Taking a deep breath, I move toward a row of lilac bushes about six feet from the back door, tiptoeing at a fast pace of about an inch a minute.

I reach the lilac bushes. Somewhere close by, a man coughs. He snaps open a cigarette lighter, and a few seconds later, the smell of the cigarette drifts over to me. I smile. Careless of him. Now I know where he's standing – just across the street behind a tree.

But what about the others? Jerry must be watching on the front porch with his finger on the trigger of his gun. And there's someone else coming around the building, evidenced by the scuff of a shoe on the cement. A low voice speaks into a phone. Or a two-way radio. They really *are* careless.

My heart is hammering in my ears, and my muscles are sore because I've held them tense for so long. I try to relax by breathing deeply a couple of times and flexing my hands.

Clothes brush against a bush. They're moving in. I've got to move.

I think I've located Jerry. He's coming around on my right. His shoes make a soft whispering sound on the pavement, and he's breathing through his nose. This time I'm not sorry if I have to use my weapon on him.

The third guy is easy. His voice and the glow from his phone give him away. He's on my left, about a half a block down, behind a big garbage bin. He showed the top of his head when he straightened to glance around.

Okay, I've located all of them. I think. Or are there more I can't find? They must have followed me when I left the FBI office. Or maybe there's a mole. *Oh, God, not that again!*

But I can't think of that. If I'm going to come out of this alive, I have to concentrate. One false step, and I'll be dead meat. One thing I have going is that they don't know I'm out of the apartment. They probably think I'm asleep already, and all they have to do is break in through a window.

I map my escape route. Can't get to my car. With a prayer and my breath held, I ease away from the lilac bush and slide across the handkerchief-sized lawn to the waist-high bushes on the property line. Beyond that is the back yard of another house.

There's a light in the back window of the house. It's from there that the theme music for CSI floats to me. Hopefully they don't have a fence or a dog. I drop to my knees when I hear another shoe on the sidewalk alongside the building behind me.

Jerry is getting close.

The grass is wet. I wrench my mind from that to focus on moving as fast as I can with little sound. I arrive safely at the low bushes, but I don't shove them aside because that would make too much crackling noise. Skirting them, I continue into the back yard of the CSI house, hoping that the lawn furniture, the above-ground swimming pool, and a stack of firewood will give me enough shelter to get away while the thugs behind me find an empty apartment.

I don't have much time. It will take them less than three minutes to discover I've flown the coop. After that, they will come looking for me. By that time, I'd better be in a safer position than hunkered down behind an above-ground swimming pool.

I think I've about got it made when my life suddenly gets a whole lot more interesting. The back door of the house opens, and a lady says, "C'mon, George. You need to go out. Hurry up, silly."

My heart sinks. *Rats!* I'm hoping George is her husband. No such luck.

It's a dog.

Chapter 25

A Tiger by the Tail

Forward Guard Ranch, June 9th

Chance hunched down by the building in the shadows and ticked off his problems. He had to free Ramone and get out of this place. Yet with the fence, the guards and guard towers, and the gated entrance, he figured they were trapped.

He studied his surroundings, taking a deep breath to calm his rapid heartbeat. He couldn't stay in one place for long. His present location was on the west side of the metal pole building that housed, he supposed, equipment and vehicles. Across a meadow were several small log cabins set amongst the trees. Ramone was held prisoner in one of them.

Farther away, beyond the open space they called the drilling ground, the lights of the Lodge shone brightly. Besides housing a dormitory and a dining hall, this building also held offices on the third floor.

A bell sounded. He glanced at his watch. 1100 hours, time for lights out. By now they would know he was missing. He snorted. Heck, they probably know where I am! But what could he do? Focus, Marshal. What's the first task?

Free Ramone.

He studied the cabins. A light shone from the window of the cabin in which he'd seen Ramone a little earlier. He'd have to approach from the side and get the window open. The guards would figure he'd go for Ramone. They would be waiting for him. But what if he could provide a little diversion?

He crept down the wall of the pole building, keeping to the shadows, around the corner, to the front doors. They were padlocked. Slowly he retraced his steps, freezing when a guard tromped by.

He let out his breath and continued down the wall of the building, coming to a window set high on the wall, too high to reach. After another seemingly endless journey in the dark, stumbling over occasional roots or sticks, he found a small door. It was jammed shut, embedded in the dirt around it.

His heart fell. *I don't need this.* He set about freeing the door from the mud with quiet determination. After digging with his bare hands, he got the bottom unstuck and edged it open an inch at a time, flinching when it squeaked.

At last it was wide enough to worm inside. He pulled a pencil flashlight from his jacket pocket. The building contained tractors, a backhoe, an old fire truck, tires, hoses, all kinds of automotive parts, gardening tools, and shelves of plastic tubs. The tubs were all neatly labeled. He shone his light on them. On one, he found the word, *Explosives.*

"This'll do," he said in a whisper. He pulled out four sticks of dynamite. Now he had to find a lighter. *Oh, God, let there be a lighter!* Yes! In a plastic bag, he found one. Now only if it worked.

He flicked the button, and a flicker of flame emerged.

Pocketing it and carrying the dynamite like it was the crown jewels, he returned to the door and stepped outside. Breathing deeply of the mountain air, he waited, listening. The guard came past again, staring straight ahead like a marionette and marching in a direct line across the drilling ground.

Easing himself from the building, Chance aimed for a row of bushes about twenty feet in front of the log cabin. He kept himself at a slow pace – no running, even though his heart was hammering in his ears and his brain told him to bolt.

Steady. Steady ...

He arrived. Took a deep breath. Put the dynamite sticks into the soft soil under a bush. Lit the fuse. This time he ran full tilt to the shadows under the window of the log cabin. Panting, he scrunched down and waited, wondering how long ...

Oh, God, the fuse went out! The sticks are duds! What's taking so long?

Boom! That was one. Three more.

He waited. Nothing. Hold on ... it will come ...

Boom! Second stick.

Shouts. The door of the cabin banged open. Two more explosions rocked the night. Footsteps. More shouts. Chance leaped up. Forced open the window. Threw himself inside, groping through the darkness. Bumped into a chair.

He pulled out his flashlight. Ropes around Ramone's barrel chest and hefty arms held him to the chair. His dark hair hung in his face and his mouth was covered with a cloth. Chance drew his knife, sliced through the ropes, and ripped off the gag. He caught the man as he fell sideways.

"Ramone! It's Chance! Wake up!"

Ramone's face was pale in the moonlight that streamed in the window. Chance felt his pulse. Yes, he was alive, but that was about all. There were more shouts from outside. Footsteps thudded past the cabin. He didn't have long, and he couldn't carry Ramone.

Chance shook him. "Wake up! Ramone!"

"Where ... where am I?" The big man rubbed his jaw and shook his head as if to free himself from cobwebs.

Chance tried to pull him to his feet. "Come on. Follow me!"

Ramone moaned and opened his eyes. "Oh. Chance. Can't get up, buddy. Can't ..." His eyes closed. Time was running out. The men outside were gathering, talking in a tight circle around the smoldering fire.

Desperately, Chance began to drag Ramone across the floor to the window. Before they got there, Ramone shook off his hands and crawled behind him, still in a daze. The shouts were dying down. The guards would soon return.

He reached the window and shoved Ramone up to it. Ramone, awake enough now to know what to do, clambered to his knees and scrambling over the windowsill. He let out a soft grunt as he hit the ground.

Chance peered outside. "You okay?"

Another grunt answered him.

Climbing out the window, Chance dropped to the ground. The guards, five or six of them, dashed toward the cabin, their flashlights glinting in the darkness as they drew closer.

One man shouted, "Here! Over here! At the cabin!"

Chance grabbed Ramone's arm. "C'mon, bud. We hafta hustle."

Scurrying like trapped rats, he led the way to the bushes behind the cabin, knowing that wouldn't be good enough – they had to keep moving. He didn't know what lay behind the cabins but figured it was a forest of pines and low-lying brush. He had to take that route – the front and sides of the cabin were now lit with spotlights.

At a crouching run, he went deeper into the bushes and small trees. Ramone's clumsy, lumbering progress sounded like a couple of elephants behind him. Yet they had to get away. Fast.

Chance stumbled and fell to his knees, smothering his cry with his hand. The bushes tore at his jeans. Branches scratched his face. He kept on, proceeding sometimes on his knees, always aware that Ramone tagged behind him, grunting now and then.

Their pursuers closed the distance behind them, using high-powered lights to see tracks in the dust. Chance hoped they didn't have dogs.

Out of breath and at the end of his strength, Chance found himself pleading with God. "Please, God! Please! Help us!" It couldn't end like this, but it would unless something happened.

The whispered words were scarcely out of his mouth when he dropped down into a gully. In the dark, he hadn't seen it coming. It was one step on solid ground, the next in the air.

He landed with a *thump!* on his hands and knees. The pain left him gasping. He almost lost consciousness. He rolled over, groaning, hoping he hadn't broken anything.

Ramone lowered himself down the bank and stumbled over to him.

"You okay?" he murmured.

"Yeah. Gotta keep moving, though." Chance staggered to his feet with Ramone's help and rubbed his elbows and knees. Up above, the men were calling to one another, using their lights.

Chance took a step forward. "We can't stop. Not if we want to live."

The pine trees that lined the gully had dropped a thick carpet of needles on the sandy ground. Chance figured these had saved him from breaking his legs, and the needles would also provide a carpet to hide their tracks.

Limping along the floor of the gully, he went only about ten feet and stopped. He looked around. There to the right in the side of the bank that now rose fifteen feet, he could make out a dark hole. A cave. It was shallow, a mere opening in the dirt and rock, yet he took it as an answer to prayer.

He crawled in, and Ramone followed. They squished their bodies tightly together in the hole and pulled their legs up to their chests. Chance slowed his breathing. If the men didn't have dogs, and if he and Ramone hadn't left too many marks of their passing, they might escape detection.

Their pursuers arrived seconds later. "Over here! The tracks disappear right here. They have to be in this gully. Spread out and look!"

The men ranged up and down the gully, above it and beyond it, but came up with nothing. A man, the leader, called out, "All right. Let's head back to camp. They can't go far. We'll have us some fun in the morning." Low laughter greeted this response.

Their tramping footsteps slowly faded.

Silence fell. Chance let out his breath. "Okay," he whispered, still afraid that one man might have been left behind. "Let's try to find a better spot for the night."

"How're we going to git outta this place, Chance? What hope do we have?" It was the first Ramone had spoken. His whisper was husky. "I'm not doin' too good, ya know? " He wiped his face. "Besides everything else, I'm hungry."

Chance could smell his fear, his desperation. "We have to take one minute at a time. Do what comes next. And next step is to find a safer spot. Got it?" He paused, listening. It was quiet outside their hole.

Ramone grunted. "Yes. I got it."

"Okay, let's go."

Chance crawled out of the shallow cave and waited until Ramone joined him before he stood. Straightening slowly, for his legs were cramped and his back hurt, he drew a deep breath and thanked God that they'd made it this far.

Together they shuffled down the gully. Chance led the way toward the buildings.

Ramone pulled back. "I don't wanta go back there, bud."

Chance helped him over a log. He rubbed his forehead. "Now think about it, *amigo.* What would they expect us to do?"

Ramone puzzled about that as he tramped behind Chance. "Probably fade back into the forest. Or try to go over the fence. That's what I'd figure."

"Yes. And so, we're going to do the exact opposite. We're going right into the heart of their camp."

Ramone stopped short. "How're you gonna avoid those danged cameras? They saw you when you was running around by that equipment shed. They was laughing about you sneakin' around. They let you do it. I figured they was baiting the trap and would get you when you came over to the cabin where I was. I didn't figure you'd have one chance in a million." He chuckled. "*Chance.* Guess you was named right."

Chance gripped Ramone's arm. "Listen. We gotta get you some food, and we have to find some bandages. You're wounded, and I'm bleeding, too. So I figure that's number one priority right now. Food, water, and some medical supplies. In the heat we've been having, we won't last two days without that." He wiped his forehead. Even though it was a cool evening, sweat trickled down his face.

"Yeah. But where we goin' to git it? You think there might be a McDonald's around the corner? Or a Taco Bell?" Ramone chuckled.

Chance sighed. "The only food I know of is in the kitchen at the Lodge. I think I know where most of the cameras are. If we sneak in before they start breakfast, when their guard is down, we might make it. They expect us to make a run for it and take off. Like you said, they'll think we'll try to find a hole in the fence and get out. We'll do just the opposite. Follow me. Keep low."

The lights of the buildings came into view, steady and bright, piercing the darkness. There were several brilliant yard lights around the drilling ground. Two more on the equipment shed. One on the porch by the main door of the Lodge. One behind it on the garage. This would be tricky.

He laid a hand on Ramone's shoulder as they crouched behind the same log cabin where Ramone had been held captive. Not far to the west was the dormitory where Chance figured the soldiers they'd seen were housed, along with their mess hall, for they hadn't come to eat in the dining room at the Lodge.

Chance settled down on the ground and pulled Ramone beside him. "This is as good a place as any to wait for a spell," he whispered. "The Lodge will be locked for the night. Can you last without food for a few more hours?"

Ramone grunted as he lowered his bulk to the ground. There was a bit of stirring as he made himself comfortable. "I'm okay. Are you? How's the knees?"

"I'll survive. We gotta wait for things to settle down. Let's stay put right here. You can sleep if you want. I'll keep watch."

"I ain't sleepy now. They drugged me up pretty good, but now I'm about as wide awake as a cat on a hot tin roof. I'll keep the first watch. How long?"

Chance settled back against a log. "Until three in the morning. We don't want to stir until dawn." He closed his eyes, thinking he wouldn't be able to sleep, but the next thing he knew, Ramone was shaking him.

"It's time, Chance! Wake up. Things are quiet. I ain't heard nothin'. Except coyotes off in the woods. You think they'd eat us?"

Chance chuckled, rubbing his eyes. "I reckon they would if we got weak enough and couldn't fight them off. But we're not going to do that. We're going to fight."

"Huh." Ramone didn't sound convinced. "I still ain't keen on goin' over to the Lodge. That's like walkin' right into the jaws of a lion."

"A tiger. We got a tiger by the tail, and we gotta out-smart him."

Ramone straightened. "What do you mean?"

"Well, it seems to me this is what we've got. The tiger is this place, this organization. It's like an army. We don't know who's behind it. All we know is that we're going to be devoured if we aren't careful. They have all the advantages. They got a good night's rest. They will get an awesome breakfast. They have the manpower, the weapons, and the know-how to track us down and eliminate us. Remember that class they offer? Tracking Human through the Wilds."

He stopped and wiped his forehead, for he remembered something that made his stomach twist and his mouth go dry. "Oh, Lord. They have the guns."

Ramone stared at him. "The guns?"

"Yeah. The Gatling and the Howitzer." He paused as chills raced up and down his spine, and it wasn't from the wind. "Anyway, we have to avoid their paws and their jaws long enough to figure a way out of here. It's going to take ingenuity, creativity, and a lot of grace. You into praying?"

Ramone closed his eyes and sank to his knees. "Okay. Let's do it right now."

Chance grimaced and pulled him to his feet. "We can pray as we go. C'mon. We're going to make our move."

Chapter 26

The Last Thing I Do

Deer Park, June 9th

Something was wrong. Bobbi rolled over and shielded her eyes from the bright sunshine coming in the window. A soft breeze wafted in the aroma of pine, grasses browning in the sun, and the corral. She stretched and tried to think why she was afraid. Oh, yeah. I'm at Gina's.

The silence caught her attention. It's too quiet. Someone's out there. Maybe they're going to set fire to the house like they did Chance's barn. Gina had told her what happened to Chance and what a narrow escape he'd had.

As she pulled on her robe and shuffled out to the kitchen, she told herself that she was imagining things. Yet she wasn't given to sudden alarms or wild flights of panic. She wasn't the sort to scream over the sight of a mouse. In fact, rather than scream, she would most often stomp it to death if she found it in the hay barn.

No, this crawling fear was real.

She started the coffee and got a shower. When she was on the second piece of toast half an hour later, she realized what the uneasy feeling was. *Gina.* She'd stayed last night up in Colville.

Bobbi expected that she would call to tell her she was okay, but then she remembered that Gina didn't have her cell phone and was restricted to calling from a land line she could borrow. She tried to pray about the feeling that made her skin crawl and her heart squeeze into a tight ball, and she did a time or two, but fear stayed with her stubbornly.

171

After she cleaned up the kitchen, she fed the horses and checked her mail on her laptop. She sent off a couple of emails and called Elton.

"I'm worried about Gina," she said.

There was a pause. Elton's slow response was typical of him. "Well, she's a big girl. I think she can take care of herself, Bobbi. Why don't you go shopping or something and take your mind off it?"

It was little comfort. She ended the conversation, saying she probably would do that. After setting down the phone, she wandered into Gina's office. There, on the desk beside the computer, she found a pamphlet. It had a picture of a dam on the front, and in big letters, the title, Boundary Dam Project. Where was this and why was Gina interested in it?

Checking it online, she discovered the dam was near the Canadian border near Metaline Falls.

She carried the pamphlet out to the easy chair and studied it. Was there something about this place that drew Gina's attention? She often spoke about the work Chance did on the border. What if someone was smuggling something into the states, and it was near this dam? Would it hurt to go and check it out?

No. Of course not. And it would be the perfect solution to her doldrums.

It didn't take long to get on her way. She took her camera, some snacks, water, and her laptop. The winding road over Flowery Trail and past the ski resort wasn't busy. She dropped down into the valley at the tiny town of Usk, turned north, and followed the Pend Oreille River as it twisted and turned toward the Canadian border.

At the road sign for the dam, she turned off the highway and drove on a paved road as it climbed above the valley. In twenty minutes, she came to the top of the dam and pulled into a small campground. She got out with her camera and snapped a few pictures.

The river widened here before dumping through the dam. Signs were abundant about the danger of entering the water. She read a huge one printed in red letters.

KEEP OUT. DANGEROUS WATER CONDITIONS.

"Well, duh." Bobbi said, sniffing at the sign disdainfully. The water looked smooth and cool, but she wouldn't want to disobey the sign's warning. The danger here was real.

One camper was parked towards the back of the campground, flanked by an older model pickup. Both pickup and camper looked abandoned.

She returned to the car and drove to a little guard shack that stood beside the road. After a short wait, a young man emerged and told her to go on down the hill to the bottom of the dam.

The dam was a massive concrete barrier that spanned the canyon wall. Three white plumes of water spurted from it, creating a spectacular view. She shifted and gazed at the mountain into which the dam was built. Giant pylons, built perpendicular to the cliff, carried electricity up and over the peak. What an amazing engineering feat this was!

She snapped dozens of pictures and joined a tour of the power house inside the dam, led by a high school girl. At the display cases next to the big glass windows that overlooked the generators, she studied the pictures that showed how they constructed the tunnels for the dam and the history of the place.

Two men entered the room, but she paid them little attention, her mind on the information she was reading. The men stood on the other side of the display cases and became involved in a heated discussion.

She finished one panel and shifted to the next. It was about then that she realized the men stood only a few feet away and continued their conversation in low tones. One phrase leaped at out her. "The girl poses the biggest threat. The boss says we have to take her out."

Girl?

She started listening, but she caught only the occasional word. Moving closer, she heard more.

The larger man said, "We have to do it *now*. Before we have to do the job here."

She didn't hear the reply, but she caught her breath at his next words.

"Boss said to take care of her. I'm gonna do it my way." He shifted slightly. She glanced around the display case. He carried a gun under his jacket! She had immediately thought of Gina, but now she wondered if he meant the girl who was their guide.

The other man saw the gun and tried to wrest it from his grip. "You can't bring somethin' like that in here!"

The big man shoved him back. "You idiot. Get your dirty hands off my gun. If I want to use it on that dirty cop, I .... " He looked over his shoulder, and for the first time he seemed aware that Bobbi was close by.

She turned abruptly and stepped away to gaze down at the huge generators below her, sensing the men were moving, too. Which way? To the door? Closer to her? Bobbi was glad the guide had remained in the room, but how could she hinder him?

The two men shoved past her and stomped out of the room. The girl followed them. Bobbi noticed she was unarmed. A young man met her out in the tunnel. They all tromped down the winding tunnel to the opening. The two men kept ahead of Bobbi and did not look at her.

She returned to her car and started out of the parking lot. Glancing in her rear-view mirror, she noticed a dark blue pickup following. She decided to re-visit the campground and heaved a sigh of relief when the pickup went on down the road. Her hands were shaking as she reversed and pulled onto the road.

"I'm not trained for this," she said in a low tone. "Not trained, not willing, and not able. Maybe I should go home."

But then she remembered the horses. And the cats.

Oh, darn, she thought. I'll have to stick around. Should I warn Gina? I've got to get in touch with her if it's the last thing I do.

Chapter 27

My White-Haired Angel

Colville, June 9th

I'm standing in the darkened back yard of a house, watching George, a fat little dog sniff around a wood pile, maybe scenting a rat.

As sweat beads my forehead, I pray that he will be more intent on returning to his warm bed than he is of signaling his mistress that there's a suspicious person lurking behind a bush in her back garden.

Unhurried, George takes his time.

I can't wait forever. Behind me, I catch the sound of the sliding glass door in my apartment closing. A whispered comment. Someone shoving a bullet into the chamber of a gun. They know I'm not in there, and they are coming – three of them. Circling, searching, listening.

Surely, they'd heard the woman let the dog out. They wouldn't want to rile up the pooch any more than I do, yet I can't wait for them to make their move. The dog squats, does his business, then waddles toward the door. But suddenly he gets interested in a scent in the grass where I'd just walked. He lifts his head. Sniffs. Barks once.

The woman appears at the door. "C'mon in, George. What did you find out there? A squirrel? Come on."

The dog is staring straight at me, but he must be near-sighted because he doesn't bark again. Feeling on the ground, I find a small stone, and toss it. It lands with a *clunk!* on the swimming pool cover.

The dog whirls. Runs to the pool. Barks. The woman calls again, and this time, George obeys her. She shuts the door.

I break through the barrier of bushes and dash to the side of the house, taking cover beside a pile of old tires and bikes. From there, I sprint to the front, to the street, and dart with all the speed I can muster down the sidewalk. If I can get to Highway 395, five or six blocks away, I can find plenty of places to hide.

I have no plan, only to flee, to hide. I'm glad I got my pack, but it bumps against my back as my breath comes in gasps and my ankle complains.

Casting a quick glance over my shoulder, I see two men emerge onto the street behind me. I race across the it, hoping to hide behind a parked van, but something tears at my right leg and a sharp pain shrieks upward. I stumble, almost fall. I'd only heard a popping sound. Silencers.

Through the pain, I keep running because I have to make good use of my lead. When they stopped and shot, they lost a little ground. Of course, I did, too. I can't believe their shot connected! What kind of luck was that?

I have the strange urge to turn around and give myself up. But of course, I can't do that. That would be suicide. Turning sharply, I enter an alley that runs behind the houses.

Oh, God, please, not a dead end!

It isn't. Coming to the side street, I turn right and flee down the hill. At the bottom, I see Safeway's gas station, lit and welcoming. But even in the street lights, I don't feel safe. I have to totally disappear. And fast.

Every step is agony. The street behind me is empty. Pausing behind a big delivery truck that's parked behind a store, I check my leg. The bullet ripped open my jeans, and the wound, on the calf below the knee, is bleeding. My shoe is squishy with blood. Tearing off the bottom part of my jeans, I make a quick bandage, wincing from the pain when I tie it.

A woman is walking a dog across from me, coming down the hill. Out on 395, cars whizz past. Music blares from someone's radio. The name of Habitat for Humanity is over the back door of the store. There's a bin for donations that sits on the corner of the parking lot.

A man emerges from a back door of the store and gets in his car. I ease past the bin and trying to walk normally, get out to the sidewalk. I need help. I'm still losing blood. Dizzy spells swoop down on me, and a weird sense of unreality, almost like I'm walking in different dimension, plague my mind. I head across the street and find myself in the parking lot of the grocery store.

People are coming and going, but I don't feel comfortable entering the store with my leg bleeding. I limp past the main doors, still in the parking lot, searching for a place to hide where I can bandage my wound and get relief from the pain.

A woman exits the store with a little boy in her cart. He points to me and says hi. I smile at him. The woman gives me a once-over and sees the blood on my leg. She sniffs and turns to her son.

"Don't talk to strangers, Justin," she says as if she's offended by the sight of me. "Let's get out of here."

I turn, shifting my body, trying to find relief for the pain in my ankle, my shoulder, my leg. The woman's rebuff stings. I remember high school days when I was excluded from close friendships because I didn't have a mom, because I wore old hand-me-down clothes, because Dad was a cop and picked me up from school in his beat-up Toyota. Besides that, I didn't have time for activities. I had to go home and make dinner and clean the house.

I shrug off the inner pain, like I always do, and hobble past the store.

My senses are sharpened by the danger that follows my heels like a hungry lion. Someone coughs as they get out of their car. A baby is crying. Clouds are whipping across the sky on the wings of the wind, blocking light from the crescent moon.

I don't know where I'm going. I find myself praying out loud. "God, you can see me. You know I need help. Please show me where to go. Please." The last comes out as a gasp as I sway and almost fall. I reach for the lamp post and look down at my leg. How much blood have I lost? I've probably left a clear trail for anyone who's following me.

I turn on a side street, still befuddled in my brain and losing control of my body. I'm thinking I'm not going to make it when someone touches my elbow. I jerk and turn around, ready to use my gun.

But it's only a white-haired lady with a kindly expression on her wrinkled face. "Do you need some help, dear?" She's holding my elbow like she won't let go of it.

My knees begin to crumple, but I straighten them and attempt a smile. "No, thank you, ma'am. I'm ... just going over there ... to my car." I nod toward the parking lot.

She isn't convinced. "I think you need some help. Come with me. It isn't far, just across the street here." She shifts her white plastic bag to her other arm and propels me along like I'm a five-year-old. I stumble along beside her, telling myself I have to be wary. Careful.

Then I see it – lighted windows. Music. Cars. What must have been an old store or shop has now been remodeled into something else. The sign in the dim light on the building front reads, *Youth Center*. On a window are the words, *A Place for Youth*. It's painted a drab yellow, and I'm not exactly a youth, but it may be my miracle.

The woman pushes open the door. "Right in here. They won't hurt you." She leads me inside. The light and music almost blind and deafen me. I stumble and catch myself on a counter that runs from the wall on my left.

There's a group of young adults gathered at the far end of the room, singing and playing guitars. One pounds on a set of drums, one is playing the keyboard. I don't recognize the song, but I hear something about Jesus. The beat of the music pounds into my head, making it spin even faster than before.

There's no cigarette smoke in the air, although I smell it on some of the kids who are closest to me. On the counter is an array of finger-foods – a plate of cheese and cold cuts, rolls, chips and dip, cookies. There's a big jug of iced tea and a coffee urn. The smells in the room are a combination of gym locker socks and a rock cafe minus the booze.

The woman glances at my leg. "Let me see to that wound. There's a place back here, if you can make it." She steers me into a small room. "Sit here, my dear."

Metal folding chairs line the walls and a water cooler stands in the corner. A small table has literature on it. Several posters decorate the walls, but I can't focus on them. I follow like a zombie because that's about how I feel.

"It's okay ... I'm fine." I sink down on the nearest chair and lean my head against the wall.

She sits next to me and presses a bottle of water into my hand. "Drink this until we can get you some coffee." A smile lights her eyes. "I'm Jane. What's your name, dear?"

I can't remember it. The first one that springs to mind is Angela, but I know that isn't right. The next is Linda, the one I used in Canada, and that isn't right, either. I can't use either because my enemies could trace me here if I did. She's waiting patiently, giving me a look like she might use on a reluctant child.

"Katie." I sigh. "You know, I think we'd better do something about this gunshot wound. I'm not going to the hospital – that's the first place he'd look. It's still bleeding. I have to put a pressure bandage on it right away."

She scurries around and brings me a couple of folded dish towels. "Do you need tape?"

I yank up my jean leg and apply pressure to the exit wound which is a ragged tear, moaning as I do. After a couple of minutes, the bleeding has diminished. "Okay. Now give me the antiseptic and tape, if you would."

By this time, she's found a First Aid kit and blows off the dust. She brings me gauze pads, water, rubbing alcohol and tape. I start to work, gritting my teeth against the pain. The wound bleeds again.

I cleanse it and fold several layers of gauze bandage over it, applying pressure so the bleeding will stop. "Ohhh. That hurts." I hold it tightly, commanding myself not to do something stupid like faint or throw up.

She waits patiently, holding my arm. Then, when I nod, she unwinds the adhesive, tears it off, and helps me apply it. Several layers of tape later, I lean back on the chair. The bleeding has stopped.

She washes her hands and rests them on her hips, regarding me with worry in her eyes. "Okay. Now I'll get the coffee."

"Yeah, that might be a good idea." I don't think I have a broken femur. That's something to be thankful for. If I can get somewhere safe, I'll wash the wound out thoroughly and re-bandage it with something better.

But what will come next? Where can I stay?

Jane returns, carrying a cup of steaming coffee in one hand and a plate in the other. It contains lunchmeat, cheese sticks, carrots, and two cookies.

"Thank you." I sip the coffee and eye the food. I'm not hungry, but I don't want to seem ungrateful. "I don't know how to thank you ... " Tears choke my throat. I blink hard to keep from bawling. "You can't know how much I appreciate this."

She smiles. In that moment, she seems like an angel with white hair, sparkling eyes, and a stained apron. "It's nothing, dear." She pats my shoulder. "My, my. Your shoes are ruined. At least that one that got drenched in blood." Straightening, she nods as if coming to a conclusion. "We have used clothes here. There's a box of shoes, too. You feel up to looking through it? There might be something in there you could use."

"Oh. Yeah. Do you want me to come and look?"

"No, I'll get one of these big strong guys to lug the box in here. You just sit and eat your dinner. I'll be right back."

I find a pair of tennis shoes that fit and don't look too bad. She also produces a box of clothes, and I discover a pair of socks and some jeans that might fit. Closing the door, she guards it while I change.

When I finish eating and change into the clothes she'd given me, she returns. "So how are you fixed for the night? I mean, it's a little late to go out looking for a motel room."

I shake my head and stand. "No, I can't do that. My ex is out there somewhere, and he'd know to check the motels. Can I stay here?"

"Well, for awhile, but we close at midnight. We're not licensed to keep people overnight. Come into the kitchen. You can sit and talk while I clean up."

I follow her to the next room and sit on another folding chair. From the sounds of things in the main room, I can tell they are winding down. Someone is speaking. There's a low murmur of voices. I glance at my watch. *11:52pm.*

I'd taken three Tylenol, but my leg still hurts. Throbs. Exhaustion lands on me like a five hundred-pound weight. It's hard to stay awake. Yet I have to find another shelter and avoid the men who are out to kill me. I don't know how I'm going to do it, but I hope an idea will occur to me soon.

People are saying their farewells as the door opens and shuts. The place becomes quiet. A man steps into the doorway of the kitchen. He's maybe in his late thirties with prematurely gray hair, an athletic body like he works out, and tired eyes behind glasses.

"Are you about finished, Jane? I'll walk you out to your car." He glances at me. "Oh. I didn't know you had a friend in here."

Jane introduces him as Bill Waters, the man in charge of the Youth Center. She explains that I'd come in and needed help. "Her name is ... oh, dear. I've forgotten your name."

I nod. "That's okay. Katie McDonald."

"Oh, yes. Katie." She turns to him. "You don't know of a place she can go for the night, do you? Is there a shelter here in Colville? She needs a place to stay."

"Just one night?"

"Yes, sir." I know I should get up and make conversation, but for the life of me, I can't get to my feet.

He shrugs and turns away. "Well, I can give her a lift to a motel."

"No, you're not." Jane steps forward, resting her hands on her hips and glaring at him. "You know the rules we got here, Mr. Waters. No man can take a single girl anywhere, least of all to a motel."

They stare at each other. I rise to my feet and hobble over to the wall where I'd left my backpack. "That's okay." I nod in his direction. "I appreciate your offer, but I'm fine. What you've done for me is above and beyond anything I expected. I know it was God who directed me here."

Jane moves closer to me like she's protecting me. "That's okay, Katie, honey. I'm taking you home." She turns to face him. "And don't you tell me I'm breaking the rules, too. I know this is what God wants me to do. So, get that look off your face and go home. You're tired, and you need to talk to your wife before you go to bed."

"Yes, ma'am." He grins. "Be careful about going anywhere with this woman, Katie. She's real bossy. Why, I wouldn't put it past her to adopt you before morning." He dodges the towel she snaps in his direction. "Let's go. I'll walk you to the car. That is, if you approve of *that*, Jane."

She sniffs in reply, hangs up the towel and gets her sweater. Then she takes my arm and helps me to the door. "Don't listen to him, dear. Come along. I don't live far away. Once we get home, I'll get you settled. I know you're dead tired."

We drive up the hill from the highway past the hospital. Her house is on a quiet street about ten blocks from the main drag. It's an older ranch-style, yet very neat and tidy and has been fixed up with a nice yard and a small unattached garage.

I'm glad her dog likes me, but I don't know about her husband yet. He's asleep. She assures me that he'll adore me when he meets me in the morning. How funny. I know she saw my gun in its holster, but she didn't say anything.

I take a shower, keeping the wound out of the water. It's hurting again. She's left gauze, tape and antiseptic on the counter. I blow dry my hair which bounces back to its usual state of insanity. It's worse now because I'd cut it and got a perm.

She knocks on the bathroom door. "I found some pajamas you can borrow. Here." She shoves open the door a bit and hands them to me.

"Thank you." I hobble back to bed and find a bottle of Tylenol on the bed stand. I shake my head as I pick it up. She thinks of everything! Yes, it is true, my rambling thoughts continue, the woman is an angel.

Lying on the soft pillows as the pain meds start to dull my brain to sleeping bliss, I marvel at God's protection this day. Saved from Jerry. Escaped after I'd been shot. Discovered a place to get help. And found Jane. I'll have to remember my new name. Katie McDonald. It's getting so complicated that I might have to write myself a cheat sheet to remember!

I sigh and roll over. What will tomorrow hold for me? I have to bring down a gang of crooks who are wealthy and highly placed. An uneasy thought comes to me. They own the cops. They own the politicians. They have power and money.

And I am nothing. I am a lone soldier to their army, a child waving a toy gun at their cannons. Yet I have something they don't.

I have God.

Chapter 28

The Hunt Is On

Forward Guard Ranch, June 10

A ray of light touched the treetops to the east as a light breeze fanned Chance's face. He was on his hands and knees, a good position, he figured, for praying. But what he was doing more than anything at that moment was trying to figure out the next step in getting out of this place.

Across an open space, about a hundred yards away, he saw the outline of the Lodge behind a hedge of bushes.

Ramone muttered, "I ain't goin' in there. I just ain't."

Chance didn't want to go into the Lodge, either. It was like entering a cougar's den. But they had to. They needed food, water, and medical supplies. Besides all that, he wanted to get some evidence about this place. The offices were on the third floor. He figured they could get up there if no one was around this early in the morning. He also wanted his backpack, but he'd have to get in his room without waking Caleb.

He started out, crawling, careful not to rustle the bushes or snap a twig. He aimed for the shadow of a big truck that was parked on the south side of the drilling ground. It seemed a journey of epic proportions as he crept from the shelter of the bushes and started into the open space.

Ramone breathed heavily behind him, keeping the distance short between them. Chance kept the pace slow and steady. Once behind the truck, he expelled his breath and glanced back at Ramone, giving him the thumbs-up signal.

Once again, he started out toward the Lodge. This time he headed toward one of the three small cabins that formed the northern edge of the compound.

They'd had their classes in the one nearest to the Lodge. He reached the classroom cottage and hunched down, thinking that any moment they would hear the tromp of feet and the shouts of the men who were coming to get them. But there was nothing.

A guard marched past.

The sky brightened steadily. The ranch was coming to life. A jet flew overhead, leaving a trail of exhaust in the pink and lavender sky. When it was clear, Chance nodded to Ramone and motioned to the Lodge. The back of it was in relative darkness, lit only by the yard light on the garage that stood behind it. Ramone shook his head.

"Not going in there," he mouthed.

"Fine. Stay out here, then." Without looking back, Chance ran to the scant protection of a row of bushes beside the Lodge. Ramone came with him.

"Think they seen us on the cameras?" Ramone whispered, breathing hard.

"I don't know." Chance shrugged. If they had, the guards watching the screens would report it, and Grant would rally his men and kill them. Or maybe they would allow them to get away so they'd have a good chase.

This could be it — the last thing he ever did. He wished he could have lived long enough to see sunlight dancing in Gina's hair and her eyes twinkling with mischief again. He longed to tell her how he felt about her.

And he wanted to talk to Dusty about the Lord, about God's love and how he could have his sins forgiven. There were so many unfinished details of his life. It couldn't end like this.

He wished he had the time to figure this out. Was it connected with the shooting on the river? With the illegal movement of people in and out of Canada?

With a jerk, he brought himself back to the task at hand. He'd better focus, or it would be over before it began. He bent his head fractionally and closed his eyes, gripping the stick he'd picked up in the gully. *Please, God. I need a miracle here.*

He got his first answer when they inched up the steps and stood under the roof of the porch on the Lodge. No alarms sounded. No heavily booted feet arrived. Chance paused and breathed, not knowing that he'd been holding his breath.

A door slammed somewhere. Ramone gripped his arm, but he merely nodded and put a finger to his lips. He motioned to the back of the building. There was a door back there, unless his guess was way off, that led into the kitchen. Surely it would be unlocked to allow the kitchen staff entrance.

Inching along about as fast as a snail on a hot rock, he worked his way down the wrap-around deck, dodging beneath the windows. Everything in him screamed to hurry. It was 4:07 am. The kitchen crew would probably arrive soon, for they had to have breakfast ready by 5:30.

His shirt was wet with sweat when they arrived at the back door five minutes later. After listening, he opened the screen door and tried the knob. It was not locked. With Ramone at his heels, he slipped inside and dropped to the tiled floor. Muffled voices came from another part of the kitchen, along with the clank of metal on metal and running water. Footsteps approached.

They were filling the big urn, making coffee. Then they would set out sweet rolls, hard boiled eggs, cheese and milk like they did every morning for the early birds.

Chance motioned to Ramone and crept along the floor, keeping low, following the line of brightly polished stoves, past deep sinks for pots and pans, to the far wall where a doorway led into the hallway.

"Hey! Come over here and help me lift this!" A man's voice called out almost above Chance's head. He ducked around the corner and flattened himself on the floor. Ramone followed him.

186

Close by, a man spoke. "They haven't found 'em yet. They're goin' after 'em this mornin'. Hope to have 'em cornered before long in the woods. Then the guys will have their sport, I figure. How many dozen did you want, sir? Five? Okay. Butter? How about the bacon? Okay."

Chance was certain now that this had all been planned. He and Ramone were supposed to run into the forest where they could be hunted like animals. The blood-thirsty killers in this crowd would love nothing better than the prospect of killing a human being. Maybe that's what they'd paid their fee to do. The class on tracking! Yes.

Like Hunger Games. He shook his head. What a thought.

The men went out to the front room. Chance was sure there were two of them, and that their tasks in the dining room would take a little while.

Motioning to Ramone to follow, he wormed his way along the white tile, trying to make as little noise as possible, praying that someone wouldn't come charging around the corner. After a bit, he came to the hardwood floor that marked the hallway. Slithering into it, he went around a corner and stood up. Now, unless someone came from the stairway above his head, they were safe.

"I'm going up," he whispered in Ramone's ear. "Stay here. If you see anyone going up the stairs, give a bird whistle."

"A bird? Won't they hear it? I can't ..."

"Just do it. I need to know. Be ready to run outside through the kitchen door when you do. I'll meet you over by the garage."

Ramone nodded wordlessly, his eyes as large as small moons. His hands shook as he wiped his face. "Be careful, Chance. They won't be nice to you if they find you."

Chance gave him a thumbs-up and, after checking to make sure the men in the dining room were not looking his direction, ducked around the corner and padded silently up the stairs, two at a time.

First thing, he wanted his backpack, because in it he carried things they could use if they had to hide out in the forest —

matches, a flashlight, his revolver, fishing line, a down sleeping bag, and a tarp for ground cover. And his wallet.

Getting it would be tricky, though. As he crept down the hallway of dormitory rooms, he heard someone in the shower. On the balls of his feet, he tiptoed past the doors and came to his room. Carefully, he turned the knob and opened the door.

Caleb was a lump inside his sleeping bag. *Good.*

Chance's pack was under his bed where he'd left it. Creeping over to it on his hands and knees, he was closing his hand over the strap when Caleb groaned and rolled over. The alarm clock went off. Caleb sat up and swung his legs over the bed.

Chance rose from the floor and thumped him hard on the back of his neck, a karate chop that he'd learned in training. Caleb sank to the bed wordlessly.

"Good night," Chance said, grabbing up his pack and making tracks for the door. Now to find the offices and get some evidence.

But someone was coming down the stairs. He had very little time to disappear. Glancing around, he saw a door that led to a broom closet about two feet away. He lunged for it and had just closed it when he heard voices.

"Good morning." Gruff voice. Captain Grant.

"Good morning, sir!" It was a woman. Rasha. "I'm ready for the hunt. When do we leave?" Eagerness laced her voice.

"Come up to my office. Want to talk with you and some of the others before breakfast."

"Okay. I'm going to get a cup of coffee first, sir."

Peeking out, Chance saw Grant going up the steps to the upper floor.

He stopped. "Oh, wait. I'll get me a cup, too." Grant moved down the hall and descended the stairs.

Now! Chance had to move fast. Taking the steps three at a time to the upper story, he dashed down the hall, praying he'd find the main office quickly. Tried one door. It led to the secretary's office.

Tried another door. Looked like a meeting room. Third door.

Yes! Grant's office. He entered on tip-toes even though he was sure no one was there. He retrieved a flashlight from his pack and illuminated the desks – a small one close to the door, and a big one over by the windows. Each held a computer.

He was tempted to snoop through Grant's desk but took the chair by the smaller one, thinking this was where the real work was accomplished. The computer was not booted up. He found the switch and turned it on, knowing he had only seconds to find what he wanted and get out of there undetected.

The computer was taking too long. Voices drifted down the hall. Grant's. Rasha's. Another man's. Footsteps thudded on the carpeted floor. Sweat beaded Chance's brow. He had to do something.

Whipping open the middle drawer, he pawed through it. Nothing of interest. First drawer on the left – file folders. Second drawer – office supplies. Now the steps were closer. He sank down behind the desk, praying they wouldn't notice the glow from the computer's screen and investigate it.

The door opened. Someone peered in. Grant's voice, loud and insistent, said, "No, there's not enough room in here. Let's go to the meeting room. C'mon." He shut the door.

Chance breathed again and climbed out from behind the desk. First drawer on the right provided pay dirt. In a corner, he spotted a flash drive, attached to a black cord. It was labeled Office Back-up. He grabbed it and shoved it in his backpack. Glancing through the remainder of the items in the drawer, he switched off his light and went back to the door.

Peering into the hallway, he saw several other people coming up the stairs. They made their way down the hall and turned into the room where the meeting was taking place. Please shut the door, he thought.

They shut the door. He inched out into the hall, feeling about as exposed as a snail on a rock without its shell. Creeping past the closed door, he heard a murmur of voices inside, and Grant's stentorian voice.

"We have lots to do today, and we'd better get down to business!"

Chance smiled grimly. The first order of business would be how to trap and kill the two humans out there in the woods. He descended the stair to the first landing and looked over the railing. To his dismay, Rasha was still in the dining room, talking to the other girl, Marina. As he watched, she ended the conversation and moved away from her.

Should he go back to the cleaning closet? Or try to beat Rasha and make it down the stairs? Neither option looked plausible. He hesitated. A low whistle sounded right below his feet. Rasha turned and looked toward the stairway. Chance froze, grateful that they didn't have all the lights on in the room below him.

Rasha started in the direction of the stairs, still staring at a spot below him where he knew Ramone hid. Suddenly something crashed against the far wall of the room. She swung around and took several steps in that direction.

"Hey! What was that?" She inquired of the cook.

He answered, "I dunno, miss. Maybe somethin' fell off the wall. You want me to check?" He came around the counter into Chance's range of vision, wiping his hands on his apron.

She hadn't moved and was still staring at the spot on the far wall. "What's going on? This is weird."

Keeping close to the wall, hoping their attention would stay riveted in the opposite direction, Chance descended the steps, crept around the corner, and dashed to the kitchen. He bent over and hurried through it, hoping the cooks were engrossed in discovering the answer to the mysterious sound in the dining room.

A young man stood at the sink, running water into it. He glanced up as Chance came to the back of the kitchen.

Chance strolled by him. "Good morning, Roger," he said, remembering the name he'd heard earlier. He counted on the fact that Roger wouldn't know one face from another in the group. "Hey, you got a sweet roll? We have some hunting to do today. I need a little extra something, know what I mean?" He chuckled and leaned toward the man like he was sharing a joke. He hoped the man couldn't hear his heart pounding.

"Oh, yeah. Sure. Hang on." The fellow dashed away.

A bowl of oranges sat on the counter. Chance grabbed up four, dumped them in his backpack, and then scooped up the fried bacon that sat beside the grill. He added a loaf of bread to his stash.

About that time, the head cook called out, "Hey, Roger, check over there by the fireplace and see what fell."

Roger mumbled a response. Chance knew he wasn't going to get his sweet roll. That was okay. He worked his way to the closet off the back door, searched the shelves, and found a First Aid kit. He stuffed it in his backpack and emerged outside.

There was no sign of Ramone.

Chance headed to the far side of the garage. The man was kneeling behind it. Chance joined him. "What did you throw?"

Ramone grinned. "A block of wood someone used to prop open the back door."

"Well, we got out with our skins intact. I even picked up some food. Here. Have an orange. Here's some bacon and bread, too."

Ramone didn't stand on ceremony. He devoured several slices of bacon and two slightly squished pieces of bread like he was starving. Then he pulled out two water bottles. "I snitched these on the way past the cooler."

With the bottled water, oranges, bacon, and bread, it was a feast.

Chance stopped Ramone from drinking all the water. "Hold up there. We may need that. Get your pants down. And don't be shy about it. I need to take a look at your wounds."

Ramone did as he was told, even though he screwed up his face funny like he didn't want to bother with it. "It ain't nothin'. Just a couple of scatches."

"Yeah, right." There was a jagged cut in Ramone's upper thigh and several smaller ones in his lower abdomen. Chance cleansed and bandaged these, but he couldn't take time for the others, the bruises and broken ribs.

"All right. That should hold for now." He put the items back in the kit and stowed it in his pack. "What do you think we should do? I imagine they'll be getting ready to start out as soon as they've had breakfast."

Ramone wiped his mouth and nodded. "Hey, I'm followin' you. You lead out. I ain't got any creative ideas in my head at all."

Chance sighed, suddenly tired. How he wanted to be away from this place! To look back on it as some sort of nightmare. But it was all too real. And their options were down to almost zero.

He figured that unless God took a hand in things, they might as well give themselves up.

"No, I don't have any ideas. The only thing I know for certain is that we can't stay in one spot for long. We gotta keep moving. So, let's go."

"But where?"

"I don't know. Let me take a look." He stood.

His knees hurt, his back hurt, everything hurt. He motioned beyond the garage to a ravine between them and the forest. "There's a stream over that way. Water is essential. The main thing is, we got to stay out of their reach." He shrugged into the backpack.

"All right. Let's make tracks."

Chapter 29

Herman

June 11th

My leg faithfully reminds me of the wound as I pull on my clothes and hobble toward the wonderful smells coming from the small kitchen. Don is seated at a round oak table, reading his newspaper.

He puts it down immediately and greets me. "Well, good morning! I see our boarder is awake, Jane."

Don is short, a little chunky around the waist, and almost totally bald. His grey eyes twinkle as he talks. As I sit at the table and receive a cup of coffee from Jane, he asks about my life, and I find the lies easy to my tongue.

The Katie McDonald I create sounds like the sister I always wished I'd had. I tell them I'm a writer for Living the Country Life magazine, and that I came here to do some stories on farms where they help the homeless and children who have been abused and are at risk.

I take my place at the table, and after we say grace, I dive into the delicious breakfast Jane serves – biscuits and gravy, bacon, orange juice, and sliced cantaloupe. The life of an FBI agent is pretty sweet at times.

But I'm dreading the day ahead.

"I understand there's quite a few places around here, orchards and such, that employ young people, or help them out. Some of them have young adults from other countries. Do you know of any like that?"

They shoot each other a glance as Jane jumps up to refill our coffee cups.

Don replies. "Well, there are quite a few orchards around Kettle Falls that employ young people. I know of one family who takes in foster children."

I gulp my coffee. "Could you write down the names and addresses? I'd like to visit them as soon as possible. I'm working under a deadline, you see. Have to get the articles and pictures back to the office as soon as I can. I'm already a couple of days late."

Jane sits beside me and takes a bite of biscuit and gravy. "Sure, I'll do that for you."

About that time, her cell phone rings. She hops up and answers it, then moves out of the kitchen and into the living room.

When she returns, she smiles as she folds her napkin onto her lap. "That was Bill Waters, dear," she says to Don. She includes me in a smile. "He told me someone called him this morning and wondered if we'd had a strange woman come in last night. It seems there's been a shooting. Someone was injured, and this woman is considered dangerous."

She eats for several minutes as silence descends on the kitchen. She glances at me. "Seems they traced some bloody footprints to the Youth Center."

My heart is pounding heavily in my ears, but I try to appear calm as I continue to devour the biscuit that I can no longer taste.

When my mouth is empty, I say, "Uh-huh. My ex-husband has connections, and he's up early. Quite a guy. Takes a pot shot at me and then blames *me*. What did Bill tell them?" There's the slightest waver in my voice.

She chuckles and wipes her mouth. "Good old Bill. He's a character. He told them we have a lot of women come in, some stranger than others, but he didn't recall any last night. I'd told him that you were running from your ex and needed privacy."

"Thanks." I expel my breath and steady my hands. "That's good."

Jane pats my hand. "Your secret is safe with us. But it might not be a good idea to go out any time soon. That leg of yours needs some rest, I would say."

I manage a laugh. "My leg is fine. I don't intend to jump any hurdles, and I'm not afraid of meeting up with the cops. I'll just have to keep ahead of that man." I shake my head. "I just can't believe he'd be so stupid as to follow me ... shoot at me, and try to get me back that way."

Jane gives me a knowing grin and refills our cups. "Okay. Is there anything you need?"

I don't like her expression and wonder what's going on her head, but I let it slide for now. "Oh, I don't think so. You've been such a help. I don't know how I can repay you."

Jane nods to Don. "She might need a vehicle. She was walking when she came in last night, so I assume she had to leave her car parked somewhere."

He rubs his chin, grinning at me. "You know, we have a van in the garage. It's not much to look at, but it runs fine, and it might get you around for a couple of days. You wanna see it?"

"Sure!" I'd been wondering what I was going to do for transportation.

It turns out to be a 2004 Dodge, the color of dog puke with a dented right fender and a cracked windshield. Not my first choice of a vehicle, but I'm glad to have it since anything I would have rented could be traced back to me. I call the van Herman.

I thank them profusely and against Jane's advice, I venture out to get some clothes and toiletries, an errand that takes me to the second hand store and Walmart. I keep an eagle's eye out for a black suburban and a man who looks like Jerry. None appear.

After I get back to the house and unpack my new belongings, I go to work on my appearance. Angela and Linda have bit the dust. I dye my hair a dark brown and apply deep tan make-up to my face and hands.

Katie McDonald is a brunette. I grin at my reflection. Now if I can only remember my name! I call Agent DeLaney on the FBI issued cell phone, but he doesn't answer, so I leave my new name and location with him and hope he gets it.

My driver's license still reads Angela Brubaker, but I have to go with that and hope that people won't ask to see it. At the Super One grocery store, I have a name tag laminated that looks fairly official with my picture, an ID number for the magazine, and phone numbers on it. All fake, of course. I punch a hole in it and hang it around my neck on a cord.

If I have to switch my ploy and begin looking for work, I'll have DeLaney send me some new ID cards.

My first stop is a farm and small orchard outside Kettle Falls. It's along Lake Roosevelt.

Silverton's Ranch and Orchard, the sign says as I drive through the gate. A white farmhouse sits towards the back, surrounded by rows of fruit trees and a neat yard and garden. To my left is a field of corn. A sign announces that you can u-pick the corn when it's in season.

It's not in season. *Aw, shucks.*

The valley stretches out around the farm – no place to hide dormitories. Yet I wonder if there are buildings behind the screen of trees and bushes towards the back of the property. Otherwise, where would they keep students?

A lazy dog hefts itself to its feet and ambles over to the car when I stop. He doesn't bark, for which I am grateful. I pat him and climb the front steps to a wide porch.

I knock twice and begin to wonder if anyone's home when the door is opened by an older man. He's taller than me with gray hair and overalls, ramrod straight, piercing blue eyes that have a question in them. I can tell he's ready to shut the door if I prove to be a religious or political solicitor.

"Hello, Mr. Silverton," I begin. "I'm Katie McDonald from Living the Country Life magazine. I'm a friend of Don and Jane Holden. They told me about your farm." I hold out my hand.

He shakes it and smiles. My reference is sterling. "Oh, oh. Right. Don and Jane sent you over, huh? Well, come in. My wife's busy right now, but she'll be down in a minute. You say you're with a magazine?" He motions to a small living room to the right.

I nod and follow him inside. "Yes. Living the Country Life. Have you heard of it?"

"Uh. No, can't say that I have. Sit down. I'll get Louise." He dashes off as if the presence of a female in his living room totally unnerves him. After a muted conversation with his wife, he re-appears with Louise behind him.

She's not as tall as he, but she's as slim and straight. Gray hair pulled back behind her neck. A no-nonsense look in her blue eyes. An apron tied around her waist. Hands that shout years of hard work.

She advances to me as I stand. "Pleased to meet you, Katie. Ted said you were from a magazine. I'm sorry, but we have all the magazines we want, and more. We don't have much time to read." She folds her arms on her chest and stares at me.

I rise. "Oh, no. You have me wrong. I want to do an interview with you and maybe take some pictures of your farm and the children. I'm writing an article for the magazine."

This changes everything. Suddenly I'm given a drink, offered cookies, given a tour, and told good-bye like we'd known each other for years.

They say they don't have any children staying with them at the moment, but they show me photos of some they'd kept and proudly relate how they are doing now.

There's a back portion of the property I can't see, and there's a road that leads back there. I also note a fence that completely encloses the property – to keep out deer, they say.

Herman purrs like he likes to ferry me around as I drive to my next stop, a church and school just north of Kettle Falls.

Pastor Dale Montgomery is young, wears a goatee, an Amour sports shirt, jeans, and a Seahawks cap. He welcomes me into the church, and when I tell him my errand, gives me a tour.

"The school is closed during the summer," he says as we admire the kindergarten classroom. "You're not looking for a job, are you? We need some help." He pulls his phone from his pocket and glances at it.

"Uh, I don't think so, Pastor. Thanks for the tour." I'm getting tired, and my leg is bothering me more than I care to admit.

The gaze he directs to me is direct and bright. "There's a meeting tonight, Katie. We're having a singing group perform. A family. They're very good. Maybe you could come. We're also having Senator Bruno Sherman here. He's not going to speak, but he'll be meeting people. He's a Christian, and we want to see him hang onto his seat in the senate this year. He can use all the help he can get, maybe even a little write-up in your magazine."

I nod, edging to the door. "That sounds fascinating, but I'm busy tonight. Maybe some other time. Thank you, Pastor. God bless."

Suppressing a chuckle, he says, "Yeah, you, too." He leans forward. "Take care."

"Sure. Bye." This parting seems to be taking forever. He follows me out onto the patio beyond the double doors of the church with more chit-chat. It makes me nervous. Is he lonely? Does he just like to talk?

On a whim, I turn to him. "Oh. I almost forgot. Do you know of any ministries around here that help children or young people in need? Like a Bible camp, or a ranch and school?"

He looks up from the phone in his hand, startled. "Yeah. There are a couple around here like that. I volunteer at one of them. You want the names? Addresses? I can get that for you. Come to the office. It won't take but a minute."

"I'll wait out here. I'm expecting a call and the reception is better outside." I wander around the outside of the building and snap a couple of pictures. When he returns, he hands me a piece of paper, brushing his hand against mine as he does.

"I listed the ones that came to mind right away. There's more, of course. You might check out a ministry they have in Colville. It's a rescue mission type of thing. Might be good for a couple of pictures." He's gazing at me with a strange light in his green eyes. "Where are you staying?"

"With some friends," I say vaguely. He's crazy if he thinks I'm going to divulge that sort of information. I glance at the paper.

"Thanks so much. See you later." With that, I turn abruptly and stride to the van, sensing him watching me all the way across the parking lot.

I stop at the service station in Kettle Falls. Sitting in Herman, my van, I look at his list. There's the Columbia Valley Bible Camp, ten miles south of Kettle Falls. Second on the list is Suncrest Orchard that (he notes) employs young people from overseas. It's south of the town on the river. The third on the list is Columbia River Ranch and School, north of Kettle Falls on Northport-Flat Creek Road. The fourth is the Youth Center, run by Bill Waters. And the last one is the Cup of Love Ministries, downtown Colville.

Since it's nearly five in the evening, I decide to call it a day. I return to Colville and pull into Don and Jane's house. The back door is unlocked, but they are not home. Strange. No note. There's no dinner in the oven or on the stove.

I decide to check out a restaurant that's located near City Hall. I order chicken cordon bleu with a salad and a glass of wine. After I eat, I drive around town, getting the lay of the land.

After about thirty minutes of that, I wonder what I'm going to do with the rest of the evening. Then it occurs to me. I have time to go to that meeting at the church in Kettle Falls. Maybe I can meet Senator Bruno Sherman. It might lead somewhere. If this gang I'm after is connected with big politics, there has to be someone at the head of it that's highly placed.

The church is moderately full when I get there at 7:05pm. I choose a pew towards the back and listen to the music. The singing family is made up of nine people – Mom and Dad and seven children, and they do a good job with Country Gospel and Bluegrass selections.

At the end of the service, Pastor Dale grips my hand eagerly and says he's so glad I came.

My attention is drawn to a tall, dark-haired man who is standing near the door, pumping hands. The politicians I've known are not people I'd trust, but this man seems honest and genuine.

He looks me directly in my eyes as he shakes my hand. "Katie McDonald, so pleased to meet you. Are you from this area?"

I chuckle as he releases my hand. "No, actually, I've just moved here. Looking for work. I'm doing some freelance writing and photography for a magazine, but that doesn't pay the bills."

He laughs like I've told a joke. I like the way his eyes sparkle when he laughs. "No, I don't suppose it does. Hey, have you registered to vote? I've got some cards here." He hands me one. "About that job. Are you interested in a secretarial position?"

"Yeah, I've done that. What're you thinking of?"

"Excuse me a moment." He turns to greet a couple who are leaving. Then he comes back to me. His attention is flattering, I have to admit, and I'm not usually bowled over by a show.

"I've got partnership in a place up on the Columbia River. Maybe you've heard of it? Columbia River Ranch and School."

A little shiver descends my spine. "Oh, yes. I've heard of it. So, there's a secretarial job open there?"

He nods, greets several more people, and comes back to me. "Yes, Miss McDonald. I'm flying to Olympia tonight, but here's a card from the place." He digs one out of his shirt pocket. I'm surprised he has them so handy, but then he might be trying to get support for the place. "Tell them I sent you." He leans toward me. I catch a whiff of his aftershave. "It might pull some weight."

"Thank you, sir. I'll go up tomorrow. And if I get the job, will I be seeing you there?"

"Oh, most definitely, Katie. I'm there whenever I can make it."

"Well, thank you again. I can't say how much I appreciate it." I lift the card in kind of a salute and smile.

I make my way out to the van and drive back to Jane's house.

There's a light in the windows, and when I come inside, I'm greeted by Jane in the kitchen, bustling about with flour on her hands.

"Oh, Katie, dear! I'm so sorry we were out this evening. I forgot to tell you we had an engagement. It was an anniversary party for some friends of ours. How's your leg? Here, sit down, and I'll get you a cup of coffee."

I plunk down obediently and let her serve me. "It's hurting, but it's okay." She serves me a warm peanut butter cookie fresh from the oven. "What are you making these for?"

"Oh, I always take some to the Youth Center when I work down there. The kids love them, but I have to keep them away from Bill."

"So, you don't take in kids to stay?" I probe gently, watching her.

She shakes her head and takes a sip of coffee. "No, but we're connected with an organization that does. Some of them are foreign kids. It's a renovated house where the young people can stay for a while until they can be placed." She rubs her forehead. "Huh. It's funny I never thought of that before. Completely slipped my mind."

I wonder if it did, or is she covering for someone? Is she truly the sweet innocent that she portrays? I shake my head. This is getting to me. I'm beginning to suspect everyone, even my angel.

I figure I'd better get to bed. I thank her for the coffee and cookie and stand, favoring my wounded leg.

She turns to me. "There are a lot of details about this that you haven't considered. I think we need to bring you up to speed. I mean, it would be unfair for you to be in the dark." She stares at me. There's an evil gleam in her eyes that is so out of character that my knees almost buckle.

"I ... I don't know what you mean."

"They're close on your tail, Gina Lindsey. You've blown your cover for the second time. Or is this the third? How many chances do you think you get? You're finished." Carefully she sets the pan of cookies down and reaches into her apron pocket.

Suddenly I'm looking down the barrel of a Smith and Wesson double-action .45 semi-automatic pistol. And it's pointed directly at my heart.

Chapter 30

Between the Fence and the Guns

June 10th

"There's lots of ways out of here, you know." Chance said, keeping his voice low.

"Oh, yeah? I'd like to hear one, if you'd care to share your great wisdom with me."

Chance smiled. He didn't have to look at Ramone to know the man was teasing. Since his rescue of the big Mexican, he knew he'd gained a friend for life. Which didn't look to be too long, considering their present circumstances.

They'd left the shelter of the garage, walked in the shallow creek, and climbed a low hill, hiding behind a fringe of bushes where they could see the ranch buildings below. Chance shifted, easing his cramped foot, and peered through the foliage. The sun climbed higher in the sky. It was getting hot. Sweat slid down his face.

He wiped it off with an impatient hand. "We have options. None of them ain't too good, but we got 'em."

They'd seen Grant's people form into teams, bring up a four-wheeler, and load their guns. A man took the forward position, his eyes on the ground. Their tracker. Probably the teacher of that class.

Chance figured they didn't have much more than half an hour lead on them. He and Ramone had to keep moving.

Ramone pointed down the hill. The team of hunters had already tracked them from the cabin to the Lodge. "We don't got time for a long conversation. Better fill me in on your ideas, cuz we have to decide pretty quick what we're goin' to do."

Chance nodded. "Well, we could return to the Lodge, hide out in a closet somewhere, and hop a ride with someone leaving. Or we could stow ourselves on that garbage truck they got sitting down there. I haven't seen them take it out yet, but it's getting full of cans. Not a pleasant way to escape, but it might throw the tracker off and get us out of here."

Ramone rubbed his bristly chin. "We don't know when they're goin' to take it to the dump. It could sit there for another couple of days. We need a fast way outta here, and I mean fast." He cracked his knuckles one by one. The men below were getting closer.

"I agree. That's the big fault in that plan. We could also waylay two of those guards, take their uniforms, and get out the front gate easy as you please."

Ramone got to his knees. "Sounds good. But not too practical."

Chance nodded and stood slowly, keeping hunched over. He figured that unless someone had glasses trained on this exact spot, they were safe enough with the brush and tree cover. He strove to sound casual and in control of the situation, but he knew they were facing something that would try them both to extreme limits.

He cleared his throat. "Another option is to fade back, far back, and wait it out. We got water and some food. We can follow the creek and hope the tracker can't see our trail."

Ramone groaned as he struggled to his feet. "Thought you said they'd expect us to do that. They want us to run so they can get some real huntin' time in. Human huntin'."

"I know I said that. But it is an option. They're on the alert at the main gate. Have you noticed the double guards? The guns? Getting out that way would be highly unlikely right now."

"Getting out any way is highly unlikely, *amigo*."

Chance grimaced. "I know. But we have to try. Another option is to fall a tree over the fence and climb out."

Ramone took a gulp of water, hitched up his pants, and paced a few feet to the brow of the hill. "What's it to be? I'm a mite nervous about them guys who know how to track."

The men below emerged from the Lodge. One of the guys studied the ground. It wouldn't be long before they headed to the creek. Chance met Ramone's eyes. Fear emanated from Ramone like a wave of heat.

Chance gripped his arm. "I'm not ready to give up yet. Let's do this. What do you say?"

Ramone's slow smile split his face. "I'm with you, buddy."

"All right. We stay together. We run like crazy. We keep low. We use our wits."

Chance led off in a northwesterly direction, aiming for a stand of pines and firs that offered some shelter. He sniffed. Smoke. It was either someone's campfire or a forest fire. He prayed it wasn't that. But he couldn't think about a forest fire now.

He led the way toward the denser part of the woods, following a creek that wound through the terrain.

It was a grueling race, but somehow Ramone kept up with him. As the sun climbed higher, and its heat increased, Chance paused after scrambling up a steep hill. He looked back and realized Ramone was not behind him. Backtracking, he found the man lying across a log. The brush was thick in this area, and so were the flies.

He rolled Ramone off the log to the ground. His face was splotched white and red. Blood oozed through his shirt. Chance stripped it off and saw the wounds. His heart fell to his boots.

Why hadn't Ramone told him he was wounded in the chest? It looked like Ramone's captors used a whip on him and practiced with their knives, too. The cuts were red and oozing, and should be stitched, but Chance would have to do what he could until they could get better treatment.

Chance retrieved the First Aid kit from his backpack and used all the antiseptic cream, gauze, and tape on the wounds. Ramone groaned as he worked.

After it was done, Ramone opened his eyes. "This is a bummer for you, Chance," he said with a glimmer of a smile. "Better leave me and make your escape. I ain't worth spit to you." He winced as he moved to a more comfortable position.

Chance shook his head. "No way. I'm not leaving you behind. We're getting out of this, and you're coming with me, whether you want to or not. We'll rest here for a spell. The tracker took a while to sort out our trail when we went in the water. Rest here. I'll be back."

With a pat on Ramone's shoulder, Chance climbed the hill again, going higher this time to a big rock that jutted out from the top. If he could get up there without showing himself, he could see where their pursuers were and plan their next move. Would Ramone be able to run? Should they just give themselves up?

He brushed these thoughts aside and mounted the rock. There, lying flat on his stomach, he studied the layout below him. The creek wound in and out of willow and laurel bushes at the base of the hill. It was almost dry, but there was enough water still flowing to drink.

Beyond that was a stand of pine and deciduous trees – mainly maples and elders. A meadow separated the trees to the southwest. He gazed north where a forested knob led to barren, low-brush country and canyons. He'd seen some of that when they ran the perimeter of the fence. Just below his position was the tangle of brush and trees that he and Ramone had struggled past.

The fence enclosed it all. It was impenetrable, hot and wired, topped with cameras and guard towers. It was like a living enemy, a lurking menace, an evil that breathed down his neck.

He spotted the dirt road they'd run the other day, skirting the property.

Down below, Grant and his men appeared. They were rounding the hill on the far side of the meadow, following the route he and Ramone had taken through the brush and the creek. They hadn't all come. Maybe Grant had allowed only those who'd paid a higher fee to join in the hunt.

Chance couldn't see them clearly from this distance, but he thought he recognized Ostranger, Rodgers, and another man. After them came two others. He noted that Rasha led the charge after Grant.

He watched them until they dipped out of sight in one of the many gullies that crisscrossed the area. Grant led the cavalcade mounted on a four-wheeler. They all carried rifles. Chance could tell from the way they progressed across the terrain that they meant business and weren't taking prisoners. When he and Ramone were murdered, Grant would probably call it a hunting accident. More than likely, he had the local police in his pocket.

Chance wiped the sweat from his forehead and went back to Ramone who had dozed in the scant shade of a tiny fir.

"Let's go," Chance said tersely, shrugging on the backpack. It was late in the afternoon. The sun was making its long arc toward the western hills. He had hoped to be out of here by now. Hoped for a miracle. But they were still on the run.

How much longer could they go?

Ramone opened his eyes and sat up with a moan. "Oh, darn. I thought it was a bad dream." He shook his head. "Did you see 'em?"

"Yeah. Maybe a mile off, in that meadow by the creek. The fence is close, maybe a hundred yards to the north. If we circle the hill, going west, we'd come out at the fence on the far side. Then we'd be forced to go south to the compound. I don't like getting boxed into a corner."

Ramone stood. "No, me neither. What are the options, then?"

"Well, we could go around the other way, east, and stay in the back forty. Don't know what's over there, except what I saw when we jogged it. I don't remember much. Dense forest, rolling hills, canyons. Lots of brush. We might have a chance that way, but it's hard going. You up to it?" He glanced at his friend who was finishing off one of the energy bars he'd found in the backpack.

"Yup. I'm up to it. Lead the way."

Chance nodded. They gathered everything, even the wrapper from the bar, brushed out their tracks, and headed east. He sensed this was the way the men wanted them to go. Again, he was being forced into doing what Grant wanted them to do.

They spent the next two hours climbing up and down gullies, fighting brush, and swatting flies, staying only a mile or so ahead of the relentless men at the backs.

Suddenly Chance stopped. "No."

Ramone bumped into him. Chance said, "I'm not going to be herded so they can play their games. We're going to do something they don't figure." He climbed a tree stump and craned his neck, looking back where he supposed Grant and the others were.

"See those big rocks over there? They're heading that way, and it'll force them to swing to the south. They'll come up the hill like we did. I know they'll go that way because they're following our tracks. Well, let's give them a little surprise. Let's circle back toward the fence like we're goin' where they want us to. Then we'll head south, straight for the ranch."

He jumped off the stump. "We'll have to fight through that brush again, but at least we won't be cornered like a treed coon back there in the canyons. What do you think?"

Ramone shrugged. He dropped his head and shuffled his feet. "Just keep goin'. If I have to stop, I'd rather be sittin' down somewhere's so I can rest."

Chance rubbed his forehead, thinking, what will we do when we come in range of those big guns and Grant's specially trained soldiers at the ranch? Can Ramone outrun them if it comes to that? Chance didn't voice his thoughts out loud. Ramone didn't need that kind of negative thinking right now.

They would have to risk going back to the ranch to search for a way of escape. It was better than being herded into an untenable position where they could be picked off at ease.

"If we can get back to the compound, we'll be able to find a way out. Remember all my ideas about that?" Chance grinned, but the big man didn't respond. "Well, anyway, let's get past that expert tracker."

With the tangy smell of pine trees on a hot day in his nose, he led out, creeping to a large rock, and from there, to a stand of laurel bushes. The men and vehicles came from behind, over the rise to the north, not more than a hundred yards away.

Chance couldn't crackle through the brush like they had going up. He put his finger to his lips and began the painstaking journey. They crossed the creek and threw water on their faces. But they wouldn't drink it because of the disease in the water, not unless they were dying of thirst.

Climbing the bank, Chance led out again, choosing his path carefully. Grant and the others should be at the place they'd rested. Maybe some of them were going to the top of the hill right now. He and Ramone had to stay under cover, for Grant would have glasses. Any slight movement would betray their position, and then it would be finished, and they would be dead.

He paused under the boughs of a big pine, mopping his brow. Ramone slumped down beside him on the ground, groaning a little. His wounds were bleeding again. Chance squatted beside him and offered him a drink, then an orange and a piece of bread.

He ate a piece of bacon, but it did little to ease his hunger. Ramone finished off the orange without comment. He seemed to be in a daze.

"All right. Let's keep moving." Chance stood. If they were going to get out of here alive, they had to keep moving. Because of the heat, Ramone's wounds, and the tracker, they couldn't tarry. Not even if Grant had his binoculars trained on them. He glanced at his watch. *5:15pm.*

With the prickly feeling that someone was watching, Chance led out again, this time along the creek, following its meandering path through the brambles and bushes. They were in a ravine that had been carved out by the creek, but eventually they would emerge into a wide meadow. And they would have no cover there.

After a half-hour's trek, Chance paused for breath, brushing off the flies that swarmed about his face. This place seemed familiar. A big pine. A meadow. Aspens along the creek. Thick bushes everywhere. Yes, they'd been this way. If that was true, they were south of the hill he'd climbed. South and a little east.

They only had to get up to the ridge above them, veer to the west a bit, fight through lots of brush, and they would arrive back at the compound. He hoped that everyone there would not have the welcome mat out for them.

"C'mon, my friend," he said to Ramone who was nodding, half asleep. "We don't have far to go. Can you make it? I sure can't carry you, and you're dead meat if you stay here for long."

Chance hefted the backpack onto his shoulders. It was a lot lighter now. He wondered what would happen in the next few hours. Well, God would show them what to do when they got back to the ranch. He hoped.

The route he'd chosen seemed full of obstacles. He tried to move carefully, but found that was impossible. Swarms of gnats and flies buzzed their faces and bit any exposed flesh as they forced their way through dense undergrowth. The sun dipped to the west, and the breeze dropped. It was silent, still, and muggy hot. His mouth was as dry as a cotton ball, and his precious body fluid ran down his back in sweat. He longed for another drink but told himself he had to wait.

It was all he could do to lift his feet for another step. Suddenly he knew he couldn't do this. He was at a dead end. And if he was at the end, what must Ramone be feeling?

Then, suddenly, he thought of something he'd been trained in the FBI. Set a pattern. Do the pattern. *Twenty-five steps. Breathe. Rest. Twenty-five more steps. Breathe. Rest.* It was a pattern.

He started out, and it seemed to work.

He prayed he could keep a straight line and was afraid that he'd veer too far to the right or to the left. They only had one chance at this. If they went too far to the right, they'd be boxed in by the fence. If they swung too far to the left, they'd be heading straight to the shooting range, a situation he didn't want to contemplate.

Yet it was hard to keep a straight line in the brush because he couldn't see the way ahead. He plowed through it for maybe twenty feet and came to a ravine. Sliding down it, hating the clatter of small stones, he waited for Ramone. Then he climbed the other side, helping Ramone up the steep part.

When they got to the top, he started off across the meadow, keeping to a row of low bushes. Suddenly he stopped, and froze as the sound, *rat-a-tat!* drifted to him on the evening breeze. He looked over his shoulder at Ramone.

"The Gatling. The big gun." Fear clamped down hard on his heart. His legs seemed rooted to the spot. "I wonder what they're aimin' at."

Ramone snorted. "Rabbits."

"Yeah, right."

Were they getting close to the back of the firing field? He rehearsed the facts he'd learned about the gun. The Gatling could fire 6000 rounds a minute, enough to cut down a small army, and the range was at least 600 yards. He wiped sweat from his forehead. They might be in range this minute.

He doubted if Grant's men would use the Howitzer. It was not designed for small targets that dodged in and out of brush. He suspected that gun was purely for show. For killing two men, the hunters could pick them off at their leisure when he and Ramone were trapped like treed bobcats.

Grant and his men had time on their hands – they also had the men, weapons, and ammunition. When those who tracked them got tired, they could call out fresh men.

Chance had nothing except his faith and his dogged determination to stay alive. *Would that be enough?* He shook his head as he gave a hand to Ramone to help him get over a fallen log. Time would tell.

Yet time was in short supply, too.

Chapter 31

Where Angels Fear to Tread

June 10th

I stand in the middle of Jane's kitchen, staring at her like I'm frozen, my heart racing.

There's no doubt in my mind that this sweet lady I'd called my angel will pull the trigger on her gun, and that the last thing I see on this earth will be her cold blue eyes.

But I'm trying to grasp why. Why didn't she kill me the first night while I slept peacefully in her guest room? Or does she want to find out what I know?

The clock strikes the hour, going through its little ditty. 10 o'clock. I clench my teeth. Her hand never wavers, and her expression never changes. Little furrows crease her brow. Her eyes glimmer with something like eagerness, and her mouth turns down in a grimace of hate.

I take a deep breath. "Well. This seems to alter things considerably. I guess I'll have to find another place of residence." I'm stalling for time, trying to think up a plan to rescue myself.

None leaps to mind. Or even crawl in.

She doesn't smile. "Sit down." The pistol motions to the stool by the breakfast bar. "Keep your hands on the counter, please."

I grope for the counter, never taking my eyes from hers. "Yes, ma'am. How about your husband? Is he in on this, too?"

"I'm the one who asks the questions. You will sit there and answer like a civilized human being, if you know how to be one." Her upper lip curls on the last words.

211

"Oh. I suppose what you're doing is the height of civilization."

She doesn't like that but ignores it. The cookies smell delicious from where they are cooling on the counter. Classical music drifts in from the living room. She stares at me. "Who do you work for?"

"I ... uh, what I told you," I begin, thinking I'll repeat my cover story. But then I remember she called me by my real name. "For the Spokane Police Department. I'm a captain of a team of officers with the Special Investigative Unit. But you know that, don't you?"

I return her glare, getting angry that she's drilling me like this. "If you know my real name, you're stalling for time. Why don't you cut to the chase and get down to the real fun of the evening? Are you going to torture me for the information?"

"That's not the point, Gina. Don't play with me. I don't want to call in the big guys. Just give me what I need to know, and I'll let you return to your little office. You're not cut out for this stuff, you know. You shouldn't have taken this on. You're not tough enough. Or smart enough." She laughs. It isn't a nice sound.

I sigh and roll my eyes, lifting my hands in a gesture of exasperation. I hope I'm making a good show, but her comments about my abilities cut deeply. "All right. Just tell me what you want to know."

About that time, Don comes wandering into the kitchen, oblivious of the little drama we're having. I tense, ready to do something if the opportunity arises, but he merely strolls to the kitchen sink, gets a drink of water, nods to me, and turns to leave.

My heart sinks. If only he would step between me and that gun, then I'd ...

He does! He reaches across the counter for a bowl of candies, partially blocking the pistol in Jane's hand. I dive behind the breakfast bar, fish my Glock from its holster, and arrive below her on the floor a couple of heartbeats later, pointing my own weapon at her.

"Drop it!" I'm panting. It wasn't easy to maneuver between the stool legs, fetch my gun, and get into position, but I can out-wriggle Houdini any day when I'm in a tight spot.

Jane places the gun on the counter as I rise. Casually she looks at her husband. "That was pretty good, wasn't it? What would you give her? B plus?"

I stare at them as they turn to me. Gone is the evil expression from Jane's face. Now it's wreathed in smiles, as is Don's.

He shakes his head. "Oh, no. I'd say an A. Definitely. Never saw anyone move so fast in my life."

I take a deep breath but don't lower the Glock. "Okay. What's going on here? If you don't mind, would you slide that pistol across to me? Slowly."

She complies, her smile widening. I lay my left hand on her gun but hold my Glock firmly in my right, trained on them. "May I see some ID?"

She nods to Don who opens his wallet to display an ID card with his picture and a number. Her card isn't far away. She fishes a leather case from her purse and shows it to me.

I slip my Glock in my shoulder holster, and Don takes the other pistol. My voice is wobbly when I say, "Okay. Mind answering my question? What's going on?"

Jane lifts the cookies from the pan to the counter. Don pours me another cup of coffee.

"I'm surprised you didn't figure it out," Jane says. "We're your cover agents, honey. FBI."

I gape at them. "You're kidding."

"No." Don's smile widens as his eyes twinkle. "Sorry Jane had to put you through that little test, but they like us to do that to new agents. Just to keep them on their toes."

"Oh. Is that so? They don't trust someone from the SPD?"

She laughs and hands me a cookie. "Here you go, dear. You deserve this. Don and I have been agents for most of our married lives. We wanted to make sure you can do the job."

"Were you following me the whole time since I hit town?"

He nods. "More or less. We knew about the apartment and kept an eye on that, and when you showed up, we covered you all the way to the Youth Center."

"You might have taken out the guy who gave me this." I hold up my leg.

Jane moves to the living room, and we follow her.

Don says, "Sorry about that, Gina, but I was too far removed from you. I couldn't stop it. We decided to keep our identity quiet, but when we saw you wandering around town this evening, we thought we'd better spring our surprise and collaborate."

"Thank you very much." My tone is dry. I'm outraged that they would pull a trick and scare me like that. "You're not fooling me. That's not the usual way the FBI conducts business. Why am I different? Is there something you're keeping from me? I hope we can be totally candid because I can't go on if we aren't."

Jane settles in her chair and pulls out her knitting. "Totally candid." She shoots me a piercing look like a thrown dart. "Okay. Undercover isn't a walk in the park. I've done it a time or two and wouldn't like to do it again. We had to be sure you're the real thing. That you know your stuff. You're going to be in a lot of danger."

"Yeah. I know. I'm probably going where angels fear to tread. But why me? Why are they sending in a rookie like me?"

Don answered with a hint of a smile. "Well, you asked for it, for one thing. You have the passion and heart for it. And you're not a rookie, not in the least. You're the best officer the SPD could come up with. We asked for their best."

I knew this was no off-hand, pretty compliment. It warmed my heart while it froze my soul.

"Now you *are* scaring me," I say, tucking my feet up under me and drawing an afghan over my lap. "So, what do we do now?"

Don stood. "I think we'd better go down to the basement. More private down there."

"Is that where you keep your prisoners?" I smile, unfold my legs, and follow him.

Jane calls after me, "Yes, dear. And it's where we torture them. Don will show you." She laughed.

For the next two hours, we bend over a large table in the basement with maps and papers, pencils and calculators spread out in front of us. From the list Jane had written and from the one Pastor Dale gave me, we compile the "top five" most likely suspects and organizations that I can target.

Don studies the list. His glasses reflect the lamp light, giving him a sort of spaced-out look. "What do you have that I don't know? We know you went north that first day you were here."

"You mean you didn't track my car? You're falling down on the job, Don." I enjoy teasing him but relent with a wink. "I went up the Columbia River, just south of where I was shot at that day. I was checking out a place that was advertised as a farm and a Bible camp, except I didn't see much evidence of a Bible camp. "

He studies the map where we'd placed little stars on all the likely locations. "Where exactly?"

I pinpoint it for him. He draws a neat star at the place. "Was there a fence?"

"Yes, around the garden, but I didn't see one around the whole property. There might be more to it on the next level down toward the river, though."

"Okay. And what about tonight? What did you find out?"

"Do you know Pastor Dale Montgomery?"

He shakes his head. "Heard of him. Haven't gone to one of their services, though. They get a little carried away there. Too loud and wild for my tastes." He stretches. "Want more coffee?"

"No, thanks. Anyway, I understand they run a day school. I asked about live-in students, and he said they didn't have the facilities for that. But there's something about him that made me suspicious. He's a little too friendly, for one thing. He was anxious to talk. Seemed lonely or something." I stop, feeling my face get warm. "Well, you know what I mean."

"But that doesn't mean he's ..."

"I know. I guess my sensors are super-active right now, and I'm picking up all kinds of things. I met Senator Bruno Sherman tonight. He was at the church trying to garner votes."

Don straightens and bends his gaze on me like I'd told him I'd found the Crown Jewels hidden away under one of the pews. "What do you know about him?"

"Not much, except that he's a senator. Could he be our guy?"

Don shakes his head and rises to pace the room as he talks. "We've taken him to the cleaners, and unless he's paid off an awful lot of people and fixed the records and books, he's squeaky clean."

"I thought there was a scandal that he padded votes to get his seat."

"No luck there, either. And no proof."

"Well, the interesting thing is that he offered me a job at his place up there on the river."

"Really!" It was Jane who'd descended the stairs quietly and came into the room. "What place is that, dear?"

I check my phone because I'd made a note of the name. "Columbia River Ranch and School. On the Northport-Flat Creek Road. Just north of where I was shot. Perfect location. Do you know the place?"

They exchange a glance. Don shakes his head. "We've heard of it but haven't checked it out."

"Okay." I can't keep the smug tone from my voice. "First thing tomorrow, I'm going to apply for the job. After that, I'll get to work on these other leads. What are you guys going to do?"

Jane sighs. "Keep the homes fires burning."

I knew there was a lot more she and Don did, even though they were semi-retired, but I let it slide. She went on in a dry voice, "I'll be busy trying to keep up with *you*. Well, now we need to get to bed. We can't keep late hours like you young people can. C'mon, Don." She straightens the mess on the table and grins at me. "Enough torture for one night?"

Don shakes his head, his eyes wide behind his glasses. "Hey, we can't stop now. She was about to tell me all she knows."

His chuckle grates on my nerves. Like I said, I'm extremely tired, my leg hurts, and I want to go to bed and forget this mess, this fear that tightens my heart and strangles my throat. Give me one tiny excuse, and I'll quit in a heartbeat.

But then I remember Sanora.

"I gave you all I have. You'll have to be satisfied with that. Yeah, I think I've had it." I push back and allow them to return all the papers to the files.

Jane pats my shoulder. "Okay. Breakfast at 7am. You've got a busy day ahead."

I groan. This is like being in school again.

As I drift off to sleep that night, I can't keep the dates, names, faces, and places from floating through my head, all mixed up like a futuristic Alice in Wonderland adventure.

But this is no adventure.

This is real life, and I know that if I'm going to be a small part in bringing this organization down and help save Sanora and children like her, I'd better roll over and get some sleep.

Something tells me I'm going to need it.

Chapter 32

Blondie and Red Beard

Forward Guard Ranch, June 11th

Chance awoke, not even knowing he'd slept. Dawn was creeping through the darkness. The last thing he remembered was falling back against the clay sides of the shallow cave where he and Ramone found refuge last night.

It seemed a nightmare, fleeing through those canyons on the northeast side of the property, trying to out-run the men with guns, fearing that they'd be made into mincemeat if they came into the range of the Gatling. Finally, he'd found a shallow gully, out of the wind, and a cave opening in the cliff wall. There they'd gone to ground. They crawled in, drank a swallow of water, and fell asleep.

Evidently Grant and his goons had decided to get some rest, too.

Now he crawled out, awakening Ramone as he did, and stood, stretching. A rising wind lifted the tree branches and stirred the bushes. It wouldn't be long before Grant got up here with his men and weapons. The Gatling lay not too far in front of their position to the south.

He faced the same dilemma as he had last night. Which way? Not much of a choice. He didn't care to die either way, facing Grant or the guns. In fact, when it came right down to it, he didn't care to die at all.

"Mornin'," he said to Ramone. "How ya doing?"

The big man grunted. He moved his limbs like he was trying them out. "Not bad. Could be worse. Any grub left?"

Chance dug in the backpack and produced a piece of bacon, the last one, two slices of squished bread, and an orange. "This is the last of it. Should we eat it all in the hope that we'll get out of here in a couple of hours? Or should we hoard it?"

Ramone eyed it hungrily. "Aw, let's eat it all. What if they get us? All that good food would go to waste."

"Okay. It's your funeral." Chance grinned. "Sorry. Didn't mean that." He bowed his head, said a short prayer, and doled out the food. "Water's low. A couple of swallows left." His mouth was so dry he wondered how he would get the bread down. He divided the orange carefully and gave half to Ramone. The juice tasted good.

Chance closed his eyes and savored this moment of peace before they had to get moving again. Gina's face danced before his eyes as he leaned against the dirt cliff.

What would she be doing about now? He glanced at his watch. *5:17am*. Probably eating breakfast or going for a run. Maybe she'd be taking an early morning ride on her mare with her long, red hair flying in the wind. She'd be laughing. Green eyes dancing.

"Hey, bub, we gotta get movin'!" Ramone jostled his elbow. His tone was low and strained like he'd used the last ounce of his strength to say the words. "I'm not sittin' around and lettin' those jerks back there shoot me like a badger in its den."

They both stood as they heard vehicles grinding up the hills. Grant was out and about already. It would be a long day.

Chance gathered up the remains of their scanty meal, stowing everything in the backpack. "Sure thing, my friend. If we move forward, we're going to get cut down with that Gatling they're so fond of. I'm sure someone's there, even as early as it is. If we veer to the left or right, they're going to close in on us with the dogs, and we'll get trapped at the fence. Can't go back. Where do you suggest we go?"

Ramone grunted and took a sip from the water bottle. "It's your call. You walk, and I'll follow."

Chance led out, going straight south, or as directly as he could, heading toward the ranch. His path would lead through the dense

219

jungle of brush and swamp in the lowlands before they climbed the last ridge and dropped down to the ranch. He figured it would take over an hour.

After about thirty minutes, they broke from the brush. As Ramone rested with his back against a pine tree, Chance climbed a small incline and gazed around. His heart fell to the toes of his tired feet. From here, the tops of some of the buildings at the compound were visible – the Lodge, the equipment building, and the dormitory for the soldiers.

It was the view of the foreground that made his knees weak and his mouth go dry. As he suspected, they were at the far end of the firing field. He could see the small building where they kept the ammunition, and he could barely make out the stands where they stood to shoot.

Closer, below his perch, was the demolished car they'd played with the other day. He and Ramone were in range. As he stood there, the gun rattled to life, and a round of fire came their way.

The Gatling.

He dropped. Had he been spotted or were they firing for the fun of it? Had Grant radioed the direction he was herding them? Chance didn't know and didn't care. They were going to die. He knew it. Tasted the sour tang of it in his mouth.

He shook his head to dislodge the thought. Not like this. *Please God, don't let us die this way!*

It was about that time that men's voices erupted from the bushes behind him. Grant and his men were closing the distance. Squeezing them forward, right into the line of fire.

Chance rubbed his forehead. If they tarried here, not wanting to face the gunfire below, Grant and his troop would pick them off from behind.

He sank to the ground and crawled to Ramone. "You ready to die? I'm askin', cuz unless a miracle comes our way, that's what I see in our near future."

Ramone pulled himself upright and groaned. "Uh. I'm not keen on dyin' just yet, Chance. Got any other options?"

"Heck, I'm out of options. I know you pray, Ramone, but do you know Jesus? I mean, personally?"

Ramone snorted and straightened, shooting Chance a disgusted look. "You have a thing about that, don't you? You know what? You just set here and talk to yourself about religion, cuz I'm tired of eatin' your dust, and I don't want to die."

"I'm tired of this, too." Chance stifled a groan and peered down the hill again.

Ramone lifted his head and sniffed. "Why'd you lead us straight back to the big guns, you idiot? Let's do somethin'. I'm not finished yet, and if they want to use the guns on us, well, they're goin' to have to hit a running target."

Chance didn't like being called an idiot, but at least he'd gotten Ramone riled. And he didn't put much hope in the fact that the men down there were poor marksmen. After taking a sip of water, and handing it to Ramone, he stowed the bottle in the backpack.

Ramone started out first. Chance was surprised to see him taking off in that long stride of his. It seemed he'd gotten his second wind. But how long would it last? Long enough? As he followed behind Ramone toward the treacherous gunfire down below, he could only hope that God would hear his cries and would help them.

But they hadn't gone more than a quarter of a mile, angling southwest, when a round of wicked gunfire seared the air and bullets zinged past his head. He dropped to the ground, flat down, telling himself they were firing randomly. Surely, they hadn't been seen.

But they had. Of course, they had.

Now they heard the men behind them, hot on the chase. Chance figured they only had a lead of about a hundred yards. They were in a gully, partially shielded for the moment from all sides.

Chance wiped his forehead. "I'd like to give them a little surprise just to make the game more interesting. What do you think we should do?" The skin on his face stretched painfully when he tried to smile.

Ramone shrugged. "I dunno. I guess we keep runnin' and hope for something to happen."

Chance shook his head. "Nope. We gotta be intentional. Think. What can we do?"

A man's voice, loud and clear, echoed from under the trees where they had stood just minutes before. "We know you're over there," Grant called on a loudspeaker. "Come out, and we'll make a deal. You're not in any danger, and you'll save us a lot of time and trouble if you come out now. I bet you're starved. I happen to know they're serving steaks for lunch. You're thirsty, too. We have lots of water. We even have some beer. C'mon over. We won't hurt you."

There was silence. Chance thought of the buffet table and closed his eyes. "Steady," he said softly to Ramone. He fought the urge to give himself up. In training he'd learned that's a natural response to extreme stress.

Ramone groaned. "Don't worry. I know their game. Dinner will be hot lead, served up by the force of the Gatling. Does he think we're fools?"

"Probably." Chance withdrew a smooth silvery object from his pocket and held it in his hand. "Well, I figure it's time to give them some work. We've been too easy on them. Ready to do some flat-out sprinting?"

Ramone swung his head around and stared at him. "You got a plan? If so, I'd appreciate it if you'd share it with me. They're gonna burst out any second from those trees over there." He mopped his brow and edged away, further down the gully.

"Hold on. I got a little trick here that might give us an edge." Chance squatted. "Now when I say go, we hightail it out of here like the devils on our tail, you hear me? Head straight for the compound. Go to the back of that big equipment shed where we were before."

Ramone froze and stared at him. Terror was in his eyes, yet he was curious. "What you gonna do?"

Chance grinned. "Watch."

He flicked open the cigarette lighter and snapped up a flame. He applied the flame to the dry brush and under-growth around his position, swinging wider and wider in the span of his movements, making sure the grass and bushes caught before he moved on.

In a few seconds, a wall of flame sprang up, fanned by the wind. About thirty feet in length, it was spreading rapidly. Already he could feel the heat of it as it snapped and crackled, feeding hungrily on the dry fuel.

He lurched back to Ramone, watching the fire over his shoulder. Yes, it was going in the right direction. Straight for Grant and his cronies.

"All right." He faced southwest, stretching out like a runner at the line. "Give it all you got. Go over this here ridge, then straight down to the ranch. We have to run so fast they can't get a sight on us. We have one chance at this, Ramone."

Giving another glance at the growing fire, and hearing a startled yell from the men who followed them, he said, "Run!"

He sprang into action, dashing up the side of the gully in great, leaping strides. At the top, he jumped over a log. The rattle of the Gatling pierced his consciousness as bullets whizzed overhead. He careened down the other side. He continued his flight down the hill, watching his steps so he didn't tumble over a hidden branch or sink his foot in a hole.

Ramone grunted behind him. He was keeping up. Good.

The compound came into view, but they had a lot of terrain to cover yet. He led Ramone to the right so they would be under more cover of trees and bushes. Yet they were still in range of the gun.

Someone over at the Gatling must have seen movement on the hillside because the gun roared to life, blasting shells their way. It could slice through the side of a tank. Chance didn't want to think of what it would do to them.

He hit the dirt. The gun went silent, probably too hot to use for a few seconds. He leaped to his feet, Ramone following his cues. Chance caught the pattern of it – *when the gun spurts hot lead, fall to the ground on your face, when it lets up, run for all you're worth. Fall. Wait. Run again.*

It was a wild dance with death.

They gained half the distance. It was hard to breathe, and his legs felt like sodden noodles. He stumbled. There was a pause from the Gatling. But it started up again, and he knew a rain of deadly bullets were coming their way. *Oh, God! Make this stop!* It seemed like the hundred-yard dash had suddenly turned into a marathon, the marathon from Hell.

Now the brush fire on the hill took precedence. Down below, men were shouting. The gun was silenced as he and Ramone dashed to the finish line.

The place looked deserted. As he approached the buildings, he aimed for a shed that stood on the far outskirts of the ranch. Reaching it, he fell to the ground, gasping. Ramone arrived a second or two later. After regaining his breath, Chance peered around shed. From this vantage point, he saw the back of the garage, and beyond that, the drilling ground and the three small cabins.

Smoke billowed from the far side of the hill. That should keep the hunters off their trail for a while. They wouldn't let it go. The wind might shift, and the ranch buildings would be in danger.

"Good idea ... " Ramone said, breathlessly. "Keep ... those buggers ... busy for ... awhile. Now ... how do we get ... outta here?"

Chance waved for him to follow and jogged to the back of the garage. Crouching when men's voices drew close, he pulled Ramone down beside him and waited behind a barrel. Footsteps thudded past. He peered out as a siren wailed mournfully.

Men poured from the Lodge, running to gather tools and vehicles. Chance used the opportunity when everyone seemed distracted to get to the back of the Quonset equipment building. He indicated an outside faucet to Ramone. "Fill up the water bottles. We're not out of here yet."

In a few minutes, they had a fresh supply of water. They both drank from the faucet and splashed some on their heads. By this time, Chance noted that the men had the fire truck out of the shed. Other vehicles started with a roar of motors. The siren stopped wailing.

Chance waited. He knew Ramone was getting antsy because he heard the man muttering and felt his nervous movements as they hunkered down behind the equipment shed. Not yet ... wait ... wait ... A Voice seemed to be directing Chance, and a Hand seemed to grip his shoulder.

A weird cavalcade of vehicles paraded from the big double doors of the building – pickups, trucks, jeeps, and the fire truck. This was driven by a guard with a stern face and a hook nose.

"Hey! That's the guy who beat me up! Let me at him!" Ramone cracked his knuckles and shifted his body like he was ready to spring into action.

Chance laid a hand on his arm. " You're not going to settle any scores until we're out of here, and I'm safely home. Then you can do what you want. *Comprehendo?"*

Ramone grunted and sagged against the barrel. "I thought you said we was in a hurry. We run like the dickens, now we're sittin' and waitin' again."

Chance grinned and said nothing in reply. "Okay. Careful now. Follow me."

He entered the equipment shed, easing open the rear door, peering inside. Dust filtered through the sunshine coming in from high windows. The big bi-fold front doors were raised.

A voice echoed eerily through the building. "Hey! Load that gear! Let's go!"

With a motion of his hand to Ramone, Chance crouched silently at the back of the building, shielded by rows of shelves that filled the back end of the room.

After a while, he led the way forward on the balls of his feet, choosing each step with care, pausing to peer into the open center area. A jeep sat in the middle, its motor chugging. Two men were busy loading equipment into the back of it. Shovels. Axes. Boxes of something, maybe retardant. Helmets. Boots.

Chance approached warily, keeping low behind the shelves, and made a dash to a stack of tires. The two men who loaded the jeep were dressed in the black uniform of the guards.

Completely focused on their task, they didn't look up or around, and they were not careful about making noise. Which was a good thing, Chance figured, as Ramone didn't have the knack of doing anything very quietly.

The two men threw the last box in and straightened, wiping their foreheads with their sleeves. The older, heavy-set man who seemed to be the leader said something. They climbed in the jeep.

Chance beckoned to Ramone, but he needn't have bothered. Ramone charged ahead and reached the jeep first. In one smooth motion, he grabbed the man in the passenger seat, yanked him out, punched him in the jaw, and was ready for the next guy.

The driver leaped from the other side of the vehicle, ready to fight. Chance didn't let him get his feet set or his arm drawn back into a swing, but waded in and delivered a blow to his chin. It was enough to floor most assailants, but this man only shook it off and bellowed. He was twice Chance's size, in excellent shape, and a trained fighter. His blond hair was long, caught in a pony tail on the back of his neck. Chance thought of him as Blondie.

His face was twisted into an angry mask, and his eyes blazed. "Come on, little girl! Let's see you fight, if you know how!"

Chance stepped back. He looked up in time to see the butt end of a rifle heading his way. He dodged it.

It glanced off his shoulder, spinning him around, but he regained his balance, clenched his teeth against the pain, and dove in close, his fists pumping. He connected, but it was like hitting a brick wall. The man was solid.

226

Chance took two blows to his ribs and decided in a hurry that he didn't want to bear hug Blondie. Backing up, panting, fighting pain and dizziness, Chance spun on his heels and kicked out, connecting with the man's knee.

Blondie went down with a howl of pain.

With the other foot, Chance delivered a blow to the man's head. Or he intended to. But the guard recovered faster than Chance thought possible, and reaching up from his prone position, grabbed Chance's foot and twisted it.

Chance leaped straight up, going with the direction of the twist. He wrenched free of the man's grasp, and landed on the man's throat. Kicked again. This time Blondie went out.

Chance leaned over to rip off his shirt, but he didn't see the man coming from behind.

"Chance! " Ramone screamed.

Chance whirled. His heart fell. A mountain of a man loomed over him. Red beard. Red eyes. Chains dangling from his waist. A huge fist, armed with steel knuckles, was aimed at his throat, a killer move if it connected. The smirk on the man's face proclaimed that he enjoyed his work.

But Chance didn't let him connect.

He dodged under the blow, dancing away. Red Beard swung again. Chance ducked, and in the same instant drove forward, head-butting the man in the face. Blood spurted from his nose. He grunted as his legs crumpled. He hit the floor solidly.

Ramone had his guy down and was pummeling him.

Chance held up a hand. "Don't kill him. Get his uniform and let's go."

He turned to Blondie on the floor and tugged off his shirt. About that time, another guard sprang inside from the front door, full tilt, heading for Ramone who was in the process of denuding his guy. The new assailant gripped a knife.

"Ramone! Watch it!"

Ramone whirled, and at the same time, grabbed a tire iron. Then Chance got busy, too.

It was Red Beard again – he'd scrambled to his feet. He drew a gun from the holster on his belt. Brought it up. Chance kicked it from his hand. "Okay, it's your fists against mine. Let's see what you have."

Red Beard was mad now. Chance liked it that way because he might get sloppy.

The giant swung at Chance's chin. He blocked it with his forearm. Bad move. A tsunami wave of pain swamped his brain. He blinked, trying to focus. Another blow came swiftly. He ducked. It connected with his shoulder, spun him around. The man grabbed him around the neck and shoulders. Strong fingers squeezed his throat.

He was aware that Ramone was alive, that he'd stopped the knife's descent into his chest with a blow with the tire iron and a kick to the man's crotch. But that's all Chance could register because his own assailant was intent on strangling him.

He tried to rear back and head butt again, but the man's arms gave him no room. Red Beard laughed.

Chance couldn't scream. Couldn't call for help. *Ramone! Please, God! Help!* But Ramone was down, felled with a blow to his head.

The strong fingers pressed harder. Roaring filled Chance's ears. Black spots danced across his eyes. He fought the dizziness that swooped with powerful wings over his mind.

The first man he'd taken out was shaking his head and getting to his knees. If Chance didn't do something soon, both he and Ramone would be captured.

This time they would die quickly – and in a lot of pain.

Chapter 33

Deep Cover

June 11th

The Columbia River Ranch and School has an attractive website. It's in the right location for the organization I'm searching for, has a dormitory live-in school, and a large staff of teachers, cooks, maintenance men, and dorm parents, besides volunteers.

At the breakfast table as I crunch Cheerios, I read to Don and Jane from the website.

"The school is a home away from home for at risk children and young adults. We want to give young people a taste of rural living, combined with down-home cooking and experiences of rural life on a farm. Above all, we want to allow the young people to grow and learn in a loving, secure environment."

Jane snorts. "Secure all right." She leans over to look at the pictures.

They reveal a school building, an interesting sports program, a full staff, and dormitories that sparkle with cleanliness and upscale accommodations. In addition to everything else, the school has a shop building where the young people make items for sale.

"The money," the information states, "goes entirely to rescue youngsters from abuse both here and abroad, and to rehabilitate them so they can re-enter life."

I sip my coffee. "If I had a troubled teen, I'd probably look into this school. In fact, it seems unbelievable for a place like this to be stuck out in the middle of nowhere. It must have cost a fortune to build and maintain."

"It isn't that far from town," Don says. "Only an hour or so."

After breakfast, Jane pulls some strings and gets me my new ID faxed to their machine. Now I'm officially Katie McDonald. I tell them that I after I checked out the place, I will try to call them and let them know how it goes.

"Maybe we should come up there on an errand," Don says. "Just to make sure you're okay. If they're in the business we think they are, they might capture you, and you'll disappear from the face of the earth."

I laugh. " I don't think that will happen. You can pray for me, though."

I pack all my belongings in Herman, the old beat-up van, and drive fifteen miles to Kettle Falls, north of Colville, and then, another twenty-five miles up the Northport-Flat Creek Road which follows the Columbia River towards Canada.

I watch the signs and finally turn into the driveway for the ranch.

As I pass underneath the sign that spans the driveway, chills race down my back. *This is it.* I feel it in my bones. But am I ready for it? I don't have Chance to rely on. Or a big sheriff like Mike Cosby from Ekalaka, Montana to cover for me. How much can Jane and Don do? Not much.

I swallow hard as I follow the long drive toward the river. *No turning back! No turning back!* I can't stop the beat of those words pounding into my brain.

There's a security fence around the place, cameras, and a gate. *Oh, no.* I hate fences, especially when I have to drive through them and get stuck inside them. I stop at the gate. A guard appears. He's dressed in a black uniform and carries a pistol on his belt.

I tell him I'm coming for a job interview, and after he duly records my name and license plate number, he opens the electronic gate. After driving through it, it closes behind me. I get the jitters again. Strange that they'd have that kind of security for a school.

A beautiful lawn surrounds the main building, which is a long, low hacienda-type building, complete with a red tile roof and arched doorways. I almost expect to see a Mexican lounging by the side of it. I straighten my hair and run my finger over my teeth. Telling my heart to behave, I grab my briefcase and backpack and climb out of the van.

No dogs, thank God. From what I can see, there is a garage close by, sheds a little further away, several large buildings off in the trees, and a big barn near what must be a bluff that overlooks the river. Over by a field, a couple of old tractors and other farm equipment are parked.

I follow a curving path past a fish pond and over a little bridge. I admire the petunias, marigolds and begonias that fill the beds on either side of the flagged walkway. At the big double doors, I raise my hand to knock, but before I can, it swings open, and a woman stands there, surveying me solemnly.

"Hello," I say, stretching out my hand with a smile. "I'm Katie McDonald. I'm here to find out about a job that was advertised online. Can you direct me to the right person?"

She stares at me without responding and without shaking my hand. Her short, wide body fills the doorway. She's middle aged, maybe around forty, with straight dark hair that is braided. She is Mexican.

After what seems like forever, my words seem to sink in. She nods and swivels her head to glance over her shoulder as if she's catching a cue from someone. Then she brings her gaze back to me. "Oh, yes. Come in, please." She steps back.

The room is done in the same charming Spanish motif as the outside. A lot of money went into this place. On one end is a large dining room filled with round tables. There's a window that opens into the kitchen where something is cooking. It smells like spaghetti sauce. At the back of the dining hall, on the far end, is a large stone fireplace.

A man emerges from a hallway that goes behind the kitchen. He strides up to me.

His big smile and outstretched hand afford me a warm welcome. "Hello, Miss McDonald! Mr. Sherman said we should be

231

expecting you this morning. So glad you could come on such a short notice. I'm Bennet Sargent." He pumps my hand until I think it will drop off.

I make all the necessary replies in response to his greeting and withdraw my hand from his. While he is not extremely tall, he has a well-built body like he works out, and he moves like a boxer. His masculine charm surprises me. His amber eyes sparkle with interest and excitement, yet they are cold like golden ice.

He motions me into the room, and motions to the woman at the door. "This is Maria, our cook. Maria, get us some coffee." He glances at me appreciatively. "Or would you like wine? We make our own here. It's the best." He winks.

"Uh. No, thanks, Mr. Sargent. Coffee is fine." I follow him across a big room to the fireplace area where two easy chairs are drawn up to a cozy fire.

The interview begins. I give him my papers. Glancing at them perfunctorily, he nods and leans forward to impale me with one of his searching gazes. "Well, Miss McDonald, or can I call you Katie?"

I nod. "Oh, yes. That's fine, if I can call you Bennet."

That brings a chuckle. "I think you will fit in nicely here. We're like a big family, and the staff who work here, they have to adjust to our situation." He draws himself up to sit stiffly, regarding me with what he might have thought is professional pride, but it comes across venomous, like a rattler about to sink its teeth into its prey.

"I'm sure that you will find this a wonderful place to live and work, Katie. We are dedicated to the Lord and feel we are doing His work. We've prayed a lot about our need for a secretary, and the Lord sends you. And to find that you have so much experience in secretarial work, well, that's a bonus."

"I don't have that much experience."

He runs his hand across his hair to smooth it down. "Well, some. The office is in a shambles, but I'm sure you can set it in order in a few days."

I finish the coffee, trying not to show how repulsed I am. "Well, I'll try to do a good job. I've been praying about getting a job, too. Do you want me to start now?"

He laughs like he thinks that's a good joke. "Yes. Of course. Come to my office and sign some papers. Then I'll have Maria show you where you're going to live."

I glance around, shocked. I'd never dreamed I'd get hired that fast. I wonder how I'm going to let Jane and Don know. Do the people monitor calls going out of here?

He continues to talk as we rise and walk to the kitchen. "I think you'll like your place. It's a little cottage just a stone's throw from this building. Private and out of the way. And you can do some of your own cooking. You won't be expected to work with the young people. They have their own supervisors. You'll meet everyone at dinner. Come along."

He's in a hurry to get me signed up. I follow him, feeling like a sheep going to the slaughter house. With my heart pounding, I put my name to his papers. My assumed name, that is, and an assumed social security number. I've had so many names recently I almost couldn't remember which one to use. *Angela. Linda.*

When I'm finished the coffee and the paper signing, Maria hands me a map of the place and without a word circles the cabin I'm going to inhabit. No. 3. On the right.

"Thanks," I say with a smile. She stares at me and doesn't say a word.

The cabin is behind the Hacienda, which is what they call the Lodge. I drive over to the cottage. There are four of them in a row, all done in the Mexican theme, with flower gardens and neat little lawns in front of each one. No. 3 is white with a bright green tiled roof, arched doorway, stone-flagged walkway, and little flower boxes beneath the windows.

Neat and cute. I'm glad I'd brought all the clothes I own at the present, along with my personal belongings. I haul my things in, thinking I'll have to go get more stuff, but the cabin is outfitted with everything a person could need. There's a tiny kitchenette that has a round table beside the window, a miniature living room with brand new furniture, a good-sized bedroom with a queen bed, and a bathroom.

No key and no lock on the door. I step outside and stand on the doorstep, looking at the big maple trees and the pines down by the river. I'd asked where everyone was and Bennet told me they were either in the garden or in the shop, and that I'd meet them at dinner, which is at 6pm sharp. *A bell will sound*, he said.

Do they have loudspeakers, too? Maybe dogs if someone gets too adventuresome? But my imagination is taking off, and I can't let that happen. If I want to survive, I have to stay alert, ready, and aware. If this is the place, and I'm convinced it is, I'm in enemy territory, behind gates and fences, deep under-cover, and alone.

I pull the door shut and walk down my little lane. The place is bigger than I thought. There are several houses over on the bluff above the river. They must be staff housing. As I proceed west toward the river, I emerge into an open meadow. In the center of that are two buildings.

I'm convinced these are dormitories, but they used to be two-story houses. They face each other across a wide patch of grass. In the center of the grass is a cement slab and a basketball hoop. I do not venture any closer.

I trudge back to my cabin and go inside. There's a Bible on the bed stand. That's strange. If this place is run by the guys who had tried to kill me with professional precision, and are running the kind of operation that I suspect they are, I wouldn't expect them to have a Bible. But it's probably window dressing. Part of the show. Like the way Bennet Sargent talked about the Lord answering prayers, being so spiritual. *Yeah, right.*

I sit at the table and clean out my backpack, for there's pieces of apples and sandwiches left in it, and it's not smelling very good anymore. There's some brochures in here, too. I take one out that advertises Boundary Dam. I'd gotten them at a grocery store rack in Kettle Falls and picked up two.

Boundary Dam on the Pend Oreille River, Seattle City Lights, the brochure reads. I've been intrigued about it since Chance went over there with his dad. He'd seen something strange going on there, but I can't figure out how it connects with what I'm doing.

A bell clangs over by the main lodge building. Show time.

Chapter 36

A Piece of Cake

Deer Park, June 11th

Bobbi shrugged into her sweater and picked up the keys. She was heading out to feed the horses. Ever since those two women tried to get into the back door, she'd gotten in the habit of locking the doors when she went out. She tried not to look over her shoulder all the time, but she couldn't shake the feeling that someone was watching her. Maybe it was her imagination, but she didn't have much of that, or so Elton told her all the time.

It was Saturday now, and she still hadn't heard from Gina. On Friday she'd poked through the stores in Deer Park and chatted with the clerks. Then, hoping she'd hear from Gina, she'd made a nice dinner of lasagna, a green salad, rolls, and a cherry pie.

But she had to eat it alone. She tried to call Chance and got his answering machine, so he wasn't back from that camp. She considered going home, but who would look after the animals? The lady next door was nice, and she'd visited with her several times, but she was elderly and couldn't do the chores.

The waiting was eating on her nerves. She called the Spokane Police Department to see if they knew where Gina was, but they gave her no information. She even tried the FBI and while the man who answered was polite, he told her nothing.

After she got back from the dam yesterday, she called the sheriff's office in Pend Oreille county and reported what she'd seen and heard, about the man who carried a gun and talked like he was going to use it. They listened politely and told her they would look into it.

"What am I doing here?" she asked Ricci that morning when he leaped into her lap and rubbed his chin on her hand, purring. "House-sitting and taking care of a you two and horses while Gina is out there, saving the world. There's something wrong with this picture."

But what could she do about it? Should she go back to Boundary Dam and... what did they call it... investigate? It seemed like the only thing to do.

Matching action to thought, she fed the cats, grabbed her purse and jacket, and locked the doors behind her. Then she drove northwest to the dam.

At the guard shack, she spoke briefly to the young man who came out, and was told there would be tour going in a few minutes. She drove down the hill and gasped as she turned the corner. Water boiled out of the dam from three places, providing an exquisite display of frothing water.

After pulling into a parking space, she walked to a low brick wall. Below her viewpoint, the river churned from its frantic race to the north. She snapped some pictures. While she was busy doing that, a female voice sounded in her ear.

"Would you like a tour, ma'am?"

She whirled, not being able to hear much over the roar of the water. A college-aged girl stood behind her, wearing a blue uniform that was emblazoned with Seattle City Lights emblem. It was a different girl than the one who had taken her through before.

"Oh, yeah, sure. I was here a couple of days ago but would like to see it again."

"That's great. We like repeat visitors. If you don't mind waiting, there's another carload of people coming down."

"Sure." While she waited, Bobbi studied the huge power poles that were built into the side of the mountain above her head.

A family piled out of their van and ambled over to where she and the guide stood. They formed a tight group and followed behind the guide as she led them into the tunnel. The tunnels were hewn from solid rock and curved inward, toward the heart of the mountain.

Once in the visitor's center, the guide directed their attention to large boards that showed pictures and information about the construction and operation of the dam. Below, through the windows, they viewed the top of large turbines, rumbling away energetically, producing the electricity that would then travel through the wires and across the state to Seattle.

"What kind of security do you have here?" she asked the guide as they were led back down the tunnel and outside.

The girl gave her a perplexed look. "Well, we don't have much. There's the guard at the top – and me, along with a couple of guys who run things here."

Bobbi nodded, and the conversation flowed to other topics. But she wondered. Why had Gina been interested in this? If the project supplied a lot of power to Seattle, what would happen if someone blew it up? But what could she do? Nothing.

She got in her car and followed the girl's pickup to the top of the dam. There she parked and followed the guide to the walkway over the dam, peering over the railing at the gushing water below, as green as the insides of an ocean wave. It was deafening and beautiful. She took some pictures and thanked the guide.

Power for Seattle. She couldn't get the mental picture out of her head of a bomb planted in those tunnels somewhere below, blowing the whole thing sky high, and the city of Seattle and maybe Olympia, too, falling into darkness. The work of terrorists. She shook her head. Her imagination *was* going crazy!

She returned to her pickup and drove to the campground near the top of the dam. Getting out, she strolled to the chain link fence that prevented people from diving or falling into the water. She shook her head. Why had she come? There didn't seem to be anything suspicious going on.

No danger. No threat from any terrorists. Maybe the conversation she'd overheard from those two men was a joke.

Yes. That's what it was. A joke.

But she'd seen the gun, and the words spoken were real.

A camper was parked not far from the sign, very near the fence. As she walked along the fence, she convinced herself that she'd been imagining everything about a bomb and terrorists. That's when a man's voice came from the camper she was passing.

He spoke in a low tone, but the window was open.

She stopped and leaned down, tightening her shoelace.

"I tell you we gotta do it soon. Time's running out. How're you goin' to go about it?"

"It's a piece of cake," another voice said. "With this, I can do it easily. And more of this is coming in the shipment today."

Bobbi didn't turn her head. Her back was killing her, but she studied a rock like she'd found a lump of gold.

She didn't catch the next muttered comments, but then the second man said, "We'll do it from inside. It's an easy enough job. No security to speak of. We got the plans of the place. We'll get down that tunnel and plant it. We'll set the timer, so we have plenty of time to get out. Like I said, it's a piece of cake." There was a pause. "When am I getting paid, by the way?"

Bobbi missed the next words. Her heart was pounding hard in her ears.

Someone slammed a fist onto the table. "Okay! Let's get to work!"

She exhaled. Should she try to see their license plate number? No, she'd have to get too close, and they would notice her.

Did they mean what she thought they meant? That they were going to plant a bomb and blow up the dam? What kind of coincidence was it that she would be here, on this very spot, when they discussed it? Or was it a coincidence?

This time she knew she was not imagining things. This time it was for real. Now she had to let someone know. Before it was too late.

There was movement inside the camper — someone was walking around. She scrunched her body as low as it would go, and after passing under the window, straightened. Her breath came in gasps, her head spun dizzily. What should she do?

She glanced back and hurried across the grassy verge to the pavement, thinking hard. She had Chance's phone number, but would he answer? As she passed behind the restroom building, she paused and, bringing out her phone, sent a hurried text to Chance.

"At Boundary Dam. Heard something strange. Think it might be someone planning to do something to the ..." But here she stopped and raised her head. Voices. Footsteps. She sent the text and pushed the phone into her pocket.

Emerging on the other side of the small building, she headed for her car. The gravel crunched under her feet. She took a quick peek back and saw that two men approached. Their faces were in the shadows of the brims of their hats. She broke into a sprint.

Only a little bit to go... The footsteps gained. *Oh, God, please!* She reached the car, fumbling in her pocket for the keys. No one else was in the campground, not even the guide or one of their guards. She should get rid of the phone, for they could probably trace her calls and texts, if they caught her.

She tossed the phone into a bush nearby. Turning back to the car, she curled her fingers around the keys. It was at that moment that she heard something like cloth rubbing against cloth and a deep grunt. They were right behind her.

She was going to spin around and kick out at them. Or scream. Or pick up a rock and heave it at them. But it was too late. The blow that landed on her head was expertly delivered. A black curtain fell across her vision, and as she fell forward, the last thing she heard was a low chuckle.

Chapter 37

Unfriendlies

Forward Guard Ranch, June 11th

Chance was suffocating.

He had only a few seconds left before he blacked out as the strong fingers of the guard, the one he'd nicknamed Red Beard, clenched tighter and tighter around his throat. He had to do something. Something drastic.

He tried to wrench the fingers from his throat, but the man's grip held. With all his remaining strength, he pulled the little finger out, away from the hand. Bent it back sharply. Heard it snap. The man screamed but didn't lessen the pressure.

Chance was losing consciousness. He broke the next finger. Everything was beginning to fade. Broke another finger. The man let go, screaming. He leaned over, cradling his hand.

Chance gulped in air, telling himself he had to act quickly. Gasping for air, he turned. His legs felt like rubber. He hoped the pain would take Red Beard out, but the man seemed invulnerable. Already he was recovering, straightening, preparing to deliver a blow that would send Chance to the next world.

He kicked the man in the head. Red Beard fell forward and lay still.

But now the first man, Blondie, regained his feet. Grabbing a crowbar from the jeep, he roared into the fight. Chance drew in two deep breaths as he dodged the crowbar. From the corner of his eye, he saw that Red Beard wasn't finished, that he leaped to his feet and rejoined the fight.

Kicking out, Chance connected with Red Beard's chest, just below the breastbone. He dropped like a lead ball. About that time, Blondie drew his arm back and with a bellow, brought the crowbar down to smash Chance's head. Chance saw it coming, but he didn't have time to stop it.

Pressed back against the wall, faint from nearly being choked to death, pain shooting from his foot, shoulder, and hands, he could only lift his arms and try to block the blow.

But the crowbar stopped in mid-air. Blondie toppled forward. Chance jumped back, staring straight into Ramone's dark eyes who held a bat and had just used it on the man's head.

"Let's get ... outta here," Ramone panted, swinging to the jeep. His two assailants lay on the cement floor, unconscious.

Chance turned to the fallen guards. "Get the uniforms off them!"

He already had Blondie's shirt, so he yanked off the man's pants and climbed into them. With shaking fingers, he buttoned the shirt and slammed the cap on his head. Gathering up his clothes, he stuffed them in the pack.

"Give me your clothes, Ramone," he called. "We'll need them if we get out of here."

"Oh, yeah." He tossed over a bundle, and Chance rammed it into the pack, too.

They jumped in the jeep. Chance slammed it into gear.

The compound seemed empty as Chance drove from the equipment shed, past the guard's barracks on the left, down the road and past the little cabins. The Lodge loomed on the right.

He resisted the urge to floor the gas pedal as he steered the vehicle carefully through the parking lot and down the long driveway, for he knew a racing vehicle would attract the wrong kind of attention. Letting out his breath, he drove across the little bridge and approached the guard shack and the main gate.

"If you were a prayin' man, pray," he muttered to Ramone.

242

Ramone shrugged. "I can pray, but if they give us trouble, I'll take them out." He grinned, a wide smile that split his face. "Look what I found back there."

Chance let up on the gas and stared.

Ramone hefted an Uzi semi-automatic rifle. "And it's loaded. Gonna git me some revenge."

Chance shook his head. "No, you aren't. This isn't about revenge. Keep your face hidden, okay? They might not have a Mexican in their army." He smiled to ease his blunt statement. "Let me do the talking."

"Okay, *amigo.* But if they start somethin', I ain't gonna be easy on 'em. They shore didn't take it easy on me."

"We're not like them, though. I hope." Chance gave him a sharp glance and rolled to a stop at the shack.

A man popped out, rifle in his hand. "What's going on back there?" He indicated the smoke. "Heard a lot of shouting. And the siren."

Chance leaned forward. "Fire up on the hill. Grant's ordered us to go around to fight it from the back. Open the gate."

The guard shook his head. He was young, maybe in his twenties, unsure of himself and edgy with caution and fear. "I don't know. You got written orders?"

"No time. Grant's up there on the fire line. Get the stupid gate open! Now!" The last was a scream in the man's face.

The guard saluted and scuttled back to the shack. Through the small side window, Chance saw him pick up his radio.

"Uh, oh. We're in trouble." He braced himself, foot on the gas, hand on the gear shift. He sensed more than saw Ramone straighten and grip the rifle tighter.

The guard came back. "Just had to check. Yeah, there's a fire up there. Sergeant Cooper says to get back to the ranch. You're needed on this side of the fence, not outside. The fire's coming down the hill. They need every able-bodied man they have. I'm supposed to go, too." He glanced around. "Hey. Can I hitch a ride with you?"

243

Chance nodded. "Why, shore. Climb in." He shot Ramone a quick look. "Get out, buddy, and make room for him."

"Yeah, sure." Ramone sounded testy as he climbed from the vehicle. As he passed the guard, he slammed his rifle butt into his head. The man fell.

"I hope you didn't kill him," Chance said.

"Nah. He'll live to be nasty another day." He headed to the shack and in a few moments, the gate rose. Chance drove through it. He paused while Ramone jumped in with him.

"So, we're out! Free! Hey, how does that feel, Chancy-boy?" He thumped Chance on the back.

"There's still a God in heaven," Chance murmured as he started down the road.

Ramone leaned back, grinning. "Yeah. This is sweet. How far to town?"

"I don't know. Probably about fifteen miles. I didn't keep track .... Oh, no." The motor coughed. Again. Chance wheeled over to the side of the road. The motor chugged one last time and died.

"Hey. Not good! What's wrong with it?" Ramone sat up straight.

Chance shook his head, studying the dials. "We're out of gas. A mile from the ranch, and we're dead in the water."

They sat in the jeep, staring at the dashboard as if for inspiration. Finally, Chance said, "Well, this won't get us anywhere. We'll have to hoof it. C'mon, Ramone. Let's go."

Ramone groaned. "Just when I thought everything was goin' good."

Chance picked up the backpack and slung it over his shoulder. They changed back into their own clothes and started out. He glanced at Ramone, wondering if he could endure a long hike in the hot sun.

At first, Ramone seemed okay, but as the day went on, his energy lagged, and he struggled to keep up. His limp increased, sweat stained his shirt, and he stopped often to catch his breath.

Chance noted that blood seeped from the cuts on his chest and back.

At one point, Chance stepped deeper into the forest and sat on a log underneath a giant pine. "Let's rest a bit. No use to hurry."

"Yeah, I think there is," Ramone said, staring at him. "We gotta get some distance between us and those guys back there who're out for our hides."

"If we don't rest, we're not going to make it," Chance responded, taking out the water bottles. "Here. Have some water. We're out of food."

Reluctantly Ramone shuffled over and sat down. "Might not get up if I stop." He blinked. "How far did you say it was?"

"Don't know. But we can't make it today. We'll have to find us a hole and spend another night in the woods." He paused. "That might not be a bad idea, you know. It'll throw those guys off if they don't find us out on the road."

Ramone snorted. "We'd better wipe out our tracks, then. Remember the tracker guy?"

As they rested, Chance's mind went back to the unfinished conversation they'd had about the condition of Ramone's soul. "You never answered that question I asked you back there. Do you know Jesus?"

Ramone heaved a huge sigh and cast Chance a rueful glance. "Yes. So, you can forget your campaign to get me saved."

"But ... why didn't you say so?"

Ramone's grin widened. "Too busy at the moment to think. I was in a lot of pain, remember."

"Well, next time declare yourself. I didn't need an added worry right then. But I'm glad to know you're in the fold."

Ramone shrugged.

They rose and trudged on, stopping now and then to listen for the sound of a vehicle coming from the direction of the ranch. As the sun disappeared and darkness crept over the hills, Chance found a place under a big pine tree to sleep.

When he awoke in the first rays of light, he groaned and rolled over. He'd been sleeping on a rock. Every bone and muscle screamed at him, especially the ones in his shoulders. Slowly he stood. It took several nudges and a kick to awaken Ramone, but finally he stretched and got up. They drank some water and started out again.

As they plodded down the road, they rationed the water carefully, not knowing how far they would have to go. The sun rose higher in a pale blue sky. Sweat slithered down Chance's back and soaked his shirt.

"Isn't there any traffic on this road?" Ramone asked after a while.

Chance shot him an amused glance. "This is the back forty. Not many people come out this way. We should try to get off it, though. By now Grant knows we've gotten away and that we're on foot. They'll have patrols out, looking for us. He probably sent some out last night, but they'll be at it again this morning. They can't let us escape." Chance looked around. "I remember this area. Seems like there were some farms along here. Do you recall?"

Ramone nodded. "Yeah. Surely there's a house where we could get help. Hey, I hear somethin' comin'!"

Chance paused. "It's a pickup. I heard logging trucks going up and down the road yesterday when we were running around in the brush."

"Whatever we do, let's do it fast. That rig's comin' at a clip."

Chance stopped. He didn't have time for a lengthy prayer, just *help!* Again, he felt like Someone was with him – it was a whisper in his mind, a hand on his shoulder. "We'll flag it down. You got the rifle. If they look suspicious, we'll try to run. Shoot if you have to."

"Don't worry. I ain't afraid to use this." Ramone's tone was grim. No joking now. He brought the gun up to his waist with his finger on the trigger.

Chance knew he wouldn't be taken back to the ranch.

A big white pickup spun around the corner, a cloud of dust billowing from the back. Chance let out a sigh of relief. Not from the ranch, he didn't think. He waved. At first, he thought the driver was going to continue on.

He motioned for Ramone to conceal the weapon.

At the last minute, the driver applied the brakes, and the truck slid to a stop.

Choking on the dust, Chance ran up to the driver's side. It was a big Dodge Ram, lifted high with added suspension and lathered with dried mud. In the back, two 4-wheelers were secured. To his surprise, he was looking into the face of a woman. Her hair was tucked into an Australian cowboy hat, and she was wearing a red plaid shirt. No make-up. Fingernails blunt and unpainted.

"You guys need help?" She squinted into the sun.

Chance nodded. "Yes, ma'am. We were hiking up in the hills and got lost. Been trying to get out for three days. We're pretty done in."

"Know where your vehicle is?" She drank from a Pepsi can and wiped her mouth.

Chance half-expected her to spit a stream of tobacco juice and pull out her Smith and Wesson revolver. "No, I ... after we get to town, we can get help to find it. We'd like a lift to Chewelah."

"Or Spokane. Whichever." Ramone said from behind.

Chance glanced back. Ramone held the rifle behind his leg.

The woman grunted. "I'm goin' that way. But I don't like the gun your friend is hiding. Bring it out and let me see it, fella, or you ain't going nowhere in this here rig."

Like a naughty child caught in the act of putting a snake in the teacher's desk, Ramone shifted the gun and held it up. "It ain't mine. A friend loaned it to me. I was just tryin' it out, ma'am."

Her eyes widened. "Hold on." She pulled the truck over to the side of the road. Climbing out, she walked back to them, staring at the rifle. "My land! You huntin' with that? What're you shootin'? Buffalo? Elephants? By the way, name's Hazel." Her grin was wide as she stuck out her hand.

Ramone shook it gravely. "Ramone, ma'am. And this here's Chance. I take a chance every time I go with him anywheres." They chuckled as Chance shook her hand.

The woman's attention was drawn back to the Uzi. Chance watched the road behind them as Ramone went into a long explanation about the weapon, which included her looking down the sights and shooting it off once.

"Uh, ma'am," Chance said, edging closer to the two of them. "We ... we're in kind of a hurry, if you don't mind. We got some unfriendlies coming on our tail, and we'd appreciate it if we could hustle on down the road. "

"Oh!" She straightened and looked around. "Sure. I need to get back, anyway. I hafta go to work." She gave him a sharp glance. "Unfriendlies? Are you police?"

Ramone shrugged. "What he meant, Hazel, was that we got wives who're mighty unfriendly if we walk in late. Mine's expectin' me for a birthday party, and I'm two days late for it."

"Sure. C'mon, then." Pulling up her pants at the waist where her stomach lopped over her belt, she led the way to the truck.

Chance allowed Ramone climb in first. Hazel eased the pickup into gear. Just as she was pulling out on the road, a vehicle approached from behind and without warning or signaling, zoomed past, veering almost into the ditch to get around them.

An emblem was on the door, a globe with two guns across it. *Forward Guard Ranch.*

She swore and pulled onto the road. "I hate those guys." After she'd got the pickup rolling, she looked over at Ramone. "Hey. Them guys your unfriendlies?"

Chance answered. "Yeah. We were up there at that ranch, and they took a dislike to our looks. We got knocked around a bit, and they used us as target practice with their big Gatling gun ..."

"A Gatling? They have a Gatling?" She swerved and almost went into the ditch.

"Yeah. And a Howitzer. But they didn't use that on us. We managed to escape. You from around here?" He figured if they had to face murder charges, it wouldn't be a bad idea to have at least one witness on their side.

"Wow. I'd like to see those guns." She shifted her attention back to Chance. "We have a little ranch in the valley. My husband drives a logging truck. Where do you want to go in Chewelah?"

Ramone wiped his forehead. "Drop me off at the service station. I'll hitch a ride into Spokane."

"No, you won't, buddy." Chance nudged him. "You're staying with me. I'll drive you to the airport." Ramone leaned his head back and in a short time, he was snoring.

That was the last they spoke until she dropped them off at the Safeway grocery store about an hour later. Chance was glad he'd taken his wallet and phone when he'd grabbed his backpack that day. Now he called Pole, and the man said he'd bring Chance's pickup. He'd gotten it from the auto body shop while Chance was at the gun retreat.

After Chance got his truck, he dropped off Pole and took Ramone to his place. It didn't take long to get showers and pack up some of his belongings, including food. They went into Chewelah and stopped at Zip's for a hamburger.

When they went out to the truck, Chance said, "Know what? I'm going to drive you into Spokane right now, if that's okay with you. Then I think I'm going to change my residence. It won't take those guys out at the ranch long to get to my place."

Chance was more tired than he cared to admit when they pulled into the Spokane airport two hours later. Ramone had checked airlines online with his phone and found a flight to LA that was leaving an hour after he arrived. Chance offered to pay for his ticket, but Ramone pulled out his wallet.

"They didn't take this off me. Had it hidden in a pocket in my jeans."

Chance parked by the curb and came around the truck as Ramone got out. They'd stopped at a pawn shop in Spokane where Ramone bought a gun case. "My souvenir for a week spent on the edge of Hell," he said with a wry grin.

"Edge of Hell, my eye," Chance responded. "More like in the middle of it." He held out his hand, but the big man grabbed him in a bear hug.

"You get that leg taken care of," Chance said when Ramone let him go. "You don't want gangrene setting in."

Ramone shrugged. "You do the same with your shoulder. And get back to that pretty girl you talked about in your sleep." He laughed and sobered quickly. "Uh, hey. Don't know how to thank you for your help escapin' from that place, Chance. If it weren't for you, I'd be six feet under about now. It's more than I deserved. I was an ornery ass most of the time."

Chance chuckled. That was the most unusual appreciation speech he'd ever heard, but he knew Ramone meant every word.

"That's okay. You would have done the same for me." Chance dug a card from his wallet. "Hey, drop me a line now and then. My email's on this and phone number. If you ever come back, give me a jingle. I'd like to show you around. And have some fun while we're at it."

"Same goes for you, although you probably avoid LA like the plague." He grinned. "You goin' after those guys?"

Chance nodded. "You bet. I got a flash drive from the office. I hope it has something incriminating on it."

"Watch your back. That flash drive might be your ticket to the grave, and you don't want to end up as somebody's back pasture fertilizer."

"Okay. You, too. They might come after you, even down there in LA. See you around!" With a final wave, Chance got in his pickup and drove out, feeling that it was over. But he corrected himself soberly.

No, it wasn't over. It had hardly begun.

Chapter 38

The Battle Begins

June 11th

Someone tromps down the walkway past my cabin. I lift the curtain. *Girls.* I count eight. Wait. No, there's two more, coming with a woman.

They don't talk much, and I hear no laughter at all. When they do speak, they use low tones, so I don't catch what they are saying even though the window is open. Most of them seem very young – one looks only six or seven. None of them are Asian.

I stride up the path to the road, following its winding curves over a small hill and across a creek. The bell rings again. I'm going to be late. I hurry across an open space, crunching across dried grass, and up the steps into the main dining room of the Hacienda.

A quick count tells me only six tables are in use – two with boys and two with girls, each with an adult. There are two more tables where the staff sit.

Bennet marches over to me and grasps my hand. "Katie! Let me introduce you. Most of the teachers don't live here and have gone home, and so has the principle. You can meet them later."

I slide my hand from his as he turns to the group.

"May I have your attention, please?" he calls in a stentorian voice. The low murmur of voices, and the clink of dishes cease instantly. "I would like to introduce to you a new face we have among us. This young lady has come to help us out in the office. Katie McDonald is our new secretary!"

They all clap. I notice some of the women smiling. They'd probably been forced into secretarial duty beyond their other responsibilities. Maria peers out the kitchen window. Two others stand behind her, a man and a woman.

I lift my hand in a feeble sort of wave and grin.

Bennet puts his arm lightly around my shoulders. "She was willing to start immediately, so we are very thankful. Katie, do you have anything to say?"

I step away from his arm, but he keeps staring at me like he wants to me to speak. I clear my throat. They are all waiting, some with forks halfway to their mouths.

"I'm ... uh, I'm glad to be here and meet all of you. Thanks for having me, and I hope I can do the job well."

There's another spatter of clapping, and they return to their meal. Bennet motions for me to sit beside him. He keeps me busy with inane chatter while I eat and furtively look around, trying to figure out what's going on here, and if this is the headquarters of the organization that is involved with human trafficking.

The adults who sit with the young people are not speaking with the children – they eat with one hand on a two-way radio, and the other shoveling food into their mouths. Their eyes rove the room, watchful and alert. It reminds me of the secret service men around important government people. Do they function more as guards than dorm parents?

I study the girls. They sit hunched over their food, hair hanging into their faces like they don't want to be seen. Some of them are mere children, while others are older. The older girls cast bold, brazen looks around the room and are clad in short skirts and tight t-shirts with low necklines.

I go over to the window to refill my coffee. This brings me in close proximity to one of the tables of girls.

The lady who is seated with them lifts her eyes to me, studying me intently. I'm chilled to the bone, for hatred glints from her eyes and seems to emanate from her pores. She's a large-boned woman, tall, with light-colored hair pulled severely from her face.

She dumps her tray and moves back to the table, carrying her weight with ease. I have a feeling she could take out a good-sized bull if she had to.

"Hello, Miss McDonald." She doesn't extend her hand or even step toward me. A sneer curves her lips. "I see you've gotten acquainted with our Mr. Bennet. He's so friendly. He'll show you around and give you a good time. Never fear."

Jealousy and bitterness lace her tone. I can't account for it. *How have I riled her to that extent? What is she hinting at?*

She picks up her napkin and dabs her mouth with it, a gesture so uncharacteristic of a big woman that I almost smile. She continues, "I'm Delphine D'Moure. Where are you staying?"

I nod. "Nice to meet you, Miss Delphine." I refill my cup and brush back my unruly hair. "They put me in one of the small cabins." I wave in what I think is the right direction. "It's cute."

She moves closer to me and lowers her voice. "Just wait. You'll see it comes with a price. They don't give nothing away here. You have a lot to learn, girlie. If I were you, I'd pack my things and get out while you can."

Again, there's a veiled threat in her tone, along with a good dose of animosity and rage. Killing rage.

The girls examine me carefully, but when I return their gaze, they look away. All of them have the same look of shame mixed with desperation written on their faces. It's then that one of them stands up, picks up her tray, and turns toward me.

Something about her raises every protective instinct I possess. Maybe it's the hunched shoulders or the tortured eyes. I make eye contact with her, and she studies me with a searching look.

I've seen her somewhere, but for the life of me, I can't remember who she is. It was recently. But where?

She freezes when our eyes meet. "Oh! I've seen you before! You came to the house ..." She throws her hand to her mouth. "I mean, you ... came to *our* house, before, when I lived with Mom."

Suddenly I remember. *Sanora!* The girl on the sidewalk in Spokane.

I chuckle. "Oh! Yeah, I remember. I was doing a survey. My, that seems a long time ago. This is a pretty nice place, right? Did your Mom pay for you to come?"

She smiles with fear in her eyes. "Oh, no. The government people, they helped me come. Mom applied for it, though. Yeah, it's fun here. Way better than the city."

"I bet." The conversation lags.

Sanora glances at Delphine. "Isn't that just something that I'd meet this lady again? She came to my house once. Mom had her come in and gave her a cookie I'd just made."

She's trying way too hard. It sounds unnatural. I finish the story with, "Yeah. It was really good, too. You're a good cook."

Delphine stands, her tray in hand. I sense she's tired of the conversation. "Yes. Very nice, Sanora. Come on, girls, let's get back to the dorm. We have things to do tonight."

She shepherds them out of the dining room without giving me another look. Is my cover blown? From the looks of it, the woman couldn't care less and wasn't paying much attention.

But maybe she was.

I return to the table where Bennet is engrossed in a conversation with a man dressed in overalls. They are discussing a burst pipe somewhere on the property.

I pick up my bag. "I better get back to my cabin. Lots to do."

Bennet gives me a wink. "By the way, we have a staff prayer meeting every night at seven in the upstairs meeting room. I know you're probably tired, but can you come?"

"I'll see. Thanks." What am I thanking him for? I just want out of there. He stands as I leave as if he's going to escort me home. I wonder where his wife is, and if they live in one of those houses over by the bluff.

So, I was right. This is the place!

Seeing Sanora convinces me. I wish I could call Jane, but I'm afraid they might have a microphone in the cabin, and they probably have the capability to monitor my calls, incoming or outgoing, along with GPS locations. As I don't want a team of assassins on Don and Jane's doorstep tonight, I decide not to try it.

I take a deep breath of fresh air when I emerge from the building and thank the Lord I'm still in one piece. I don't *feel* in one piece, though – more like I'm torn and shredded.

I desperately want to do something physical to something ... or someone, like call the cops and have them arrest the crooks who have captured these kids under the guise of helping them.

At the cabin, I set down my backpack. Inhaling deeply, I remind myself that I have to keep a clear mind. Focus! Your life is on the line here, and you have a job to do!

I flip open the notebook Bennet Sargant gave me on the ranch – the rules, constitution, staff pictures, and other legal matters. But I can't get my mind off the sight of the girl, Sanora, and the other kids. Some of the boys I'd seen couldn't have been more than ten. They must be in training to do domestic work in the home or on a farm or as sex slaves. They are slaves, all of them, of that I am sure.

It's not until I get ready for bed that I discover that someone has searched my things. The job was done thoroughly and skillfully, but I'm organized enough to know when my belongings have been moved.

Plopping heavily on the bed, I rest my head on my hand and look around. Enemy territory. The battle has begun. I tell myself to calm down. They are probably watching me. Are there cameras in here? If so, they're going to get an eyeful because I'm going to act like they don't exist.

Loneliness descends upon me like a ten-ton boulder. If only I could pick up the phone and chat with Chance. I can't even call my back-up agents.

Alone. Scared. Yes, a big tough FBI agent like me is scared out of my wits. The only one I can call for help is God. It's comforting to know He's never too busy or too far away, but tonight a friendly face and a warm hug from a real, live person would go a long way to cheer my desolate heart.

Chapter 39

Stand and Fight

Chewelah, June 12th

Someone is in the house. Chance sets down his flashlight. He'd been out to check on the horses, and when he returned to the house, he heard a noise.

Cautiously he crept forward, every nerve tingling, his breath coming in shallow gasps. The boards squeaked under his weight. He reached the door that led to the living room and opened it, glad he'd left a lamp lit. Carefully he checked each room. Nothing.

He sighed and locked the doors and windows of the old farmhouse on his ranch. It was good to be home, to see the horses, to relax in his living room. But he couldn't shake the feeling that someone was watching. Someone was out to get him.

He turned on his laptop and inserted the flash drive he'd retrieved from his backpack. The screen came up with dozens of file folders, but they were not titled. When he tried to open them, he found they were all encrypted.

He could not break the code. He had a feeling that the information on this was important. Why else would they go to the trouble of coding it? Maybe it was Grant's master plan, spelled out to the last digit.

He rose and stalked through the house, his nerves twitching. He had to get this to the FBI. But how? He couldn't call Gina. He wondered when Grant would discover the loss of the flash drive, because when he did, Chance's life wouldn't be worth a dog's flea.

He picked up his phone and after locating the number, called the FBI office in Spokane. An agent answered on the first ring.

Chance told him an abbreviated version of his experiences at the ranch and said he had, what he figured, was hard evidence that incriminated those at the ranch with the intent to commit federal and state crimes, including murder.

He concluded, "The information on the drive is encrypted. That won't bother you, though. I'm sure you guys can break it."

The agent asked his name, address, and phone number. After duly recording this information, he said someone would be in contact with Chance and set up a meeting.

"I might not be around," Chance said. "Could we do this right away? Like tonight?"

"No, I'm afraid that's out of the question. This is a mobile number you gave me, right?"

"Yes, sir.

"All right. We will contact you and set up an appointment. Thank you." He clicked off.

Chance strode through the house again, checking on the doors and windows. First thing he had to do was get to a position of strength, and this wasn't it.

The farmhouse had always felt more like home to him than the fancy house his dad and step-mom had in Seattle. But now it was a death trap. He couldn't secure it sufficiently, and the presence of the horses increased his vulnerability.

He called Bobbi. She didn't answer. All he got was her cheery answering message. Stymied again.

What should he do about the horses? He called Pole, and the man said he could watch them for maybe a week longer.

Chance lifted the curtain in the living room and peered into the long June evening. Now that he knew the horses would be taken care of and out of danger, he bent his mind to what he should do next. He had to stay in the area, but he also wanted to become invisible.

He'd have to adopt a new identity, and he happened to know some sources in Spokane who could help him with that. He would call them in the morning.

He hated to go undercover, but he supposed it was the only way. If he could find Gina, bring those scumbags at the ranch to justice, and get his life back on track, he'd be happy.

He looked at his phone one last time before crawling into bed. To his surprise, he noticed a text message had come in. When he clicked on it, he discovered it was from Bobbi. Thinking she was replying to his message, he read the text.

At Boundary Dam. Heard something strange. Think it might be someone planning to do something to the ...

He read it through twice. Why hadn't she finished the sentence? Or texted another one? He texted back, "Please call me. What's going on?"

Boundary Dam. Maybe he needed to go up there tomorrow. But would tomorrow be too late for Bobbi?

As he was getting ready for bed, he heard something outside. *Someone.* They were trying to be quiet, but the old windows screeched when you forced them up, especially when they were locked. They'd jimmied the lock.

He crept out to the living room and threw on his shoes and jacket. Then he grabbed his .500 Smith and Wesson revolver. Tiptoeing back through the living room, he retrieved his rifle that he'd left by the recliner. In the kitchen, he found a box of ammo in the cupboard drawer and shoved it in his pocket along with his keys and wallet.

The window that was being forced open an inch at a time was in the porch off the kitchen. Good choice, since it was ground level and had nothing blocking it inside. He took a deep breath, held it, and exhaled.

Low voices drifted to him like a buzz of bees, but he couldn't hear what they were saying. He wondered how many had come. Should he call 911 or handle this on his own? How long would it take the sheriff to get here? He could be pretty dead by then. Go out the front door. Circle around. Surprise them.

But it wasn't going to be as easy as that if they had several guys in the yard, probably watching his truck to prevent him from getting away.

First thing was to get to safety. Call the sheriff. Then take care of his house and horses. He crept to the front door through the living room. The men made little noise as they crawled through the porch window. The old floor boards squeaked in the kitchen. How many were there?

He could handle two, he figured, but he didn't want to fight in the house. Didn't want to kill anyone, either, if he could avoid it. He put his hand on the doorknob and turned it slowly. Opened it. He stepped outside on the front porch, crouching as he did, trying to stay as silent as possible.

He waited, breathing softly through his mouth. Listened.

Two men stood by the big maple tree beside the driveway. They weren't trying to be quiet – their low voices carried across the yard on the still evening air. This told him that they were sure they would bag their game tonight.

Holding his rifle in the crook of his arm, Chance stepped off the porch. "Howdy, fellas. Can I help you with something?"

They whirled. They hadn't expected him to choose a frontal approach. One leaped to the left, behind the truck, the other crouched down and brought up his gun.

"I wouldn't try that, if I was you," Chance said. He shot from his waist without sighting, the bullets kicking up dust at the man's feet. "Oh, shucks. I missed. But I won't next time. And you! Behind the truck!" He flattened himself on the ground as a round of bullets sprayed him from that direction. Rolling, he found shelter behind a stack of wood. After arriving there, he dashed, hunched over, to the garden shed that was about twenty yards from the house.

He groped in his pocket for his phone, but his heart fell to his toes. He'd left it in the house! Now the two who'd entered the house emerged on the front porch.

"He's behind the shed. Hey, Rob, you take the left, and I'll take the right."

"And I'll take you both!" Chance shot twice toward the dim shapes on the porch. Got one. The man went down with a yelp. The other dropped and returned Chance's fire. Another dark shape emerged from the left of the house.

Chance was sweating now. Three to one. He had to even the odds or get out of there. If he ran, what would they do to his house? His horses? He couldn't flee. Had to stand and fight.

Clenching his teeth until his jaw hurt, he sent another round of bullets at the guy behind the pickup who'd tried to lunge out and get to the stack of wood.

Shattered glass was all he got. The assailant made it to the wood pile. He shook his head. It was the second window to get blasted out in less than a week – that was a record he wouldn't care to beat.

He brought his attention back to his assailants. They were closing in. Two were inching around the right side, one on the left. Very precise. Leaving no loopholes for him to escape.

His ammo was running low. Was this the end?

But he had so much more to do. Gina needed looking after. His job. There were people who needed to hear about the Lord, like Dusty, and his dad. It couldn't end now.

But it looked like it would unless something happened. And happened fast.

Chapter 40

Deadwater Pond

June 13

I can't believe it's been three days since I came to work here.

Every day I tell myself that I have to get busy and get hard evidence on the gang that's running this place, find a way to rescue the kids, and report to Jane and Don. Yet I've been so swamped, learning the job and setting the office in order, that I can hardly find time to brush my teeth.

I've looked through the files, both on the computer and in the cabinets, but I can't find anything that would be in the least way incriminating. There is one locked file cabinet in the office. Bennet told me that they keep the confidential information regarding the students in there. Only Mr. Cummings, the principal, Bruno Sherman, and himself have keys.

This morning I came into work with a huge headache. I don't have any ideas on how to investigate this organization and not get caught. I've thought of sneaking into one of the staff homes, but that's too risky.

I settle down to work because it's payday tomorrow, and I have to get the checks out.

It's late, around 2pm, when Bennet comes into the office and wanders over to my desk. "Hey, you want to go for a spin in my new Ranger?" He leans over me in a proprietary way. "I'll take you on a tour of the place. You haven't seen it all. I bet you've only just walked from your cabin to here. Come on. This is Monday. Supposed to be your day off."

I dredge up a chuckle. "Sorry, but I have too much to do." I turn back to the computer.

He lays his hand on my shoulder. "It won't take long. There's something I want to show you."

I shrug off his hand. I've told him not to touch me, but he does it anyway just to annoy me. "All right. But I have to get these paychecks out by tomorrow."

"Oh, you'll get it done. I have confidence in you." He laughs and leads the way to where his Ranger is parked. It's like a four-wheeler yet has a top and a steering wheel. I climb in and fasten the seat belt.

He glances at me and turns it on. "First we'll head over to Bruno Sherman's place. You haven't seen that, have you?" He raises his voice above the engine noise and nods toward the bluff.

"No."

"He owns this place," he says with a grand wave at the buildings and gardens as we pass them. He follows the road that leads past the dorms and continues on, heading toward the river. "He's a senator, you know. Flew in this morning. He's going to come for dinner."

"Am I supposed to wear my backless silk gown and spike heels?"

He laughs and gives me a look that makes my skin crawl. I wish I hadn't mentioned that. He says, "Yeah, I'd like to see you in that. I'd take you for a spin on the dance floor."

"If we had one, which we don't."

After about ten minutes, during which he keeps up a commentary on everything we see, he turns into a paved driveway that leads one way to the main road and the other way to the Mr. Sherman's house. He doesn't pull all the way up to the house, or I should say mansion, but stops and tells me about it as if he owns it himself.

"He bought this place about five years ago with the dream of creating a ranch and school for children who are at risk. He used his own money to bring it to where it is today. We've already helped over one hundred young people create stable lives for themselves, and he is proud of our work. We won't go in. I just wanted you to see it."

I nod as if I'm impressed. In fact, I am, but a sick feeling is crawling up from my stomach. Bennet's presence gives me the willies to start with, and then to have him hunched over me, selling me on the many wonderful aspects of the ranch, is almost more than I can bear.

The house is truly something to see. It sprawls out in majestic splendor, a Mediterranean style house, built of white stucco with a red tiled roof. It has several levels, huge picture windows, a wrap-around covered deck, fountains and gardens and probably a swimming pool and tennis court in the back. It overlooks the river valley. Bennet says he wishes he could show me inside because the interior is even better than the outside.

I scrunch away from his arm that rests on the of the back seat. He starts up the Ranger, and we trundle back to the Lodge.

For dinner, I put on my best skirt and top for the occasion, an outfit I'd purchased in Spokane. The flowing skirt has bright colors in it, a Spanish creation that fits the decor. The top is a simple white peasant blouse with puffy sleeves and scoop neckline.

Mr. Sherman makes his grand entry after we say the blessing. Some of the kids are starting through the line. They all stop and face him when he enters, frozen in the midst of their conversations. Silence falls on the room.

I half expect them to salute or call out a united greeting, something like, "All hail, most revered and honored leader! Welcome!" But, of course, they don't.

His smile is calculated to sweep women off their feet. I see it has its effect on most of the women and girls present. All I feel is slightly nauseous. I wonder at that because I've been feeling that way a lot here. Maybe I'm coming down with something. Or maybe this place is getting to me.

Bennet introduces me. "Mr. Sherman, this is Katie McDonald. She's our new secretary. Katie, meet Senator Sherman."

"Hello, Mr. Sherman," I say breathlessly.

He shakes my hand, bending over it like he might kiss it. "Ah. So, we meet again. I see you took my suggestion. So glad you did, Katie McDonald. You can call me Sherm. Most people do."

I liked the guy when I saw him at the church that night, but now shivers run up and down my spine as he looks intently into my eyes as if to gauge my worthiness.

"Oh, yes, Mr. Sherman. I mean Sherm." I giggle like a school girl. *Don't overdo it, missy!* I remember what Dad told me about undercover work. *Take it slow and easy.*

But Bruno Sherman, with his massive ego, seems pleased. With his hand on the small of my back, he guides me to the table. We sit down, and immediately there are two women from the kitchen at his elbow, bringing him wine, salad and rolls. This table has a white linen tablecloth, crystal wine goblets and shining silverware.

We chat pleasantly about our backgrounds. I eat sparingly. We discover that we are related. He says has a nephew whose name is William McDonald.

I play along with that. "Oh, yes! William! Let me see... he's related to my uncle, but I can't remember ... oh, yeah, he's my cousin on my dad's side. What a coincidence! But I haven't seen him for a long time." *Yeah, like never.* What a liar I've turned out to be.

He picks up on that immediately. "This is awesome! You wouldn't believe how many relatives I've found around the state. I must have sprung from a large family. You'll have to come up to the house for lunch tomorrow."

The others at the table eye me enviously while I preen in my new-found glory.

I set my glass on the table. "Oh, Mr. Sherman! I'm so honored. Bennet took me over to see your place today, and it's just ... well, I don't have words to describe it. Yes, I'd like to come. Is your wife with you?"

He chuckles and looks at me like he thinks I'm a cute child. "No, but my secretary is here. You'll like her. Come on over and have a bite to eat with us at about 12:30."

He turns to Bennet, who is seated on the other side of him. They begin a conversation about the school.

After dinner, I make my farewells to Mr. Sherman and return to my cabin. I make some notes on my iPad and check the news on the internet. I can't access my Facebook page or send any emails.

After about an hour, I change into jeans, a warm flannel shirt and comfortable walking shoes. I'd noticed that Bennet hadn't taken me to the northern part of the property, and when I asked about that area, he said it wasn't developed and probably wasn't safe.

I want to see what's over there. Besides, I'm itching to get out and stretch my legs. It's getting dark when I zip up my jacket. At the last moment, I grab my flashlight and my revolver and shove them into my pockets. I head out the door.

There's a group of girls going up to the Hacienda in company with Delphine. I nod and smile as I pass them. They are dressed in short skirts, high heels, and flimsy tops.

A band of light lingers on the far horizon, and a sliver of the moon is rising over the hills to the east. Something rustles in the bushes, and mourning doves coo from the low branches of the firs.

I hike toward the bluff, following a path. But I find this will take me right past the boy's dorm, and I don't want to be seen. I leave the path and cut through low under-brush.

After fighting the tangled bushes, I find another trail, maybe one deer have made. It zigzags down the cliff to the river. I wonder if I'll run into the fence before I go very far, but I don't see any sign of it.

I come at last to the river and walk out on the sandy beach, noting a black-scarred circle on the ground. Someone's had a fire here recently.

The river is a wide band of water, flowing smoothly, glimmering in the light of the new moon. There's no house or building of any kind on the other side. A fish breaks water in its bid for a tasty bug. I hear an owl in the forest behind me on its nightly hunt.

There. The fence looms in front of me, ten feet tall, topped with hot wire. It meets the river so closely that you'd have to wade out into the water to get around it. I imagine there are cameras along here. Still, if one of the young people wanted to escape, this might be the way, if they could make it across the river.

It's at least a half mile wide here.

But I hadn't counted on the guard. As I stand and contemplate the escape route, I hear gravel crunching underfoot. A man approaches rapidly, coming down the cliff. He's carrying a rifle and is dressed in dark clothing. When he draws near, I recognize him. He's a guard. His name is Gunther.

He shines his powerful light on me, then turns it off. There are no niceties here as there were at the dinner table.

"Miss McDonald, I need to warn you that it's against the rules, coming down here near the river. It's off limits. Surely you know that."

"Off limits?" I put the right amount of incredulity into my voice. "Why wasn't I told? I just wanted to stretch my legs and see the river."

He nods grimly. In his stern face there is no leniency for cute little secretaries, no budging on the rules. "Yes, ma'am. But now you know, so I'd appreciate it if you left."

I want to say, *my aren't we being serious?* but I don't. I edge away from him, putting fear into my voice. "Okay! I'm leaving! I didn't mean any harm. You won't ... use that thing on me, will you?" I eye his gun and grip my arms around my chest as if I'm terrified of him. Wouldn't the real Katie McDonald be fearful of a threat like this?

He stands stiffly, watching me.

I give him a little wave and whirl, taking off in my best stumbling run, not looking back to see his reaction. When I'm out of his view, I stop and breathe deeply.

I'm not scared of Gunter. Yet this encounter convinces me that I'm dealing with an outfit that is ruthless and cruel.

I hike back up the cliff but instead of returning to the cabin, I veer off to the right and climb down into a gully. There's a stream at the bottom of it, flowing toward the river. I follow it inland for a short way and find a lake.

As I approach, I see it is more like a stagnant pond.

Reeds bristle from its edges. A clearing widens out on the left side and there's a bit of a beach. My nose twitches at the smell. It stinks like a dead rat. It's not a nice place to linger, but I'm tired. I look around for a place to rest.

Finding a boulder the size of a small table, I perch on it and watch the moon climb higher in the sky, wondering where I'm going with this investigation. I have to find something concrete to take to the DA.

Should I use my portable tape recorder and get a confession from one of the girls? Would Sanora do it? I've taken some pictures, trying for clear shots of the faces of the young people here, but it's hard to do it without being caught.

I hear brush crackling behind me and think immediately of Gunther and his cold eyes. I'm partially hidden behind a stand of bushes on the verge of the water, which is good as I don't want to get caught because there's no escape route except to dive into the water. And I really don't want to do that!

Footsteps. A girl emerges, coming down the bank from the direction of the dorms. She's one of the older girls. Long, dark hair swishes around her face in the light breeze. I almost call out to her when she steps closer to the water. It seems she's in trance, or maybe she's sleepwalking. She lifts her face to the moon and spreads out her arms as if praying to it.

Now I know who it is because she works in the kitchen at times. Her name is Jenny. I thought she was mentally ill, but had not talked with her enough to know for sure or asked anyone about her. She seems to live in a dream world of her own. Maybe it's her way of coping.

Tonight, something is definitely wrong with her. She looks at the water near her feet and takes a step into it. Then she rapidly advances. The water comes to her knees, then to her waist. Suddenly I know she's going all the way.

I stand. "Jenny! Stop! What are you doing?" I might as well have been speaking to the wind. The girl doesn't flinch or turn in my direction. She keeps walking into the water. Chest high.

"Stop! Don't do this!" I scream.

But she pays me no heed.

I dump my jacket on the ground and fling myself into the water, shuddering at the impact of the cold. I'm making swifter progress than her, but I'm not going to make it in time. Her head goes under with a soft swirl of water.

I lunge and dive.

Thank God, my groping hands touch her. I pull her to the surface. We are both coughing up the horrible water we've swallowed. She doesn't struggle to get away from me. I start for the shore and find the bottom, towing her along.

But I'm not alone. Someone else is standing on the shore. Two people. Girls.

Gasping for air, Jenny and I slosh our way to the bank. She coughs and splutters but follows willingly behind me. I still have hold of her shirt. Her wet hair is plastered flat against her head. She swipes it away and looks around when we're ankle deep in the water.

"Jenny!" One of the girls runs into the water and grabs her, obviously not minding her wet clothing. "Oh, Jenny! What are you doing?"

I step onto dry ground and let go of her shirt. The girl who has her arms around Jenny's shoulders is younger, maybe twelve or so. I know her name, but I can't remember it. The second girl helps Jenny get higher on the bank, further away from the water.

Now I know who the second girl is. *Sanora.*

Jenny coughs again. "I ... I wanted to ... die. Why did you come, Ophelia? I thought I'd gotten away without anyone seeing me. And you!" She turns on me ferociously. "I hate you! You ... you ...!" She coughs, unable to find a word strong enough to describe me. "Why did you come in after me? I was going to ... find Kathleen ..." She starts to sob, crumpling to her knees on the shore.

I step back, surprised by the vehemence of her attack. " Is this how I get thanked for saving your life?"

Her face twists into a mask of hatred. "I don't want to live! And you have to go and drag me back to ... to this place, this Hell. Thanks for nothing!"

I get my jacket from the ground, squishing in my wet tennis shoes. The breeze is cold. I'm shivering. The stink of the water clings to me like a dead thing. There's nothing to say in reply to her.

"She was only trying to help, Jenny," Sanora says. "Come on. We gotta get you back." She turns to me. "Don't say anything about this to anyone, okay? Jenny would get ... well, she'd get into a lot of trouble, and we would, too. Please?"

I nod. "I won't breathe a word. But what ... why ..." My voice trails off.

Sanora gives me a scathing look before turning away. "You don't understand. This is the place where they ... where they bury dead people. It's dead here. And her sister, Kathleen ..."

She chokes on the name. "They ... beat her up, and she didn't get better from it. Then she disappeared. They dumped her here. I don't know why you came, but you're not making it any better. You should go home. At least you can."

Her words come from broken heart, and they stab my heart like knives. I clutch my jacket around my chest and start off behind them.

Silently we file up the path. The moon sails directly overhead. I can't see how I'm making it worse for them. Maybe Sanora expects that I'll do something, like magically help them all escape.

I'm at the end of my rope. I can't go forward. I can't get out. I can't solve this mystery or bring these people to justice. I've failed.

With these dismal thoughts ringing in my head, I let myself into my cabin. But the moment I step inside, I realize I'm not alone.

Bennet is sitting at my table, smoking in the dark. He puts out his cigarette. "Hello, sweetheart," he says in a low voice. "We need to talk."

Chapter 41

Tying It Together

Chewelah, June 13th

Chance lay prone on the ground, listening to the footsteps crunch in the gravel of the driveway, counting his last few bullets. They would take him soon. He prayed it would be a quick death.

He got a shot off at a shadowy form that flitted across the driveway toward the shed where he was sheltering. Didn't connect.

He blasted again on the left side when he heard the bushes crackle. Still nothing. Taking a deep breath, he told himself to wait. Wait until they were so close he could see their eyes.

But by then, it would be too late.

He figured they had night vision goggles on and could spot him as clearly as they would on a sunny day. He thought of getting into the woods that ringed the place, but knew he'd never make it the twenty or so feet to the nearest cover, a row of small bushes.

The men were closing in. Soon they would be able to pick him off with ease. There'd be three slugs, hitting his body almost simultaneously. Sweat dripped into his eyes. He gripped the rifle and took a deep breath. It wouldn't be long.

Oh, God! Help it to be fast! His last prayer. His last anything.

But suddenly a shot rang out from the woods behind him. Bullets slammed into the house. Two more shots followed the first, expertly placed. They thudded against the side of the shed. Who? Pole? No. Pole was visiting his kids in Colville tonight.

"Put your guns down and your hands up! This is the police!" The call came ringing from the shelter of the trees near the road.

Silence. Rapid footsteps pounded across gravel. He waited.

271

He got to his knees. "Chance Marshal here, Sheriff! Seems like they left. Can I come out?"

"Come out, Marshal. Put your weapon down and your hands up."

Chance got to his feet and stepped out from behind the shed. There were two of them, the sheriff and his deputy. He'd gone hunting with Sheriff Bob Wilson often, and many times he stopped by the office to chat with the deputies.

They advanced slowly, cautiously.

"What's going on here, Chance?" Wilson asked, lowering his gun when they were close enough to see each other. "We were driving by, doing a routine check, when we heard the shooting. Who were those guys?"

Chance shook his head, telling himself to breathe. His knees were wobbly as he walked to the officers and shook Wilson's hand.

"I can't tell you how relieved I am, Bob. Come in for a cup of coffee, and I'll fill you in on the details."

The deputy, Tim Watts, drove the patrol car down the driveway as Chance retrieved his rifle. He was glad his truck hadn't suffered too much harm, but he'd have to get the shattered windshields replaced.

In the house, he poured coffee into three mugs and sat down with the officers at his kitchen table. He told them the rudimentary facts of what he'd experienced at the weapons retreat, the barn fire, and the disappearance of Bobbi at Boundary Dam, even showing them her text.

Wilson finished off his coffee and stood. "Come by the office and file a formal report tomorrow morning, Chance," he said. He seemed anxious to get going. "In the meantime, batten down your hatches and stay alert. We'll be checking up on you."

"Thank you, sir." Chance shook the man's hand again and nodded to Tim. "Sure appreciate your help tonight."

After they left, he checked on the horses and locked up the house. Not that it would do much good. The assailants could get in. He had to move.

The next morning, he called Pole.

"Hey, buddy. I'm calling to ask another favor of you," he began. He wasn't comfortable leaving his horses alone and unattended. "Would you mind if I moved my horses over to your place? I was attacked last night, right here. If it's inconvenient for you, that's okay. I'll think of something else."

"Hey, Chance! You don't have to apologize. That's what I'm here for, and any way I can help, I'm willing. You want to do it right now?"

"Sure. Come on over. We can ride two and lead the other one."

It was done before the sun had risen very high in the sky. After that, Chance packed his belongings, locked the house, and drove his old pickup to Spokane. It took him most of the morning to locate his contact and get the fake ID cards.

While he waited, he checked online and found a furnished apartment in Colville that he thought was not only a good price but also gave him a good place to hide out for a spell.

After a quick lunch at Zip's in Chewelah, he drove to the apartment building. It stood on Walnut Street across the street from the city park. It was old and in need of paint, but it would do. He paid in cash and pocketed the key.

After moving his things into the apartment, he drove to Boundary Dam in search of any clues he might find about Bobbi's disappearance. In the upper parking lot, he strolled to the chain link fence and gazed out on the river that was running broad and smooth before it plunged over the dam. Had someone killed her and tossed her into the water?

He shuddered and began a thorough search in the campground around the bushes and underneath them, in the soft soil along the chain link fence, and around the restrooms. There had been rain, so he found no footprints, no cigarette butts, no handy little notes. Nothing.

Suddenly he caught the glimmer of something red underneath a bush near the restrooms. He fished it out. Her phone. The batteries had run down. He pocketed it and turned to look for more clues. But once again, he came up with a big fat zero.

He drove back to Colville and charged her phone. When it was charged, he turned it on, but there was nothing on it that gave him an idea of where she went. He called her husband, Elton.

Elton was concerned because Bobbi didn't usually disappear like that for any length of time, and because she hadn't come home or called.

"What are you going to do about it?" Elton asked.

"Well, there's not much I can do. I'm going to report her disappearance to the sheriff, but I doubt if they'll take it seriously. Probably think she's off on a trip or something. Her rental car isn't here. Could be she decided to go somewhere."

"I shore don't know where she'd go," Elton drawled. "Have you checked Gina's house? Maybe she's back there. Maybe she's sick or something, which is why she can't call."

"No, I haven't gone over there yet, but I will. Okay, Elton, I'll call if I hear anything. If she turns up on that end, please give me a call, would you?" He gave Elton his cell phone number.

"I'll do that. Thanks for looking into it, Chance."

He drove to Deer Park and out to Gina's house. He found a couple of lonely horses, looking for grain. When he forced open the lock on the dining room window and got into the house, he was assaulted by a pair of hungry cats. After feeding them and giving them fresh water, he headed out to ask around the neighborhood.

No one had seen Bobbi. Or Gina.

At one place, about a mile down the road, Chance found an older couple in the garden. When he asked about Gina, they brightened and said they knew her.

"Have you seen her aunt around? She drove a red car. She was visiting, but now it seems like she's disappeared."

The man straightened and wiped off his hands. "Disappeared?" He gazed down the road toward Gina's house. "No, I haven't seen her or the red car. We wondered what was going on because of the horses. Gina's so careful to take care of them usually."

Chance removed his hat, fear striking his heart like a dagger. He wiped his forehead. "Would it be too much to ask you to take care of the animals for her? The horses need grain once a day. It's in the barn in a bin by the door. A canful each. The cats will need to be fed once a day, too. The key to the back door will be under the mat. Can you help us out until we find them?"

They nodded. The woman said, "Oh, yes. Glad to. Let us know when she comes back, okay?"

"I'll be sure to notify you when she returns. I think you might get a pie out of the deal."

On the drive back to Colville, he mulled over the situation. He had to find Gina and solve this mystery, but how?

After taking a pain pill, he drove over to the sheriff's office where he filed a missing person's report on Bobbi.

There wasn't much he could tell them about her. He didn't even know her real name, but assumed it was Roberta. He gave them her description and Elton's phone number.

The deputy took the information. "We'll investigate, but it will take time. Call us if you get any new information."

"Okay." Chance rubbed his forehead. "The sheriff asked if I'd write out a report of an attack at my house last night. Okay if I do that now?"

"Sure." The officer handed him a clipboard and pen. It took about a half an hour to write out the detailed account of the attack.

The deputy read it, asked a few more questions, and had him sign it.

In the parking lot, Chance shook his head, wondering what to do next. He was out of time. Out of patience. He felt in his bones that things were moving, but he was powerless to stop them.

He decided to check with the Border Patrol office and see if he was on the schedule. At the office, he found his name missing from the roster, and everyone seemed too busy to talk.

When he got back to the apartment, he called Dusty. When Dusty answered, he said, "Hey, partner! I'm glad to hear that you're home! Last I saw you, you was flat on your back in the hospital with a dozen tubes running into your body! How're you doing these days?"

Dusty laughed, a low chortle that Chance recognized. "Good to hear from you, Chance. You in the area? I heard you took some time off."

"Oh, just a few days. Now I'm back, and I find they don't have me on the schedule yet. They say I'm still on leave. But I'm itching to get back to work."

"Yeah, I can imagine. I want to get back to work, too, but this danged injury has kept me on the sick list."

"Hey, about that. I was wondering if you could help me out. Could I come out and have a chat?"

There was silence. Then Dusty cleared his throat and said, "Uh, I got some things I gotta do today. Friends coming over. Maybe another time?"

"Oh, Sure." Chance paced to the window and glanced out. "I went back in to the place, Dusty, where you was shot, and I found some evidence. Things they dropped. I wondered if you remembered anything, or could give me some information about what happened."

A low, gravely chuckle came across the line. "I can't remember nothing from that night except you sittin' there, holdin' my hand and prayin' like mad. I'm not much use to you, I'm afraid, if you're trying to find out who did it."

"I've got to find out who did it. My friend, Gina, was shot and almost killed that very same day. People have been disappearing. My barn was burnt to the ground. And at that weapon's retreat, they tried to kill me and my friend. There's gotta be a connection in this, and I aim to find out what it is. I think the patrol is trying to cover their tracks and keep this hushed up."

"Well, I've learned to let things go," Dusty replied. "I mean, it don't do no good to buck the bosses. And it ain't my job to bring to justice the crooks who break the laws. I'm the one who was shot, and I'm not goin' off on a danged head-huntin' expedition."

"Yes, I know. I just wondered if you remembered anything. Saw anything. I see this from a different angle, I guess. I thought maybe you could give me some help."

There was another pause. Chance could see him hefting his belt up and striding to the window to gaze out on the Columbia River.

"Wal, sorry to disappoint you, buddy. Don't think I can help you out. See you around."

"Okay." Chance punched the button and set his phone down. So, they'd gotten to Dusty. Silenced him. Probably threatened his job. *Man, this must be something big.* The hairs on the back of his neck prickled as he thought about it.

He sighed as he opened his laptop, determined to find something, anything on the gang. He searched for Forward Guard Youth Ranch. After scrolling through hundreds of sites on Google, he found what he wanted. The website was professionally produced.

The words in large print read, "Dedicated to helping the unwanted, serving the people, standing guard for our America, and meeting the needs of those who come to us for shelter and safety. Forward Guard stands ready, able, and willing to serve our country."

He clicked on the tabs and found pages dedicated to a school, a rehabilitation facility, a second hand store in Seattle, and a factory in Los Angeles where they employed Asian people to make furniture. He couldn't find who owned the organization, only that it was based in Seattle.

As he got off the site and pushed back the chair, he realized the only one who could help him was Dad. He put the call through, but only got a message. He hung up without leaving one of his own. Striding across the pocket-sized living room and back, he couldn't find peace. Couldn't think. He had to do something. But what?

Time is running out and things are piling up. What could he do?

Staring out at the big trees in the park, he stopped pacing. His head hurt. So did his ribs. He'd bruised them from the fall he'd taken last night when he avoided gunshot. Who owned Forward Guard?

He called his dad again and this time the senior Marshal picked up.

"Hey, Chris. What's going on?"

Not an extremely friendly greeting, but Chance figured at least he had his father's ear for a few moments. He'd better get straight to the point. "Hi, Dad. I just wanted to run something by you and see if maybe you could help me out."

"Yeah? What do you have?"

"Uh, I got myself in a world of trouble the other day when I went to that weapon's retreat at a ranch outside of Chewelah. It's run by some scumbags, Dad. The organization calls themselves Forward Guard. I wondered if you could check it out for me and find out who's behind it. I'd like to get the FBI and the ATF in there."

"That drastic, Chris? They were probably testing you."

"No, it was more than that. They were serious about eliminating me, and they pretty darned near accomplished it. C'mon, Dad, it won't take you long."

Senator Marshal sighed heavily. "All right. What do you want to know?"

"Find out who owns it. If we can get some hard evidence about the place, we can call in the feds and have them shut down. Maybe arrest the guy —"

"Heck, why don't you call in the army, too?" Mr. Marshal chuckled. "Slow down, son. I'm not going to be a whistle-blower on some little —"

"It's not little. It's huge. They're behind the attack on the border. Smuggling. Drugs. Human trafficking. Who knows what else? Can't you give me some help here? I feel like —"

"I'll see what I can do."

Chance knew from his tone that he'd expired his three minutes of his father's time and patience. "Okay. Call me. I need to know. Someone I care about —"

"I have a call coming in. I'll be in touch."

The phone disconnected. Chance felt like throwing the phone across the room, but he shoved it in his pocket and rumpled his blond hair, striding to gaze out the big picture window. The wind was picking up outside, whipping the giant pines in the park and tossing paper debris down the street. With a groan, he sat on the old couch.

What could he do? He was stymied at every turn, and if he didn't hurry and find the solution, he would be dead. And Gina, too. He had to help her.

He'd thought for most of his life that he could handle anything he encountered. That he was smart enough, strong enough, brave enough to do it. But this – this was too much. Despair settled over his heart like a blanket, suffocating his small hope.

He could only turn to God. He picked up his Bible that he left on the coffee table and flipped it open. It fell to Nahum 1:7. He read through the verse twice. "The Lord is good, a stronghold in the day of trouble, and He knows those who take refuge in Him."

Another verse sprang to mind. He turned to Prov. 3:5-6. "Trust in the Lord with all your heart and do not lean on your own understanding. In all your ways acknowledge Him, and He will make your paths straight."

He closed the Bible and his eyes. "Lord, but this verse says that if I trust in You, You will direct me. So please show me, Lord. Help me. Give me strength. I can't do this on my own. I need You." He waited awhile and said, "Thank You." Peace flooded his soul.

Stretching his long legs on the couch, and leaning back on the cushions, he thought he'd rest for a moment. He closed his eyes and opened them when his phone rang.

He jumped, swung his legs to the floor and after locating his phone, turned it on, thinking it was Dad.

"Yeah? You got something?"

"I understand you have something for me," a deep male voice said. "Meet me outside your apartment in five minutes. I'm driving a dark blue Toyota."

Chapter 42

At the Bottom of the Well

Flat Creek/Northport Road, June 14

Bobbi didn't know how long she'd been in the room. It was dark, except for a little light that leaked in under the door. She was lying flat on her back. She moaned and tried to roll over, tried to find a more comfortable position, but she couldn't. Something rattled when she moved. Her head ached. Her body ached.

Slowly she sat up and swung her legs over the cot. She was thirsty, oh, so very thirsty. But it was the darkness that ate at her soul. Made her want to scream. And it was very quiet. Where am I?

Bobbi reached down and felt her ankles. Chains. Running her fingers up the chain, she found it was connected to the wall. There were blankets on the cot. She was shivering with cold. Yet it wasn't chilly in the room. Maybe it was shock. Maybe it was fear. Her teeth clenched together, she tried to calm her nerves, tried to remember.

It was all so fuzzy. How had she landed up here? What had she done to ... *Oh!* Now it came flooding back like a horrible nightmare.

She'd gone to Boundary Dam. Heard the man say something. What was it? It escaped her now. She ran across the parking lot and texted Chance. She got to her car, was unlocking it.

Then... the blow to her head. Those men in the camper had seen her, knew she'd overheard their conversation, and brought her to this place.

"They say you can see the stars from the bottom of the well," she said. Her voice was low, scratchy. She looked up. Nothing but blackness. "I can't see anything, but You can see through the darkness, can't You, Lord?"

Gradually her eyes adjusted to the gloom. The room was small, maybe ten feet square. No window. Only this cot she sat on. The walls were unadorned. It smelled like urine and vinegar. There was the faintest whiff of Pinesol. Would they feed her? Bring her water?

Forcing herself to a more cheerful subject, she remembered a Bible verse she'd memorized. "When I am afraid, I will trust in Thee." Simple words, but they gave her hope and comfort.

She lay back on the bed and pulled the smelly blanket up over her body. Muted footsteps thudded above her. Once in a while, she heard the clunk of something, maybe a motor turning on, maybe it was the old building groaning under the weight of its sins.

She smiled. What a fanciful thought. And she wasn't given to fanciful. Strange what darkness and solitude did for a person.

Thirst gnawed at her like pain.

She tried to sing but couldn't because her throat was too dry. She thought of Elton and got teary-eyed. Last summer he'd been the one missing. Now it was her.

Tears oozed from her eyes and dripped down the sides of her face. She sat up again and thought, Oh, my land! Lying around crying won't help anything! I've got to get out of here. She studied her chains. Yanked on them. The chains held firmly.

What could she use to help her get free? They'd taken everything she'd had on her except for her clothes. She grimaced. At least they'd left those!

The cot. Surely, she could do something with it. It was made of wood and metal. She examined it, but it was too dark to see clearly, and she knew she couldn't get the screws out with her fingernails.

She sighed and leaned back. "Well, here I am, Lord. I always said I wanted a few days to myself, so I guess now I've got them. I can either moan and groan and cry myself to sleep, or I can use this time for a good purpose. It seems the only thing I got left to me is prayer. So, I hope You don't mind, but I'm just going to talk to You about a few things, Lord."

She drew a deep breath and began. But she hadn't gotten more than ten words out when she heard footsteps clomping down a stairwell. A few minutes later, the light at the bottom of the door grew brighter. The jingle of keys was like music to her ears.

She sat up.

A woman entered, carrying a bucket, a flashlight, a jug, and a plate. She didn't look at Bobbi as she set her load on the floor. Liquid splashed on the floor as she plunked a plastic milk jug down near the cot that was filled with water.

"Oh! I'm so glad to see you!" Bobbi said, trying to keep her voice level and her tone light. "What's your name? I'm Bobbi. How are you doing? Where am I?"

The woman was dark-skinned and had graying hair and a bent back. She seemed not to have heard. Maybe she was deaf. She didn't make eye contact with Bobbi as she swung the light over her briefly.

"I'll be back for the dishes. Use the bucket to..." Without finishing the sentence, the woman trudged out of the room and shut the door.

"You can't leave now! I need to know a few things." But the woman and her light were gone. Bobbi was alone again.

She lifted the water jug and drank deeply. Then she felt for the plate and lifted it to her lap. The food was not bad – she was faintly surprised, suspecting that she'd be given watery soup with fish eyes floating in it.

She found two hot dogs, each on a dry bun. Potato chips. And, *glory be!,* an apple. She found she was famished and soon finished off the meal. Not the most nourishing, but certainly more than she'd expected.

With food and water and the comforting thought that she could relieve herself when she needed to, she lay back on the bed and took a deep breath.

"Well, Lord. Here I am, like I said before. I hope you got your listening ears on, because I'm going to blister them right now. I can talk for hours, you know." She chuckled. "You see, I only have You, and I need to talk."

But her intentions were greater than her strength, for she hadn't prayed for more than ten minutes before her eyes closed, and she fell asleep.

***

From Gina's Journal, Monday, June 14th

Bennet and I stare at each other. He's seated at my small kitchen table in my cabin, and I'm standing in the doorway, still damp from my swim in the pond. His presence in my cabin unnerves me more than anything I'd encountered yet in this place. I keep my face still, allowing only outraged dignity in my tone.

"What are you doing in here? Get out. And take your stinking cigarette with you." I can only think about the Glock tucked away in my backpack. Little good it will do me. He'd be on me before I could get it out.

Bennet grins and stands slowly like a cat stretching itself after a long nap. "I like a girl with spunk, and you got spunk, I hafta say that." He moves past me, going out the door. "But I still need that little chat. You wanna do it out here in the open, that's fine with me. I ain't choosey." His Cheshire grin turns my stomach.

My heart beats so loudly in my ears that I think he can hear it. He leads the way to a park area near the cabins where there's a picnic table. There he sits on the bench and stares at me. I can't fathom why he wants to talk. Or maybe he wants something more than talk.

Standing about three feet away from him, I shrug out of the backpack and hold the strap in my left hand. If I have to, I can go for the gun with my right. The pack is unzipped, and I know where the gun is.

The moon is playing peek-a-boo with the clouds, and the wind is lashing the tree branches above us about with gusto. My hair is blowing into my eyes. I glare at him like he's a coiled rattler.

"Yes? What do you want, for pity's sake? I'm tired, Bennet, and I'd like to get some sleep."

I don't mention my need for a shower to wash off the smell of the pond as I'm afraid that will give him ideas.

He nods. "Yeah. Tomorrow's goin' to be quite a day, ain't it? You'll be trottin' up to the boss's house and fluttering those long lashes at him, right? Ain't you the big enchilada all of a sudden? And what about us poor workin' wretches that makes his life possible? We don't get any sweet talk and eye flutters, do we? What you got for me, Katie McDonald? Every time I try somethin' on you, it falls flat like I'm dirt. Well, let me tell you, little girl, I run things here. I tell the senator what's what. And we got a deal. I get a cut out of his take, which means I got a claim on you." He moves closer to me.

I don't know how much of what he's saying is the truth. I hold my ground, even though his presence sends chills down my spine. From the smell of his breath, I know he's smashed.

"I don't know what you're talking about, Bennet." I look up at him, which I hate to do because it puts me at a disadvantage. "My job doesn't include catering to your lusts. If it does, then I'm resigning on the spot."

I hold my breath, hoping he doesn't call my bluff.

Chuckling, he staggers as he tries to grab my arm. I step back. He's panting when he says, "C'mon, missy. I'll give you a good time. Hey, I'm not forcin' you or nothin'. I'm just sayin'. I got a bottle of wine from the store room. C'mon." He grabs my arm.

I twist away from him, tempted to go for my gun. But I can't. It would give me away. "I'm not Mr. Sherman's property, and I'm not granting him favors, at least not the kind you're suggesting. I know how to defend myself, Bennet, and I'm not shy about doing it. So, stay away from me, you hear?"

He laughs again and lurches toward me like he's going to embrace me. I kick and connect solidly with his crotch. With a howl of pain, he goes down to his knees. I follow up with a kick to his head – not a hard one, I could kill him that way – but just enough to teach him a lesson. That does it. He crumples to the grass, writhing and moaning.

"You're not going to mess me with, Mr. Sargent. You try this again, and you'll be looking for another secretary and an emergency room."

I'm shaking when return to my cabin and fall onto the chair by the small kitchen table. All the bravado, the smart ass answers, the cocky attitude has drained from me like water from a slashed plastic bag. I'm in over my head. I can't fight this. I can't win.

Yet I know that this is just the beginning. What will come next? I can't try a trick like that on Mr. Sherman. But what if he comes onto me the same way and wants the same thing? Will they enslave me, too? I rest my head in my hands and give way to a bout of tears, so unlike the real me that I think I'm coming unglued. That I have to get out of here before...

Before what? Before they capture me, enslave me?

I raise my head, tears still on my cheeks. *Oh, God! I need You. I need You now. Please help me. I can't do this alone.*

The tears are gone. I'm numb and cold.

Tomorrow I have to do something. I have to break this case and get out of here. Time is running out.

Chapter 43

The Lady in the Cheese Aisle

Colville, June 15

Chance glanced at the clock on the bedside table. *7:36am*. He'd slept all night! He clutched his phone tightly and tried to identify the man's voice. *Ramone? No. Dad? No. McClurry?*

"Who is this? I don't meet with nobody unless I know who I'm meetin'."

The man snorted. "The FBI. You called us, remember?"

Chance didn't like his snide tone. "Why didn't you say so? Okay. I'll be out there in a moment."

He tied on his shoes, slipped his gun into his shoulder holster, got on his jacket, and picked up the evidence envelope from the table. After retrieving the flash drive and dumping it in the pocket of his jacket, he stepped out into the morning sunshine.

The man was sitting in a dark sedan, parked beside Chance's old pickup. The windows were tinted, so Chance couldn't see him until he rolled his window down. He was fair-haired and wore a t-shirt with a blazer over top. Chance noted he had a shoulder holster and a gun.

"You have it?"

"Have what?" Chance squinted against the sun that shone in his eyes, moving a bit so he could study the man. There was something wrong. His senses on full alert, he stepped back.

The man snorted again. Chance was beginning to hate that sound. The agent held out his hand. "The evidence. Hand it over."

Chance leaned one hand on the car. "I'd like to see some ID, if you don't mind."

With a muttered swear word, the agent dug in his front pocket, retrieved a business-card case, and flipped it open. He was going to return it to his pocket, but Chance snatched it from his hand, bringing it up close and studying the fine print and the picture. The card looked official. *Agent Brian Peck.*

But people can get these made up, Chance thought. In fact, he carried a false ID driver's license at the moment.

"Satisfied?" The agent retrieved the card case and put it in his pocket. "The evidence, if you don't mind. And after this, stay out of our way. We don't like amateurs."

Chance fingered the flash drive in his pocket, undecided. He looked away, trying to gain time. "I'm not sure about this. I've been hunted down and almost killed for it, and I'm supposed to hand it over to a... to the first person to come calling? I think I'd better just take this in myself. Sorry about your wasted trip here, Agent Brian. Just call me suspicious." He attempted a laugh, but it ended as a cough. He edged away.

Agent Brian climbed out of the vehicle. Chance wondered if the two of them would have one of those old-fashioned gun fights, going for their guns and the fastest draw stays alive.

Chance turned sideways, drawing his revolver smoothly from its holster. As he completed the turn, he saw the man's foot coming toward his head and had just enough time to dodge it.

Whirling, he slammed his elbow back and caught the man in the throat, snapping back his head and slamming it into the car. As he crumpled to the pavement, Chance leaped back. Sprinting to his apartment, he glanced back.

The man lay still on the pavement.

He entered and locked the door behind him. Returned the flash drive to the evidence envelope, he put it in the briefcase that held his laptop. He threw his belongings into suitcases and boxes.

When he returned to the parking lot, the sedan and the fake FBI agent were gone. He placed his suitcase and laptop in the pickup, hiding it under the seat, and returned the key to the office.

"I decided not to take the apartment," he said.

"Oh!" The girl turned to him, wide-eyed. "I'm sorry. Do you want a refund?"

"No, thanks. I figure it's donation to your establishment. Have a good day." He strode to the pickup and jumped in, wary of every moment, watching the shadows in the park, ready to fight or flee. But no one showed themselves, and he drove away, his heart hammering.

It was while he was driving downtown, before he reached Highway 395, that his phone rang. He looked at it and didn't recognize the number. Punched the button.

"Yes?" The question carried the weight of his frustration and fear. He pulled over to the curb. "Who is this?"

A low chuckle reminded him of a hot afternoon on a baked hillside where a fire raged. "Hey, Chance, don't you know your old buddy? What's going down? Your voice sounds like you're still in the battle."

Chance let out his breath with a *whoosh!*, not even knowing he'd been holding it. "Ramone! Yeah, you might say that. Man, it's good to hear your voice! I sure could use your help. Can you come?"

He smiled. Is this God's answer to my prayer for help and guidance?

Another chuckle. "I'm already here. Where do you want to meet?"

"Here? Where here?"

"At the airport. Gettin' me a car."

Chance's mind raced. "Okay. They traced me to an apartment I got in Colville. So, I'm clearing out. Tell you what. I'll meet you in the city park after dark, let's say 9:30. Wander around. I'll spot you. It's good to hear you! I can't believe you're here."

"Colville Park at 9:30," Ramone repeated carefully. He whistled low. "They have you runnin', don't they? Just like at the ranch. See you soon. Keep your head down."

Chance laughed, relief washing over him. Yes, this was a God thing. Just when he was at the end of his resources, Ramone shows up!

He glanced around. They knew his pickup. Maybe even had it bugged. How did they know he'd called the FBI? Did they have a tracer on his phone? Or had they overheard him at the house?

Where should he go now? He'd have to leave the truck somewhere. After making sure he wasn't being followed, he drove to the edge of town and rented a storage space. It seemed strange to leave his few belongings in the large compartment, but it was better than lugging it around with him all over town. He saved out a suitcase and his briefcase that held his computer.

Then he drove to Walmart, thinking he could grab something to eat for lunch at the deli. He wandered to the meat aisle, made his way to the frozen dinner aisle, and from there to the cheese and lunchmeat shelves. It was while he choosing the kind of cheese he wanted that he became aware of a woman who stood next to him.

He'd noticed her as she approached, but his mind only registered that she was a young lady, very thin, dressed in jeans and a baggy shirt with dark hair and a funny kind of hat.

She bumped him with a mumbled, "Excuse me."

It was enough for Chance to glance at her sideways. Just a quick peek, then he swung his eyes back to the display, staring at variety of cheeses like he was trying to decide what to buy.

But, in actuality, he didn't see a thing.

"*Gina?* Is that you?" He whispered, hoping he was correct.

"Yeah. Hi, Chance." She, too, stared straight ahead. "Finding what you want?"

"Uh, not really. How about you?" From his surreptitious, fleeting glance, he noticed her clothes. She wore a shirt that was too large and pants that were too long, stuffed into boots that were muddied and worn. Her dark hair was tucked into a baseball cap.

Chance nudged her. "Can we talk? I've been worried sick about you."

She shook her head. "Not here. Meet me in the Safeway parking lot in about ..." She pulled her phone and checked the time. "Twenty minutes."

Making way for another customer, she snatched a brick of hard cheese from the shelf and left. Not too fast. Not too slow. Just as you would if you'd finished a casual conversation over the prices of cheese these days.

Clever girl. He made his choice, and without looking at her again, went to the aisle where a thousand kinds of chips were displayed. Mindlessly he grabbed a bag and pushed his cart to the bread aisle, finishing at the fresh vegetables, picking up some apples and bananas.

His heart hammered wildly in his chest as he waited in line to check out, resisting the urge to search for her in the other lines. At least, he could solve one mystery today! *Maybe.* Another answer to prayer? *Definitely.*

Something about her appearance bothered him. It wasn't that she was unkempt or that she was a brunette – that was her new look. It was her posture, the expression on her face, the way her hands shook. She was different, and a gut feeling told him it wasn't entirely due to going under-cover.

He arrived in the Safeway parking lot early. He didn't have long to wait until he saw her standing beside an old yellow van that she'd parked several rows away. He got out and moved a bit until she saw him. Then he got back in the truck.

A couple of minutes later, she opened the passenger door and climbed in.

"Hi, ya, Chance," she said in greeting, not meeting his eyes. "This can't take long. I'm supposed to be back soon. What's going on?"

He wondered where to begin. Her abrupt manner threw up a wall between them, as if they were strangers and had to start all over again with the real things of life.

When he didn't respond, she took off her hat and brushed back her hair. She sighed, staring straight ahead. "How'd the camp go? Was it fun?"

He laughed. "That's not the word I'd use to describe it. Interesting, maybe. Whacko, certainly." He shifted and fiddled with his keys. "Almost lost my life about a dozen times and had to break out of it like a jailbird. Met a nice guy, though. From LA. A big policeman. We had a grand time avoiding being shot by a Gatling gun and mowed down with Uzis." He paused. "I should've listened to you. You had a gut feeling it wouldn't be good."

"A Gatling? You're kidding."

He chuckled at her shocked expression. "Nope. I don't make jokes about things like that. I can tell you one thing, though. That experience sobered me up, good and proper. I rarely smile anymore." He belied that with a grin. "The place was called Forward Guard. I called my dad, and he said he'd check it out for me."

"Forward Guard? Hey, that's the organization behind the ranch and school where I'm working now." She met his eyes. "Small world, huh."

"It's fitting together, Gina. I want to get to the bottom of this." He jiggled his keys. "So how about you? You're undercover? Where's the location, just in case I get lonesome and need to pay you a call?" He rolled the window down and took a deep breath of air.

He hated this cat and mouse game with her! Why couldn't she just open up? It was like before, in Montana, when he first got to know her, but this was worse because he wanted her friendship. Needed her feedback. Her humor. Her life and vitality, which was pointedly lacking right now.

"I don't want you coming out there, Chance," she said, giving him a direct glare with her sea-green eyes. She leaned back on the seat with a sigh. Then she said, "Well, okay. I'll tell you if you promise not to come."

He shook his head in disbelief. "I don't get you, girl. You doin' this alone again, like you tried to do in Montana. You know that doesn't work. I'm not promisin' nothing. If you want to tell me, fine. Otherwise..."

He let the sentence dangle and turned his head. He clenched his teeth against a wave of hot-white anger that scalded his senses, knowing it came because he was so afraid for her.

She riveted her gaze on the roof of the cab. "All right, but don't blow my cover. It's up on the Columbia River, the Northport-Flat Creek Highway. It's called the Columbia River Ranch and School. It's owned by a senator named Bruno Sherman. I met him last night. He's quite ... interesting."

She passed her hand over her forehead like she was in pain. "The guy who manages the place gives me the willies, but I can handle him. Chance, I'm so angry about the kids that I don't know if I can ... do this. They have maybe twenty there, some young ones. They're trained to ... well, I can only guess at what they're trained to do. Some of the older girls go out at night. There's Asian girls at a neighboring ranch that they bring down from Canada."

"Canada? Hmm. Our traffickers must bring them in over the border."

"Yeah. I went to that motel in Trail, Chance. The one on the card you gave me. I saw this girl there – she was Asian. Then I came back, and the next day, I was exploring on the river where I'd been shot at, and this boat came up onto the shore, and they unloaded some girls. I recognized one of them. It was the same girl I'd seen at that motel."

"Did you get proof? Evidence?"

She nodded. Her words came fast and furious, stumbling over each other in their hurry to get out.

"I got some pictures and sent them to the FBI. But it doesn't help much. The place is tighter than a drum. If anyone tries to find out anything, they'll slam down the lid. Those kids are slaves. I'm sure of it. I saw that girl I met on the sidewalk in Spokane. Sanora. Then last night, I rescued a girl from drowning herself in this horrible pond they have. She said it's called Deadwater because they dump bodies there. They have chain link fences all around the place and armed guards." She stifled a sob. "I have to break this case and do it right away. It's ... it's getting to me."

Chance nodded. "You need back-up. How about if I come and offer to work? Like I did at the Bible camp in Montana? Shoeing horses or somethin' like that." He removed his hat, rubbed his head, and replaced the hat.

"No. I'll get hold of you somehow if I need help. They probably can trace my calls, so it's just when I come to town that I can contact anyone. I'm afraid if I make a wrong move, my chance will be gone." She smiled. "By the way, I'm going by Katie McDonald now."

Her tone changed, was more like her normal voice, but weariness edged it. "I'm glad we could connect. I really needed it. How are you doing? I mean, really?"

He returned her smile, liking the way warmth crept into her pale face, the way her eyes lit up like he remembered. "Okay, I guess. Last night the gang from the camp found my place and almost killed me. The sheriff showed up in just in time. I was going to give my evidence to an FBI agent this morning, but he was impersonating an agent. They traced me to the apartment I rented. I got away, but I can't stay in one place for long. They're keen to get my evidence, the flash drive I picked up. Must be important."

She grimaced. "I'm sure it is."

He shook his head. "This is getting too weird. Oh! I got a text from Bobbi on ... let's see, it was Saturday, the day I got home. She went up to Boundary Dan. She heard or saw something suspicious and sent me a text. Here. I'll show you."

She read it. "Oh, no! What're you going to do? You've got to help her! Something must have happened to her. Did you go to the police?" She fixed wide eyes on him, almost willing him to find her aunt that moment.

"Yeah, I filed a missing person's report, and I called Elton. There's not much else I can do. I went back to the dam and looked around, but all I found was her phone beneath a bush by the parking lot. I checked on your place, and she hadn't been there for several days. Got your neighbors to feed the horses and the cats until you get back."

She exhaled, leaning back against the seat. Her hands shook when she retrieved her backpack and got out a water bottle. "Well, that's one good thing, I guess. But I'm worried about Bobbi. I wonder where she is. I'd feel terrible if she ... " She drew a breath like she was fighting against tears. "If she was hurt because of me. What do you think she meant about the dam?"

He shrugged. "Don't know. I'm out of clues."

She rested her forehead on her hand. "This is ... awful. I've got to find the answers. It's all part of the same plot but how does it tie together?" She sighed and gripped the door handle. "Look, I gotta go. When I figure this out, and if I get out alive, I'll get in touch with you. By the way, would you call these people?"

She pulled a pen and a piece of paper from her backpack. "They're my backup agents. Retired. Tell them you heard from me and that I took the job. That I'm okay and if I need them, I'll give them a call." She handed him the scrap of paper with the number on it. "Hey, you can give them your evidence. They'll get it to my boss."

He nodded. "Okay. Anything else?"

"Don't misplace that phone number, okay?" She grinned, almost like her old self.

He smiled. "Got it memorized already, sweetie."

"Sorry I've been so ..." she stopped and turned her head.

"It's getting to you, Gina," Chance replied, laying his hand on her shoulder. "Give it up before ..."

She turned back to him, her eyes blazing, tears streaking through the dark make-up on her face. "Before what? Before they murder me? Before the girls are taken away? Before they blow up the dam and ..." She stopped again, for she'd seen something beyond him, something in the parking lot.

"Oh, no. I gotta go!"

Leaping from the truck, she landed on the pavement and hunched over, she ran to her van, unlocked it and got in. Without looking in his direction, she drove from the parking lot and turned on Highway 395, going north.

A truck followed her onto the highway. Two men were in it.

Chance leaned forward on the seat and cradled his head in his hands, fighting against the despair that tore into his heart. He couldn't shout curses. Couldn't scream. But he wanted to. After a bit, he straightened and pulled himself together.

God was in this, and that gave him courage. First, Ramone was coming to help. And now, Gina told him where she was located. But what was he supposed to do with this information? He sorted through what she said. At least she had back-up. But would she call them?

Making sure no one followed, he turned south onto Main Street and drove past the Toyota dealership on the right and the Goodwill store on the left. One truth pounded over and over in his brain. I'm not going to let her go.

Even if he was the only one to tackle the problem, he had to do it. And time was running out. He could almost hear a ticking clock. Someone had a scheme, and it was up to him to figure it out and stop it before things exploded and people died.

He drove to the fairgrounds where someone was having some sort of an event.

He ate the cheese and meat sandwich that he'd purchased and washed it down with a Pepsi, munching his way through a bag of chips. Pulling out his cell phone, he called Gina's back-up people.

"Don," a man said on the second ring.

"Hi, this is Chance Marshal. I'm a friend of Katie McDonald."

There was silence. The man cleared his throat. "I don't know any Katie McDonald. You must have the wrong number."

Chance felt like he was walking on hot tar. "Look. I can't talk over the phone. She gave me this number and asked me to call you. Can we meet? I have ... something for you."

There was a long pause. Chance thought the man had hung up. "No! Don't hang up! Please. I need your help."

The man cleared his throat. "Okay. I'll meet with you. Bring whatever it is that you have for me, plus evidence that you are ... who you say. Give me... half an hour. Meet me in the Safeway parking lot."

That will give you time to check me out, right? He cleared his throat. "Okay. Walk inside the store, okay? I'll meet you in the produce aisle."

"Very well."

Chance was surprised when he saw Don, or the man he thought was Don. He was older, maybe in his late sixties, and bald. He inspected each item he put in his cart like it was a possible bomb.

Chance met the man's eyes. "Hello, sir. Want to get a cup of coffee?" He looked toward the deli where there was a coffee shop and tables.

The man nodded. "Sure." He didn't smile, but Chance caught a twinkle in his eyes. Enough to go on for now.

When they were looking at each other over the rim of their coffee cups, Chance waited for Don to begin. He was, after all, a senior agent.

"ID?"

Chance chuckled and pulled out his fake driver's license. "I had to go undercover, so this says I'm ... Bob Young. Sorry. Would you like to see the real one?"

Don shook his head. "How did you meet Katie?"

"In a snow storm last year in Montana. She'd gone out to investigate the disappearance of her uncle, and I ... well, I was tryin' to track down a drug cartel that killed my little brother in Columbia. We discovered we were after the same guys, and after she started believin' that I was on her side, we got along real well. And now..." He took a sip of coffee.

"Yes? And now? How do you fit into this?"

"You know how I fit into this," Chance said in a low tone. "You checked me out, didn't you? I used to work for the FBI. I'm a border guard. I went to a retreat on guns and weapons and found a place where they kill for the fun of it. I'm beginnin' to connect the dots and figure the same guys are involved in the human trafficking ring that Gina ... I mean, Katie, is looking into. Before I left that ranch, I got into the office and snatched a flash drive from a desk. That's my evidence. I looked at it, but it's all encrypted. Figured you guys could puzzle over it." He grinned. "Give you something to do."

Don nodded soberly. "Yeah. In our spare time. Why don't you hand it over, and I'll pass it on?"

"I wish there was some way I could know for sure that you're her back-up people."

"You're getting a little edgy, aren't you?" Don fished a wallet from his front pocket and shoved it over.

Chance took it. "After getting nearly killed several times in the last couple of days, I'd say I *am* a little edgy."

He opened the wallet and studied the card and the badge the man showed him from the inside of his jacket. He said, "All right. Here it is." His fist closed around the flash drive in his pocket. He slid it across the table.

Don received it with the flat of his hand. "Thanks." Shooting Chance a quizzical glance, he continued, "You said you're on the run. Need a place to hang out? We don't have much, but you're welcome to what we have. Katie stayed with us for two nights."

Chance grinned. "Anything that's good enough for her is okay with me. To tell the truth, I was wonderin' what I would do. I'm going to meet a friend of mine at 9:30. Mind if I bring him along?"

Don's smile was wide and genuine. "More the merrier. My wife, Jane, loves to cook. I'll show you to the house, and then you can come and go as you want."

As Chance got in Don's red Buick, his mind returned to Gina's pretty face and sea-green eyes. She needed him, and he was stumped as how to help her. How to rescue Bobbi. How to bring down this mammoth organization. He couldn't do it alone, and even having Don and Ramone to help didn't solve the problem. It was a good he had God on his side.

He didn't want to think about what he would do without God. His strength, wisdom, and grace would carry him through this.

It had to. It was all he had.

Chapter 44

In the Lion's Den

June 15

I keep my emotions tightly in check as I wind through Colville and head north. Shoving the conversation I'd had with Chance to the back of my mind, I concentrate on the task at hand – getting back to the ranch in one piece, hopefully not shot or pushed off the road on one of those curvy spots where a cliff drops down into the river.

I've learned most of the names of the people who are on staff at the school, and the kids who live there, except the Asian girls. They keep those separated at a different place.

Once, at dinner, I'd overheard two of the dorm parents talking about the Asian girls. They said they were moved out quickly to their destinations, some of them traveling by van as far as New York City. That made sense because they wouldn't want them to learn English.

Noting that a pickup hangs close behind me, I smile grimly and keep the van at a steady pace – not too fast, not too slow, not trying to lose them. Of course, it would be difficult to lose someone in the traffic of Colville or Kettle Falls. The truck behind me is black. *They like black, don't they?*

After I pull out of Kettle Falls and descend the long hill to the bridge that crosses the river, they disappear. I wonder if they called someone else to follow, but no other vehicle takes the black pickup's place as I start up the highway following the Columbia River.

As I drive, sobs well up from my chest and tear at my throat. Chance's face comes rushing back – the intense look in his eyes, the tight way he gripped the steering wheel, the grim line of his mouth. He said he was worried about me. Well, I'm worried about him, and I wonder what he is doing and how he can cope.

At a wide spot, I drive down by the river where there is a fishing access and picnic area. After I get my emotions in control and blow my nose, I roll down the window and breathe deeply of pine and fir and other forest smells I love.

Chance was hurt by the way I pushed him away and wouldn't confide in him, yet I can't allow him into my life right now. I have to do this alone. If he came to the school, I'd risk everything. Just one look or one comment when the wrong person was near, and my cover would be blown.

I shake my head, tears wetting my face. "*No!* I don't want it to be this way!"

What makes it worse is that I think I'm falling in love with him, and I realize for the first time that he's the kind of guy I could spend my life with. I can't allow him to slip through my fingers while I'm chasing bad guys around the country.

I don't want to go back to the school. I want to keep driving and blot out from my memory the task I've set myself to do.

But I've got to solve this mystery. I've got to help the kids escape, and I've got to bring this organization down, even though it might mean my life, and maybe Chance's, too. Yet I'm the only one who can do this. As Dad was fond of saying, you choose this path, now you have to live with your choices.

I wipe my face and re-apply my make-up.

Arriving at the ranch, I unload the groceries I'd bought and carry them to the kitchen. Maria helps. I just have time to change my clothes and get over to Bruno's for our lunch date.

Choosing the Mexican skirt and peasant blouse I wore last night, I brush my hair and grab my black shoulder bag that I use for a purse. I'll have to walk this time, as I don't see Bennet or his handy little Ranger anywhere.

It's a quarter past twelve when I ring the doorbell at Bruno's impressive front door, wondering as I do if I should've gone around to the side door, the servant's entry.

After a short wait, a man opens the door.

He studies me without expression, standing straight and stiff. He's tall with dark hair and dark eyes, very wide shoulders and muscles on muscles. The bodyguard. Definitely not a butler!

He steps back. "Come in, Miss McDonald. Mr. Bruno will see you in a moment." I enter the foyer, a well-lit space with a flagstone floor, a full-length mirror, a coat rack, and a big painting of a hunting party.

"In here, miss," the man says, leading me down a hallway and into a large room that can only be called the formal living room.

"Thank you." I nod to him. He turns and strides away.

The room is like something out of a Fortune magazine. It has a white carpet, leather furniture, Chinese vases of real flowers, lamps, two paintings that look like masterpieces. I admire a huge rock fireplace.

I step to a pastel blue chair that's facing the fireplace, but before I sit down, I hear soft footfalls behind me. Turning, I see that Bruno has entered the room from a different doorway and is advancing upon me with a huge grin. He holds out his hand.

"Katie! I'm glad you can come over! Let's go to the sitting room. It's more comfortable and has a view of the river." He leads me, with a hand on my elbow, to a smaller room that opens off the living room. One whole wall is devoted to large windows that look out on the river and valley below the house, looking south.

After I'm seated in a plush easy chair, an older woman enters with a tray that holds two cups of steaming coffee and a plate of cookies. I take the cup and one cookie and thank her, meeting her eyes and smiling. She returns my smile.

Bruno engages me in a conversation of small talk, but he seems uneasy, disturbed. Like a pacing panther, he moves around the room, laughing at times, other times impaling me with an intense stare. My stomach growls with hunger, and I wonder when we're going to eat. It's about then that Patti Jo enters.

It's the first I've seen her, and I'm surprised she's so young. I'm guessing she's maybe twenty or twenty-one. Her tawny hair flows past her shoulders, and her eyes are greenish blue. She sweeps into the room like a queen, every inch of her faultless body tanned, groomed and clothed to perfection. She's gorgeous, and she knows it.

Bruno introduces her as his personal secretary. I have to choke back a snicker as I'm thinking she's probably very personal!

She meets me with a dip of her head and an outstretched hand, flashing white teeth in a wide smile. I don't know if I'm supposed to shake her hand or kiss it. Rising from my seat, I opt for the first.

"Hey, it's great that you could come over, Kathy," she says, sweeping her hair behind her shoulders.

"Katie." I respond.

"Oh. Yeah. Anyway, make yourself at home. We don't stand on ceremony here, as Bruno says." She flashes him a dazzling smile, then includes me in it. "I just *love* it when I can meet the staff here and get to know you a little bit better."

"It's gracious of you to have me," I respond, thinking I can gush as well as she can.

She receives a kiss to her cheek from Bruno. I follow behind them as they stroll into the dining room. The meal is delicious, as I expected, barbecued salmon on toasted buns with a lacy salad of greens, arranged artistically with orange slices. The same older lady who served us previously brings out wine and pours it into our glasses. Her name tag reads Evelyn.

Bruno dominates the conversation with talk about the mutual relatives he thinks we have, the ranch, and his work. I get in a word occasionally, but he's not focused on me. Patti Jo doesn't seem to mind – she spends most of the time on her phone.

It's late when we're finished lunch. Bruno rises first, rather suddenly, and exclaims that he'd forgotten about a meeting he had scheduled. Patti Jo stands with him and gives me one of her million dollar smiles.

"It was nice to meet you, Katie," she says regally.

"Yes. Nice to meet you, too, Patti. I hope you enjoy your work." That slides out before I can check it. She jerks her head to give me a quick glance, but I pretend ignorance.

I get to my feet and pick up my bag, which looks old and ratty in this setting. "Thanks so much for having me. This has been fun."

Liar! a voice says in my head. It was actually more like having lunch with a ravenous wolf. "Would you mind if I paid my compliments to your cook?" I glance toward the kitchen door. "I was wondering if I could get the recipe for that delicious salmon."

Bruno laughs. "Oh, sure. Please forgive us for rushing off. You can find your way out, can't you? If you need anything, my man, Hugo, can help you."

"Oh, no. I'm fine."

They leave abruptly, and I'm alone. But I have to be careful because of My Man Hugo.

I find the kitchen and chat amiably with the cook, a lady whose name is Phyllis. She's flattered by my compliments and promises to write out the recipe for me. I tell her that I can let myself out and leave the room.

Creeping down a long hallway that leads to what I figure will lead to the bedrooms and office, or maybe a gym or home theater, I look back. Did My Man Hugo know when I left the kitchen? Will he come looking for me?

I peek into every room and find a spacious office at the far end of the house, complete with two desks, file cabinets, a bulletin board, potted plants, leather chairs, and an aerial photo of the ranch on the wall. Heading straight to what I figure is the Bruno's main computer, I sit at his desk and tap the space bar.

A screen comes up, asking for a password. I stare at it, trying to think. There's a commotion outside – dogs barking, someone shouting. Sweat forms on my brow. I try a few obvious ones like Columbia River School. *Nope.* Replace *school* with *ranch.* No again.

The commotion settles down. I dislike the silence more than the noise. On the edges of my consciousness, I realize I shouldn't be here, that if someone found me, I could be dismissed rather abruptly. But the burden of needing to know something that will help me crack this case drives me forward.

I blot out all the extraneous sounds and concentrate.

Address of the ranch? *No.* Date of Bruno's birth? I guess and come up negative, hoping the computer doesn't shut me out after so many wrong guesses. I try numbers that I think would apply. Dates. Words. *Nothing.* I hear voices in the house. It sounds like Hugo is talking with someone. *Is there a guard nearby? Are they searching for me?*

Wait. This might be his personal computer. If so, he might have used something less formal and more private. What about Patti Jo? I type in her name and what I guess would be her year of birth. Nope. What about the date they met? I find an appointment calendar of his personal events on the computer and go back ... maybe April? No. May? There it is — date with Patti Jo. May 25th and the year.

Hearing footsteps in the hallway, I jump up and look out the sliding glass door, thinking I can escape that way. It leads to the back deck with steps going down to an enclosed yard. I open the door for a breath of air as the room is stifling hot. Then I return to the desk.

Now the voices I hear are closer. Doors opening and shutting. A vehicle drives up — is it Bennet's Ranger? More voices. Footsteps on the deck outside the sliding glass doors. I'm sweating profusely now, and praying silently as I type in words and numbers. *Please, God, help me get it right! Please!*

Bingo! The right combination opens the window. Now I'm in. I scan the various files he has on his desktop and open a few. Nothing here of interest. *Darn!* Shoving back from the desk, I freeze when I hear someone approaching the door, calling out to someone.

"Have you checked the office? Okay. I'll look."

Maybe there's something I can find in the drawers. Opening the center drawer, I push aside the usual office supplies – pens, erasers, paper clips, note pads – and see a small key. The guard is at the door. The knob turns.

Grabbing the key, along with my bag, I sink down behind the desk and squish into the tiny space, thankful there's a front on it. The door opens. Someone enters. He stomps around the room and stops at the sliding glass door. I remember I'd left it open.

"Hey! This door is open!" He calls to someone outside. "She must have gotten out this way!" Another person comes into the room but stands quietly by the door. The first man approaches the desk. I hold my breath and hide my eyes.

"The computer's on. He never leaves it on. She must've heard us and ran." He straightens. "Check the back yard. Then get your guys out on the road to the school. She's got to be around here somewhere!" He pauses, listening. He glances under the desk.

I know this is it. I've been discovered.

But to my surprise, he straightens and heads straight for the sliding glass door. His footsteps fade as he descends the steps.

I am shaking like a corn stalk in the wind. My legs begin to cramp, and my breath comes in gasps. But I try to stay still for a few more minutes, waiting until the hue and cry has diminished.

After enduring the pain as long as I can, I unwind myself from my hidey-hole and crawl out. With my bag looped over my arm, I stand slowly and creep to the sliding glass door. Silence has descended on the place. Even the birds are quiet. I wonder if they've left someone watching. No matter. I have to get out of here as soon as I can.

Taking a deep breath, I step out on the deck and jump down the steps to the ground, expecting any moment to hear the dogs and men coming for me again.

Chapter 45

The Person in the Basement

Colville, June 15

Ramone was not in the park when Chance arrived. It was nearly dark, and the silent old trees stood with branches outstretched, providing shade and a cool breeze in the warm, soft night. He moved toward the restrooms, thinking his friend might have gone in there, when a movement caught his peripheral vision.

At the same moment, he heard the sound of cloth rubbing against bushes as something moved through the underbrush that lined the path. He dropped to the ground and rolled to the shelter of a big rock that had been placed artistically beside the playground, expecting to hear the blast of gunfire. He waited.

Silence. A low chuckle. A man slid from the shadows of a giant pine and stepped toward him. "What's the matter, Chancy-boy?" he said. "Your nerves a little edgy tonight?"

Chance stood, relief washing over him. He advanced to shake the big man's hand and give him a one-armed hug. "Ramone! It's good to see you! Why'd you come?" He sat at a picnic table near the parking lot where he could watch for cars and pedestrians.

Ramone shook his head. "I got your message, and you was so mysterious, I figured I'd better hightail it up here. Besides, it was gettin' hot down there, and I don't mean the temperature. I had my apartment broken into and was followed one night. Then someone blasted out my truck's windows when I was in it."

"Yeah. That's one of their favorite tactics. I've had two windshields shot out."

"So, what's been goin' down with you? You look... haggard, like you haven't slept for awhile. Same thing as my troubles? What about your girlfriend?"

Chance sighed. "C'mon. Let's not stay in one place too long. You got a car? Let's go get some coffee, and I'll fill you in on all the gruesome details."

"Sounds good to me." Ramone led the way to where he'd parked the vehicle he'd rented, a red Toyota Highlander.

It was after ten in the evening when they returned to Don and Jane's house. There were no lights, except a glimmer from a basement window.

As they sat in the driveway, Chance shook his head and glanced at his friend. "You sure you want to help? This might get dangerous. Someone might even get killed."

Ramone stared at the sky where a full moon was playing peek-a-boo among the clouds. "I wouldn't have come all this way unless I wanted to help. Just tell me what to do." He got his suitcase out of the back.

Chance rang the doorbell. "Okay. Like you said, I could stand some sleep, so let's crash here for the night and figure out what we're going to do tomorrow. But we can't drag our feet on this. They're moving fast toward some sort of deadline, and we've got to figure it out, or we'll get blown out of the water."

Ramone grunted. "I'd rather you not use that metaphor, Chance. A little too close to home." He yawned. "All right. Show me where to go. I'm ready."

***

From Gina's Journal, 5:33pm

I make it back to my cabin without being seen, at least not immediately. I imagine I'll be traced on their security cameras, and everyone from Bruno down to Gunther the guard will know my movements. But I'd tried to stay in the shadows, and, of course, I avoided their men who were beating the brush for me.

"And now you'll see me," I whisper as I slip inside, resisting the urge to wave at the camera above the door.

I change clothes and head up to the Hacienda for dinner.

Bennet approaches my table as I'm buttering my roll. "Katie! Where have you been? We searched the whole campus for you! We thought something had happened to you, like you got drowned or something. You had us worried." He sits down beside me and flings his arm on the back of my chair.

I straighten. "You want my itinerary for the whole day? I thought that's what the cameras were for." I glance at him to see a reaction, but he keeps his face impassive.

Continuing in a didactic tone, I continue, "I went to town to get some groceries. When I came back, I had lunch with Bru ... I mean, Mr. Sherman and his secretary. After that, I visited with his cook, and walked back here. What's the deal? Are you tracking my every step? I don't appreciate that. There is such a thing as personal privacy." I decide to take the high road of offended dignity which always seems to work with him.

This time it doesn't. He presses his face close to mine and speaks softly. "Well, you listen up, girlie. You're not going to pull your tricks on us anymore! You better toe the line here, or we've got some surprises in store for you." He leans back. "And I promise you won't like them."

I return his hard glare as best as I can. "What are you going to do? Toss me in that nice little pond you have down by the river? I wouldn't try that, if I were you. I've got friends, you know." I bite into a crusty roll and turn away from him.

He isn't finished. As he stands, he says, "I know you do. Those friends are being taken care of, too, and they won't be able to protect you. Just watch your step. I've taken a liking to you, so I'm giving you this friendly warning."

I snort. "Friendly? That's rich coming from you. Okay. I hear you. I'll watch my step. Is that what you want me to say?"

He grunts an obscenity and marches off, across the dining room and out the door. I'd pushed him too far. He's no longer an ally, a friend. But it's all I can do to be civil to the man, knowing what they're doing here. Knowing the lives they are wrecking just for greed. What do they know about me? Is everything he said a bluff, hoping I'd cave in and spill my guts to him?

Should I call in my back-up and try to get out while I can? But I don't have much evidence. I'd taken some photos, but nothing else. It would be my word against their big lawyers, and it doesn't take much imagination to figure out who would win that case.

I'm mulling over my choices when Maria, the cook, touches my shoulder. I jump. "Oh! You startled me, Maria. What can I do for you?"

"Brenda is sick. She cannot come tonight." She pauses as if that explains it all.

"Yes?"

Wiping her hands on her apron, she continues, "She usually comes to help with dishes after supper. We are rushed. Mr. Sherman has a meeting tonight, and we have to get things ready. Do you think you could help, Katie? This one time?"

"Oh, yes. I don't mind at all. Let me finish, and I'll be right there."

Relieved, she thanks me and returns to the kitchen. Half an hour later, I find myself at a deep sink, elbow in hot, sudsy water, scrubbing on a pile of pots and pans. Two girls, who helped serve the meal, are wiping the tables and counters. They finish and leave.

The only other ones in the kitchen are the older couple, Gerri and Gary, who volunteer when needed. They are putting the finishing touches to the meal that will be served at the meeting, and they pay me no attention whatsoever.

I don't mind the work – it gives me something to vent my anger on. Yet I'm not expecting what happens next. Maria makes a funny sound as she stirs the soup at the stove next to me. I glance at her. She is holding her hand to her stomach, and her face is as white as pastry dough.

She meets my eyes. "I need to go —" With that, she dashes to the bathroom.

When she returns, she turns the heat down under the soup and steps over to me. "I ... I am not feeling well, either, Miss Katie. Maybe I have the same thing Brenda has? I do not know, but..."

I straighten and set the last pan on the counter beside the sink to drip dry. "What do you want me to do? Are there others who can come in?"

She nods. "Yes. We can call other staff to help with the dinner. Gerri knows who can help. The bad part is that I'm supposed to take a meal to someone who..." She stops and glances around as if afraid she'll be overheard. She whispers, "Someone who is in a room down below. In the basement. Can you..."

"Take dinner to them?" I can't quite believe my ears. What are they doing in the basement? I didn't even know the building had a lower floor. "Yeah, I can do that. But I don't know where..."

"Oh. I will show you. You must do this tomorrow morning, too. For every meal. This person is... very sick. They have to be quarantined until they get better."

Maria opens a drawer and removes a key that's been wired to the inside of the drawer, hidden behind a stack of papers. She slips it in her apron pocket. Then she takes a plate of food from the oven and places it on a tray along with a plastic bottle of water. "Come with me."

Chapter 46

Busted!

Columbia River Ranch, June 15th

As I follow Maria's broad back down the long hallway that leads to the back of the building, I long for my revolver. It's in my backpack in the cabin, tucked under the bed.

Maria opens a door. It reveals a stairway descending to the basement. She flips a switch and without a word, starts down. I follow her. We enter a darkened hallway. I expect to see bare light bulbs and maybe spider webs, but the lighting is good, and there's carpet underfoot. She reaches into a recessed cupboard to get a flashlight, which she hands to me.

At the third door, she uses the key from her pocket and opens the door. There's no eerie screeching of door hinges, yet an awful smell assaults my nose, like an outhouse gone bad. I gag and hold my nose.

She glances over her shoulder. "Bad smell. Lady is very sick. You wait here. I will take the food in."

I want to tell her it isn't disease I'm smelling — it's a lack of bathroom facilities. She enters the room as I hover near the doorway. Chains clink as someone says something softly like they've been awakened.

My curiosity is overwhelming. I lean around the doorpost and look inside, using the flashlight. A woman is lying on a low cot. She sits up when my light hits her face. I gasp.

Maria hurriedly sets the tray on the floor and whirls to me. "Get back! It is dangerous in here!"

But I've seen the woman. Her dark hair, sprinkled with gray, falls into her face as she turns to the light, squinting against its brightness.

She glances up at Maria. "Oh! Oh, I'm so glad to see you! I must have fallen asleep. What do we have for dinner tonight? Not fish soup with eyeballs in it again?" She chuckles, and I marvel that she can, for chains manacle her ankles to the wall. How long has she lived in this fetid darkness? I study her face. I've seen this woman before.

Then it hits me. I stagger and grab for the doorpost. *Aunt Bobbi!* I almost cry out, but realize in time that there are probably security cameras in here. I can't say a thing, and she hasn't seen me. She's looking up at Maria in a bewildered way.

"Yes. Eat, lady," Maria says, backing away, shoving me out the door. She gathers up the previous meal's tray and begins to shut the door on Bobbi's words.

"Don't leave me! Please! Oh, I beg you! Don't leave me in the dark! I can't stand it. Leave me the light. Please!"

But the door closes on her frantic entreaty. Maria's panting by the time we reach the top landing of the stairs. "When you take food, just put it down on the floor. She can get it. Then get the used dishes and get out. The disease is very bad, Miss Katie. Very bad."

I think I see tears streaking her face, but maybe it's sweat.

"It is not sickness, Maria," I say in a low tone as we hurry down the hallway. "Didn't you see the chains? How can you do this?"

But she merely deposits the tray on the counter in the kitchen and removes her apron. "I am going home, Miss Katie. You will do as you have been instructed." Her eyes are glistening, and her face is white. Yet there's a steely will in her words. "Good night."

I want to grab her by her throat and demand she help me free Bobbi. What monsters run this place? How can they manipulate the staff like they had Maria? Why does she choose to believe them?

Maria flings the key into the drawer in the kitchen and walks away. I have to free Bobbi soon. She can't last very long as she is. Yet the cameras watch my every move – those blasted cameras.

I take the key, slip it in my pocket, and go back to my cabin.

***

Columbia River Ranch and School, 9:35pm

"I've seen her before. Somewhere." Bennet rubbed his forehead and studied the computer screen in the guard's quarters in the Hacienda. Two men accompanied him – the guard, Gunther, and Tank, the manager from the neighboring ranch where they kept the Asian girls.

"Yeah? Where?" Gunther leaned over him, breathing down his neck.

"Give me some space, you idiot," Bennet snarled. "I know I've seen Katie's face before. But she looked different. Hey. I'll check the security photos. The ones from Spokane."

He had to do something to appease his boss. The man had been furious when he reported that they'd lost track of Katie, that she'd gotten through their net at Bruno's house, and that she'd turned up at supper like she'd never done anything wrong in her life.

No, the boss wasn't happy about it at all. In fact, he hinted that Bennet could be replaced. Demoted. Maybe even killed. His whole future flashed in front of his eyes like smoke, disappearing with a breath of air. His wealth, the fancy house he wanted to build that would rival the senator's, the women he could have, the things he could buy – it could all vanish in one swift stroke if he didn't find some answers and find them quickly.

"Why you lookin' at them, boss?" Tank asked, leaning close again. "She ain't from Spokane. Her resume says she's from Billings."

313

"Yeah, right, and I'm from Mars. It's her cover story. Don't you get it?" This could take hours, pouring over every inch of footage from surveillance they'd been sent from their men in Spokane, but he had to keep going.

Suddenly a face emerged on the screen. Gina Lindsay, a cop with the SPD. She was getting into her car, her face turned upward. Bennet stopped the camera. Froze the face. Enlarged it.

"That's her!" He yelped, jumping up, bumping into Tank. Gunther ambled over from his position. Bennet's finger jabbed toward the computer screen. "This is Katie McDonald. Look! She's changed her hair color. Puffed out her cheeks a bit. Wears different kind of clothes. But I bet it's her. What do you think?"

Tank nodded slowly. "Could be. What about it? Why'd she change...?"

"She's an undercover cop, you fool!" Bennet resumed his seat. "Let's see ... she works for the SPD, with their Special Investigative Unit, now on leave of absence." He flipped to another camera. "Oh! And look at this one. This is from our house in Spokane just before the police closed it down."

The camera showed a girl meandering down the sidewalk. A woman stopped and talked with her. Bennet zoomed in on the woman's face. *Bingo!* Gina Lindsey again!

He leaned back. "I'm buying beers all around! Then I'm calling the boss. We got her nailed. And, boy, am I gonna have fun with her when we throw her in the holding room! She won't karate chop me then! C'mon over to my house for a round, guys. We're gonna have us a party!"

***

Colville, June 16

"I'd like to ride into that place where I saw some men unloading boxes," Chance said over his third cup of coffee the next morning in Jane's kitchen. He turned to Ramone. "I'll need to go get my horse. But I'm worried about Gina. She might need help if she tries to

314

escape. Do you think you could stake out the school? It's on the river. I'll show you where. I was thinking you could find a place, either above the ranch or below it, and watch it. Could you do that for me?"

Ramone shrugged. "Shore, if that's what you want. Show me the place, and I'm off." He shot Chance a sharp glance. "Are you going to take your truck to pull the horse trailer?"

"No, I'm leaving my pickup parked at Safeway. I think I'll rent a truck." He got out his map and marked where the Columbia River School and Ranch was located. Then, after packing their gear and telling Don and Jane good-bye, he and Ramone headed out.

As Chance filled out the rental agreement, he considered the danger he might be creating for himself. Renting the truck might lay a trail for their enemies to find him, but it would take a few days for them to track him through this means since he was using a fake ID.

He found his horses well fed and content at Pole's place and chose Santiago for the trip. Leaving a note on the door, for the man was not home, he loaded the horse and started north, stopping long enough at his house to get his .223 Remington semi-automatic rifle that Dad bought him for Christmas last year, along with several boxes of ammo.

Before he left town, he called the Nelway border patrol station north of Metaline. He alerted them to what he'd seen and that he was planning to go and investigate the beach just north of the dam.

The border guard seemed busy and distracted. "It might be best to run this by the Field Operator in the Colville office, Agent Marshal," he said.

Chance shifted, anxious to get going. "I feel we need to move on this, Mike. If these are the same people who shot Dusty, they aren't afraid to kill, and they're bringing in contraband from Canada. I'd appreciate some back-up if you have it."

Mike didn't respond immediately. Then he said, "Have you contacted your Supervising Agent in Charge? Or the Field Operating Supervisor? We can't authorize a patrol going down on the river without written notice. Call your office over there. When we hear from them, we'll send a patrol. It might be best to delay your investigation a day or two."

Chance reined in his impatience. "No, I haven't cleared it with the D-PAIC or the FOS." He liked and trusted McClurry, but he knew it would end up on the Whitley's desk or in DeMoss's office, the two top administrative bosses at his post. "I'll just do surveillance today. If I find something, I'll report it. Thanks."

"Yeah. Take it easy. I'll let the SAC over here know you called."

It took two hours to drive to the overlook on the east side of the dam. The border was only two miles across open country from here, an easy run. The sandy beach where he'd seen the men unloading the boat was about a mile below him.

Santiago was ready to go when he got the saddle cinched and his rifle in its case. "Easy, boy," he said. He loved to ride, and this was a fair day to do it. Yet the knowledge of what he might encounter tightened his muscles and sharpened his senses. He didn't mind fighting for what was right, but he didn't like killing people. Even bad people.

A tiny logging road led north from the parking lot, winding through the trees. He directed Santiago into it, every sense alert and his spine stiff. There'd been vehicles driven up and down the rutted trail recently. Who would be using this road? There was no logging done up here anymore, yet they might be hikers or people looking for hunting places and huckleberry picking spots.

Or it might be the gang he'd seen down on the river.

He kept watching for a smaller trail that would lead off the logging road and slant down to the river, and sure enough, about half an hour later, he found one. Directing Santiago onto it, he discovered it descended steeply in places. Santiago didn't like the loose shale which they encountered, and once Chance had to dismount and lead him to the side where there was more underbrush and safer footing.

At one point, he stopped and drank from his water bottle, studying the terrain below. If someone was smuggling contraband into the country from Canada, how would they transport it out of here? On his search on Google maps, he'd seen a clearing to the north and a good-sized road leading from that.

Before the trail leveled off to the sandy beach, he caught glimpses of the river through the trees. When he figured he was as close as he wanted to get with the horse, he found a shady place beside a big pine tree and dismounted.

He started down the last one hundred yards toward the river, stopping now and then to listen. Crows cawed from the trees and a squirrel scolded him, but otherwise, the woods were silent.

He paused as he reached the edge of the forest and gazed down at the beach and the stretch of the Pend Oreille River, flowing north. The dam was to his left, south. Three plumes of water gushed from the dam face.

Sweat streaked his face. He wiped it away with an impatient hand and found a stump to sit on, wondering how long he'd have to wait. He had water and an apple in the saddle bag, but he couldn't get it. The end of the lower parking lot for the dam was directly across the river from his position. At the far end of the parking lot, there were two storage buildings near the river. He studied them with his glasses, but no one drove in or out, and he couldn't spot any cars in the lot.

He wanted to go down to the beach and search for signs of a boat or a camp where the men waited for shipments, but he held himself still. Waiting was the hardest thing he ever did, and now, with danger clanging in his head like tolling of a bell of the dead, he clamped down hard on his jittery nerves and bent his mind to listening.

It wasn't long before he heard it. The sound of a motor out on the river. It drew closer, the motor stopped, and oars dipped in and out of the water.

It was not a large boat, but there were boxes piled in the center of it. Two men rowed with powerful strokes, both wearing wide-brimmed hats. He suspected that if they were from Canada, that a larger boat was around the corner, and that this one was used on the approach to the beach where they stowed the goods and got them to the highway.

How did they pack the boxes to the road? They must have a four-wheeler and a trailer parked somewhere.

The men remained silent as they beached the boat and tied it to a stump near the shore. Chance crept down the bank slowly, making sure he didn't break a twig or roll any stones. The two men unloaded the boxes, not caring if they got their feet wet when they waded into the river. They piled the boxes on the bank out of Chance's view.

He inched closer, staying in cover behind scraggly bushes that lined the bank. He wanted to get a good picture of them, and had his camera out, but he couldn't see their faces, not even with his binoculars.

When they were finished, they mopped their brows. One took out a cigarette and lit it. The other disappeared for a short while in the bushes. Their voices came to Chance in fits and pauses as they were raised and lowered.

"... when they get here ... yeah, let's get this ... when ..."

"Tonight ... eight pm. Yeah ... when they close the ... lot." This from the big man who gazed at the dam. He laughed. "Can't wait to see it go ... will be quite sight .... All right, let's move it out."

Chance sneezed. It came too suddenly to stop and sounded like a shot in the clear, still air. Before the men on the beach could register the sound they'd heard, he'd started to move, forcing caution into his movements, watching every step. One of the men swore loudly.

Glancing over his shoulder when he reached denser cover, Chance saw one man had dropped to a knee and held a rifle firmly against his shoulder.

The other man, the big guy, was heading up the bank, carrying his rifle in the crook of his arm, a grim expression on his face. "I'll get him," he called back to his partner. "Stay here and guard the shipment."

We'll see about that. Chance darted up the hill through the trees. He had to get to Santiago, mount, and run before the man who aimed to kill him could cut him off from the horse.

His shirt dripped with sweat as he flitted from tree to tree, trying to keep in cover, yet he had to get across the bare hillside, the one he'd slid down on the way to the beach. As he started across it, a shot rang out and a bullet singed his head. He ducked, lunged upwards, clinging to slender bushes to pull himself higher.

Finally, he fell behind a large rock at the top of the slope.

That was close. He'd been spotted, and now he had to run for it. Keeping his rifle up and out of the way wasn't easy as he mounted the next set of rocky steps. He expected any minute to feel a bullet tearing into his back. But he made it to the top and glanced around. Where had he left Santi? Yes. Over there, by that big pine.

Sprinting to the tree, he found Santiago. The horse edged away from him, his eyes showing white. He'd heard the rifle shot and didn't like it.

"Easy, boy. We gotta ... get out ... of here." Chance was gasping when he leaped into the saddle and turned the horse up the slope.

Another rifle boomed below him. He caught a glimpse of the man and wanted to return fire, but he didn't like the prospect of his horse going berserk. Santiago wasn't keen on the noise of a big gun right by his ears.

He kicked the horse. "Okay, boy. Let's go!" Santi knew what that meant and took the hillside in long, lunging strides as if he was born to flee an armed assailant.

They broke out onto the logging road and without pausing, Chance turned him right. Santiago thundered down the track like it was a race course. They were out-distancing his pursuers, but Chance knew they wouldn't let him live. They couldn't let him live.

Would they call someone to kill him as he drove down that long East Side Road to the highway? Or would it be on the way to Metaline?

319

Well, all he could do was get to the truck. Load the horse. Make a fast exit. The truck looked a welcome sight. It was probably the fastest job he'd ever done of unsaddling, loading the horse, and getting the rig going out of the parking lot.

It's funny what adrenalin will do, he mused.

As he drove south, he had time to think about what he'd learned. *Tonight! At eight!* He was sure the man meant blowing the dam – *I can't wait to see it go,* he'd said.

It didn't give Chance much time. In fact, hardly any time at all. He kept a close eye on the traffic coming towards him as he wound down the hill into the small town of Metaline. No one followed, and there seemed to be none that threatened his progress. Yet it was not over. Not by a long shot. They would get him.

He gripped the steering wheel, sweat dripping into his eyes and clouding his vision. His dad hadn't responded with information about Forward Guard, and the border guard wouldn't help. Not much, anyway. He doubted if the sheriff would get his act together to bring aid, either.

Not in time.

Chapter 47

Impossible!

From Gina's Journal, June 15, 5:23am

Jolting awake, I leap out of bed, fully dressed. I didn't think I'd sleep, but I must have dozed off around two in the morning.

As my feet hit the floor, the scene I'd witnessed in that dark cellar room below the Hacienda hits me like a mad bull. Bobbi didn't know I was there, as I hadn't spoken. I wish I'd said something — anything! It would have given her hope during those long, tedious hours. Or I could have shoved the flashlight through the door. I doubt if Maria would have noticed.

I have to wait to free Bobbi until breakfast is delivered to her because the guards would expect to see someone going down the stairs and into her room at that time.

I stretch and pad over to the window, lifting the lacy white curtain. The sun isn't up, but light is growing in the east, and the sky is robin-egg blue. I'm cold, chilled by the reality of my situation. I must think through my next moves carefully, and I have to devise an exit plan. One by one, I tick off the things I have to do. Get evidence. Free Bobbi and get her out of here. Get in touch with Sanora. Get out myself.

I take a shower and dress. While I'm brushing my hair, a wave of frustration and anger engulfs me. No! This is impossible. I can't do all of that — I can't even do a part of it.

I blink back sudden tears. Gritting my teeth against the searing weight of responsibility thrust upon me, and getting angrier by the second, I pace the small living room, picking up a stray sock here and a cushion there. I fling the covers up on the bed and punch down the pillow.

Then I take a deep breath. Oh, God I've got to stay calm. Focused. Anger isn't going to get me anywhere. In fact, it will open the door to fear and cause me to make stupid mistakes.

As I start a pot of coffee, I mull over the questions that bombard my mind.

How did Aunt Bobbi get captured? Why hadn't she stayed home and taken care of the animals, like I'd told her to? How am I going to get her out of that room with all the cameras they have around the place? Anything I try will be disastrous, unless I eliminate the guards who sit watching the security cameras.

No, not eliminate. Neutralize. I smile grimly as I try to bring my brain into gear. Rubbing my head, I wish the searing headache would go away. I sure don't need that today!

One of the few things I'd accomplished during my time here is that I found where the security screens are located. I'd come upon it quite accidentally one day when I was looking for the broom closet along the hallway that comes off the dining room. I opened a door and looked inside. It was dark in the room, except for the blue glow of the screens on the far wall. Three men sat in office chairs in front of the screens. They didn't look around or say anything as I softly closed the door.

I bring my mind back to my problems. How can I escape? Swim the river? It's wide, deep and cold. A person would have to be in excellent shape to swim across it, as it's probably at least a half a mile wide right here. There's a long, shallow beach, and it would take several minutes to get to deep enough in the water to submerge. They'd thought of all the angles and had them covered.

What should I do?

Do the next thing!

I remove a container of yogurt from the refrigerator and rip off the cover. This will have to do for breakfast. While eating, hunched over the table, I carefully grind up all the sleeping tablets I have on hand, the over the counter drugs that I seldom use. I'll put this in a drink and try to get it into the guards. It won't be enough to knock them out completely, but I'm hoping it will be enough to make them sleepy and inattentive to the screens. I wrap the powder in a napkin and lace on my boots.

After packing my backpack with everything I can think of that I might need if I don't have time or opportunity to return to the cabin, I sling it over my shoulder and start out for the Hacienda, watching the shadows as daylight sifts through the tall pines and birds awaken with song.

I notice, on the fringes of my consciousness, that it's a lovely morning, filled with a small breeze that lifts my hair, with sunshine and the scent of pine. Down below, the river reflects the colors of the sunrise. But my mind is set on what I have to do, and nothing shakes my focus, not even the beauty in nature that surrounds me.

Or Bennet with his not-so-veiled threats.

This is it. Once I spring Bobbi from her prison cell, there's no turning back. I wonder if I can get word to Sanora at breakfast that she has to be ready to get out with me. I'm still trying to come up with a scheme to help her escape, although there are maybe ten or eleven other girls who need to get out of here, too. Not counting the boys.

Do the next thing!

The office. I need to get evidence, and no one is ever in the office this time of the morning. After donning the denim floppy hat I have in my backpack, I enter the building through the back door which leads into the kitchen and hurry through it to avoid being seen by the lady who's taking Maria's place to prepare breakfast.

Slowing to a sedate saunter, I emerge into the dining room, cross it, and duck into the hallway that leads to the office.

I hesitate, a little out of breath, in front of the office door, fishing my key from my pocket. There are three in my pocket. One is the key that I'd lifted from Bruno's desk, hoping it will open the secret file cabinet, another one will unlock the door going down to Bobbi's cell, and the last is the office door key. I start to insert it into the lock.

But then I see the door is ajar an inch. *Strange!*

I put up my hand to push it further open when I hear voices inside. I freeze and listen. Two men are in there. I'm thinking it's Bruno Sherman and Bennet Sargent, the two masterminds of this horrible organization. I grip my hands so tightly that my fingernails dig into my palms and lean closer to hear what they're saying.

It's Bennet's voice that drifts through the crack in the doorway. "I tell you, she's an undercover cop, and we gotta do something about it!"

I can't hear the murmur of the reply from the other man.

"Well, we can't wait," Bennet says. I hear him striding around and hope he's not coming to the door. "We strike at eight tonight, and nothing is going to stop us. Not even the cutesy little cop we have running around here. Let's see where she's at now. It shouldn't be too hard to find her on the cameras and take her out."

Footsteps thud across the floor.

I jump back and look around frantically. The door to the broom closet is ajar. Leaping into it, I hide just as they stride past. They unlock the guard's room door and disappear inside. I'm convinced that the only camera in the hallway is one at the entrance to it. I ease out of the closet and let myself into the office.

Eight tonight! Is that when they're going to blow up the dam? Every nerve in my body is jangling. It's 6:33am by the clock on my desk. The computer is old and takes a few minutes to boot up. I pace about the office and try my key on the file cabinet. It works!

Inside, dozens of files are labeled with the name of the children who have gone through this place. But I can't take them all as evidence. I'm closing the top drawer when I see the corner of a piece of white paper, tucked in the front. I withdraw it. On it is written: *forwardguard101. Forward Guard!* Of course, I should have guessed!

Back at the computer, I try the password on the secret file. It doesn't work. I try numerous times, thinking in my haste that I'd made a mistake, but nothing opens the file. Maybe they'd changed the password and hadn't written the new one down.

Voices! I duck behind the desk, but this one doesn't have a front on it, and I feel exposed, sure that I'll be seen when the owners of the voices enter the room. But they don't come in. The voices and footsteps fade. I let out my breath.

My whole body is shaking. I can't stop it. Crawling from underneath the desk, I make my way to the door and peer down the hall. Dishes are clanking from the kitchen as they set up for breakfast. People are moving about, talking. The door to the guard's room is shut.

Hoping my hat will conceal my identity long enough to do what I need to do, I make my way to the kitchen. There I find Brenda, the substitute cook, flying about in a dither. She's a good cook, but she hasn't prepared meals for large groups much, which makes her overly controlling and bossy. She doesn't pay any attention to me.

7:05.

People are drifting into the dining hall. Pretty soon they'll ring a bell, and the kids and their house parents will come. The kitchen helpers arrive and manage to bring a semblance of order.

Two girls enter the kitchen to help serve – Ophelia, the older sister to Jenny, and Rita, a rail-thin girl whose lank blonde hair falls into her eyes. She's Sanora's room-mate.

I get a tray and fill three coffee cups, dumping in the powder from my napkin judiciously, attempting to make it even. I hand it to Rita. "Take this to the guard's room, okay? Compliments of the cook." I attempt a smile and know it comes out like a grimace.

"I... I don't know where it is," she says, her hands shaking as she receives the tray.

"I'll show you." I take her to the door and knock on it, leaving when someone unlocks it. I hear her voice and glancing back, see a man receive the tray.

Back in the kitchen, I help serve the food after the blessing has been said, watching the time, waiting for the drug-laden coffee to get inside the guards and do its work.

8:06am.

I can't wait any longer. I grab a tray and place on it a bottle of water, an orange and a biscuit, things I think Bobbi will be able to stuff in her pocket and eat on the run. While everyone's busy with breakfast, I figure it might be a good time to make my move.

They take a meal to the guards, too, and I'm hoping that while the men are eating, their eyes will stray from the screens. With a prayer that God will cause that to happen, I start out, my hands shaking almost as much as Rita's had.

The same key that unlocks the cell door also opens the door at the top of the stairs. No one pays me any attention when I open it, fetch the flashlight from the cubby-hole, and close it again, balancing the tray with my left hand. I turn on both the flashlight and the light above the stair and descend, sweat dampening my shirt and running into my eyes.

At the cell door, I set the tray down and use my key. With my flashlight, I enter, the stench taking my breath. This time Bobbi is sitting upright. She faces into the light almost like she's hungry for it.

"Breakfast is here," I say for the benefit of the camera. "Just wait a second, I'll get it."

She looks beyond the light, sees my face, and gasps. "Oh, Gi..." She covers her mouth with her hand. "Gee! My breakfast!"

"*Sh!*" I grab her hand and squeeze it, bending close to her, not brushing away the tears as they stream down my cheeks. "Camera!"

She relaxes and nods.

I continue in a whisper. "Yes, it's me. But we have to be careful." Straightening, I raise my voice. "I have your tray." I turn and fetch the tray.

"Oh, my dear lady!" She's using her pleading voice and does it well. "Thank you so much! Will you talk to me? I get so lonely down here! Please stay!"

"I can't stay," I reply harshly, handing her the food. I lean down as if to assure myself that she has it. Lightning quick, shielding what I'm doing with my body, I bring out the key and unlock the chains that are around her ankles, laying them carefully on the cot so they don't clink.

"Take the food," I say softly, "and put it in your pocket. When I say go, let's get out of here. We won't have much time. You think you can run up the stairs?"

She nods, her face wet. I know she wants to hug me and cry out loud, but she holds in her emotions. "Yes," she whispers, obeying my suggestion to take the food. "I think I can."

She's breathing hard. I'm hoping she isn't so weak that she can't ascend the stairs and get out of the building with me.

"Follow me. Don't move fast until we get into the stairwell. We'll take it slow through the dining room, too. If someone yells at us, we run. Are you ready?"

She nods.

"Okay, let's go!"

***

6:23am

Ramone perched on a rock and swatted mosquitoes. The weight of his Israeli-made Uzi, a semi-automatic rifle he'd taken from Forward Guard ranch, was comforting as it lay in the crook of his arm. A pair of binoculars hung from his neck. He was cold.

Yesterday, he'd found a road that led off toward the river not far from the main gate, and hid the car there. Then he sat in the vehicle and watched the entrance to the school and a portion of the fence. He slept the night in the car, and this morning he awoke with the dawn, longing for a hot cup of coffee, but only got water and a handful of nuts and raisins for breakfast.

The wounds he'd received at the Forward Guard Ranch ached – the one in his thigh, especially. He rubbed it hard and got out of the car, stretching and looking around. The school was quiet, almost too quiet.

He peered through his glasses at the buildings – a structure that looked like a lodge and a couple of smaller houses that might

327

be staff homes. He wondered why there'd been so little traffic from the school, either in and out, and he had no answer, although a sense of dread grew upon him with every passing minute.

He couldn't call anyone from here, as there was no cell service.

Hitching up his pants and shrugging into his backpack, he grabbed his rifle and slung the glasses around his neck. The pack held water and food, yet he knew it would be a long, hard day. Surveillance was one of the most difficult things for him to do, yet he was glad to help Chance.

He crept through the dense forest that grew on the plateau above the river, staying out of sight of the fence in case they had security cameras mounted on it. Just above the river, he climbed a rise of ground and perched on a big rock. This afforded him a view of a big house built on a bluff above the river, several smaller cabins among the trees, and a path that wound through low bushes to the river beach.

If Gina tried to escape this way, he would have her covered.

That was a big if. She couldn't get out the main gate. It was guarded day and night. There was a barrier across it that was activated electronically from the guard shack. Much like Forward Guard.

As the morning wore away, he grew colder. The wind, just a whisper in the boughs of the trees earlier, was picking up and bringing with it a smattering of rain, and the heavy clouds overhead promised something more.

At 8:45am, he decided to change his position.

He crept up to his car, got in it, and drove down the road past the main gate. About a mile further down, he pulled off the highway when he found a wide spot. Getting out, he grabbed his rifle and his backpack and hiked back. The rain was coming in earnest now. He was glad he'd brought his water repellent jacket, but he was cold from sitting all morning.

Following the fence on the northern side of the property, he dropped lower into a gully, then climbed out, keeping the fence in view. Finally, as before, he found a hill that overlooked the river down below and also gave him a view of the school. From this vantage point, he could see what must be two dormitories, a road that twisted and turned among the trees, and the big house on the bluff.

He had barely gotten settled on a fallen log when something happened. They were using a bull horn. He couldn't make out the words.

Suddenly shots rang out. Men shoued. Two women emerged from the trees and dashed down the small road that led from the main school buildings to the back of the property. They were too far away to see clearly, yet it seemed one was having a hard time keeping up.

He stood up and used his glasses. The lead one was young, slender, with dark hair. She looked back repeatedly at the other woman who was older, and seemed to be urging her on. They were being pursued. He swung the glasses. A posse of men with guns, mounted in a jeep, followed close behind them. The women were aiming, it seemed, for the big house.

It was Gina, he was sure of it. He had to get inside the fence. Even his high-powered rifle wouldn't be accurate this far away. He raced to the fence, and heedless of the cameras, followed it for some distance. It was a ten-foot high chain link barrier topped with coiled wire. They were serious about keeping people out. And in.

Impossible. He couldn't get over it or through it. How about the main gate? Should he force his way in? No. He couldn't do that unless the whole place went up in flames.

He stopped almost mid-stride and caught his breath. There was no point in running up and down the fence, hoping there would be a way in. Obviously, they patrolled it and removed anything that might breach their security. Even brush had been cleared from around it.

He went back to the car. There was nothing he could do except call Chance, alert the sheriff's office, and wait for the officers to arrive.

But Gina could die by then.

He opened the car door and started the motor, looking back towards the school for inspiration. But none came. Driving out to the highway, he started for Northport.

Chapter 48

From the Fire into the Furnace

Boundary Dam, June 16, 12:42pm

Chance tapped the steering wheel of his rented truck. What should he do? Take the horse and trailer back to Chewelah, contact Don, Gina's FBI agent, and return to the dam? But that would take four or five hours. By then, they might have infiltrated the dam, taken out the guards, and planted their explosives. He wiped the sweat from his forehead and slowed down for the tiny burg of Metaline Falls.

Should he stop and call from here? What if they'd alerted their gang and someone was on his tail already? He couldn't stop. Watching his rearview window, he drove slowly through the town, across the bridge, and turned up the road that led to the dam.

Parking in the campground at the top of the dam near the back where there was grass, he ate his lunch and then unloaded Santiago. Tying him to the back of the trailer, Chance filled a bucket from the water spigot and put out a pan of oats, glad he had some in the trailer. He unhooked the trailer from the pickup. The horse was busily chomping on his own lunch when he left.

1:44pm.

Driving to the guard shack at the top of the hill, he chatted with the young man who appeared, a clean-cut fellow with a smart uniform. No gun. After proceeding to the lower parking lot, he chose the place to park with care so he could watch the entrance to the dam and also be free to leave in a moment's notice.

He wished he could have contacted Ramone and found out what he knew about Gina and the situation at the school. But Ramone would be out of service, and unless he could get to Northport, he wouldn't be able to call anyone.

Chance fetched his rifle from the gun rack and made sure it was loaded, shoving several boxes of ammo in his pocket.

2:12pm.

It was hard to wait. He filled in the minutes with prayer for Gina and Ramone, for the situation he was facing, for the capture and conviction of the vermin who ran the organization. Several cars arrived. People got out, met a guide, and followed her into the tunnel for a tour. Several tours came and went.

3:02pm.

He jiggled the keys that dangled from the ignition, his nerves jumping, his heart thudding heavily in his ears. Something was about to happen. He could feel it.

Where's Gina? Has she escaped? He couldn't get her from his mind. He swiped at his nose and tried to bring his mind back to watching the people and cars that arrived, but she invaded his thoughts. She was laughing at him, tilting her head in that way of hers, her hands perched on her hips.

He wanted to protect her. But it was more than that. Suddenly he knew. He loved her. Yet would she push him away again? Did she want a close relationship with him?

Well, after this was over, he promised himself he'd find out.

A motor home drove into the lot across the way and parked, but no one got out. He studied it and decided he needed to keep an eye on it. The gang could gut a motor home and use it to stack boxes inside. It would be less noticeable than a big truck.

Two men stepped from it and stood on the pavement. One was Captain Grant, and the man beside him was Caleb Ostranger. Chance picked up his rifle. About that time, a vehicle pulled into the slot next to his. It was a small red Toyota pickup, one he recognized. Dusty sat in the driver's seat.

As he watched, Dusty picked up a rifle and loaded it. He meant business. *A good man to have on your side.*

Yet whose side was he on? Chance drew in his breath as a black SUV arrived and stopped next to the motor home. The two men from the RV went over and talked to the driver.

Chance drew a deep breath. *Here we go. This is it!*

***

8:55am

From Gina's Journal

Bobbi and I climb the stairs. I pause before opening the door that leads into the dining room. A buzz of voices and the clink of dishes erupt from the big room. People will be leaving as they finish their last cup of coffee and head to their jobs. The young people will be making their way to their work assignments.

It's now or never! I glance back at Bobbi and nod. She responds with a glimmer of a smile. I'm surprised at how good she looks after her ordeal, except for the fact that she needs a shower and a change of clothes. I'm determined to see she gets them, too. It's the least I can do for her.

"Follow my lead." I open the door and head straight for the kitchen.

Bobbi stays close behind me, her head down. The ladies who wash dishes don't look up from their work, and the cooks have left. An old man, the husband of one of the ladies, nurses a cup of coffee as he sits on a high stool beside the back counter, shuffling his way through a magazine. He doesn't seem to notice us, either.

I take a deep breath and grab my pack from the shelf by the back door. *We've made it this far.* I lead the way outside. Dark clouds have covered the sun, blown in by a brisk wind that moans through the treetops. I try to avoid the cameras on the way back to my cabin. I'd seen a map of where they were placed, but I hadn't had time to commit it to memory.

Once at the cabin, I shield the camera's view on the porch with my body and motion for her to run inside. She does. Without saying anything, I nod towards the bathroom. She takes my meaning immediately and hurries across the room. I'm glad she's small and slender, built sort of like me.

I gather a pair of my jeans and a shirt from my bedroom, along with some socks, and shove them through the bathroom door, still without saying a word to her. The shower starts. At least the cameras aren't audio – for that I'm grateful. I pace the room, picking up this and that while she finishes. Should I put my evidence in the van for safe keeping?

Thinking that might be a good idea, I run outside and find that it's raining. I unlock Herman and shove the evidence under the front seat. It includes files from the computer that I'd been able to copy, the digital camera I used to take pictures of the students and the school, and a flash drive I'd picked up from Bennet's desk one day.

9:10am.

Back in the cabin, I knock on the bathroom door. "Bobbi? Can I come in?"

"Sure."

I stand beside the sink while she finishes dressing. "We have to get out of here," I say. "They'll be at my door in a few minutes if they've noticed the empty room in the basement on their security screens. The problem is I don't know how we're going to get out of the property."

"Why not just drive out like you're going for groceries?"

"Can't do that, I'm afraid. You have to show a signed statement at the gate if you want to go somewhere."

I rub my aching head, trying to think. The pressure of having to do something and knowing it probably won't work is fraying on my nerves. "There's the river, but we'd have to swim. Can you swim?"

She shakes her head and sits down on the toilet. "Not as far as that. And it's cold. Can you? If you can, I'll stay here and you can get help."

"No. I'm not leaving you alone." I sigh. "I have to find Sanora and take her with us, too. She's a girl I met in Spokane. She was kidnapped and brought here. We have to get to the dormitory, which won't be easy. If we can hide out somewhere with her, maybe Chance will bring help. He should be around somewhere. Or maybe my back-up agents will call in the troops. What do you think?"

She shrugs. "You're calling the shots. I'm just along for the ride. I guess I made things a whole lot more complicated for you, didn't I? I'm always doing that."

I give her a quick hug. "It's okay, Bobbi. I like excitement. Don't you remember that about me? C'mon. Eat an apple as we go. You're hungry, I bet."

"Yeah, I never got my breakfast." She shoots me an amused glance, her eyes twinkling. "Fish eye soup."

I have to admit it — she's gutsy. I want to sit down and get everything right between us, to say I'm sorry for the times I'd been impatient and disrespectful to her and for the times I'd put her off when she tried to get involved with my life. But there's no time. If we are going to stay alive, we have to move. *Now.*

I give her a coat and shrug into my jean jacket. After stuffing an apple and two water bottles in my pack, I sling it on my shoulder and lead out. At least I have my gun. Not that it will do me much good, but maybe I can take out one or two of them before they get us.

I'm still trying to avoid the cameras. She follows like a shadow behind me, her steps light. With the rain lashing my face, I keep to the woods and low bushes, picking my way, heading in the general direction of the river and the dorms. I don't know what I'm going to do when we arrive, but I have to find Sanora and give her the chance to escape with us.

Avoiding the road, I follow a dim trail made by wildlife. Wet bushes slap my face. Bobbi is panting behind me. Suddenly we come out on the bluff that overlooks the river. I've gone too far to the left. Not far away is the pond where I'd encountered the girl who was trying to drown herself.

Turning right, I head back toward the dormitories, thinking I can skirt them and come up behind the girl's dorm. Bobbi mumbles something when she trips and almost falls over an exposed root.

"Be careful," I say as I pause for her to catch up with me. The rain slants straight across, blown on a cold wind from the north. We're both wet clear through and starting to shiver. I stop and take stock of our position.

She sniffs. "Is it very much further?"

"No. Just over that rise. C'mon."

"Wait ... a moment. I have to rest." She wipes her nose on a tissue. "I love you, Gina. You know that, don't you?" Her voice wobbles, and I think she's going to cry.

"Yes, Aunt Bobbi, I know you do. I love you, too. Now let's do this."

I start moving. She's right behind me. We jog across the field and come to the next danger point – the road. The dorms are in a clearing about half a mile down the road.

I decide to follow the track, as it's a direct route to the dorms and will save us a lot of time. But we hadn't taken five steps on the road when the sound of a vehicle approaching fills me with dread. I glance around, ready to jump into the bushes, but it's too late. A jeep rounds the corner. It's got four guys in it, and they've seen us.

Before we can dash to the cover of bushes, a man's voice bellows through the air, amplified by a bullhorn. "Stop where you are, or we will shoot!"

I jump down a steep bank and slide into a cover of bushes, hoping Bobbi will follow me. A big gun booms behind me as I clamber down the bank. She lands in the same bush about a second later. There's a gully here. We dash down it, leaping over rocks, and finding a hiding place behind a massive pine tree.

I wait, holding my breath. They're coming, hollering to one another. In a few seconds, they'll find us.

"C'mon," I say, pulling her up the side of the steep bank. "Let's get back to the clearing. It's not far to the dorms now." We swing south through the trees and emerge at the clearing. It seems like we've shaken our pursuers.

"See those houses? That's the dorms. We're almost there." But what will happen when we arrive? I wonder if we're not running from the fire into the furnace.

We're only halfway across the clearing when a shot rings out. I drop to the ground. Bobbi follows my lead, groaning as she hits the muddy turf. I glance over my shoulder. Two men leap out of the jeep and are coming now on foot, their rifles ready. But they don't see us. We've fallen into a ditch that crosses the field. Heavy grasses shield us from view unless they stand right over us.

We wait. My breath comes in gasps. I try to breathe quietly, but I can't. The men shout to one another. The jeep arrives. Someone honks the horn. Then silence. The jeep pulls away.

After making sure they're gone, I climb to my feet and help Bobbi stand. The two large homes that were remodeled into dormitories sit on the other side of the clearing. I head for the trees that ring the field, aiming to come out behind the houses.

Bobbi lags behind me. She's panting. "Just go on, dear," she gasps, holding her side. "I'll ... keep them ... busy for a while."

"No way!" I grab her arm and pull her along.

After what seems an eternity, I stop in the bushes behind the girls' dorm. "Now we gotta figure out how to get inside." They'll have cameras on the outside by the entrances, and I bet the guards are watching the screens intensely and communicating with the men who are searching for us.

She stumbles and collapses onto the ground beside me. I reach down to help her up. "You're going to get wet down there. Here. Let me help you."

"I'm fine," she says, refusing my hand. She manages to get to her knees.

The jeep comes into view again, driving slowly, the men studying the trees. I recognize Gunther. There's another man with him. Not Bennet. They don't come as far as the dorm. After they wait for about five minutes, they hold a brief conference with each other. Gunther talks into a two-way radio. Putting it down, he yanks the gear shift, turns around, and heads back down the road.

The clouds lift, and the rain lets up a bit. I'm so cold that I think if I had to shoot, I couldn't hit anything with my hands shaking like they are.

"We'll die of exposure if you wait too long," Bobbi says and sneezes.

"I know. But I was hoping to see Sanora. Oh, wait. Here she comes."

She steps out the back door and looks around as if she's watching for someone. She's frowning. Her face mirrors her pain, but there's also concern written there, too. It strikes me that she's seen more grief and anguish in her thirteen years than I've known in my whole life.

I stand up. "Sanora! Over here!" I don't want to raise my voice, but I have to. I call twice before she hears me.

She swings her head around and stares. When she sees me wave, she hurries over to us. "What's going on? What are you doing?"

I notice she doesn't ask who we are. She knows what's going on, knows we're on the run. She's not sure if she wants to trust me. I realize I have to win her over, and I have about five seconds to do it.

"Hi! I've been looking for you! This is my aunt. They held her in a prison cell in the basement of the Hacienda in chains. This place is evil, Sanora. We're getting out of here for good. Do you want to go with us?" I say this without taking a breath, holding her eyes with mine.

Her face is drawn, the color of old cheese. She shakes her head. "But... you can't! Don't you see? It's useless to fight them. They'll get you, Miss McDonald. You better turn yourself in."

"Yeah, and end up in Deadwater Pond?" I want to shock her into some kind of positive action, but her reaction is so extreme that I think I've overdone it. She sways and closes her eyes as her face loses all color.

I grasp her arm. "I'm sorry, Sanora, but it's true. Listen to me. I've got to get you out of here. What they're doing is wrong. You're going to end up like ... those girls who go out at night. They're not going to win this time. We need someplace to hide until they stop looking for us. Can you help us?"

Bobbi steps forward and puts her arm around Sanora's shoulders, nodding to me. "This lady knows what she's doing, sweetie. She can help you. But you need to be brave. Okay? Can you do that?"

The girl stares at Bobbi. Her nose is red like she's been crying, and her shoulders shake like she has a chill. But she nods like she's reached a decision.

Her voice is thin when she speaks. "Okay. I messed up my chance once to get away from them, and I don't want to do it again. And they ... they killed my best friend. I want to make them pay for what they did. Come on." She straightens. "Talk and laugh as we go in. I hope no one's around."

"Yeah, we do, too." I trail behind her as she emerges from the shelter of the trees and starts across the open ground.

Bobbi and I speed up so we're walking with her. We chatter like the girls would do. Sanora pulls open the door and allows us to go first. We keep our heads down like we're studying the faded carpet.

She strides down a short hall and turns to the right. Her room in the first one that opens from a common room. We tag along after her. Inside, she opens a closet door and motions for us to get inside. I crumple to the floor. Bobbi plops down beside me.

She brings us a couple of blankets and a pillow. "Do you need anything else?"

I shake my head. "I have water and some food. We're fine."

"Okay. Be quiet! I have to go to work, or they'll come looking for me. I'll come back for you in a while." She leaves the door open a crack. There's the rustle of clothes. The door opens and shuts.

We're alone.

I can't believe we found a place to get dry, to rest, and to hide until the hunt dies down. In the dimness, I can barely make out Bobbi's face. I grin at her, and she smiles back, giving me a thumbs-up. All day, I've tried to keep up a brave front for her, but it's only bravado. All of it. I know it. She knows it. Our chance of escaping this place alive is about as good as jumping the Grand Canyon.

Bobbi lies down and closes her eyes. Her face is grey, and her breathing is shallow. I feel her pulse. She groans and gets more comfortable but doesn't open her eyes. Her heart is beating steadily and strong.

I roll over and stare into the darkness, telling myself I have to stay awake. Yet the warmth, the mad dash through the woods, and the release from stress affects me like a sleeping pill. My eyelids drift shut. My last thought is, *Stay awake! Focus!*

But it's impossible.

Chapter 49

On the Run

Boundary Dam, June 16, 3:36pm

Chance opened the door of the red pickup and climbed inside. Dusty shot him a startled glance.

"Hi, ya, partner," Chance said, smiling. He braced himself for an attack, wondering if Dusty would swing his weapon around and turn on him.

"Chance? What're you doin' here?"

"Saw you drive up and thought you needed some company." He glanced at the gun Dusty held. "Goin' huntin'?"

Dusty grimaced. "Yeah. I think there's some varmits around here that need to be taken out." His eyes slid to the motor home and the two men who stood beside the black SUV. "Know them guys?"

"Yeah. Met them a while ago. They're the ones who run that retreat I went to. Forward Guard. They tried to kill me and a friend of mine before we was able to get out."

"Nice guys."

"Yeah." Chance turned to him with a wry grin. "I thought you weren't going to fight this one. What happened?"

Dusty rolled down his window and spat. Wiping his mouth, he returned Chance's smile. "Thought about it some. Those people who were gettin' over the border with drugs are in with this gang, right? The ones you said might be goin' to blow the dam for some fool reason?"

"Yeah, I think they are. What of it?"

Dusty ran his fingers down the rifle lovingly. "There's an informer, a spy, in our department somewhere. Someone's lookin' the other way when they come across. I aim to find him. I'm gettin' riled up about it. It ain't right."

"You got an idea who it is?"

"Nope. You?"

Chance shook his head and glanced at his watch. "I don't." He thought about Roger Whitney. The man had a disagreeable personality and was hard to work under, but that didn't mean he was in with the crooks.

Maybe it was the top brass himself, Patrol Agent in Charge, Henry DeMoss. Chance remembered how he acted the night he was told he wouldn't go on a patrol. But that alone was not enough to suspect or convict him of collaborating with smugglers, let alone being part of the gang that was going to blow up the dam.

He shrugged. "I really don't know. But I agree with you. It has to be one of the bosses, that's why it got hushed up, and why I was sent off. Hey, it was one of them who gave me the brochure for that weapon's retreat. McClurry handed it to me, but he said it came from one of the top guys."

Dusty rubbed his chin, keeping his eyes fixed on the two vehicles across the way. "Okay, so what are they plannin' to do now? And how can we stop them?" He got out a bag of chips, grabbed a handful of them, and handed them over to Chance.

"I figure they've got explosives in that RV over there." He took some chips. "I saw two of them down on the river, hauling boxes off a boat. They said eight this evening was when they were going to strike. They've got to disarm the guard at the top, get inside the tunnel with their vehicle, neutralize whoever is on duty there, and plant the bomb."

Dusty nodded. "What are we going to do about it?"

"I don't know. For now, let's keep watch. Nothing much else we can do. Unless you want to drive over to Metaline Falls and call the sheriff, the state police, and whoever else might spring to mind. There's no cell service here."

"If they ain't goin' to do nothin' until eight, I might as well."

Chance dug a slip of paper from his pocket and handed it over to the older man. "Here's a number for Gina's back-up agents with the FBI. Give them a ring, okay? Tell them to alert their people. Okay?"

"Sounds good." Dusty turned on the motor as Chance stepped out, keeping his face turned from the motor home. Dusty kept his voice low as he said, "Be careful and keep your gun handy. These guys mean business, and I bet they're loaded to the teeth."

Chance nodded. "I will. Get back here soon. I'll need you."

Dusty grinned as he gave Chance a thumbs-up signal.

Chance climbed into his pickup and watched as Dusty drove slowly out of the parking lot. He hoped the men across the way didn't make their move sooner than planned because he was alone now. And he figured Dusty was right. They'd probably arrived with an arsenal of weapons.

He wondered what Ramone was doing and thought about the Uzi he carried. He would give a year's wages to have that Uzi in Ramone's capable hands as his back-up!

He took a deep breath and sagged back against the seat. Three against ... how many? A dozen? Two dozen? Well, he would try and do his best. That's all he could do.

***

From Gina's Journal, 1:44pm

I wake from a deep sleep with a jolt like a stab of lightning. Someone had entered the room outside the closet where Bobbi and I are hiding. The door slams shut. I glance at the digital numbers on my watch and resist the urge to swear. How much has happened while we slept?

Sitting up, I peer out the crack of the door and ease it open another two inches. *Sanora.* She paces the room, then plops on the bed and stares straight ahead like she's coming to a difficult decision.

Her head drops into her hands, and her shoulders shake convulsively while the sounds of heart-rending sobs reach me. I'm struck again with how fragile she is, yet at the same time, how grown up. She's a thirteen-year-old with a woman's broken heart and smashed dreams. And now she's lost her last slender lifeline of hope.

"Sanora!" I'm hoping the camera doesn't have audio.

She raises her head, searches for the source of the voice, sees me, and shakes her head. "Go away! Just go away!"

"Come over here. Please. I have something to tell you."

At first, I don't think she's going to obey me. But finally, she blows her nose on a tissue and shuffles over to the closet. I scoot back. Bobbi mutters something in her sleep, rolls over, and is quiet.

"I come in here quite often," she says as she lands on the floor beside me. "They can't see me in here."

I nod. I have only a few minutes to speak with her, for we have to get moving. Leaning forward so I can look in her face, I say, "I'm sorry I've complicated your life. You don't need to worry about me. Or my aunt."

She shrugs. "There's nothing that can hurt me anymore. Not, I mean, more than it already has. What're you doing here? How do you figure you can get out? Nobody escapes this place unless they die." The way she says it sends cold shivers down my arms. She's seen murder.

"You want out?"

The answer takes longer to come than I thought. She seems almost reluctant to admit it. "Well, I guess so." With a sigh, she continues, "I'd hate to leave my friends. But I want to get out. Of course, I do. How would you like to be ..." She slants me a glance that says she doesn't want to talk about the uglier parts of her life.

She continues in a heavy voice, "I want to get back to Mom and my little sister and brother. I worry about them, you know. But I can't get back to them, and if you don't do what they want, they beat you up. There was this girl, Kathleen, and I really liked her, you know, and they beat her up because she was keeping back some of the money. I haven't seen her since then. It's bad here. If I was you, I'd get out and not worry about me. I'll be all right." She lifts her chin.

I have to fight back the smile that pulls at my mouth and the tears that sting my eyes.

I lay my hand on her arm. "I'm not leaving without you. We're going to close this place down and send these people to jail. You can give testimony, Sanora. Without you, we might not have much of a case if they can destroy the evidence. It will look just like what they say it is — a school and ranch home for kids who need help."

I take a deep breath, choosing my words with care. "I care about you, and I want to see you free of this place. But that's not the most important thing going on right now. The most important thing is, do you know God? I mean, really know Him? Do you pray to Jesus?"

She nods, dropping her head again like she's ashamed. "Yeah, I do, but He don't hear me."

"Yes, He does, Sanora. He sent me to help you. But what I want to tell you is that even if you get out of here, you'll still be in prison. A different kind of prison, one in your heart."

She looks at me, startled. "No, I won't, I'll go back..."

"All of us are prisoners to sin, Sanora. You are Satan's prisoner. I was, too, before I met Jesus. Only He can free you. When He forgives your sin, you are free from the inside out. And even if you have to live like a slave, you can be free in your heart. And you can know that when you die, you'll go to heaven."

I wait, not looking at her, praying.

Silence fills the little closet while a clock ticks loudly from the room outside, reminding me that time is fleeting by. But I'm not going to rush this. Bobbi moans and mumbles under her breath.

I lift my head. "So, what do you think? Do you want to give your heart to Jesus? He died to save you from sin. You need to ask Him to forgive you and come into your heart. Do you want to do that? Now?" I wait, telling myself that this is so important, nothing else matters. Not even staying alive.

"He wouldn't take me! I'm too dirty!" She says it vehemently and cringes away from me like she's warding off a blow.

"Jesus will forgive anyone who comes to Him. He did me. And I was a worse sinner than you." That fetches a wide-eyed look from those blue eyes. "It's true. I was a rebel, and I hated everything. I hated God because He took my mother from me."

She nods. Light is starting to penetrate the darkness she's lived in for so long. But she still isn't ready. Fear stalks her. She's afraid to trust anyone. "I... don't know, Miss McDonald. I... can't... it's too hard."

She's fleeing from the very One who can heal her.

"Don't put it off, Sanora. Please. He loves you. Don't turn away from Him! Ask Him to forgive your sin. Do it now!" I lean closer. "Then you can write your mom and tell her what you did."

She straightens, a look of horror flooding her face. "Oh, darn! I forgot! I left my notebook in the kitchen. Just a minute. I'll be right back." With that, she leaps out of the closet, opens the door to the room, and thuds down the hallway.

Bobbi moans and rolls over, her eyes fluttering open. "What's going on? What time is it?"

I glance at my watch. "Two-fifteen. We have to get going."

We eat the apples, and I pass her a water bottle. I'm listening for Sanora's return footsteps, but instead the outer door to the dorm crashes open. Heavy footsteps approach.

A man's voice, right at our door, bellows, "All right! Come out! We know you're in there!"

***

3:36pm

Chance kept a low profile as he watched the RV across the way. After Grant and Ostranger returned to the RV, he glanced at his watch. Four and a half hours to wait.

He was glad the pickup he'd rented had tinted windows, but he wondered if they were watching it as much as he was their

346

vehicles. Would they ask themselves why no one went into the dam on a tour?

His eyes felt gritty. Sleep dragged at his senses, but he couldn't close his eyes, not for a minute. He wished he had a cup of strong coffee.

The wind blew in showers of gusty rain and scuttled pieces of garbage across the lot. Two cars drove down the road and parked. The guide, a girl, met them beside the overlook of the dam. She wore a hoodie and held a two-way radio. After a brief conversation, during which she indicated the tunnel, she clipped the radio to her belt and led the way inside the tunnel with four adults on her heels.

4:12pm

After the tourists returned to their cars and drove away, a dark blue Ford Super Duty pickup arrived. The bed was loaded, and a tarp covered the cargo tightly. It did not park next to the SUV but pulled toward the tunnel opening and stopped a few feet from it.

The guide emerged from the tunnel and ran to speak to the driver. It wasn't a long conversation. She said something, waved her hand, and dashed back to the shelter of the tunnel. Three men emerged from the cab. They strolled leisurely to the overlook, gazing up at the cliff above them like most tourists did, to see the electrical lines and poles climbing the mountain.

Chance trained his glasses on them. Two of them he did not recognize, but when the third, it seemed the leader of the group, turned toward him, he drew in his breath sharply.

DeMoss!

***

2:36pm

From Gina's Journal:

As I struggle to my feet, I'm praying that Sanora doesn't return and walk into this. They will punish her, if they can find her. Bobbi flings her arm around my waist as if she's trying to protect me, and so we emerge from the closet. I have my pack around my left shoulder, hoping they don't see it.

347

But, of course, they do. It's Bennet himself in all his pumped-up glory, gripping a Beretta m9 semi-automatic revolver. His face is wreathed in a smile of triumph, but his eyes are hard, cold, and angry.

"Have a nice little nap, girls?" He asks between gritted teeth. "Well, your fun is over. We're going to take a little walk – to the pond you like so well, Miss Lindsey, and maybe we'll take us a dip in it. Hey, Tank, relieve this lady of her backpack, will you? Who knows what she has in there."

The large man with a black beard yanks it off my shoulder.

I glare at Bennet, not revealing the way my heart is hammering in my ribs or the dread that clamps down cold and hard on my soul.

"Are you proud of yourself, capturing two women? Is this going to go down in your memoirs as one of your greatest deeds?"

I shouldn't have mocked him. He is truly dangerous when he allows his anger to drive him wild.

He grabs my arm and almost twists it off. I yelp with pain and adjust my body so the pain eases up some. He snarls in my face, "I'll show you, you know-it-all cop. You think you're so smart. You won't think that when you're floating face down on the water of that pond."

He glances over his shoulder at Gunther and Tank. Their mouths are hanging open as they drool with anticipation.

Gunther ties my hands behind my back none too gently, but I don't cry out. Bobbi is handled in the same manner, her hands bound brutally behind her back. She's in pain, there's no doubt about that, but she clenches her teeth and won't make a sound.

They hustle us out of the dorm, past two girls who are entering. The girls stare. Rain washes my face as we step outside. Clouds are hustling through the darkened sky like they don't want to witness what is about to happen. We are shoved into the back of a jeep. I'm praying.

Bobbi is, too. Her lips are moving, and there are tears on her cheeks. She glances at me. "It will be okay, honey," she says. "God will get us out of this."

I can't answer. My throat is so tight I think I'm going to strangle. I nudge her with my shoulder. "Keep praying, Aunt Bobbi."

It's a short drive to the pond – only about ten minutes, but it seems to take a lifetime. Tank rides with us in the back and keeps his rifle trained on us. I'm surprised it's not an Uzi. It's a hunting rifle, a 30.06 Remington, but the bullet from it will kill just as good as a slug from a higher caliber gun. In fact, a .22 rifle would work, too. Funny the things you think of when you're going to die.

The marshy pond is ruffled along the edges with tiny waves and sudsy ripples that lap through the high weeds. They stop at the water's edge, where I'd rescued Jenny. Bennet leaps from the front and, with a stony face, orders us out.

Bobbi's shoulder is next to mine as we stand at the brink of the water with our backs to the pond. The three men face us, standing up the bank a little way – Bennet with his Beretta, Gunther with his Winchester 300 mag repeating rifle, and of course there's Tank with his 30.06.

All three weapons are trained on our hearts without wavering. All three men are grinning, their faces like the demon masks I've seen at Halloween. The clouds part in that moment, revealing a weak sun that's heading for the horizon. A bird trills a sweet melody from the reeds by the pond. It's a meadow lark. I wonder if that's the last sound I will hear on this earth.

The breeze lifts my hair. A Voice whispers in my heart, "I am with you." I take a deep breath of clear, fresh air that's softly scented with pine.

"Got any last words?" There's a chuckle in Bennet's voice.

"You are pitiful," I say, my voice steady even though tears stream down my face. "You will pay for this, and for everything else you've done, when you meet God."

He laughs. The other two don't move a muscle.

This can't be happening. I'm not really going to die, am I? Will they find our bodies in this stinking pond? I wish I'd been able to find Mom – that's a grief I will carry to my grave.

Bobbi moans low in her throat. "Gina," she says, "there's something I have to say..." She closes her eyes and leans into me. "But there' no time. I'm so sorry, honey ..."

"It's okay," I say, my voice muffled in her hair. "It will be over soon, and I'll see you on the other side. Where's there no more night."

She glances at me. Her eyes are shining like she's already glimpsed Glory. "I love you."

"I love you, too."

"All right." Bennet lifts his revolver and sights. His muscles tense. "On the count of three, gentlemen. One. Two ..."

Chapter 50

A God Thing

Boundary Dam, June 16, 5:05pm

Chance searched the pickup and found a bag of nuts he'd forgotten in the glove compartment. That would have to be his supper. At least he had water. He finished his little meal and checked his watch. Time to go check on Santiago.

He drove up the hill and over to his trailer. The horse lifted his head, glad to see him. He'd tangled the rope on some brush and couldn't get to his feed pan. Chance patted him, untangled the rope, and saw that he had water. At least it had stopped raining.

The sun was dipping towards the west when he refilled Santiago's oat pan. Then he drove back to the guard's shack at the top of the hill.

The young man who came out recognized him. "Going back?"

"I've been waiting for some friends of mine to show up," Chance said as a way of explanation. "When do the tours end? Do you close the lower parking lot then?"

The guard arched his eyebrows as if those were improper questions. "The tours end at eight. We close the lot soon after that, when all the guests have left."

Chance nodded. "Okay. I'll clear out before then. Too bad I can't call. No cell service."

The guard smiled. "No, afraid not." He waved him on through.

Back in the lot, Chance parked in a different spot, one that was behind and to the left of the RV and the other vehicle. He turned off the motor and prepared to wait.

6:12pm

He hadn't sat there long when another pickup entered the lot. It stopped about five spaces over from where he sat. Three young people – two boys and a girl – were laughing and talking as they got out. They walked over to the tunnel and met the guide.

Chance was watching them with absorption when the passenger door was flung open and someone climbed in. *Dusty.*

Without preamble, Chance said, "You back? Where's your rig?"

Dusty chuckled without mirth. "Ditched it up top. Took me this long to work my way back, and then I had to hitch a ride with those kids."

"You didn't make it out to Metaline Falls? You haven't called anyone?"

Dusty took off his cowboy hat and sighed. "Nope. They're stopping traffic at the top of the hill, just after the entrance to the dam. When I saw what they were doin', I made a u-turn. But they'd seen me and someone came after me. I ditched my pickup and took off through the woods. They stopped followin' me, and I came out by the dam. I waited until it got darker, and then asked these kids to take me down. Said I'd injured my leg. They were willin', so I hopped in the back, and hid as we came past the big RV over there. Didn't want the gang to see me return."

"Okay. That leaves us without any backup. You up to this, or should we leave it for the pros? We can leave now and call the police."

Dusty shook his head, his mouth thinning into a stern line. "No way. I'm goin' to see this out, even if it means facing their guns. How long do we have to wait?"

"I figure about an hour and a half. They pulled that big pickup in over there. It's loaded, and the cargo is covered. Three men got out. One of them's our boss, DeMoss. They went into the tunnel. I guess on a tour, although I didn't see the guide come out and get them."

"DeMoss, huh." Dusty snorted. "It figures. Someone high up had to be coverin' for them to get stuff into the country." He leaned back and closed his eyes. "You don't mind if I close my eyes for a moment, do you?"

"Go ahead." Chance wanted to rest, too, but Dusty was not in top shape and probably in more need of it than he.

Dusty had not been asleep for more than five minutes, though, when Chance straightened. He reached over and shook Dusty awake.

"Hey, wake up, partner! We got something goin' on, and it don't look good!"

***

3:21pm

The blast of a siren shatters the quiet air.

I've shut my eyes, ready to enter the next world because three men have their weapons trained on my heart. I grab Bobbi because she's swaying like she's about to topple into the water.

Bennet lowers his gun and glances around. He makes his decision like quicksilver. "You. Gunther. Stay here and guard these women. Tank, come with me. Someone's breached the fence. We have to deal with it."

He vaults to the jeep.

"But ... can't I shoot them now? And come with you?" Gunther's tone holds disappointment.

"No!" Bennet doesn't bother to look back as he leaps into the driver's seat and turns the key. He raises his voice over the engine. "Stay here, you idiot! Don't let them get away! I'll be right back!" He roars off.

I feel like I've died and been reborn. Wiping my face, I look around, noting the gold and blue clouds in the sky, the little bird that's still singing his heart out, the ripples in the water. There's the rock I sat on when I was here before.

Gunther crouches, his rifle cradled in the crook of his arm. "Go ahead. Try to get away," he says with a crooked grin. "See how far you can get, running scared. I'd love to mow you down." He pats the weapon.

I glare at him. "You're nice, aren't you? Can we sit while we wait? I promise not to run. Just moving over there about ten feet to that rock. You won't shoot us for that, will you?"

He grunts. "Go ahead. But I warn you, that's all."

I nudge Bobbi out of her stupor, and we tiptoe to the rock, wading through the shallows of the water. "Sit back to back," I whisper. "That's right. Now let me see if I can work on your rope."

Gunther gets up and saunters toward us, but he doesn't want to get too close because he'd have to get his feet wet. "Shut up, you two!"

We do. But my fingers are busy on the knots on her rope. It's tight, and it hasn't helped that the rain has gotten them wet. Almost impossible to loosen, but God has been doing impossible things for me all day.

My fingers are tired and bruised as time wears on. Gunther strolls back to his place by the beach. He tosses a rock into the water and stares at us like he's willing us to try to escape.

I figure it will take Bennet about ten minutes to get over to the Hacienda and into the security camera room, and another ten minutes to round up some guys and go hunting for the critter that got over the fence.

I'm wondering who or what did it at such an opportune time when a shot rings out and Gunther slumps to the ground. Still bound, I leap up and dash over to him, prepared to kick him in the head if he's moves.

He's shot high on his right thigh. Blood gushes from the wound as he writhes on the ground. He lifts his gun. I kick it from his hand. Bobbi joins me.

"Let's get out of here!" Her hair has come out of its braid and is flying about her head wildly. She starts to take off.

"Wait!" I say sharply. "Who did this and why?"

"I did." The answer comes from a tall man whose skin is burnished brown and who wears a cowboy hat. He approaches rapidly from the northern border of the property.

"Who are you?" I'm floored. It's as if an angel has suddenly appeared.

A grin splits his face. "Name's Ramone. Friend to Chance. He sent me over here to help if I could." As he speaks, he slashes the ropes on our hands and ties them around Gunther's wrists and ankles. "No time for chatter, though. Those gents who were about to shoot you are on my tail, and they're madder than a herd of bulls in heat with no cows." He grins. "Sorry. That just sprung to mind." He has a nice smile with white teeth.

He glances at the man he's shot. "I guess I better do somethin' about that gunshot wound. Wouldn't want him to die and miss bein' prosecuted." He kneels and cuts off pieces of Gunther's shirt, then ties the strips around his leg. The man groans once and passes out.

Ramone straightens.

I hold out my hand, feeling a little giddy. "Howdy, Ramone. I'm Gina, and this is my aunt, Bobbi. Thank you for coming. Which way should we go?"

After he shakes my hand, he leads off toward the forest. "I got my car parked up on the road. Can't go back out the way I came in, though. They'll be watchin' that now. Do you have a vehicle here?"

"Yeah, but it'll be hard to get to, and even more difficult to use." I'm having a hard time keeping up with his long strides. The siren stopped, but now at least two jeeps are approaching. From the pond, they'll fan out and canvas the whole property.

By that time, we'd better be up by the Hacienda, the last place they'd look for us, and the most dangerous, yet I have to find Sanora.

He stops in a thicket of tall bushes just behind the building. While I catch my breath, he fills us in on how he'd been able to get inside. "I was goin' up to Northport to call the police, but then something told me to turn back. I came back and piled some brush and dead trees over the fence so I could climb it. Guess I set off the alarm."

I pat his arm. "You came at the right moment, believe me." The shakes, the after-math tremors that plague me, begin in my legs and work their way up my body. I want to sit down and re-coup, but I don't have time.

I glance at Bobbi to make sure she's recovered. Her eyes are sparkling like diamonds. "It was a God thing," she says, wiping her nose. "A God thing."

I nod. "Yes. But we'll need another miracle to get out of here. I'd like to take Sanora with us. How many miracles are allowed, I wonder?"

Ramone has no answer for me. He has been scanning the area, and he's holding that Uzi like he intends to use it again. Two jeeps have come and gone from the back of the Hacienda.

"My van is over by the cabins, just through the trees over there." I say, pointing. "But I bet they're watching it."

Ramone nodded. "Yes, they probably are. Which means we'll have to find another way out."

"I need to find Sanora, too. She said she was coming to the kitchen. If we try to find her, they'll see us, and we're dead in the water."

"I don't like that analogy, my dear," Bobbi says.

"We need to stay together," Ramone says. "Let's get closer to the building. Maybe someone will pull up in a vehicle and leave it running. In that case, we'll jump in and drive out, even if we have to ram the gate." He looks at us. "Okay?"

I'm not happy with his solution as I don't think I'll see Sanora again. But it's all we can do at the moment. I throw an arm around Bobbi's shoulders as she's trembling, at the limit of her strength.

"With Bobbi's prayers and Ramone's Uzi, I think we might do this." I put more bluster in the statement than I feel, but it seems to cheer her up. "And maybe the police or the FBI will come. Maybe Chance called them."

Ramone grunted. "Yeah. I haven't contacted him, and he said if he didn't hear from me, he would call or come if he can. He's at the dam."

"The dam." I'd almost forgotten about the drama going on at that location. "He might need help, too." I glance at Ramone. "Your weapon would come in handy over there, I suspect."

"That's what I figure, once we get clear of this place."

"Okay," I respond, wishing I still had my backpack and my revolver. "Let's do this."

We move closer to the building, staying low in a fringe of brush. Bobbi sneezes. Ramone looks at her with eyebrows raised. She returns his look and shrugs, blowing her nose into a tissue.

There doesn't seem to be anyone around.

"I'm going to the front," Ramone says, hefting his rifle. "You stay here. If someone leaves a vehicle running, do what I said, okay? Beep the horn, and I'll get in. I'll do the same for you." He disappears through the trees, circling the building.

"I'm going inside," I say through clenched teeth. "I have to find Sanora and get her out."

"What about me?" Bobbi's voice is thin and wobbly like she's scared.

"You stay here and warn me with a shout or something. I won't be gone for long. Okay?"

She nods and plunks down on a fallen log, hugging herself. "Just hurry. I don't know how much more of this I can take."

I feel bad, leaving her like that, but I tell myself I'll be in and out in a jiffy. Hopefully with Sanora in tow.

When I open the back door into the kitchen, an alarm goes off. I crouch down beside the sinks. Maria arrives and sees me, but she says nothing, only gives me a look with raised eyebrows.

A man accosts her from the window to the dining room. "Why did the alarm go off?"

"I let the cat out," she says with a deadpan face.

"Well, leave the stupid cat alone. Do you hear?"

"Yes, sir." She winks at me. I give her a smile and a thumbs-up.

Leaving her, I creep through the kitchen and arrive at a place where I have a view into the dining and activity room. It looks like the entire school is here – staff, personnel, students, overseers, maintenance. Yet for the amount of people, there's very little talk, only just a few low comments passed from person to person. Guards stand at all the doors, legs spread apart and guns gripped in their hands.

Shielded by the crowd as most of them are standing, I straighten and step forward, searching for Sanora. Then I see her! She's standing near the back wall.

She sees me. I motion her toward me and without waiting to see if she follows, I back-step into the kitchen, crouching again on the floor behind one of the counters. Sanora grasps my hands when she joins me. Her eyes look like they're going to pop from their sockets, and her hands are icy.

I whisper, "Why do they have all the people in here?"

Maria stands beside us, her wide hips and full skirt shielding us from the view of the camera.

"I didn't know at first," Sanora says, "but then I saw Mr. Sargent go to the office with some of his men. And I saw their wives leaving in cars, fast, like they knew something was going to happen."

She takes a breath and looks around with that hunted, wild look she has. "So I snuck down the hallway toward the office and listened at the door. Mr. Sargent said something about clearing out for good, and that they were going to set it off."

My heart drops. "Set what off?"

She shakes her head, tears forming in her eyes and dripping down her cheeks. "I don't know. Honest. But they said something else about the evidence going up in flames. I'm afraid, Miss Gina! Really afraid! Can I come with you?"

I notice she uses my real name. She's recognized me. Smart girl. "Yes! Yes, of course."

I can't believe it. Do they plan to blow the building sky high with all the staff, students, and evidence? And afterwards claim it was an accident?

The thought about knocks me over. "Did they say when? That's important."

"No. I didn't hear nothing like that. They came toward the door and the last thing Mr. Sargent said was to get the computer program going and get out. Then I ran and went back to my group."

I rock back on my heels, my mind spinning. We will have to wait until Bennet and his cronies leave the place. Then I can disable the program and get out with Sanora. But will there be enough time?

I lean toward her. "I have to talk to a friend of mine who's helping us. You go back to your group so you won't be missed. Wait for me. Watch the kitchen, and I'll come back for you. Okay?"

She grips my hands tighter. "You'll come back? Promise, Miss Gina?"

I smile. "Yes. I promise." With a hug, I leave her and go back to the door.

Maria follows me. "I will let cat back in, no?"

"Yes, please."

She opens the door, and I'm outside. I motion to Bobbi who joins me at the corner of the building. In a rapid sentence, delivered in one breath, I tell her what I've discovered. We creep around the side of the building. I'm hoping there aren't any cameras along here. Before we get to the front, I hear a whistle. Ramone stands on the edge of the trees, motioning for me.

"Don't run," I say to Bobbi. "They'll notice that. Just walk calmly."

She lets me take the lead as we make our way across the gravelly parking lot and enter the woods. I repeat to Ramone what Sanora shared with me.

"I have to disarm that computer program after they leave," I say, looking back at the Hacienda. "We can't let fifty people die."

Ramone's brow furrows. He shakes his head. "No. You leave. I'll stay and take care of this because I know computers. This is for me to do. Then I'll go over to the dam." He grins. "If you'll tell me how to get there."

I give him the directions, still thinking I should be the one to disable the program. Yet by the time I'm done, he's ready to go in.

I pull on his sleeve. "There's an alarm on the back kitchen door when you open it. The cook, Maria, knows me. Tell her you're my friend, and she'll make some excuse for opening the door."

"Yes, ma'am." He salutes me.

I'm thinking of the quote, *We who are about to die salute you, O Caesar.* As he takes off towards the kitchen door, tears sting my eyes. Then I remember Sanora.

"I have to go back for Sanora! Stay here, Bobbi. I'll get in with Ramone. Be right back!"

Ramone enters the back door and for some reason, there's no alarm. I'm right on his heels. He raises his eyebrows when he sees me but proceeds forward, keeping low.

I find the reason for the disabled alarm. Ricardo, Maria's husband, is dismounting a ladder, holding wires that are attached to a unit of some kind in his hand. A wide grin spreads across his face.

"We will try to smuggle people out the back way," Maria says in a whisper. "Sanora told us what she heard." Her eyes bulge from her head, and her hands tremble as she grips my arm.

I gently peel her hand away. "Have courage, Maria. That man, Ramone, is going to try to stop the computer program."

I proceed forward, but duck down quickly when Bennet and his two lieutenants charge out of the hallway and head for the front door.

As he passes the kitchen, he says, "Ten minutes. Tell the men at the exits so they can clear out just before it goes off."

I catch Sanora's eyes as Ramone starts for the offices, trying to hide behind the crush of people in the room. Sanora see me and makes her way to the kitchen, sidling along the wall, then dropping behind the counter. Together we get outside.

I put my arm around her thin shoulders as we stand in the rain near the back door. "We need to get a vehicle. Aunt Bobbi should be over there." I nod to the trees.

A car is coming down the lane. Fast. It's my van, my old loaner car! I'd left the key on the driver's seat, thinking I might need it in a hurry. Aunt Bobbi is driving it, and her face is set like she's intent on ramming whatever is in her path.

She pulls up beside us and motions frantically for us to get in. Sanora and I run around to the passenger side. I fling open the door. But just then a loud, booming voice shatters my nerves. The bullhorn again!

Two pickups pull to a skidding stop a few feet from the van, and the voice booms out. "Get away from that vehicle! Put up your hands! Now!

Chapter 51

Into the Depths of the Dam

Boundary Dam, June 16, 6:31pm

Dusty jerked awake. "What? What's going on?"

Chance nodded toward the front entrance to the dam. Three men stood beside the black SUV, their hands in their pockets, caps pulled low over their faces. "Looks like the hit team is getting ready to strike," he said in a low tone.

"What're we goin' to do? Sit here like a couple of dummies?" Dusty gripped his rifle. His other hand went to the door handle.

"Stay put. We can't make our move yet." Chance tapped his fingers on the steering wheel.

The sun was going down, but the long summer evening had just begun. There was plenty of light. Enough to see that the young girl who worked as a guide appeared in the tunnel mouth and was eyeing the group of men opposite her.

She brought a radio to her ear.

Two men from the pickup walked over to her. She lowered the radio. There was a short conversation. Chance was sure he saw her shake her head. She stepped back and looked over her shoulder like she hoped someone was coming.

One of the men approached her swiftly and grabbed her arms. The other man gagged her and bound her wrists. Then they marched her into the tunnel. It hadn't taken more than a minute.

There was only one other car in the parking lot. About five minutes later, a group of people emerged from the tunnel and walked over to the vehicle, got in, and drove away. Besides that, there was the RV, the big blue pickup, and the SUV. Chance guessed there were ten or twelve men, ready to carry out whatever plan they had in place.

A man from one of the vehicles strolled toward the tunnel. He held a satellite phone in one hand and a rifle in the other. Several times he looked in their direction. Chance drew in his breath. *Captain Grant! That will make Ramone happy, if he ever gets here.*

Chance grew increasingly uncomfortable, as his pickup now was alone in the lot. Had they closed off traffic at the top of the dam?

"I'm getting out of here," he said as he turned the key. "We're too obvious."

Dusty lifted his gun. "I'll give 'em something to remember."

"Not now. We're going to try to stay under the radar. I'm going to drive out, nice and easy. If they stop us, you have my permission to use that rifle." He pulled slowly out of the lot and up the winding hill.

No guard came out of the white shack as they passed. Chance glanced at his watch. *6:45pm*

The gang was moving to the target early. Yet they had to get a ton of dynamite into the dam and the bomb set. That would take a while.

He drove to the top and pulled into the campground. It was empty. "I'm going to move my outfit back over there," Chance said with a nod to a row of trees on the far side of the campground. "Why don't you hop out and lead Santiago over there for me?"

Dusty helped him hook up the trailer and led the horse as Chance pulled his outfit past the designated slots, halting behind a screen of bushes and trees. From this location, the truck and trailer weren't visible from the top of the dam, and if it blew up, his horse would be safe from the destruction. He hoped.

"I wish I could make a phone call," he said. Worry for Gina consumed his mind. What would she think when he didn't show up, and she needed him? But he was trapped here.

When all was situated with the horse and trailer, he and Dusty started out on foot, weapons in their hands, creeping down the hillside toward the lower portion of the dam and the parking lot.

They arrived in time to see the Ford pickup being driven slowly into the tunnel mouth. They were moving the dynamite into the dam.

And the worst of it was that Chance could do nothing to stop them.

***

4:21pm

Ramone waited, crouching on the floor of the dining room behind a group of boys at a table. Bennet and his men left. Gina found the girl, and they disappeared into the kitchen. Time to make his move.

With his rifle cradled in his arm, he scuttled into the hallway, praying that the guards would not see him. Sweat beaded his brow as he entered the office.

The outer office held a desk, several chairs, and a computer. He eyed it speculatively. Gina's computer? Off to the right was another door on which an engraved metal sign read *Bennet Sargent, Manager*.

He opened the door, surprised it was unlocked, and stepped inside. It was empty. The computer was turned off. Leaning the rifle against the desk, he sat down and turned on the computer. The first screen came up. Asked for the password.

Gina hadn't told him the password. He guessed several, but they failed. His shirt clung to his back as sweat ran in rivulets. He leaned back. *Oh, God! I need to get in!* He glanced at his watch, for he'd heard the man's muttered comment to his henchmen.

He had ten minutes. *4:24.* No, he had seven minutes. He tried Columbia River School and Ranch in several combinations. Denied. *What about ... Forward Guard?* He tried that and sat back when denied.

Now his breath came in gasps, and his hands trembled. *4:25*. Six minutes. The office door opened. Someone stepped into the room.

Ramone gave the man a passing glance, barely aware of him, as he was so engrossed with his problem.

"Who are you, and what are you doing?" The voice was stern, one used to giving commands.

"I'm trying to access this computer," Ramone said without rising or lifting his rifle. He knew he was caught in the act, but he was desperate. "I was told to get to a file on this computer, but I don't know the password. Who are you?" He glanced up.

The man was well dressed, had black hair and snapping dark eyes. He strode purposefully into the room. Ramone reached for his gun, but he froze when he saw a Glock G37 semi-automatic pistol pointed directly at his head.

"I am Bruno Sherman. *Senator* Bruno Sherman. I own this place. Leave that weapon where it is and get out of here! I don't care what you're doing or who you are! Leave immediately, or I will call my men."

Ramone leaned back and lifted his hands.

***

4:26pm

Bobbi and I stand with our arms raised above our heads while Bennet covers us with his gun.

"You got away from Gunther with the help of a friend. You think you're smart, don't you?" Bennet glances around as if he's afraid Ramone will appear again with his rifle. "But he should have killed Gunther because we found him."

He glances over his shoulder. "We've patched him up, going to take him to the hospital as soon as this other ... deal is finished."

Two other men, all carrying guns, emerge from the other pickup and stare at us. Tank and the other guard, Pete.

Bennet tosses them a tie-down he finds in the back of his truck. "Use this and make it tight. We'll take them over to the dam. I know a perfect way to take care of the problem of nosy cops."

He turns to us as Tank obeys his order, tying our hands tightly behind our backs. "I knew you wouldn't be able to escape this place and that we'd bump into each other again." He laughs and tosses my backpack into the cab of his truck.

I say through gritted teeth, "You might laugh, but you aren't going to get away with it. I'm an undercover FBI agent, and I've contacted my back-up." It's a lie, but I pray that God will forgive me. "They're coming, and they're going to shut you down, Bennet."

He snorts and turns to his pickup, anxious now to be off. "Throw them in the back, Tank, and tie them to the bed. They can't get out of that."

There are loops on the bed of the truck for securing loads. After Tank and another man dump us roughly into the back, he threads some rope he has around our wrists and then through the loops on the bed of the truck.

About then, I realize Sanora is not with us. She'd vanished the moment Bennet stopped us with his bullhorn. I don't blame her, really. She's just a kid, and she's scared out of her wits.

Bennet opens the door of his truck, but stops suddenly. "Tank! Search that van. I'd bet anything she's hidden something in it."

My heart falls to my shoes as I watch the big man search, praying that he won't find my evidence folder. But he does. Bennet casts me a triumphant grin as he grabs it. Then he climbs in the cab. He backs up.

Allowing the other pickup to lead, he jams the gear in drive, the turn complete. Just then a slim shape slips over the side of the truck bed and ducks down beside us.

Sanora!

I lift the corner of a tarp that's lying at our feet with my toe. She crawls underneath it. We start out, the pickup swaying as we turn south on the main road. My stomach lurches. I hope that apple

I ate doesn't come up. I'm still damp from the rain, and the wind is chilly. I shiver. Bobbi puts her arm around my shoulders.

Sanora peeks out from under the tarp.

"Stay down! They're watching." I nod with my chin to the window on the cab. She disappears.

"It's a miracle she got in," Bobbi says.

I nod. "But I don't know what she can do. There are lots of men with us, plus those from that ranch where Chance was. He said there were twenty or thirty of them over there. They must have a small army at the dam."

She shakes her head. "I don't think so. Didn't you say that blowing the dam was only part of their scheme? That they want to disrupt Seattle and Olympia? I bet he's moved the majority of his men over there."

"Well, let's hope so."

It's nearly seven when we pull up to the first barricade on the road above the dam. With a few curt words to the guards, Bennet drives on – past the guard shack and down the hill. He stops at the mouth of the tunnel. A large RV, a black SUV, and two pickups are parked near the entrance. Two men in black uniforms stand guard, holding semi-automatic rifles. Ammo belts circle their shoulders.

The pickup stops. Sanora surfaces from under the tarp and slides over the side of the truck. I hold my breath. Will anyone see her? I let out my breath when no one calls out an alarm.

Bennet, Tank, and the other two men swarm from the two vehicles. Tank, his face angry red, slashes the rope that's held us to the bed of the truck and lays down the tailgate.

"Get out," he says gruffly. "And hurry up about it. We ain't got all day."

Stiff and sore, badly in need of water and food, I climb out, my hands still bound behind my back. Bobbi follows me to the ground.

I look over the area, hoping to catch a glimpse of Chance. But the place seems deserted. Tank and the guard called Pete grab our ropes and yank us toward the tunnel. Bobbi puts up a struggle, but it's useless, and in the end, we follow behind the men into the depths of Boundary Dam.

***

Sanora heard Miss Gina say something about a man who was at the dam. A man who would help them. A funny name. Chance.

As she crouched behind a small fir tree near the entrance to the tunnel, she glanced around. The parking lot was empty except for a motor home and two pickups. Were there people inside the dam? She didn't know and couldn't assume that there was anyone she could call for help.

How could she find that man, Miss Gina's friend?

Her attention was drawn to the tunnel entrance. She knew the bad men were going to blow up the dam. That much she'd understood from listening to them talk.

It seemed all she could do was listen, but she desperately wanted to do something else, something that would help free the kids at the school and save Miss Gina's life.

The guards who stood at the tunnel mouth left and went inside. Probably they thought all danger was past of anyone stopping them now.

She dashed to the tunnel and entered it.

Inside, she was amazed at how large it was. It was hewn out of solid rock and lit with a row of light bulbs down its length. The big generators throbbed from the heart of the dam.

The tunnel curved. Maybe now she was right under where the water flowed through the massive concrete slab above her. It gave her the jitters. She hugged herself and went on. I have to have courage! I have to help Miss Gina, like she helped me.

She came to a door that led off to the left. It was open, blocked with a brick. She entered and proceeded slower, listening with all her might for the sound of voices or footsteps. The roar of the generators swamped her senses. Every so often there was a little closet in the cement tunnel wall where she figured they kept the tools they might need to fix things.

On tiptoes, she turned a corner, and there was Miss Gina and her aunt about twenty yards ahead, sitting on the cement floor, their hands and ankles tied. A bunch of men huddled over a large pile of something. Boxes? No. It looked like dark red sticks. They had them lying in bundles, laid out in rows on the floor, connected with wires along the wall.

One man seemed to be in charge. He worked on something without looking up, saying things in a low voice to the other men from time to time like he was telling them what to do. Mr. Bennet stood off to one side, watching intently. The big man who was named Tank studied him, too, his gun gripped tightly in his hands like he could use it to ward off the explosion if the dynamite went off too soon.

A guard, dressed in a black uniform, stood close to Miss Gina and her aunt, his rifle pointing directly at their heads.

Sanora drew back. She couldn't do anything to help them. She had to find that man named Chance and get him down here.

She took a deep breath and peeked around the corner of the cement wall for one last glance. Several men were edging away from the dynamite. The man who knelt beside the gadget on the floor stood.

She had to get out of there. She fled down the tunnel the way she had come.

***

7:10pm

"Hey! More company." Chance nudged Dusty's elbow as two pickups arrived and pulled up to the tunnel entrance. "What's goin' on now?"

They crouched in the grass behind a small building about a hundred yards from the tunnel entrance. It was a restroom, one door only. Chance wished for more ground cover so they could creep closer to the tunnel, but there was none — only carefully manicured grass that ended at the pavement.

On the left, a stone parapet guarded the drop-off that fell to the river below, and overhead towered the massive concrete dam. Water gushed with white foam from two sides, meeting in the center.

Soon after the two pickups halted, the slender figure of a girl emerged from the second truck bed and disappeared behind a row of small fir trees that were planted beside the sidewalk. Chance wondered who that was and thought immediately of Gina. Could it be her? No. She was too small.

His attention was drawn back to the vehicles.

A large man leaped from the cab of the second pickup, laid down the tailgate, and climbed up. Chance noticed that two people sat in the bed of the pickup. The big man used his knife to cut something. Then he motioned to them. They managed to get out of the truck even though their hands were bound behind their backs. The men jerked them toward the tunnel.

His heart fell, and his mouth went dry. *Gina and Bobbi!*

He could do nothing about it, though, for the occupants of the pickups, three armed men, guarded their prisoners. Bobbi struggled, but they overcame her, and the two women were yanked inside the tunnel. The guards at the entrance left their posts and followed behind the group.

"Let's go after 'em!" Dusty said, straightening as if he would stand.

Chance shook his head and pulled him down. "We wouldn't have a chance in a million to rescue them, not even with a surprise attack." He wiped the sweat from his forehead, even though the sun was now down below the level of the trees, and the breeze was cool along the ground. "We can't do anything but wait."

"Wait for what? Judgment day? Isn't there something we can do?"

"Well, I was going to say *and pray*, but I don't think you do that."

Dusty spat into the grass and grunted. "You don't know what I do or what I don't do. Ever since that night ..."

"Look!" Chance pointed. "There's that girl!"

She crouched on the sidewalk and gazed around curiously. Was she looking for them? He was about to stand and call to her when she darted inside the tunnel and disappeared.

Chapter 52

The Ticking Bomb

Inside the Tunnel, 7:22pm

I'm freezing.

The shivers haven't stopped since we were loaded into the pickup at the school. As we're shoved down the curving tunnel, Bobbi sobs quietly, and I feel like crying, too, but I tell myself that isn't going to help anything.

What can I do? What would Dad do? I come up with a blank for the answers.

We are herded past another tunnel that bends to the right, and continue on, going deeper under the dam. The generators throb through the stone wall beside us as the men lead us through a side door which has been propped open and goes deeper under the dam.

I wonder about the people who work here. Are they being held somewhere in a room to be blown up along with the dam when the bomb goes off? Or were they killed?

We turn a corner. Ahead in the tunnel, there's a group of men crouched together, studying a coil of wires on the floor. Strung out on the floor are sticks of dynamite, connected with wires.

A man kneels beside the wire, connecting it to a device. *The bomb!*

They push us to the floor beside the wall and tie our ankles with sturdy rope Tank has brought with him. Then he secures the other end of the ropes to a pipe that runs along the wall.

One of the guards stands over us. He's wearing a black uniform with an emblem on the pocket of the shirt that displays two rifles

372

crossed over a globe. *Forward Guard*. So, I finally get to meet Chance's friends from the ranch.

The guard's rifle is almost resting on my head. Now that I'm closer, I get a view of the man who is working on the bomb. He's the one who tried to kill me on the Columbia River the day this all began, an explosives expert, probably smuggled from Canada down the river.

I glance over at Bobbi. "It's okay. Keep praying. We'll get out of this."

She wipes her nose with her sleeve. "I am praying, but I don't feel like God is hearing me." She tries to smile, but it comes out a grimace.

"Shut up, you two!" The guard menaces me with his weapon.

I glare at him. "Look, mister. You might be able to kill us, but you can't keep us from praying. And we've got a big God. So, you better say some prayers yourself because He's watching out for us."

I should have saved my breath. There's no change in his expression. Cold black eyes stare at me. He *wants* to kill me. I see it in his face.

The explosives expert stands. "I've set the timer, Grant. It will go off in twenty minutes. Time for us to get out of here and away from the dam."

Now I know that the man who is in charge is the captain from the retreat that Chance attended.

"All right," Grant barks. "Let's go. I'm headin' up top, across the dam, then to the overlook across the river. Perfect place to watch it go. I have a chopper comin' for me there." He turns to Bennet. "Where are you goin'?"

Bennet straightens from leaning against the wall. His face is the color of white cheese. He clears his throat.

"Headin' to the top, sir. I've got men out on the road. I'll meet you at the capitol building in Olympia in the morning."

Grant nods. "Very well. I have my soldiers in place over there. Several bombs will be detonated at the same time this one goes off. We'll move in and mop up the wreckage."

He tips his hat to me. "Sorry you ladies won't be around to see it. My brilliant plan is all set to go. It's been in progress for about ten years now, and when it's done, it will land me square where I want – at the top of the heap in charge of this whole country." He grins.

"You're crazy," I say. "What about the US military? Got them in your hip pocket, too?"

He acts like he doesn't hear me and gives final commands to his men.

Bennet steps closer. "He has the military angle figured out, if you need to know. The first step is the state government, and all the other states will fall to his command. It's all been planned. Down to the smallest detail."

I twist my head to stare at him like I would an ugly bug. "You like killing, don't you, Bennet? You know the first thing Grant's going to do when he gets into power? Kill you. You won't be necessary to him, and you'll be a threat to him."

Bennet laughs. "That's a lie. You and this other woman will be blown to pieces in twenty minutes. That threat will be removed." He looks at his watch. "No, more like eighteen minutes." He turns to his men. "Let's go."

He's anxious to leave. They all are. It doesn't take them long to exit the tunnel. As their footsteps thud away, and we sit alone, all the brave words and hopeful thoughts vanish from my mind.

We're going to die. There's no one, not even Chance or Ramone, or my FBI back-up agents, who can help now. The minutes tick away. I'd noted the time they set the bomb. It was 7:40 then. It's 7:44 now.

Bobbi sniffs. She has her face screwed up funny like she's going to cry. "Gina," she says. "There's been something I've been meanin' to say to you, and I couldn't get it out. I've got to say it now."

"Well, you better spit it out fast, Aunt Bobbi, because we don't have much time." I'm thinking more about trying to undo the rope that's around our hands than I am of what she's about to say.

"That's the problem, you see," she says, her voice stronger. She doesn't look at me. "I ... I'm not your aunt. I'm your mom."

It doesn't register at first, but when it does, I stare at her and swing my head away. The generators throb in time with my heart beat. She doesn't say anything. My throat closes. I'm falling into a deep, dark pit.

I cough and shake my head. "You're joking, right?" When there's no response, I say, "Bobbi, c'mon, what's going on?" My voice is sharp, the sound a person might make if they'd been stabbed. I inch away from her.

It isn't true. She's saying this to get my attention or because...

But it *is* true. I recognize it, but I veer away from it like poison. I realize in that moment that I never really wanted to find my mom. She was a fictional figure, a willow-the-wisp dream that I could fantasize about but never would have to deal with.

Sitting there in the dank, cold hallway beneath the dam, keeping company with a bomb that's ticking my last minutes away, the shakes begin in my soul and shudder throughout my whole being.

"I'm sorry," she says with another sniff. "I... I know I did wrong to leave you, but I couldn't go on like I was. I had to get away. And... I knew Tom's brother lived in Montana, so I found him and came out here. He took me in. We wasn't... in love then. That came later." She glances at me. "Will you forgive me, Gina? I love you. I've always loved you. And I've kept track of you."

I fight against angry tears that sear my eyeballs. "I can't believe you'd come back into my life and tell me you're my..." I can't say the word *Mom*. I drop my head onto my upraised knees.

"Gina, please!" She leans toward me, but I increase the distance from her, as far as the rope will allow. "Please forgive me!"

I lift my head, staring at the ceiling, hating the tears that flood my face. "Look, Bobbi. I've wanted to find my mother all my life. I dreamt about her, longed for her, wanted to feel her arms around me. But she wasn't there. I hated God because He allowed her to go away from me. I've come to see the error of that, but I can't deal with this. It's too hard. I've carried this pain for most of my life. I had a picture of you that Dad overlooked when he destroyed them all, and I've looked at that picture and imagined ...."

"Imagined your mom would be beautiful? Talented? Like some model you see in a magazine?" She sighs and shakes her head.

I answer sadly with a sigh. "No. I thought of my mom as a warm person, someone who would welcome me back into their life if they could."

"I'm sorry I disappoint you." There's a pause. "I don't suppose you can understand. I hoped one day you'd find out, and things would be good between us."

Another minute ticks past. I'm finding it hard to breathe. Hard to think.

She says, "Hadn't we better try to get out of here? That thing is going to go off in a little while, and I don't want to die."

"I do."

She gasps and stiffens like I'd plunged in a dagger.

I raise my head and try to swipe the tears from my face. "Yeah. We have to get out of here. Then we'll deal with ... whatever."

But how can we get free? I'd managed to loosen my bonds a little bit on the way over in the truck, but they still held. "Turn your back to me. I'll try to work on yours."

She dutifully shifts around, and I feel her ropes. I wrestle with them, sweat dripping into my eyes.

7:47

I lean back, my fingers sore. "It's not going to work. At least we'll be together as we die." I look toward the ceiling. "Here. You try to work on mine. It's all we can do."

It isn't long before she gives up. I close my eyes, defeated. Everything that I've lived for — my career, my faith, my family, such as it is, drifts before my eyes and vanishes like smoke. I'm going to die.

7:49

I can't forgive Bobbi for what she did to me and Dad, but I know I must. God's Spirit tells me to do it. I shudder, the pain I'd suffered for all those years like a weighted chain around my heart. I have to think about this. Process it. I need some time.

But I'm running out of time. I screw my head around and look at my watch. The bomb will explode in exactly ten minutes.

***

7:46pm

Chance leaned forward. There was a movement by the entrance to the tunnel, but it was getting darker, and he wasn't sure if his eyes were playing tricks on him. A second later, the girl stepped outside.

"She's comin' out. She don't know where we are," Dusty said.

Chance stepped out from behind the building. "Over here!" He waved.

She lifted her head and started for them, dashing across the pavement like she was in a race. She was in a race. Against time.

She stumbled just as she arrived. Chance caught her and drew her back behind the building. She was trembling and breathing hard.

"Catch your breath." He waited. "Who are you? What's going on?"

She looked at him, her eyes wide. "Are ... you Chance?"

He nodded. "And this here's my friend, Dusty. Are you Sanora?"

Surprise flooded her face. She gave him a ghost of a smile. "Yes. I saw them take Gina and that other lady inside, so I followed them, and I saw the ... the bomb. I figure that's what it was, anyway." She drew a breath and pulled away from him.

"They were tied up?" Dusty fidgeted with his gun like he wanted to use it.

"Yes. I couldn't get very close, so I didn't hear nothing that they was saying, but it was like real scary. There was this big pile of ...

like, maybe dynamite. You have to get in there and get them free! They're going to be ..." She choked and turned her head.

Chance patted her shoulder. "We'll figure out what to do."

"But there's no time!" Sanora tugged at his sleeve. "You have to go! Now!"

"Hey, wait. Here they come." Dusty nodded toward the tunnel and drew back.

Chance peered around the corner. A group of men emerged, some of them almost running toward the vehicles.

"They've set the timer, and they're clearing out," he said in a low voice. The men hurriedly climbed in the pickups and the RV.

"What're we goin' to do?" Dusty stepped out from behind the building when they were gone.

Chance mopped his brow. "We have to free Gina and Bobbi first, and then deal with the gang. I suspect they're not going far. They'll want to watch the fireworks." He lifted his rifle. "Sanora, you stay here with Dusty. I'm going inside."

"Do you know how to take care of that bomb?" Dusty's eyes were large in the dim light. "Because if you don't, we're dead, and they've won."

"I know. But I've got to try. Get the girl to the top. Wait for me. I'll come. I promise."

Dusty snorted. "Some promise." He hitched up his pants. "You're wrong, Chance. I'm goin' to take a look at it. Worked some on them in the military. In Afghanistan. Maybe I can do somethin'."

"But I don't want to lose you. You can't die yet." Not until you accept Christ and are right with God! But he didn't have time to talk about the man's soul.

All he could do was stare as Dusty trotted off to the tunnel.

***
7:51pm

I shift so Bobbi can see my hands. She says, "I think I'm getting this. Here. See if you can help me. Use your teeth if you have to."

She works on the ropes frantically. Her teeth bite into my wrists. Sweat pours into my eyes. I swipe at my face with my shoulder.

She pauses. "Stay still! My land. You wiggle around so much, I can't do nothin'."

"Anything." I say, correcting her grammar.

"What?" She sounds incredulous.

"Anything," I repeat stubbornly. "You can't do anything."

"Hey, don't talk to your mom like that!"

I shift again. "But that's what you said."

Bobbi sighs. "No, I didn't. I said I can't do nothing ..." Her voice trails off. "For Pete's sake! Does it matter?"

We are back to our old fights. In a way, it makes me feel better. The cold anger I'd felt a few minutes ago burns now like a hot wave. I use it to fuel my desire to live, thinking about what those men are getting away with.

Suddenly my wrists move. The rope is coming off! There! She does it!

Without a word, she turns, and I grab her wrists. She's worked on the knot a little bit, so I don't have much to do. It takes less than a minute before her rope falls off. We both frantically untie the knots on our ankles.

7:55pm

When my rope falls off, I wipe my face and stand. We're still attached to the rope that's tied to the pipe along the wall. I yank on it, hoping the pipe will give, but it doesn't.

"We have to get out of here. Before ..." I allow my eyes to slide over to the dynamite that's strung along the wall of the tunnel, connected with fuse wire.

"We don't have time." Her voice rises to a wail. "Gina! It's five to eight right now. We can't get out in time!"

I force composure into my voice. "We're not going to die. Calm down." I take her arm and shake her gently. "Let's both yank on this. We can get it off. Look. There's a coupling. It should give there."

We're yanking on it when we hear footsteps. Out of breath, I whirl, ready to use my feet if I have to on this new threat.

A man charges around the corner. He stops and stares at us. Then he says hoarsely, "You must be Gina. I'm Dusty. Chance's partner from work."

"Pleased to meet you and all, but could you help us here?"

He whips out a knife and slashes the rope. "Get going. Chance is outside. I told him to go up top and watch the gang up there. I'll see what I can do here." Kneeling on the floor, he stares at the bomb.

I smell his fear from where I stand.

Under his breath, he says, "Man, this is a monster! I've never seen anything like it!"

I shake my head. There's no way he can do anything to stop the bomb. It's suicide to defuse a bomb like this unless you have a robot. Usually they take it out and blast it from a distance. But we have no time for that.

"Okay. Good luck!"

Turning, I sprint down the tunnel, hoping Bobbi can keep up with me.

I shouldn't have worried. She not only matches my speed, she passes me.

Chapter 53

The Shooting Gallery

Boundary Dam, June 16, 7:57pm

Chance didn't waste time. He started away from the restroom, angling up the hill, the girl following. "We have to get on top, away from the blast and the water if all that dynamite goes off." He wished he hadn't mentioned that possibility, because Sanora hesitated and looked at the tunnel mouth.

"They were tied up. I didn't even try to help them."

"You're not going back. Come on." His firm tone got through to her. They climbed the hill and came out to the road near the guard shack.

7:58pm

He wanted to stop and say a prayer for Dusty, Gina, and Bobbi, but he kept going. Sanora panted along after him, not saying a word, but casting glances over her shoulder as if she were watching and hoping for someone to appear from the tunnel.

He ducked behind the guard shack because he'd spotted some of Grant's men near the top of the dam, positioned far enough away that they wouldn't be in the collapse when it blew. They had all their vehicles parked on the roadway, some of them with motors running, ready for a quick get-away.

He clenched his fists. Here he was, alone and helpless to stop them. They had won, and he was unable to stop them. Again.

He had to do something. He turned to Sanora. "There's going to be some gunfire," he said in a quiet voice. "You circle around those cars and get over to the campground. Over there." He pointed south through the trees. "I've got a pickup and horse trailer parked over there. You find my camp and get into the truck." He handed her the keys. "I'll be there soon."

He didn't wait for her to respond.

7:59pm.

One more minute before the explosion. He couldn't wait to see if the bomb was going to go off or not. He had to stop them. Lifting his rifle, he began to shoot. Systematically, he blasted out the tires of all the vehicles within range. With that done, he reloaded as fast as he could, for he heard a shout. They were coming for him.

8:01pm

On the edge of his consciousness, he realized that the dam hadn't blown. That's when heavy gunfire started his way. The whole gang with high powered, semi-automatic rifles was aiming for him. And they were mad.

Not much of a chance he'd get out of this one alive.

They shot out the windows of the little shack and riddled it with bullets. He hunched over and rush for a pile of pipes to one side of the road, and made it, but they'd seen him. And the pipes were no match for the hot lead that seared through them. He returned fire, noticing that some of them were circling his position. In a few minutes, they would have him cornered.

He peeked out to see where next he could run, wishing he had Ramone or Dusty as back up.

8:06pm.

The dam stood solidly. No blast from deep within. Had Dusty done it?

He returned fire and caught one man as he ducked between trees on the left. The man fell. But there were others. How many? Did it matter? One well-placed bullet would take him out. It gave him a little satisfaction to know he'd disabled their trucks and blasted out the windshields. A bit of payback, but it came at a high price.

They let up on the gunfire. Someone yelled. He thought it was Grant. Maybe the man realized the bomb hadn't gone off. Maybe they were going back inside to make sure it did.

He dashed to the shelter of one of the bigger pickups. But here he was exposed on three sides. Not good. He took a few shots at a man who was circling ... missed. Getting low on ammo. Sweat in his eyes. His breath came in labored gasps.

Had to stay focused. Had to stay out of their line of fire.

The next place of refuge was a large rock sitting near the entrance to the campground. If he could get there, he might be able to creep back into the woods and find more cover. Big if.

Chance aimed at the closest man who appeared briefly from behind a building. The man twisted and fell. But it was only a brush. The next shot was for Grant who stood out in the open.

Grant took the shot and fell, but he leaped up and found refuge behind a building near the top of the dam. He returned the fire to Chance, who kept low.

The men in the woods began firing. Chance dashed out of cover, hit the dirt, and rolled. Crab-walking, he made it to the ditch beside the road. Flattened out in it. Reloaded. Last time. Then out of ammo.

He took careful aim at the shadowy shape of one of his assailants who dodged through the woods on the right. Hit his target. The man fell with a scream. Enraged, Grant sent another rain of killer bullets his way, blistering the air, seeking him out.

If something didn't happen soon, he was dead. But he didn't let the thought sink in. He had things to do. And he aimed to do them.

***

7:58pm

I arrive at the tunnel entrance, holding my side, panting great gasps of air into my starving lungs. Bobbi sags beside the opening, grasping the lumber struts that frames it. I glance at my watch. Two minutes before the bomb goes.

"We have ... to get out ... completely." I motion to the top. "Up there, or the water will ..."

"I know." She straightens. "Okay... but not running ... can't ... anymore."

"No. We'll walk. Let's go." I lead off with her close behind me. We stay near to the trees planted at intervals along the winding road. Chance is here somewhere. Dusty said he was going up top to watch the gang. Watch them? Or stop them?

Suddenly shots ring out. Coming from the top of the dam. Now I see Chance who is sheltered by the guard shack, firing steadily at an unseen target.

"You stay low," I say, turning to Bobbi. "It might be best to go back to the tunnel. Stay there until we come for you. Seems like we've got a gun fight going on up here, and I've got to give Chance some back-up. You okay? Can you wait?"

She shakes her head, sniffling with a new batch of tears. "But what can you do? You don't have a gun. Are you going to ... yell and draw their fire? That's suicide, Gina."

"Just get back down there so you're safe!"

She reaches for me. "It's just so ... different than what I thought ... what I wanted. I mean, you and ... me. Gina, please."

I step back. "Just do as I say. We can talk later." My tone is harsher than I wanted, but I can't help it. There's more gunfire now. Grant and his men are returning Chance's fire, and it sounds like it's heating up.

Bobbi starts down the slope without replying, her shoulders slumped. I have the urge to call her back, to try to explain how I feel, but I can't. Not now.

I climb the slope, aiming for the forest that borders the road on the other side. Chance is receiving a lot of heavy fire now, and Grant's men are getting into position to take him out. There's one of them just ahead of me. He's angling toward the shack, keeping in the trees.

Chance sees him in time and shoots. The man falls. Chance dashes to the cover of something on the ground. I can't see what it is. He's out of my line of vision. But I can see the assailant he took out.

I creep up to the fallen man, watching to see if he will move. When he remains still, I approach and feel his pulse. He's alive but unconscious. I help myself to his gun, a Ruger semi-automatic tactical rifle. I take boxes of ammo from his pockets and shove them in my own.

It's about that time that I hear someone coming behind me. I turn, the weapon in my hands. It's Dusty.

"There's some pretty steady gunfire going on," he says, holding his rifle steady, his eyes on the slope above us.

I nod. "Yeah. Chance stirred up a hornet's nest. You got the bomb disarmed?"

"Nah. Couldn't do that. But I figured I could change the time on the timing device. Gave us a couple more hours. Maybe we can get a bomb squad in here by then. You think?"

"We have to find a satellite phone. Grant has one, but I don't think he'll let us use it." I let out my breath, not even knowing I'd been holding it. "Well, that's a relief. Now we just have to disarm those thugs up there. You ready?"

He gives me a lop-sided grin. "Oh, yeah."

I lead out warily, eyeing the surroundings. The steady blast of gunfire hasn't lessened. As we draw near to the top of the dam, I spot Chance taking shelter behind a truck parked on the road, along with the other vehicles the gang had driven to the dam.

All of them have shattered windshields and blown tires. This must have been Chance's first objective – disable the gang's get-away cars. He accomplished that, but he also managed to make them steaming mad.

I was just about to call out to him when he dashes from the truck, which didn't give him much protection, and falls into a ditch about twenty yards away. There are two men in the woods near me. They are working their way forward, using their fire power to blast the way to Chance and get a good shot at him.

I take out one, and Dusty targets the other. They both fall.

Chance twists around, gun pointing at us.

"We've got your back, buddy!" Dusty calls out.

"It's me, Chance. Gina! Work your way to the trees. We'll cover for you."

He's cautious, but the blistering attack from the buildings lessens as Dusty and I pepper them with bullets. Grant and Bennet have to stay undercover while Chance sprints to the nearest large tree, and from that, to our position behind an outcropping of rocks.

"Gina! Dusty!" He sinks to the ground like his legs have given out. "You're two mighty beautiful people to see!" He glances up at Dusty. "The bomb? You got it taken care of?"

"For now. Delayed the timer. That's all I could do. We gotta get a team in here pronto to take care of it for good."

I plop down beside Chance. "In the meantime, we need to deal with those bozos over there. You sure know how to raise the dust, Chance."

He grabs me and holds me close. He smells of sweat and gunpowder and horse, yet I figure it's the best scent I've smelled for a long time.

When he releases me, he clings to my hand like he won't ever let it go. "I thought I wasn't going to make it, Gina. And I realized how much ..."

Dusty swears softly under his breath. "Uh, I hate to interrupt this tender moment, folks, but we got trouble comin'. Take a look, you two. This is ain't good."

I lumber to my feet and swish my hair from my eyes. Grant and two of his men, along with Bennet, Pete, Tank and someone else I don't recognize, have stepped out onto the open pavement in front of the buildings. Tank is holding someone ... *who?* ... and then I know.

Sanora!

"Hey, you! Chance! And Gina Lindsey!" Bennet calls out. "Come on over and see who we have. You might find it interesting!"

"We better go," I say to Chance. "We have to finish this, one way or the other."

"How did they get the girl?" Dusty glances at Chance. "Wasn't she with you?"

"I sent her to the campground. She must have come back, looking for Gina. She wanted to help you escape."

"Those ... jerks!" I can't find a word strong enough for the rage that explodes in my head. For a moment, it blots out everything, but I force myself to control it.

With an effort, I bring the forest, the buildings at the top of the dam, the smell of gunpowder, and Chance's pale face back into focus. "I'm not going to let her go! Come on."

I lead out as we thread our way forward, staying undercover. Five or six guns are trained on us, ready to blow us to the next world if we so much as show an eyelash. Sanora struggles. They slap her down.

"Leave her out of this!" I call out. "She has nothing to do with it. Let her go! You can have me!"

Bennet laughs. "Yeah, right. Come here, and we'll talk. But we ain't lettin' her go. Not until we get free passage out of here!"

Chance calls out as we get to the first building near the top of the dam and shelter behind it. "What do you want? We can't fix your vehicles."

"You throw out your guns and let us change those tires. Then we'll leave, and you can have the girl. Deal?" Bennet sounds pleased with himself.

Grant calls out, "You get nothing, Chance Marshal, except a free ticket to Hell if you don't do as I say. My man is goin' to fix that bomb, and my plans are going ahead. Now throw your weapons out onto the road and stand down. Or we will toss this girl over the railing. You understand?"

Even as they speak, they move back until they're standing on the walkway that leads over the top of the dam. Sanora screams. I peek around the building.

Grant is holding her up like he's about to toss her over. I gnaw on my lip, trembling with anger. I can't do anything. Not when they have Sanora.

***

"Stop!" Chance called out. "Put her down, you swine! Now!" His finger itched to blast the men away, but he couldn't. Again. Couldn't do anything.

Grant laughed. "Who's calling the shots now, big boy? So you got away from me once, but you can't do it again. This is my show, and I'll do it my way. Throw your guns out, or this girl's going over the edge."

Chance wiped his brow, singling out a gray-haired man who crouched beside Grant. "DeMoss? Is that you? How can you lower yourself to be a part of this madman's schemes? I thought you were a decent person. You're throwing a lot away. You can still get out. Nobody knows about this but me and Dusty, and we won't say a word."

DeMoss answered by sending a round of bullets towards them which nicked off the edges of the block building. Chance ducked back.

"I guess I got my answer," he said to Gina.

"Keep them busy for a bit," she said, eyeing a ladder that climbed the far end of the building. "I think I can get up this."

"No, wait! You'll be ..." But she started out, clambering up with her rifle in one hand. He'd been going to say, "blown away because they'll see you," but she was determined to do it. The Lone Ranger again.

"Hey, Gina!" He called in a low tone. She stopped, halfway up the ladder. "Grant has a vest on. I swear it. Aim for his head. Or legs."

She nodded and kept going.

Chance engaged Grant in a conversation, hoping for a moment when his attention was diverted from the girl, the window they needed to rescue Sanora. It was easy to get him to talk – he liked to brag about his accomplishments and his plans.

As he talked, Chance glanced around. There should be more of Grant's men here. Have they faded back into the woods? Are they ready to spring a trap on us, attacking front and back, when we yield our weapons? It was a possibility that raised the hairs on his neck.

A chopper appeared overhead and landed in the small parking lot behind them. Chance heard it coming, but he'd been so engrossed in the drama being played out that he hadn't realized what the sound was.

Grant glanced at it. "That's my ride out of here, boys." He turned and addressed Chance and Dusty who were hunched behind the building. "She's going over, boys. You better make your move soon." He pinioned her arms and lifted her off the pavement. She screamed.

Chance wondered what Gina was doing and when she would make her move. Not now. Not unless she wanted Sanora to die.

"Okay! You've had your chance!" Grant lifted the girl clear of the pavement and shoved her into Bennet's arms. The other man hesitated to take her, and finally did with a look of utter hatred and repugnance on his face.

"Gina! Help me!" The girl screamed as Bennet hefted her out over the edge, over the long fall to the sheer concrete wall and the rushing, roaring water that sent spray to the top.

"Stop!" A booming voice reverberated against the cliffs.

Chance whirled. Two men had hopped down from the helicopter, holding their guns with both hands. At first, his heart dropped. They were Grant's men. Then he saw someone he recognized.

"Ramone!"

Ramone advanced despite Grant lifting his rifle to get a shot off. Chance did not know the second man. He was tall, dark-haired, and seemed accustomed to giving commands. Both of them strode toward the walkway, seemingly unconscious of the danger.

"Get over here!" Chance called. "They're aimin' to kill you!"

The stranger and Ramone ducked behind the building just as the first bullets whizzed overhead.

"Bruno Sherman!"

Chance twisted his head and looked up at the voice. Gina's face peered over the edge of the roof.

She grimaced. "What are you doing here?"

"Good afternoon, Miss McDonald," Bruno said with a wry grin.

"Gina Lindsey, sir," Gina replied.

Ramone gazed up at her, a smile spreading across his face. "He's on our side, Gina. Mr. Sherman came in the office just in time to stop the computer program so the bomb didn't go off. Bennet Sargent was doin' all the bad stuff," he motioned widely with his hand, "without Mr. Sherman's knowledge. We called the police and captured some of Bennet's men. Everyone's safe."

Ramone looked at Chance. "So what's the score here?"

Chance briefed him as Bennet called out that he was going to drop the girl. Gina's face disappeared.

Bruno's voice boomed out again. "Bennet, you fool! What's going on? Get over here and talk to me! Now!" His voice quivered with rage.

Bennet laughed. "You ain't my boss no more, Mr. Sherman. I'm with this fellow who's going to take me to the top. Meet my new boss, Captain Grant."

"Commander Grant to you!" He thrust his head forward like he would ram anyone who opposed him. "We have a problem, Senator. My friend's arms are getting tired. If we don't see some weapons come out on that pavement in five seconds, she's going to meet her Maker. You savvy?"

When Bruno made no reply, Grant called out, "On the count of five! One! ... Two!... Three!... Four!" He paused. "I'm not joking, gentleman. She's going over!"

Chapter 54

Lights and Sirens

From Gina's Journal:

I'm watching Bennet's arms. He's getting tired and rests on the parapet. Sanora grasps the edge. Good girl. Now if only Chance is ready.

I take aim at Bennet's heart and squeeze off the shot. But he turns fractionally, and I miss! I can't believe it. He extends Sanora beyond the railing. She screams and struggles to keep her hold while he tries to pry off her fingers.

I shoot again. This time I connect with Bennet. He drops. Sanora clings to the edge of the railing, screaming.

"Chance! Get the girl!" My cry draws Grant's attention.

The man drops to one knee, shielded by the cement wall of the walkway from the fire erupting from behind the building. I take careful aim, for I have a clear shot of him.

But before I can pull the trigger, he swings his gun up and shoots. A bullet sears through my chest, blasting me backward. I roll away from the edge and manage to get on the far side of the roof, where Chance and Ramone are kneeling. I'm falling. Blackness descends on me like a curtain.

I have to hold onto consciousness, but I can't. My last sensation is sliding down the sheet metal roof toward the ground.

***

In response to Gina's call, Chance charged from behind the building, Ramone and Bruno with him, all blasting away with their weapons. DeMoss fell. Grant twisted, cried out, and partially fell, his gun clattering to the cement. He managed to stand, but he'd been shot in the leg.

Gunfire erupted from the rear. Grant's men. Or maybe Bennet's. Chance didn't know, couldn't think. Ramone and Dusty swiveled almost as one and returned fire.

Chance leaped to the walkway, barely aware that Grant was fleeing, that he was running with a limping gait to the far end of the walkway where a gate led to a path up the far side of the mountain.

The girl!

Her hold was slipping on the smooth railing. She screeched again. "Please! Help!"

He leaped to her and grabbed her wrists just as she lost her hold. The weight of her pulled him forward. He lost his footing, was being pulled over the edge with the girl.

Chance yelled, "Ramone! Need some help here! Ramone!"

A rifle clattered to the cement. Ramone grabbed his waist. "I'm here. Hang on." In two seconds, he landed on the cement walkway, the girl beside him. She sobbed. He gathered her in his arms.

"Take it easy, Sanora. You're safe now. You're safe!"

"But Miss ... Gina ... she was shot!" She wiped her face and pointed up toward the roof of the building. "I saw her fall! We need to help her!"

Chance left the girl and charged down the walkway. He stopped by the ladder where Gina had crawled to the roof. It seemed the road leading to the dam was swarming with emergency vehicles, their sirens and lights filling the night.

"Bruno called them," Ramone said in his ear. "Thought we might need some help. He told them to bring in a bomb squad. Sure hope they did."

Chance looked up to the roof of the building. Gina's body had stopped just before plunging over the edge. He and Ramone lifted her down. Blood poured from a wound high on her chest. Something seared his eyeballs, and he realized it was tears. He gasped as pain shot through his chest, almost like a bullet had lodged there, too.

Holding her in his arms, he gazed at her pale face. Her breathing was shallow. No, this can't be happening! Oh, please, God! He tried to get a grip on himself, tried to shake away the light-headed dizziness, but it persisted. He had to be alert. Had to help her.

"Gina, oh, my darling," he said under his breath. Tenderly, he laid her down and brushed back her hair. A thin stream of blood trickled from the corner of her mouth. Her lungs. But not her heart. Please, not that. He ripped off his shirt, folded it, and pressed it on the wound. She groaned.

Her eyes fluttered open. "Chance ...." She reached up for him.

He grabbed her hand and kissed it. "Don't leave me. I need you, girl." His face was wet with tears he didn't know he was shedding.

She shook her head weakly. A smile touched her lips. "No ... won't leave ... you have to ... get Grant. Said a ... chopper would meet him at the ... upper parking lot ... by the overlook. Go ... get him, Chance. Don't ... let him get away with ..." She tried to form the next words, but they would not come. She turned her head and moaned again. Her eyes closed.

Medics shoved Chance aside.

He wrenched his gaze from Gina's grey face. Grant had fled down the walkway. Two men, both dressed in Forward Guard uniforms, met him at the end and opened the gate for him. They would get away up a path that led to the overlook.

He tore away from the crowd, aiming for the campground. When he arrived at his pickup, Bobbi popped out. Her eyes held questions, but there was no time to talk. He grabbed Santiago's lead line and vaulted onto his back.

She held up a hand like she would stop him. "You can't overtake them! There's no time! Take the truck!"

"I can't. He's cutting up to the upper overlook. Gina's been shot. Bad."

He kicked the horse. Santiago thundered across the campground. Chance used the lead line and his knees to guide him past the crowded area of the parking lot and the medics who lifted Gina to a stretcher.

"Here, *senor!*" Ramone called as Chance passed, and tossed him a rifle. "The Uzi might come in handy! I'll be right behind you!"

He caught the weapon. Santiago thundered across the top of the dam. Chance slowed him down as they exited through the open gate on the far end. The path zigzagged up the cliff above the dam on the northeast side.

He had to pause once and let Santiago take a breather as he climbed the hillside. After that, they entered the footpath that went to the lower overlook area and kept flying upward. The way was clear now, an easy path for tourists to use. At times, Chance caught glimpses above of Grant and his two cronies who hurried to the rendezvous place in the parking lot.

At the top, Chance broke out from the path and pulled Santiago to a halt. He slid from his back and dropped the rope, ducking immediately behind a boulder.

The two men held Grant upright as they scurried across the lot. Chance recognized Caleb Ostranger and Chang, the Korean. "Halt where you are, or I'll shoot!" Chance called out, the Uzi firm in his armpit and Grant in his sights.

They whirled, staring.

Grant shook his head, unable to admit defeat. "Oh, no, you don't! Boys, take him out! Then we're outta here!"

"Drop your guns. Now!" Chance stepped out, drawing closer, his finger on the trigger of the Uzi. "Your vest won't protect your head, Grant, and I have it in my sights."

He had the satisfaction of seeing Ostranger's eyes widen. They dropped their guns on the pavement. A chopper descended. Chance wanted to cuff the men before it landed, as he figured it was Grant's chopper. It touched down, and two men jumped from it, rifles in their hands.

"Throw down your guns! Raise your hands!" The man to hit the ground first was an officer, dressed in combat gear, with a yellow vest that proclaimed AFT. He looked at Chance who lowered his weapon and lifted his hands.

"Chance Marshal here, sir! I'm a border guard and apprehended these three men. They are leaders of the gang from down below." He motioned to the dam.

The man turned his weapon on the three men who were trying to step back into the woods. "You! Down on the pavement! Now!"

They dropped face down to the ground.

Two police cars and an unmarked vehicle entered the lot with sirens echoing against the trees and lights casting eerie, pulsing colors through the evening shadows. The officers who emerged from the cars joined those from the helicopter.

Chance stepped back to Santiago and held his reins, for the horse didn't like either the sirens or the lights. "Easy, boy." He tied the horse to a slender birch and glanced across the parking lot in time to see a third man climb out of the chopper.

Chance blinked.

"Chris!" The man sprinted across the intervening space. "Are you all right?"

"Dad!" Chance met his forward charge. "What ... why are you here? What's going on?"

Josh Marshal took him by the arm away from the noise of the officers and their vehicles. "I got to thinking about your phone call ... about the threat to the dam and the other thing, the smuggling and human trafficking business. I decided to do an inquiry on the organization, Forward Guard. I didn't find much, but something smelled rotten, so I rallied the FBI, the ATF, and the state police. It seemed like things were coming to a head, so I had them come to the dam."

"But how did you know to come to here?"

"We flew over the dam and saw sufficient police force in position there. Then we spotted that man hoofing it up the trail with you in pursuit."

He smiled and put his arm around Chance's shoulders. "Like something out of a western. We decided to give you a hand."

"Well, you sure did. Came just in time." Chance turned to his horse. "Hey, I've got to get back. Gina's injured. I want to see how she's doing."

Josh nodded, concern wrinkling his brow. "Okay. Are you going home afterwards?"

"Yeah. Then I'm going into Spokane. I'll call and let you know. Meet you at my house. Go and make yourself a cup of coffee. Thanks, Dad. Thanks a lot. "

"Okay. Glad I could help." Josh nodded, his face flushed. "I'm very proud of you."

A warm glow filled Chance's heart as he jumped on Santiago. With a thumbs-up to Dad, he rode back down the trail to the dam, going a little slower now, yet every fiber of his being bent toward the ambulance that was still parked on the far end of the walkway.

Gina! Oh, dear God. Please help her. Don't let her die. Please.

***

Bobbi held Gina's hand for as long as she could, but in the end, she had to give way to the medics as they treated her. When Bobbi stepped back, she noticed more police vehicles in the lot – the Border Patrol, unmarked vehicles with lights on the top, State Police, and county sheriffs.

Officers leaped from them in full combat gear. They combed the woods and brought in the wounded. More ambulances arrived, and along with them, the media. Bobbi figured this would be big news in Spokane and probably go national.

A fire truck pulled to a stop. The fireman spoke briefly with an officer who stood at the dam's entrance, then drove down to the lower level. They were going to take care of the bomb, she hoped.

"Is she going to be all right?" A voice penetrated her thoughts that whirled like the lights on the emergency vehicles.

She looked down. It was Sanora, hugging herself in the chill evening air. The girl's eyes were wide with shock, and her body trembled. Bobbi marveled that no one paid any attention to her.

"Sanora! Where did you come from?" Bobbi wrapped an arm around her thin shoulders.

"I saw Gina was hurt and ..." She wiped her eyes. "I ... wanted to find out what happened to her."

"I don't know if she's okay or not," Bobbi said. "But we need to get you somewhere safe."

She straightened and spied Chance's friend, Ramone, talking to one of the sheriffs. Dusty was there, too, filling out a report. She walked over to the group of men with Sanora. "Ramone?"

He turned. "Yes?"

"Is it safe at the school? Sanora would like to go back. Is anyone going over that way? She needs someone. I can't take care of her because I have to be with ... " She glanced at the paramedics treating Gina. "With Gina."

"I'm goin' that way, ma'am," Dusty said, nodding to her. "As soon as I finish my statement. In the meantime, she can get in my car. It's right over there, the blue Toyota. Turn on the motor and get the heat goin'." He handed her the key.

Bobbi was unsure about the propriety of sending Sanora with Dusty, but it was the only option, so she unlocked the pickup and climbed in with Sanora. She hoped and prayed that the ambulance wouldn't leave with Gina before Dusty was finished with the police.

There was a heavy wool jacket on the seat. Bobbi pulled it over Sanora's shoulders and turned up the heat. "It won't be long now," she said. "Maybe he'll stop in Chewelah and get you a bite to eat. I bet you're hungry."

Sanora nodded. "I suppose I am, but I'm more worried about Miss Gina. You'll let me know, won't you?" She leaned closer to the heat. A smile curved her lips. "I knew who she was right off when she came to the school. I'd read her card and repeated her name like it was a prayer. *Gina Lindsey. Gina Lindsey.* So, I never forgot her name, and when she came, well, I thought it was like an answer. It was, wasn't it?"

Bobbi smiled. "Yes, it was."

The girl rubbed her arms. "What will happen to us? To the kids at the school? Can I go back to Mom?"

"I suppose they'll let you go as soon as they sort everything out." She glanced up. "Oh, here's Dusty. You'll be okay." She climbed out of the driver's seat. "Goodbye, Sanora. You are a brave girl. Pray for Gina, okay? We'll let you know how she's doing."

To Dusty, she said, "Stop and get the girl something to eat. I think she's not only in shock, but she's hungry."

Dusty nodded. "Yes, ma'am. See you later."

She went back to the ambulance. They had Gina inside now. Stepping forward, she said, "I'm her Mom. Can I ride with her?"

The paramedic, a young woman with dark hair and snapping brown eyes looked at her and said, "Do you have a vehicle here?"

Bobbi shook her head. "No. And I ... really need to be with her."

"Okay," the lady said, cleaning up the mess they'd made on the pavement. She glanced up. "Go ahead and get in. There's a seat in the back. Strap in."

"Where are you taking her?"

"To Spokane, Sacred Heart."

Bobbi climbed in ambulance, studying Gina's pale face. Her eyes were closed. The lady entered and sat beside Gina, adjusting the oxygen mask that went over her nose. Gina was hooked up to IV's and a monitor. The doors closed, and they started off.

"Will she be all right?" Bobbi said loudly over the roar of the motor and the siren.

The paramedic did not smile. "We don't know. If you can pray, I'd suggest you do that."

Bobbi nodded. "Oh, yes. I know how to pray."

***

When Chance rode across the parking lot to the campground, he saw that the ambulance had left already. At his pickup, he dismounted and loaded Santiago into the trailer. He'd rush home, drop off the horse, and hightail it to the hospital. An officer held up his hand at the roadway entrance from the dam. He stopped.

It was Don, Gina's back-up agent. He was holding a radio to his ear and a rifle in the other hand.

Chance extended his hand. "Don! It's me, Chance. How're you doing, buddy?"

Don nodded. He finished the conversation and tucked the radio on to his belt. "Good work back there, Chance," he said with a ghost of a smile. "Hey, you want to see the bomb explode? Just got word they have it and are transporting it to a field."

Chance shook his head. "I have to get the horse unloaded and get into Spokane to be with Gina. She's hurt bad."

Don nodded. "I know, but this won't take much time. It's on your way out. Follow me if you want." He waved the next police car on by, and climbed into his green Ford pickup.

"Lead the way!" Chance yelled through the open window on the passenger side. He followed Don's pickup up the road to a field that opened to the right. Don pulled off and stopped.

Two police vehicles, pickups, and a fire engine were already in the center of the field. Chance stopped and hopped out. He and Don walked a short distance toward the officers who climbed down and carried large crates into the field.

Chance waited, shifting his feet, wishing he hadn't said he would come, yet wanting to see this more than anything he'd ever witnessed in his life. It would surely blast a hole in the ground.

The explosion rocked the earth. A soaring tower of flame lit the night sky. The sound was deafening. Chance clapped his hands to his ears, hoping Santiago was okay in the trailer.

When it was over, Don grinned at him. "That surely would have blown the dam to smithereens. Too bad Dusty didn't get to see it."

"But I did." Dusty approached from the rear, a wide grin on his face. "Best show I've seen for a long time! I hope it didn't leave a crater."

"I imagine it did," Chance said. "You should get a medal for what you did, Dusty! Best job ever."

"Well, I prayed a bunch while I was doin' it, that's for sure!"

"You did!" Chance grinned. "That's good news." He told Don good-bye.

Don patted him on the back. "I'll be thinking of Gina. Maybe Jane and I will come in to check on her. She's a good officer. The best."

Tears stung Chance's eyes. "I know. See you." Wiping his face, he drove over Flowery Trail highway and dropped down into Chewelah. At his ranch, he unloaded Santiago and went to the house.

His dad pulled in behind him. Chance unlocked the door and stepped inside, turning on lights as he went. "First time I've been here since ..." He stopped, thinking. "Since they set my barn on fire, and then tried to kill me right here in my front yard."

He started a pot of coffee and checked the refrigerator. Nothing in it to eat. "Afraid I'll have to do some grocery shopping. Hey, Dad, are you okay here for the night? I'm going to drive into Spokane and check on Gina. Sleep in my bedroom, okay? I might be gone a couple of days."

Josh Marshal plopped down on a chair and folded his long legs under the table in the kitchen. He leaned his head on his hands and only glanced up when Chance mentioned staying the night.

"No, I'll drive you in, Chance."

Chance stopped and turned to him. It was the first time his dad had ever used his nickname. "You sure?"

"Yes. You're in no condition to drive. I'm tired, too, but not nearly like you. You can catch some sleep on the way in, and we'll get a motel near the hospital."

Chance sat next to Josh and looked him straight in the eyes. "Thanks. I appreciate it."

Josh smiled. "It's the least I can do for not believing you. For not being there when you needed me."

"It's okay. You don't have to do this. I mean, for me."

"Well, it's not entirely for you. I got a shock the other day, and I need some time to process it." He paused, then shook his head and rose to pace the small kitchen. "Brenda told me that ... that she wants a divorce."

Chance could not reply. He watched his dad's slow progress across the room, his shoulders bent, stumbling once or twice like an old man. Finally, Chance said, "I'm ... sorry. Really. I had no idea."

Josh shrugged. "It's my fault. I've lost ... everything for my career. But I have it made. Got to be a big time senator." His short, derisive laugh came out as a snort. "A big, fat idiot, that's what I am. Can't even keep Brenda. And I nearly lost you, too."

He sat down again, his head in his hands.

Chance touched his arm. "I'm here for you. Take all the time you need. God will help you. Hasn't He said that He will? Do you believe in Him? In His Word?"

Josh lifted his face. His eyes were weary, red-rimmed. "Yeah, I do. He's calling me back. I've been away so long. But it's ... hard."

Chance refilled their cups. "I know. But we'll get through this. You have to throw your burden on the Lord." There was another pause. Then he stood and said, "Well, I'm going to grab a quick shower. You want one? Off to the left you'll find a guest bathroom. There's clean towels in there. I want to get to the hospital as soon as we can, so I can be by Gina until she's ..."

His throat closed up, shutting off his words. What was he about to say? Until she's out of the woods? Until she's home with the Lord?

He couldn't think that way. "I imagine Bobbi has Gina's cell phone. I'll try calling that and see where they've taken her." He jotted a note on a scrap of paper and taped it to the kitchen door. "This is for Ramone. He'll probably stop by tonight."

Josh nodded, finishing off his coffee. "Okay. Let's do it."

Chapter 55

A Soft Summer Night

From Gina's Journal, June 18th

I'm in a deep, dark pool. So black I can't see. But I hear things from time to time, like from a great distance. I'm breathing hard, struggling to reach the top. There's a glimmer of light up there. If only I can get...

But I can't. It's too far. I sink down again, allowing the suffocating darkness to overwhelm me. I don't know how long I'm like that, but again, I awake and hear something from a long way off. Someone's weeping.

I have to see who it is. I have to comfort them.

I exert all the energy of my being to swim to the top. Now it's closer. Closer. The light grows.

My eyes pop open. The brightness about blinds me, so I shut them again. There's a machine beeping close by my right shoulder. A voice crackles over a loudspeaker. Bennet with his bullhorn? Grant?

No. This is a woman's voice.

I peek through my closed lids. A window is shuttered against the sunshine. The walls are white. I take a deep breath. I'm alive!

But there *is* someone weeping nearby. The sound comes intermittently along with a mumbling sort of chant. I open my eyes wider and turn my head. Bobbi is seated next to me, so close I could touch her if I could raise my hand. But it won't obey me.

I moan. She swivels her head and stares at me.

"Gina? Are you awake?"

402

"Uh-umm." It's all I can get out.

Her eyes and nose are red. She grasps my hand tightly. "Oh, Gina. I've been so afraid ... that you would leave me, and I can't go on like this. I told God I can't. I told Him He had to bring you back. And your breathing was so shallow, and your heart rate went down. I thought you were dying. They came in and gave you another shot. I don't know how it happened, but God brought you back to me." Tears ran like rivers down her cheeks. "Can you hear me?"

I nod. "Yes, Aunt Bobbi." I try to smile. "I mean ...″ I try to say *Mom*, but for the life of me, I can't.

"That's okay, honey," she says. "I wanted one last chance to say how sorry I am." She wipes her nose, but she doesn't let go of my hand. "I was so young and foolish. And selfish. I thought all my problems would be solved if I could just get away. I was wrong, though. They just got started."

There's a pause like she expects me to say something.

"It's all right, Bobbi," I manage to say through a dry throat. "Honest. God's forgiven you ... how can I hold it against you? Maybe ... maybe this ..." I try to wave at the hospital room, "is for the best. Maybe we're ... getting a new life. A new start." It's a good statement from someone newly awakened from death, but it isn't enough.

Drawing a breath, I force myself to say the words God has burned into my mind. "I forgive you, Bobbi."

In that moment, all the bitterness and anger drain out of me like air out of a blown tire. I don't cry – I'm too tired for that, but I manage to squeeze her hand and smile.

She can't speak. We just sit there and gaze into each other's eyes for a long moment. She leans down and kisses my cheek.

She's saying something about forgiving me when my eyes close. Peace fills my heart and mind. And I sleep.

***

"Is she asleep?"

A young voice jars me awake. I open my eyes. Sanora stands beside my bed with a worried frown creasing her brow. Behind her, Bobbi peers at me like I'm the queen of the universe.

"Hi, Sanora," I say weakly, extending my hand. I'm surprised it obeys me this time.

She comes forward and grips it. "Miss Gina! I'm so glad you didn't die." She stops suddenly and looks at Bobbi. "Oh! Maybe I shouldn't say that!"

"No, it's all right," I say reassuringly. A nurse appears at my bed. I motion to her that I want to sit up. She pushes a button, and the head of the bed rises. She gives me a glass of water.

"I see you made it out of there all right," I say to Sanora with a smile, pushing back my hair. "Is everything okay? Are you back with your Mom yet?"

Sanora shakes her head. She looks happier than I've ever seen her, and I'm thinking she's pretty when she's dressed nicely and has her hair done.

"No, I'm still with the foster people. But they say I can go home soon." She edges nearer me. "They closed down the school, Miss Gina. Mr. Bennet, he died on the way to the hospital. And so did that big man, Tank, I think they called him. It's in all the papers! Your name and picture and everything!"

"You helped so much, Sanora. You should have your picture in the paper, too! You were like a ... soldier. You came through for me. Thanks so much." I squeeze her hand.

She beams. "Oh, it was nothing, really. Well, I better go. Miss Bobbi here, she came and got me when I told the CPS lady I needed to see you. Now maybe I can sleep at night."

"Yeah, I hope you do. Come and see me again, okay?"

She nods and starts for the door. Then she turns back, grabbing up something from a chair. "Oh! I almost forgot, Miss Gina. This is your backpack with that other folder. I took it from Bennet's truck and hid it. But then Miss Bobbi and I got it before we left the dam, and we gave it to the police. They took out the things in it and gave it back to me. So, all your ... what do you call it? ... clues and stuff, they're safe."

I accept the pack like it's a million dollars. "Wow, you really were on the ball! Thanks, Sanora!"

I'm getting tired. Bobbi kisses me and tells me to get some rest and that she'll be back. I nod. She puts the bed down, and I fall asleep.

***

"It took you long enough to get here." I grin at a familiar face that peers around the door jam.

The face frowns. It emerges into the room, followed by a tall, broad-shouldered young man carrying a cowboy hat. I suspect he's wearing boots, too, but I don't notice those because I'm captivated by his blue eyes.

In two loping strides, he's by my bed and has a hold of my hand. "What do you mean a long time? I've been here day and night, right by your bed while you enjoyed a nice, long sleep." His tone sounds aggrieved, yet light sparkles from his eyes like stars on a dark summer sky.

"Oh. Sorry. How are you doing?" I try to remove my hand from his, but he hangs onto it.

"Well, a lot better since you decided to rejoin us in this life." He releases my hand long enough to wipe his brow. "I can tell you that you had us worried. Worried sick. Couldn't sleep. Couldn't eat. Prayed God's ears off."

He grins. "You get under people's skin, you know that? And we nearly lost you. The doc said if the bullet had come a fraction of an inch lower, you would have been gone. Next time, you're wearing a vest."

I laugh and then groan because it hurts to laugh. "Like I had a lot of time to put one on!" I reach for his hand. "I'm glad you weren't injured. I hear they all got arrested? Even Grant?"

"Yeah. I took off on Santiago, across the dam, and up the trail to the upper parking lot like a cowboy, riding him without a saddle or bridle. You were right. Grant was expecting his chopper to land up there. Well, one came, and I thought it was his, but it was the police, and my dad was with them!"

"Really!"

He nods and sits down in the chair by the bed. "I had them disarmed by the time the police got out of the chopper. They arrested Grant and two of the others from the ranch. I took Santiago home. Dad's been with me through all this. He took some time off from his job just for me. And for you." A slow smile spreads across his face.

"So, you and him ... you're doing better now?"

He nods. "He ... his wife wants a divorce. We're praying together about it, and I think he's coming back to the Lord."

"What happened with the bomb? And all the stuff that was going to happen in Seattle?"

He leans back, crossing his long legs. Yes, he's wearing cowboy boots. "They got the bomb out of the dam and took it to a field. I got to see it explode. Made quite a show, I can tell you!" He grins. "The police arrested twenty-three guys in Seattle. In all, the arrests for the gang totaled thirty-five. And they've shut down the porno and human trafficking ring that Bennet was running. Of course, without Grant and Bennet, it's over. They shut down the school, too."

"How about the people at the dam? Did they get them out okay?

"Yeah. Found them in an office inside, all tied up. They were a group of very grateful people, I can tell you that!"

"I imagine so. Well, I'm glad." A wave of tiredness sweeps over me. "Well, I have some news. While we were inside the dam, sitting there with that bomb about to explode, Bobbi dropped one of her own on me. She told me she's my mom! Can you believe that?"

406

He doesn't look surprised. "Yeah, we got to talking out in the waiting room the other night. She told me. You okay with that?"

I grimace. "I wasn't at first. But God helped me forgive her. When I did, it was like this huge weight rolled off my shoulders." I yawn.

"I better let you get some rest," he says, standing.

"You get some, too." I look up at him and wish he would kiss me, but I look awful, and my breath would probably slay a dragon.

"I'll be here. When you're ready to go home, I'll take you out there." He leans down and kisses my cheek. "Get better, Gina girl. Okay?"

"Okay."

***

It's a soft, warm summer's night. We're all together at my house – Bobbi, Elton, Chance and his dad, Sanora and Lucy, her mom, and Sanora's siblings, Jamie and Bonnie.

Ramone had gone back to LA a few days before my homecoming, but not before he visited me in the hospital, and I'd had a chance to thank him for his help.

Bobbi cooked a wonderful turkey dinner in honor of my return home, and Sanora and Lucy made a huge "welcome home" banner across the front of the house. The cats seemed glad to see me, but of course, you can't ever tell with cats, can you? Maybe they were just glad they'd get fed more often.

Sanora was bursting with her news. Soon after I arrived home, she told me. "Aunt Bobbi and Uncle Elton have asked us to come out to Montana to help on their ranch," she says, her eyes shining.

I glance at Bobbi. She nods with a smile.

Sanora dances around the room. "And we're going to get to ride horses and everything!"

"I'm so glad for you, sweetie," I say and give her a hug.

Later, while I'm sitting in the kitchen, watching Bobbi make gravy, she says, "She calls me Aunt Bobbi. Isn't that cute?"

"You're going to hire them to work?"

She nods. "I figure Lucy can help with housework, and I bet she can find other house cleaning jobs, too. They can live in Tim's trailer. He's not home anymore, what with goin' to college and all."

I hear sadness and loneliness in her tone. "Well, I have some time off coming, so I might come out to visit. Help you with your garden. That is, if Chance will let me. He's kind of taken charge of me lately."

She sniffs. "Well, someone needs to watch out for you."

I haven't come to the point of calling her "mom" yet, and she says it's okay. We get along a lot better now. I figure that her domineering ways were to get me to pay attention to her and to get me to include her in my life. Anyway, we're committed to learning how to love and forgive each other like Christ did for us when He died on the cross.

When we bow our heads to pray that evening for the meal, holding hands around the table, Sanora says she wants to say the blessing.

I smile. "Of course."

She looks around with a wide grin. "I wanted to tell you that Gina told me how to pray to God, and she helped me accept Jesus and ask Him to forgive my sins. I did that when I was under that tarp all that longs ways when we was going to the dam, and I was so scared I about peed my pants."

We all laugh. Tears come to my eyes when I tell her how glad I am for her and that I'll give her a Bible.

When the kitchen is cleaned up, Sanora and Lucy leave to return to Spokane. Josh, Elton and Bobbi settle in front of my TV to watch a football game.

I ask Chance if he'd help me walk down and see the horses.

"Shore," he says with his characteristic slow smile.

He puts a strong arm around my waist as we stroll to the pasture gate. He opens it, and Gypsy Rose comes up to greet me, nuzzling my hand. I don't disappoint her. I have an apple ready, and one for Pecos Bill, too. Then I lean against her and breathe deeply. I missed her a lot.

Chance hooks a boot on the lowest rail of the fence and studies me. "How are you and your mom doin'?"

I move to stand beside him. "Okay. It will take some time, but I think I'm learning to love her." I pause and watch Gypsy. "It's like I was sinking lower and lower in a murky pond, like that Deadwater pond at the school. Only mine was in my heart. It was self-pity and bitterness, and I couldn't get out of it. I couldn't let people near me. But now that's changed. Maybe now I can let people get close to me."

He puts his arms around me. "Like this?"

"Yeah. That feels good."

Crickets tune up their little violins over by the creek, and Gypsy wanders off to see what Pecos has found to munch on. A full moon rises over the low hills to the east, casting a golden glow over everything.

"Too bad we don't have dance music," he says in my hair.

"I know. The crickets are making a nice sound, though."

He chuckles and squeezes tighter. I groan, for the wound in my chest hasn't healed.

"Oh! I'm sorry!" He relaxes his arms.

"No. Don't be sorry. Please."

He sighs. "It's just that I thought I was going to lose you, and I never want to let you go again." His voice is gentle like he's afraid he'll scare me off.

He kisses my forehead.

"That's funny," I say a little breathlessly. "I don't want you to let me go." I lift my face to look into his eyes.

I'm not totally prepared for his kiss, but I like it. A lot.

He wipes the tear that escapes down my cheek and smiles. "We either got to get us another profession, or I'm buying you a full suit of body armor. I can't stand the thought of anything damaging you. I love you and will to the day I die."

I can't speak because he claims my lips again. When I can talk, I say in a low tone, "I love you, but I'm not wearing body armor. You'll just have to learn how to pray, that's all."

He laughs. It reverberates deep throughout his body. "I've learned a lot about prayin' with you around! You keep me on my toes."

I step back and punch him gently on the arm. "That's my gift, bringing drama into your life. Okay, let's head back to the house."

"Are you ready?" He loops his arm around my waist.

I laugh up into his eyes, joy bubbling from my heart like a fountain. "I am. Ready for whatever God has for us. Let's go."

The End

A Note to My Readers:

I first thought of the location and theme of this book when my husband and I visited Boundary Dam near the Canadian border. Later, I was pleasantly surprised when God brought a border guard into my life! This kind man helped me with many of the details in the book. Project Noble Mustang, described in the book, is still in operation in the Spokane Sector of the Border Patrol.

I became aware and burdened for the victims of human trafficking when my daughter visited Thailand on a mission's trip. The ministry she was working with provided help for trafficked women off the streets of Bangkok and for victims around the globe who are captured into slavery of the worst kind.

With that in mind, I would like to create a fund called **Sanora's Legacy.** I will donate 5% of every book sale of Deadwater to the ministry, *Remember Nhu.* This ministry is located in Bangkok, Thailand and reaches children and women from the streets. They train women to learn a craft and support themselves. The items they make are brought to the US and sold.

To find out more about Remember Nhu and to read her true story, visit the website: www.remembernhu.org

Thank you for purchasing this book. God bless!

Virginia Ann Work Chewelah, WA Jan. 2016

Made in the USA
Middletown, DE
27 September 2022

11324124R00235